**He lowered his head and brushed
his mouth over hers.**

It was the merest whisper of mouth to mouth, but the instant their lips touched, everything changed.

And then, as if in slow motion, his arms came around her and he dragged her against him while he savaged her mouth.

God in heaven, she tasted so good. He couldn't seem to get enough of the taste of her. His lips moved over hers, drawing out all the sweet, tart flavor that was uniquely hers.

With a growl of pleasure he backed her roughly against the closed door. He had his hands in her hair, though he couldn't recall how they got there. He lowered his mouth to the soft curve of her neck, and heard her throaty sigh. The sound of it was enough to make him dizzy with need.

She'd anchored her arms around his waist as the kiss spun on and on. The feel of her, all wrapped around him, had him sweating. He breathed in the heady fragrance of her perfume that reminded him of a field of wildflowers. Right this minute he would happily drown in her.

He knew he had to stop, but not just yet. He wanted one more touch. One more taste...

RAVES FOR
R. C. RYAN'S NOVELS

Josh

"There's plenty of hot cowboys, action, and romance in this heady mix of a series that will leave you breathless."
—*Parkersburg News and Sentinel* **(WV)**

"A powerfully emotional tale that will connect with readers...Love a feel-good cowboy romance with a touch of suspense? Then pick up *Josh*."
—**RomRevToday.com**

"This story is action-packed and fast moving. Just when you think it's safe, it isn't...a good solid story with fantastic characters and an interesting story line...Another really good romance with enough suspense to keep you waiting to see what will happen next."
—**NightOwlReviews.com**

Quinn

"Ryan takes readers to Big Sky country in a big way with her vivid visual dialogue as she gives us a touching love story with a mystery subplot. The characters, some good and one evil, will stay with you long after the book is closed."
—*RT Book Reviews*

"*Quinn* is a satisfying read. R. C. Ryan is an accomplished and experienced storyteller. And if you enjoy contemporary cowboys in a similar vein to Linda Lael Miller, you'll enjoy this."
—**GoodReads.com**

"Engaging...Ryan paints a picturesque image of the rugged landscape and the boisterous, loving, close-knit Conway family."

—*Publishers Weekly*

"I thoroughly enjoyed reading about the Conway family and their ranch...a wonderful introduction to a new trilogy that looks to be unique and full of surprises."

—NightOwlReviews.com

Montana Glory

"The child adds a lovely emotional element to the story, the secondary romance is enjoyable, and all loose ends are nicely tied up."

—*RT Book Reviews*

"[The Montana Trilogy] is a good series of hunky cowboys and nail-biting mystery. Zane and Riley have great chemistry and are a read that you can't put down."

—*Parkersburg News and Sentinel* (WV)

"These not-to-be-missed books are guaranteed to warm your heart!"

—FreshFiction.com

"Wonderful romantic suspense tale starring a courageous heroine who is a lioness protecting her cub and a reluctant knight in shining armor...a terrific taut thriller."

—GenreGoRoundReviews.blogspot.com

Montana Destiny

Montana Legacy

A *Cosmopolitan* "Red Hot Read"

ALSO BY R. C. RYAN

Montana Legacy
Montana Destiny
Montana Glory
Quinn
Josh

JAKE

R. C. RYAN

FOREVER

NEW YORK   BOSTON

Copyright © 2013 by Ruth Ryan Langan
Excerpt from *Quinn* Copyright © 2011 by Ruth Ryan Langan

Forever
Hachette Book Group
237 Park Avenue
New York, NY 10017

www.HachetteBookGroup.com

Printed in the United States of America

First Edition: February 2013
10 9 8 7 6 5 4 3 2 1

OPM

Forever is an imprint of Grand Central Publishing.
The Forever name and logo are trademarks of Hachette Book Group, Inc.

The Hachette Speakers Bureau provides a wide range of authors for speaking events. To find out more, go to www.hachettespeakersbureau.com or call (866) 376-6591.

The publisher is not responsible for websites (or their content) that are not owned by the publisher.

*For my three sons, Tom Jr., Patrick, and Mike,
who make me so proud and happy.
And for my darling Tom, who hung the moon.*

PROLOGUE

Conway ranch—The Devil's Wilderness
Wyoming—1982

Q uinn. Josh." Big Jim Conway's voice had his two grandsons looking up from their chores in the barn.

"Yes, sir?" Quinn paused, and the hose in his hand continued spilling water across the floor of the barn.

"Watch what you're doing there, boyo."

"Oh." The boy turned off the spigot and dropped the hose. "Sorry."

"Where's your little brother?"

"Don't know." Quinn glanced guiltily toward his brother Josh, and the two boys waited for the explosion they knew would follow that admission. Since the day their mother, Seraphine, had vanished without a trace two years earlier, they had been charged with keeping a close eye on seven-year-old Jake. Not an easy job on a ranch this huge, especially since their youngest brother had a habit of wandering off to find all sorts of mischief.

"Sorry, Big Jim." The boys never called their grandfather by anything other than that. There were no warm, fuzzy nicknames for this tough rancher, even by the youngest members of his family. "Last I saw Jake, he was out behind the barn."

The old man walked away, muttering in frustration. A search of the area behind the barns came up empty, and Big Jim climbed the hill to the spot where a gleaming headstone stood, with five smaller stones forming a semi-circle around it.

As was his custom, the old man lay a gnarled hand on the headstone that marked the resting place of his wife, Clementine, who had borne him six sons, five of whom had died in infancy. "I swear, Clemmy, that boy will be the death of me. He's too damned independent for his own good. Do you have any idea where he's gone this time?"

As if in answer a small head popped up from the far side of the hill. Jake was carrying something in his arms that appeared to weigh more than he did.

"What's that you've got there, boyo?" As the boy drew closer Big Jim's jaw dropped. "Is that what I think it is?"

"It's a cougar, Big Jim. He's just a little one, and he's hurting."

The old man's growl was a combination of rage and fear. "Put that critter down before he devours you."

The boy merely continued toward his grandfather. "I can help him, Big Jim."

"I said put him down."

The boy halted, then knelt in the grass before depositing the animal gently on the ground.

The old man ventured close enough to see that the young cougar was bloody and mangled, but still alive. "Looks like he tangled with something big and ornery. Probably a mother bear, and the bear won."

"His ma was dead."

"You know that for a fact?"

The boy nodded. "Looks like she fought hard to save him. He was lying beside her, licking her face. Can I take him to the barn and doctor him?"

"Listen to me, boyo." The old man's voice lowered, hoping to soften the blow. "It's a fine thing you want to do. But this is a wild critter. He may be too weak to keep you from doctoring him now, but if he should survive, once he's well and strong, he'll do what wild things do. He'll try to kill you. It's his nature."

Jake turned those wide, trusting eyes on his grandfather. "I know, Big Jim. But I still have to try to help. Look at him. He's hurting something bad. And he doesn't have a ma either."

And he doesn't have a ma either.

The little boy's words were a knife to Big Jim's heart. How could he possibly refuse a motherless boy's request to help a motherless creature? Besides, there would be plenty of time for the lad to learn that nature could be cruel as well as beautiful.

"All right, boyo. I'll help you build a cage and lend a hand with the doctoring. But you're not to forget that he's a wild thing that sees other creatures as food. As soon as he's strong enough, he'll bite the hand that doctors him."

"I won't forget, Big Jim." With great tenderness the boy lifted the heavy animal.

"Let me give you a hand with him."

As the older man reached out, Jake shook his head. "I can do it."

He carried the big cat toward the barn. Inside, he applied ointment to the worst of the bite marks, and then went in search of Ela, an Arapaho woman who cooked for their family and had been with them since Big Jim's wife, Clementine, had died some thirty years earlier.

Ela showed Jake how to use a needle and some fine thread to close the gaping wounds and stem the bleeding until they could heal.

For the next week Jake slept in the barn beside the cage his grandfather had made, and he even took his meals there, hand-feeding the cougar and applying ointment whenever its curious tongue weakened the stitches and opened another wound. Jake's father, grandfather, and brothers reported hearing the lad talking to the animal late into the night.

A week later, when the young cougar had passed through the crisis and began to grow restless, Jake persuaded his grandfather to load the cage into the jaws of their front-end loader and drive it out to the range, near where the animal had been found.

Once there, they deposited the cage on the ground and then sat trying to figure out how to open it without risking their own safety.

"I'll just lift up the door," Jake said calmly.

"Like hell you will, boyo." The old man shook a finger in his face. "You'll stay up here on this machine with me, and we'll figure out a way to snag the door with a rope and hook."

While his grandfather was pondering the situation,

Jake jumped to the ground, walked to the front of the cage, and lifted the door before stepping back.

For a moment the cougar stared at the boy, and then at the man, who was swearing a blue streak.

With a last look at the boy, the cougar calmly stepped out into freedom, before sprinting off.

Big Jim hurried to stand beside his grandson as the cougar made a great leap onto a rock ledge, where it lay panting in the afternoon sunshine.

Before they could turn away, the cougar lifted a paw and began licking it. It seemed, to the old man, that the animal wasn't so much grooming itself as waving to the one who'd saved his life.

Or maybe, the old man thought, he was merely getting a bit dotty in his old age. After all, this predator would probably thank them by killing off more of their cattle.

Still, he'd swear that young cat was smiling and purring. And all because an innocent lad with a passion for healing couldn't bear to see another living creature suffer.

CHAPTER ONE

Paintbrush, Wyoming—Present Day

Thanks, Jake." The grizzled rancher pumped Jake Conway's hand hard enough to have him wincing. "Figured old Scout here had seen his last sunset. I tried every home remedy I could think of." The old man grinned. "Hated having to give in and pay a vet. You know how it is."

Jake nodded in understanding. Every rancher in these parts knew how to birth a calf, treat a lame horse, and cure the hundred-and-one things that could go wrong with ranch animals. A veterinarian was called only in extreme circumstances, or when an animal had to be put down and its owner couldn't bear to do the deed.

"Looks like I'd better start calling you Doc." The old rancher winked at his teenage granddaughter, who was practically swooning over the handsome young veterinarian as though he were a Greek god.

His wife, standing beside their daughter, thrust a covered plate into Jake's hands. "Brownies," the older woman said with a shy smile. "Our Tina here baked them herself."

"Thank you, Anna. And thank you, Tina. How'd you know about my sweet tooth?" Jake turned that famous Conway smile on both females, who audibly sighed.

The old rancher couldn't suppress a grin. The women in his household were all smitten with Cole Conway's youngest son. Word in the tiny town of Paintbrush was that Jake Conway had the same effect on every female there from sixteen to sixty. It had been that way since Jake was twelve or thirteen, and still trailing his older brothers around town wearing a sweaty T-shirt, dusty denims, and one of his grandfather's cast-off frayed, wide-brimmed cowboy hats. As he'd matured, he'd grown into a tall, muscled cowboy, whose rugged good looks were enhanced by a spill of curly black hair always in need of a trim, and devilish blue eyes that sparkled with unmistakable humor. A big part of his charm was that good-natured, roguish smile. Women just gravitated to him like bees to honey.

"I guess what I've heard around town is the truth. You're some kind of miracle worker."

"Not me. I've got miracle drugs." Jake smiled and patted his pocket before tucking away the syringe and vial. "Just doing my job, Will."

"The way I see it, thanks to that fancy vet school in Michigan, you're doing it even better'n old Doc Hunger did. And that's saying something."

Jake couldn't hide his pleasure at the compliment. It meant the world to him that the ranchers accepted him without question. Not an easy task when they still thought of the youngest Conway son as a lightweight compared to his father, grandfather, and two older brothers.

At his truck, the two men shook hands again before Jake climbed inside and started toward home.

As he drove along the dusty road he played back his phone messages. One from Phoebe, their housekeeper, reminding him that Ela was baking her famous corn bread to go with the ham she'd put in the oven, and he'd better not be late.

His mouth was watering as he played the second message, this one from his brother Quinn, reminding him of dinner Saturday night as a surprise for his wife's birthday, and that if Cheyenne had so much as an inkling of what was planned, he'd know it was all Jake's fault for having a big mouth.

Jake was still grinning as the third message began. A woman's breathy voice, sounding either stressed or annoyed.

"This is Meg Stanford. I've just arrived at my father's ranch to dispose of his estate, and there's a colt out in the barn that appears to be lame. I'm not sure there's anything you can do for it, but I'd like you to . . ." The voice paused for so long, Jake thought the call may have been interrupted. But then the message continued. ". . . do whatever it is you do with animals that are beyond help."

Unsure of what he'd heard, he played the message a second time before dismissing all thought of Ela's corn bread and ham from his mind. He made a sharp U-turn and headed toward the Stanford ranch.

As he drew near, it occurred to Jake that though Porter Stanford had been his family's nearest neighbor, he'd never before set foot on the property. He and his brothers had been warned when they were just boys that they were to stay clear of the rancher, whose volatile temper was well-known around these parts.

In the town of Paintbrush gossip spread quicker than a prairie fire, and the juicy tales about Porter Stanford before his sudden death days ago had all been negative. Folks around these parts just shook their heads over his hair-trigger temper, the hellish life his two ex-wives had endured at his hands, all of which they'd been eager to share with anyone who would listen, and of the fact that his third wife had been young enough to be his granddaughter. She'd died two years ago of a brain hemorrhage, leaving Porter with a young son.

Jake wondered about the woman claiming to be Porter's daughter. He could vaguely recall hearing about a wild child who matched her father in looks and temperament. But that was years ago, before Porter's very public first divorce, when she and her mother, Virginia, had taken themselves off to parts unknown.

Jake turned his truck onto the lane that led to the rustic ranch house. Nestled on a bluff, the house overlooked some of the richest grazing land in the territory. Now in early spring, the land was just turning green and was dotted with buds of Indian paintbrush and towering cottonwood. No wonder Porter Stanford had thought of himself as a king and all of Wyoming as his fiefdom. Maybe, Jake thought with sudden insight, that was another reason why Stanford had a particular dislike of the Conway family. Not only were they his nearest neighbors, but they owned all the land around him, leaving him unable to expand his kingdom.

Jake followed the curving driveway to the back door

of the house and stepped out of his truck. A sleek, candy-apple-red rental car was parked beside the porch.

He climbed the wide porch steps and knocked.

A sexy female voice called, "Come in."

He stepped into a kitchen offering a spectacular view of the Tetons in the distance. Finding no one there, he stepped through the open doorway into a massive great room, where a woman was walking toward him, carrying a cardboard box that was bigger than she.

"Hello." Though he couldn't see the face, the view from the waist down was enticing. A tiny waist and long, long legs encased in narrow denims.

"Oh. Hello. If you want to take a look at the farm implements, you may as well start tagging the things out in the second barn."

"You're planning an auction?"

She peered around the box. "Aren't you from the auction house?"

"No. Sorry. I'm the vet. Here. Let me help you." He took the box from her hands. "Where do you want this?"

"The kitchen table will be fine." She led the way and Jake followed.

As he set down the heavy box he shot her a grin. "What've you got in there? A safe?"

She sighed. "Sorry. I should have warned you. I found several locked metal boxes in an upstairs room and thought I'd bring them down before opening them to see what's inside." She offered her hand. "I'm Meg Stanford."

Jake accepted her handshake and took the moment to study her. She had her father's fiery red hair, pulled back into a ponytail, and green eyes the color of prairie grass.

"Jake Conway." He was fascinated by her lips. Soft,

pursed lips that, though bare of makeup, were absolutely enticing. "I'm sorry about your loss."

"Thank you." She spoke the words in a flat, unemotional tone. "You said you were the vet. I was expecting Dr. Hunger."

"He retired. His service directs his calls to me."

"I see." She nodded toward the door. "I'll take you to the barn."

Jake trailed behind her, enjoying the view of her trim backside in the shiny, new denims. They were so crisp they looked as though they'd just come off a store rack, as did the cotton shirt buttoned clear to her throat and tucked precisely into the waistband.

He glanced at her feet. Even the sneakers were brand-new, though they wouldn't remain that way once she stepped into the barn.

"How long have you been here?"

"Since this morning."

"Where are you from?"

She paused, her hand on the barn door. "Washington."

"As in Spokane?"

She smiled. "As in D.C."

"You're a long way from home. What do you do there?"

"I'm a lawyer."

His smile deepened. "That explains the new duds. I'd never mistake you for a rancher."

That brought a smile, transforming her face from pretty to gorgeous. "My usual wardrobe runs to tailored suits and heels. I figured I'd need something more practical for the week I plan on being here."

"A week?"

She nodded. "My vacation time. Not exactly the way I'd hoped to be spending it. I haven't been back to this place since I was a kid. I honestly never expected to see it again."

She lowered her voice. "As you can imagine, I've forgotten more than I can remember about ranch animals. The colt has a pronounced limp. I thought I'd ask a vet to take a look and advise me as to the best way to...deal with it." Her voice lowered to a near-whisper, as though she were sharing state secrets. "If you have to euthanize the colt, I'd appreciate it if you would take it with you rather than do it here. There's the boy..." When she faltered, Jake waited until she composed herself. "My father's sudden death wasn't my only surprise. I've learned that I have a half brother. I'm not sure of his birthday, but I'm guessing he's about seven. I suspect that he was alone here when our father had his heart attack. That may be why he doesn't speak—at least not to me. But he seems really attached to the colt. That's why..." She looked at the ground. "...I'd rather not add to the boy's suffering."

"All right." Jake nodded toward the door. "Let's have a look."

She opened the barn door and led the way to a stall. As Jake's eyes adjusted to the gloom, he could see the colt lying in the straw, its head cradled in the lap of a blond, shaggy-haired boy in dirty denims and an even dirtier T-shirt.

Meg's tone was cautious. "Cory, this is Dr. Conway. I asked him to take a look at your colt."

"Hey, Cory." Jake knelt beside the boy and ran a hand gently over the colt's forelock. "Does your horse have a name?"

The boy merely stared at him.

"Can your horse stand?"

Cory shuffled out from under the horse's head and got to his feet before tugging gently on the animal's mane.

The colt scrambled to its feet.

Jake pointed toward the door. "Would you mind leading him outside?"

Without a word the boy led the horse out into the sunshine, with Jake and Meg following.

The animal's limp, Jake noted, was pronounced.

He watched as the boy led the colt in a wide circle. When they were close, Jake ran a hand along the animal's neck. "He's a real beauty."

The faintest flicker of a smile touched the boy's eyes before he looked away.

"Has he always had this limp, or is it a recent injury?"

The boy shrugged.

Jake decided to try again. "Was he born with this problem, Cory?"

The boy shook his head.

"So, this happened recently?"

"Yeah." The boy sighed, as though the weight of the world rested on his shoulders.

"Okay. It's a start." Relieved that the boy could speak, Jake glanced toward Meg.

She covered her mouth with her hand to hide the slight trembling, and he thought for a moment she might cry in relief. Instead he saw her suck in a quick breath and compose herself.

Jake bent to the animal's leg and began gently probing. When he touched one particular spot the colt flattened its ears and sidestepped.

"Tender. Did your horse take a fall?"

The boy shook his head. "No."

"Was he hit by something?"

The boy shrugged his thin shoulders.

"Maybe by a stone thrown by a truck?"

Seeing that the boy didn't intend to reply, he added, "Maybe he was attacked by a flying saucer?"

That had Cory smiling before he ducked his head.

Jake glanced at Meg, who stood with her arms crossed, watching the interaction between the two with quiet intensity.

"All right. Let's try something else. Walk him again, Cory."

As the boy did so, Jake moved along beside the colt and probed not only the leg but the animal's underbelly as he took each step.

When he straightened, Meg asked in a low voice, "Will you be able to take him with you?"

Jake shrugged. "I'd like to try treating him here."

"Treating? I thought . . ." She looked at Cory, then away before whispering, "I thought vets had to put down a horse when it was lame."

"I guess that was the treatment of choice back when women didn't have the vote, and ranchers chewed tobacco and played poker in the town saloon. Nowadays, ma'am," he added in his best drawl, "you wouldn't believe the miracle drugs we have."

She had a rich, throaty laugh. "I guess I deserved that. All right, Dr. Conway. I'll leave you to your patient. I have work to do in the house."

When she walked away Jake watched until she'd climbed the steps. Turning, he saw the boy staring at him.

He winked. "You've got a pretty sister, Cory."

The boy hung his head and absently patted the colt.

Jake touched a hand to the boy's shoulder. "I'm sorry about the loss of your dad."

Cory glanced up at him. There was an eager, almost hungry look in his eyes. "Did you know him?"

Jake shook his head. "Not really. I knew who he was, and saw him in town a time or two, but other than that, he was a stranger. I guess he kept to himself a lot."

The eager look in the boy's eyes was gone in the instant before he looked away. "Yeah."

After a pronounced silence, Jake sighed. "While you take this little guy back to the stall, I'll get my bag of tricks."

He walked away and retrieved his supplies from his truck. Spying the plate of brownies, he took them along.

In the barn he took his time, examining the colt while trying to find ways to engage the boy in conversation.

"How old are you, Cory?"

"Seven." His gaze followed every movement of Jake's fingers as he touched and probed the colt's leg.

"That would make you a second grader?"

The boy shrugged. "Don't go to school."

"Yeah. I never did either, when I was your age. Too far to town." He looked over. "So, you're homeschooled. Did your dad teach you?"

Another shrug. "Now that I can read, I get the lessons out of books and do my class assignments online."

"Who checks your homework?"

"I scan it and send it to the teacher assigned to me."

"Did anybody live here on the ranch with you and your dad?"

"Yancy. But he doesn't live with us. He stays in the bunkhouse."

Jake heard the warmth in the boy's tone and nodded. He'd heard that Yancy Jessup had taken over some of the ranch duties after Porter's young wife died. Yancy was one of the last of a dying breed. A cowboy with no desire to own his own spread. An old man who preferred living in a bunkhouse with other cowboys. A drifter who loved tending other rancher's herds, until the itch to move on became too great. Yancy Jessup had worked ranches all over Montana and Wyoming, and his work was universally praised. Nobody had ever had a bad word to say about him.

"I suppose Yancy's up in the hills with the herd?"

"Yeah."

"Does he know about your dad?"

The boy looked stricken, and Jake realized that the cowboy had no idea that his boss had passed away.

Jake pulled out his cell phone. "Give me his number and I'll see that your sister calls him as soon as I'm finished here."

As Cory spoke the numbers, Jake programmed them into his phone. "I'd call Yancy myself, but I think this call should come from a family member." He looked over. "Do you have a cell phone?"

Cory nodded.

"Good. While I'm thinking about it, why don't I give you my number? That way, if you need me, just call."

He spoke the numbers and watched as Cory punched them into his phone.

"Now give me yours." Jake added the numbers as Cory said them aloud.

For the next hour, while Cory soothed the colt, Jake applied ointment and wrapped the injured leg. When he was finished, he closed his bag and got to his feet.

"That's the best I can do for now. I'll look in on him tomorrow and see if he's improving."

The boy kept an arm around the colt's neck. "His name is Shadow."

Jake paused. "That's a good name. And you're a good friend to Shadow, Cory. I can see that he trusts you. Now I'd better report to your sister." He offered his hand. "Thanks for your help."

The boy looked surprised before giving him an awkward handshake.

Jake pointed to the plate of brownies. "I'll leave those for you and your sister to snack on."

"You mean it?" The boy's gaze fell on the food like one who hadn't eaten all day.

With a thoughtful look Jake turned and made his way from the barn.

It was plain that the boy was feeling scared and confused. And he was probably in a lot of pain. And why not? In a matter of days he'd lost his father, gained a sister who was a stranger to him, and had to watch his colt going lame. It must have seemed as though his whole world had toppled. To make matters worse, his future would be decided by a woman who apparently didn't know much about the care and feeding of a seven-year-old, one who couldn't wait to get away from here and back to the life she'd left behind.

But Cory Stanford wasn't the only person in pain. His sister was, too. She might have spent her childhood on this ranch, but after so many years away, she had become a stranger in a strange land. That city woman looked as out of place as a designer dress at a rodeo.

A week. Did she actually believe she could contact an auction house to dispose of a ranch, a herd, and an entire way of life, in the time it took to vacation at some tropical beach?

Jake paused on the porch and watched through the screen door as Meg struggled to pry open a metal box with a rusty screwdriver. Several other metal boxes, empty and misshapen from forced entry, littered the floor around her feet.

Taking a deep breath, he knocked and stepped inside. "Would you like a hand with that?"

Meg's head came up sharply. "Sorry. You startled me. I'd appreciate any help you can give." She handed him the screwdriver. "There are probably dozens of tools around here, if I knew where to look."

Jake nodded toward the door. "Probably the equipment barn, up the hill. That's the usual place to store tools."

"Of course. I'll check it out later." She gathered up a pile of papers and documents, clutching them to her chest. "It looks as though my father's filing system was a lot like his life—careless. When I was a kid he never would have dreamed of just throwing things into boxes with no apparent rhyme or reason."

"Maybe, as you sort through them, you'll discover some sort of order to them."

"Not likely." She deposited the papers on the kitchen counter before returning to stand beside him as he pried open the metal box. A haphazard stack of papers spilled out, littering the tabletop.

"See what I mean?" She eyed the papers before turning to Jake. "What have you decided about the colt?"

"There's a small wound with swelling and redness that suggests infection. I've given him an antibiotic and wrapped the wound. I'll look in on him tomorrow and see if there's any improvement. If there is, I'll continue the treatment. If not, I'll try something else."

"I'm so relieved that you were able to get Cory to speak to you. From his reaction to me, I was really afraid he might be deaf and mute."

"He hadn't spoken at all?"

"Not to me. But he opened up to you right away."

Jake gave her one of his devilish smiles. "All part of my charm. Kids and animals just can't resist me."

She glanced at his ring finger. "I see that you can't make the same claim about women."

Seeing the direction of her gaze he chuckled. "It's been tough, but so far I've managed to resist their advances." He winked. "I keep a club in my truck, just in case I run into a really aggressive female who won't take no for an answer."

He was rewarded with her deep, throaty chuckle, which transformed her from pretty to absolutely gorgeous.

"Thanks for my laugh of the day. I needed it." She crossed her arms over her chest and tapped a nervous foot. "I'm at a loss as to what to do about Cory. And I get the distinct impression that he isn't about to give me any help at all."

"He'll come around. You've already learned that he can talk."

"To you. But I need him to open up with me about what he's feeling, and what he wants to do going forward. So far the only thing I've heard from him is silence."

"Give him a little time. In his short lifetime he's lost his mother and his father. And the colt he loves is suffering. The kid is scared. I'm betting he's convinced that all the really important things in his life are going to be taken away from him."

"I'm his half sister, not his enemy."

"He doesn't know that. He knows only that a stranger will be the one to determine his future."

"I hadn't thought of that." She frowned. "I guess I've been so busy dealing with my own feelings, I was overlooking all the things he must be going through."

"Does he have any family other than you? Grandparents? Aunts?"

Meg's lips turned into a pretty pout before she chewed her lower lip. "I'll ask him. I would've before but I didn't think he could speak. So far I've found no documentation of any other family. That's why I'm so desperate to find all my father's legal documents. I have a frightened little boy, a sprawling ranch, and who knows how many debts I might encounter, and I don't have a clue what to do with any of them."

"I hate to add to your burden." Jake saw the way her eyes narrowed slightly. "Cory tells me that there's a wrangler up in the hills with your father's herd. His name is Yancy Jessup. A good man. Folks around here will tell you that he's someone you can trust. But right now, he doesn't even know that your father has passed away." He handed over his cell phone. "Cory gave me Yancy's number. I think you'd better give him a call."

She plucked a cell phone from her pocket and deftly

added Yancy's name and number before extending her hand. "I'll call him. Thank you. I appreciate your help."

"You're welcome." Jake accepted her handshake, while keeping his gaze steady on hers.

She'd probably intended it to be a purely businesslike handshake, but it had become something else entirely. At least for Jake.

Was she feeling that same searing pulse of heat that he was?

He couldn't help smiling at the startled look that came into her eyes before she removed her hand from his and stared pointedly at the floor.

It would seem that she and Cory shared another family trait. Neither of them was very good at hiding their feelings.

With a last look at her bowed head Jake turned away. With his hand on the door he paused. "My family's ranch is just over those hills. We're your nearest neighbor."

She shot him a startled look. "The Conway ranch? Of course. Jake Conway. I was a little distracted when you introduced yourself."

His smile grew. "I gave my cell phone number to Cory. So if you need anything, just call."

As he made his way to his truck, he glanced toward the barn and felt a wave of sympathy for the boy caught up in all of this. He knew what it was to lose a parent at a very young age, and he could clearly recall the pain and confusion of those early days as he'd struggled with grief and fear of the unknown, and an unreasonable sense of loss and emptiness that had never gone away.

As his truck ate up the miles to his home, Jake decided that he would make the Stanford ranch his first stop in the morning. Not just to soothe a frightened little boy's fears, he realized, but also to indulge himself with another glimpse of the boy's gorgeous, pouty-lipped sister.

The thought of tasting those lips ought to be enough to fuel his dreams all through the night.

CHAPTER TWO

Meg climbed the stairs and stepped into her old bedroom. Not that it resembled the room she remembered from her childhood. Then, it had been painted pale pink, and the walls had been plastered with pictures she'd cut out of magazines. Photos of horses had littered not only the walls but the top of her dresser and her desktop, and had been taped to her vanity mirror. She'd been totally horse crazy.

The floor had been hardwood, with a pink fuzzy rug under a canopy bed. A princess bed, her father had called it. And she was the princess who ruled all the land that could be seen outside her window.

Now the room was painted a dull shade of pale green, and the sparse furniture consisted of a bed, a dresser, and a bench under one window.

Not that it mattered to her what the room looked like. She wouldn't be here long enough to settle in. It was merely a place to park her things until she could take care of business and get back to the life she'd left in D.C.

She undressed quickly and pulled on the sea foam night slip she'd tossed into her suitcase before leaving home. The sexy, tissue-silk fabric seemed as out of place here on her father's ranch as she felt.

She pulled out her ponytail band and made her way to the bathroom carrying the overnight case that held her bath essentials. A short time later she turned out the light and climbed into bed.

After the day she'd put in, she expected to fall asleep instantly, but there were too many things weighing on her mind, dragging her down.

Her father—her big, strong, tough-as-nails father—was dead. It just didn't compute. Not that she hadn't faced death. But the loss of her mother and stepfather in a boating accident, though shocking, hadn't been nearly the jolt to her system that this news had been, delivered over the phone by Everett Fletcher, chief of police in the little town of Paintbrush.

Instead of tears, her legal training had kicked in, and she'd calmly, dispassionately, made her plans to fly here and handle the burial of her father and the disposal of his estate. Clean. Simple. Final.

What she hadn't counted on was Cory. She hadn't even known about him. And now that she did, she had more questions than answers. Burying a long-estranged father was one thing. Dealing with a scared, angry little boy was simply outside her realm of expertise. Would he go willingly to a big city, or would he fight her every step of the way? If he did go, how would he fit in? What sort of schooling had he had so far? She could easily afford a tutor, but school was only one small part of the equation. How would he fit into her lifestyle? She was single, by choice, and deeply involved in her career. She often brought her work home with her and spent endless hours prepping before a trial. What was she supposed to do with a frightened, lonely little boy? A nanny? Boarding school? She'd been saddled with both as a girl, and she found herself rejecting them out of hand.

As she pondered all this, she tossed and turned, willing herself to relax. It was impossible. She felt...twitchy. Uneasy.

To distract herself from her unsettling thoughts, she focused instead on Jake Conway. That cowboy had been one of the sexiest men she'd ever met. And that was saying something, since in her line of work there had been no shortage of handsome, successful guys, all of them eager to impress her with their wealth, their success, their...educational and social pedigrees, she thought with a smile.

What set Jake apart was the fact that he was so down to earth, despite the fact that his family ranch was one of the most successful in the country. In those faded denims and a plaid shirt with the sleeves rolled to the elbows, he'd exuded more sex appeal than the men in her firm in their custom-fitted suits and Italian leather shoes, smelling of expensive cologne and sporting razor-sharp haircuts, fresh from their workouts with their personal trainers.

She rolled to her other side and clenched a fist. The minute he'd started examining that colt and she saw those muscles flexing, she'd been mesmerized. And when he'd dazzled her with that killer smile, she'd actually felt her heart do a slow, dizzying flip.

It was a good thing she wouldn't be around long

enough to actually get to know Jake Conway. He could be a real heartbreaker.

Still, while she was here, he would certainly make things a lot more interesting.

She fell asleep smiling, with thoughts of an earthy, sexy cowboy playing through her mind.

"We missed you last night. Not like you to miss supper, boyo." Big Jim looked up from the breakfast table as Jake ambled into the big, sunny kitchen.

"Had to visit a lame colt." As was his custom, Jake brushed a kiss over old Ela's cheek before reaching for a foaming glass of freshly squeezed orange juice sitting on a tray. He lounged a hip against the counter and downed the liquid in one long swallow.

"You might want to take the time to actually taste that, bro." Quinn stepped in from the mudroom behind his wife, Cheyenne, and unrolled his sleeves after washing up at the big sink.

"Take time? What a concept." Jake grinned at his oldest brother and sister-in-law. "I'm learning how to eat and drink on the run."

"I don't know why you're in a rush, son." After morning chores in the barn, Cole Conway bypassed the juice and went straight for a cup of steaming coffee. "It's not as though your patients can run out on you if you're late."

"So many cows, so little time." Josh, just entering the kitchen with his wife, Sierra, winked at her, and the two of them laughed at his little joke. "You know, Jake, before you became a veterinarian, we used to say that about you and every woman for miles around. But now, I guess, the only females you have time to charm are the cows."

Everyone in the room burst into gales of laughter.

Jake joined them before saying, "Oh. I don't know about that. Last night's colt had an . . . interesting owner."

Seeing that he had their attention, he turned away and busied himself pouring a cup of coffee.

"Okay, bro." Quinn shot him a withering look. "Out with it. What heart are you about to break this week?"

Jake managed to tear off a corner of Ela's corn bread and pop it into his mouth before she rapped his knuckles with a wooden spoon. He shot her one of those famous Conway grins before turning to the others. "There's a certain new redhead in town that's looking mighty . . ." He licked the crumbs from his fingers. ". . . tasty."

That had them all moaning at his bad joke.

"The only redhead within a hundred miles of us is Blanche Eastman, and she was a teenager when Big Jim drove his herd here back in 1950."

Josh's remark had them all chuckling.

"Go ahead. Enjoy your little joke." Jake took his seat at the table as Phoebe and Ela began passing platters of scrambled eggs, crisp bacon, fried potatoes, and cinnamon toast. "Maybe I'll just keep the name of the lady secret, and you can hear it from old Flora the next time you visit the diner."

"If anybody would know, it's Flora." Cheyenne grinned as she helped herself to eggs and bacon. "But I'd rather hear it from you, Jake."

Cole glowered from his position at the end of the table. "Stop the teasing and spit it out, son."

Jake played out the waiting game until he had everyone's attention. "I paid a call on the ranch of one of our old neighbors."

Big Jim's lips thinned. "Of course. Porter Stanford. His sudden death is the talk of the town. I heard he left everything to his kids."

Around the table eyebrows were lifted.

Jake paused with the fork halfway to his lips. "You sure about that?"

"That's what Thibault Baxter told me over at his hardware store yesterday. And he said he heard it from Flora, so it must be gospel."

Jake shook his head. "If she knows that, why in the world was she tearing into all those metal boxes?"

"She?" Cole stared at his son.

"Porter's daughter. Her name's Meg. She's in from D.C. to dispose of the estate."

"And she called you?" Cheyenne shot a look at her sister-in-law, Sierra, who returned a knowing nod.

"About a lame colt. Only she didn't know she was calling me. She left a message with old Doc Hunger's service, and it was forwarded to my phone. It turns out the sudden death of her father wasn't her only surprise. She didn't even know she had a seven-year-old half brother until she got here."

"Wow." Sierra had forgotten her breakfast. "I guess since I'm the newest member of the family, I'm missing some history here. Who is Porter Stanford? And what kind of woman doesn't hear that she has a sibling for seven whole years?"

"The kind of woman who hadn't spoken to her father in fifteen or twenty years. Porter is—*was*," Jake corrected, "our nearest neighbor. They say he died of a heart attack. His daughter left Wyoming when she was ten, along with her mother, after a divorce—"

"A nasty divorce," Big Jim put in.

"Yeah. That's the impression I got." Jake sipped his coffee. "Anyway, his daughter Meg is a lawyer in Washington, and when she got here she discovered Cory. That's the seven-year-old."

"What about his mother?" Sierra asked.

Cole picked up the story. "Arabella. Pretty little thing. Nobody knew much about her. She and a boyfriend drifted into Paintbrush, looking for work. That was about the same time that Porter's second wife, Sherry, divorced him, and he hired Arabella to clean his house."

"He hired a pretty drifter to...clean his house?" Sierra exchanged a look with Cheyenne before the two women broke into laughter. "Is that the story he gave everyone?"

"That's the story." Cole chuckled. "Next thing we knew, they were married very quietly by Judge Bolton and shortly after welcomed Cory. Folks who saw Porter said he was a changed man. Everybody figured his new young bride was a tonic. Then, a couple of months ago, she died suddenly. Doc Walton said it was an aneurysm. After that, Porter lived like a recluse, and the boy along with him. They hardly ever went to town. Nobody called or visited. The rumor was that Porter couldn't even muster the energy to eat or fix a meal for his kid. He grew so depressed, he even hired old Yancy Jessup to oversee a crew for the ranch chores and herd, something he'd have never considered in earlier times."

"Speaking of Yancy. When I learned that nobody had notified him about Porter's passing—" Jake took a bite of his breakfast "—I got his number from Cory and told Meg she needed to make the call."

"So, as I understand it, you went out to a ranch to

treat a lame colt and just happened to find a pretty red-head?" Cheyenne shot a questioning look at her brother-in-law.

"Yeah." He nodded. "That's just the kind of dumb luck I always seem to have. I will say this for Meg Stanford. She looks damned fine in a pair of jeans. Almost as good as you and Sierra."

That had his two sisters-in-law laughing.

Quinn shook his head. "Only you, little bro, can fall into a pile of manure and come up smelling like a rose."

"It's a curse." Jake grinned. "And the hell of it is, I have to drop by again this morning. Just to make sure the colt is healing, you understand. And I promise," he said to his sisters-in-law, "if Meg Stanford is wearing tight jeans and an even tighter T-shirt, I won't even look." For emphasis, he covered his eyes with his hands in a see-no-evil pose.

They were all roaring as they finished their breakfast.

Jake was whistling as he drove his truck toward the Stanford ranch. He hoped Meg was wearing those denims that fit her like a second skin. The thought had him grinning.

His smile faded at the sight of Police Chief Everett Fletcher's car parked by the back door. As he drove closer he could see that all four tires of the pretty little rental car had been slashed, the windows shattered.

As Jake sprinted from his truck, the chief, who'd been talking quietly to Meg, looked up. "Hey, Jake."

"Chief." Jake looked from Everett to Meg. "What's going on?"

Her brows were creased, her voice tight with nerves.

"When I came downstairs this morning, the back door was open. That's when I spotted the damage to my rental car."

She drew her arms around herself and shivered, despite the warmth of the morning sun. "Look at it. This isn't just petty vandalism. This was vicious."

Jake nodded. "Was anything else vandalized?"

The chief took up the narrative. "After Miss Stanford came inside, she realized the door to her father's office was open, and his files tossed everywhere."

Jake studied Meg's pale features and could see the lines of worry and fear. "I'm sorry you have all this to deal with on top of your father's passing. Any way of knowing if anything was stolen?"

She turned away to hide the overpowering worries that had her by the throat. This, on top of what she was already dealing with, had her tied up in knots. "I've already told Chief Fletcher that I'm willing to go through my father's things to see if I can identify anything missing, but without knowing what he kept in there, I don't see that I can be much help."

Everett eyed Jake. "What brings you here?"

"There's a lame colt out in the barn. I treated him yesterday, and I promised to look in on him again today to see if he was improving." He glanced around. "Has Cory already gone out to the barn?"

"He spent the night there." Meg flushed. "I tried to get him to come in to bed, but he just clung to that colt's neck and dug in his heels. Knowing how much he loves that animal, I didn't want to make a fuss, especially since he seems so resistant to anything I say or do, so I gave up and let him stay in the barn."

The police chief lifted a brow. "Porter's boy resents you so much he slept in the barn?"

Meg shrugged. "I don't know if it's personal, or if he just dislikes people in general. Whatever is going on in that brain of his, I seem to be the focus of his distrust at the moment."

"If he was out there all night, the boy may have heard something." The chief turned to Jake. "I believe I'll just go along with you and have a talk with the boy."

"I'll go, too." Meg led the way to the barn, giving Jake another chance to admire her backside. It was the perfect distraction from all the crazy things going on here.

Today, instead of the prim shirt buttoned clear to her throat, she wore a skinny tee. Not one of those souvenir shirts with cute sayings on them. This one was the color of a ripe peach and had an interesting ruffle around the modest neckline. To Jake's way of thinking, that modest neckline just made what was inside the shirt all the more interesting.

When Meg tried to roll open the big barn door, it didn't budge. She glanced at the men before pounding a fist and shouting, "Cory? You in there?"

They heard a shuffling sound and then a scraping sound before the door opened. As the sunlight filled the gloomy interior, they saw the boy, his hair sporting bits of straw, rubbing his eyes.

"'Morning, Cory." Jake noted the manure cart shoved to one side. It had obviously been used to secure the barn door from inside. "This is Police Chief Fletcher."

The boy nodded toward the tall, muscled man in the police uniform, who was an imposing sight with his gold star winking at his lapel, his police-issue gun in a holster at his side.

"Cory." Everett extended his hand. "I'm sorry about your daddy."

The boy hung his head.

Jake stepped into the stall. "I hear you spent the night with Shadow. How's our patient?"

The boy shook his head before mumbling, "No better."

"If you'd like to bring him outside, I'll take a look at his wound."

Cory looped an arm around the colt's neck, and the boy and the horse walked out into the yard.

This morning the limp seemed even more pronounced than it had been the previous day.

Jake unwrapped the dressing and began examining the colt's leg.

As he did, the chief cleared his throat. "Did you leave the barn at all last night, Cory?"

The boy shook his head.

"Not once? Not even to get a drink of water? Or maybe to use the bathroom?"

Another shake of the shaggy head.

"Did you hear anything unusual? A car approaching? Someone walking around outside?"

Cory glanced toward Meg, avoiding the man whose size and uniform were intimidating. "Something wrong?"

Meg tried for a reassuring smile, though her lips trembled slightly. "Someone vandalized my car and broke into the house while I was sleeping."

Cory merely gaped at her.

The chief lay a hand on the boy's shoulder to get his attention. "Can you think of anybody who might want to do damage or steal something that belonged to your daddy?"

At his touch Cory cringed before staring hard at the ground. "No."

Everett studied him for a moment. "Well, if you think of anything I ought to know, you call me." He turned to Meg. "I'd like to go through the house with you now, Miss Stanford, and see if we can spot anything that might look out of the ordinary."

"Do you think someone might—" she swallowed "—still be hiding somewhere inside?"

"Not likely. Most intruders get in and out as fast as they can, so nobody has time to identify them." The chief put a hand under her elbow. "But if it would make you feel better, I'd be happy to do a walk-through, just to be sure."

"Thank you." She turned away and walked with the chief back to the house.

Jake watched them leave before returning his attention to the colt. Beside him, he heard the boy let out a long, slow breath.

"So." Jake knelt and ran his hand along the colt's leg. The colt flinched when his fingers came in contact with the wound, which appeared to be festering. "Did Shadow give you any trouble during the night?"

"No."

Because Jake had noticed Cory's reaction to Everett Fletcher, he deliberately kept his back to the boy to ease any discomfort. "Did you notice if Shadow was restless? Unable to get comfortable? Did he seem to want to pace?"

"Maybe."

"Did you let him out of the stall to walk a bit?"

Cory paused, as though weighing his words. "I opened

the stall door so he could move around. But just inside the barn."

Jake turned to look up at Cory. "You're saying he took a turn or two around the barn?"

"Inside." The boy nodded. "But we never went outside."

"So the two of you didn't actually sleep through the whole night? You were up at least a couple of times to walk?"

"I guess so."

Jake was watching the boy carefully now. "How many times? Three? Four?"

Thin shoulders shrugged uncomfortably.

"Five times?"

"I didn't keep count."

"And all those times you were awake, you never heard anything out of the ordinary?"

"I...guess I heard some things. But there are a lot of sounds in the night."

"Yeah. I know what you mean." Jake gave Cory a boyish grin. "Owls in the trees. Cattle in the fields. An engine idling. Footsteps on the gravel. Back doors opening and closing."

Cory flushed and looked away, but not before Jake saw the distress in his young eyes.

Whatever the boy had seen or heard, he was too afraid to talk about it.

Jake stood and wiped his hands down his pants. "Lots of cracks in that old barn door. Wide enough to look through. I guess if I heard someone drive up and walk around, I'd watch from a safe hiding place. Did you recognize the night visitor?"

Cory jammed his hands in his pockets. "I don't know what you mean."

Jake kept his tone soft. "You need a friend, Cory. Someone you can trust to share your burden. Otherwise, the load you're carrying is going to be too heavy."

When the boy refused to look at him, Jake turned. "I'll get my bag. Shadow needs another shot of antibiotic if he's going to beat this infection."

He sauntered toward his truck and took his time removing his bag. He wanted the boy to have plenty of time to ponder his words.

When he returned, Cory had his arm around the colt's neck, his face pressed to the warmth of its velvet muzzle.

The boy and horse watched Jake's approach with wary eyes.

"You might want to hold his leg while I inject this, to keep him from kicking me. Sometimes, in order to help, I have to do something painful."

Cory took hold of the colt by the hoof, immobilizing the leg while Jake plunged the needle.

"Ever been kicked by a horse?" the boy asked.

"Too many times to count." Jake began wrapping the colt's leg.

"Then why do you keep doing it?"

"Because I know that what I'm doing is a good thing." Jake looked over at the boy. "We all have this inner voice that tells us when we're doing right or wrong. It's called our conscience. Ever hear of it?"

Cory nodded. "My mom talked about it."

"What did she say?"

"That sometimes, when we're doing something wrong, we start to feel bad about ourselves. That's our conscience telling us we need to change, even if it means we'll be in big trouble when we tell the truth about what we did."

"Your mom was right. But there's one more thing. Even though we may get in trouble for telling on ourselves, that bad feeling will go away, because we'll know in our hearts that we did the right thing. So if you're tempted to keep secrets that might cause harm, find somebody you can trust and ask for their help. You'll be glad you did."

Jake could see the way Cory was absorbing his words. He offered his hand. "Thanks for all your help, son. Do you have a horse trailer in the equipment barn?"

"Yeah. Why?"

"I'd like to borrow it to haul Shadow to my ranch."

Seeing the alarm that darted into the boy's eyes he spoke quickly, to soothe his fears. "I know you want to be with him, but it would be a whole lot easier for me to check on him if I had him close by. The fact that the wound didn't respond to the first injection tells me that it's in the bloodstream and needs some serious attention. By having Shadow at my ranch, I can spend more time with him, and see that he gets better. Think of it this way. My ranch is like a hospital for sick animals. Do you understand?"

Cory hung his head. "I guess so."

"Okay. Let's get Shadow comfortable, and go find that trailer."

A short time later, Jake drove Cory in his truck to the equipment barn and located the horse trailer. After hitching it to his truck, Jake opened the passenger door for Cory. "Let's find your sister and let her know what I'm planning to do."

As they drove to the back door of the house, Jake glanced at the boy beside him. "I know you haven't had breakfast yet, since we woke you."

Cory nodded.

"Want to ride along to my place? I'm sure Phoebe and Ela would have something cooking. They always do."

"Who are Phoebe and Ela?"

"Our housekeeper and cook. They make the best pecan pancakes and warm maple syrup in all of Wyoming."

He could see the boy hesitating.

"You'd be helping me, too, by getting Shadow settled into his new stall. I'm sure he'd feel better having you around."

Cory gave a quick nod of his head. "Okay. I'd like that, too."

"I'll just tell your sister." Jake turned off the ignition and stepped from the truck.

He was smiling as he sprinted up the steps.

It was clear that the boy had secrets. And the best way to uncover them, one by one, was by using his secret weapons—Phoebe and Ela, and their Conway-tested food. What kid could resist such a winning combination?

He had an idea that Cory's sister might be in need of that very same magic. So far, her homecoming had been a nightmare.

CHAPTER THREE

Hearing voices at the rear of the house, Jake ambled through rooms filled with dusty old photographs. Rooms with dark paneled walls and heavy draperies that kept out the sunlight. Rooms that smelled musty and old and lifeless.

He stepped into what must have been Porter Stanford's office. The walls were lined with shelves and cabinets. A heavy oak desk was littered with books and ledgers and papers. They spilled out of drawers and half-opened cabinet doors. There were more papers on the floor, and a trail of them led from the desk to a set of floor-to-ceiling glass doors, which were still locked, their heavy draperies half-closed against the light.

Meg was stone-faced, while the chief looked grim.

Jake paused by the door. "Looks like the intruder was busy."

Everett Fletcher nodded. "Apparently. But how can we know if he got whatever it was he came for?"

"You think someone's looking for money?"

"I'm sure he wouldn't turn up his nose at it. But Porter was meticulous about his profit-and-loss records. Anybody who knew him would know that he believed in keeping his money in the bank in Paintbrush." The police chief pointed. "From the looks of this mess, our intruder was after something else. A legal document maybe. That seems the most likely reason to break into a dead man's house and rifle through his files."

Jake glanced at Meg. "Do you have a copy of your father's will?"

She shook her head. "My father and I never communicated. But Chief Fletcher said that Judge Bolton handled my father's legal work." She paused to look at the police chief to fill in the blanks for her.

Everett Fletcher nodded. "Kirby Bolton was your father's lawyer long before he became a judge. If anybody would know about a will, it would be Kirby."

"Or Flora." Seeing Meg's arched brow, Jake added with a smile, "Flora owns the diner in town. She knows what happens in this part of Wyoming as soon as it occurs, and considers it her solemn duty to spread the news as fast as is humanly possible. Folks in Paintbrush don't need to read a newspaper or watch a TV news show. They just drop by Flora's Diner."

A smile touched Meg's lips before the look of worry returned. "I remember Flora from my childhood. But, if it's well-known that Judge Bolton has my father's legal documents, why would an intruder want to break in here?"

The chief shrugged. "Maybe he figures your father

kept other things. Coins. Collectibles. I can't really say, Miss Stanford. Could your mother fill you in on some of your father's background?"

"My mother is dead," she said matter-of-factly. "I hope you'll consider sending an officer to patrol the area until this is resolved."

Chief Fletcher was already shaking his head. "This isn't Washington, Miss Stanford. I don't have an officer I can spare—"

"I'm not asking for a full-time bodyguard. But at least at night—"

"You don't understand. I'm the only lawman around here. Just me. My only deputy assistant, Burk Truman, fills in while I grab some sleep. If he needs backup, he calls me at home. As you can see, I'm spread thin as it is. I can't possibly promise to be out here for even one night. But I'd like to give you Thibault Baxter's number. He owns the paint and hardware store in Paintbrush, and he'd be happy to come out and change these locks for you."

"Thank you." She turned away, but not before Jake saw the stricken look in her eyes. It was obvious that she was feeling completely out of her element.

"Miss Stanford . . ."

Before Everett could finish, Jake put a hand on his shoulder and gave a quick shake of his head.

He kept his tone soft and easy. "I came in here to let you know that I'll be taking Shadow to my place."

She whirled. "You mean you can't treat him and you're going to . . . put him down?"

"Not at all. What I'm saying is that this is a nasty infection that hasn't responded to my first line of treatment, so I want the colt close, where I can keep an eye on him.

I've asked Cory to ride along and help Shadow settle in. I think you should join us."

When she seemed about to refuse he added, "Chief Fletcher will tell you that our cook and housekeeper serve some of the finest food around. You've had a lot to handle in just a matter of days. Why don't you and Cory take a break from all this, and enjoy a good meal while you have the opportunity?"

The chief seemed relieved for the distraction. "Jake's not just bragging, Miss Stanford. I find an excuse to stop by the Conway ranch at mealtime whenever I can. Between Phoebe's pot roast and Ela's corn bread, those two would put those fancy TV chefs to shame."

"Food." Meg touched a hand to her stomach. "I haven't eaten a real meal since I got off the plane. And that was some trail mix and a glass of cheap chardonnay."

"There you go." The chief looked over at Jake. "I think a visit to your place is just what Miss Stanford and the boy need right about now, before they have to deal with changing the locks and figuring out what safety measures to take."

Jake glanced at Meg, who was biting her lip and trying to come up with a decision.

Jake decided to nudge her a bit more. "I can't imagine that the intruder would risk coming here in daylight."

After considering her options, Meg started across the room. "You're right. I'll get the keys." She frowned. "Not that a locked door will make much difference to the intruder. It didn't stop him last night."

The police chief called, "Maybe he already got what he came for and is long gone."

Meg paused and turned to the man with the badge. "I hope you're right, Chief Fletcher."

He followed her from the room, leaving Jake to trail slowly behind, as he dug out his cell phone and called Phoebe to let her know he was bringing guests for lunch.

Meg and Cory stared out the truck windows, watching the passing scenery with avid interest.

Cory, sandwiched between Jake and Meg, turned to Jake. "How far to your place?"

"We're on it. Have been ever since we left your ranch."

"This is all yours?"

Jake nodded. "Not technically mine. It belongs to my family. My grandfather, my father, and my two brothers and their wives."

The boy's eyes widened. "You've got brothers?"

"Quinn and Josh. They're both older than me."

"Wow. It must be cool having older brothers."

"Sometimes." Jake chuckled. "And sometimes I used to wish I was an only child." He looked over. "How about you? Ever wish you had brothers?"

Cory shrugged. "It would've been neat. My dad didn't do a lot with me. Sometimes I thought it was because he didn't like me." He sighed. "But my mom said it was because he was old and tired."

Jake looked beyond the boy to the young woman who hadn't spoken a single word since leaving her father's ranch.

She looked pensively out the side window, and it occurred to him that she and the boy didn't interact, except through him. Maybe they'd already given up trying to communicate with each other.

"How does it feel to be back in Wyoming, Meg?"

She forced herself from her reverie to shrug her shoulders. "It feels strange. For years after my mother and I left, I begged to be allowed to come back, if only for a few weeks. I missed it so much. I'd had a pony..." She stopped and glanced at the boy beside her. Her tone lowered. Softened. "I'd almost forgotten, Cory. I called her Strawberry. She was a roan. A gift from my father on my seventh birthday." A long, deep sigh escaped her lips. "I loved that pony."

Cory shot her a timid look. "That's how I feel about Shadow. Did you take her with you when you left?"

She seemed more surprised by the fact that he spoke directly to her than by the question. "I had to leave her behind. My mother made it clear that we were leaving everything except the clothes on our backs, and starting our new lives with a clean slate. And so we did."

"If you had asked Dad, he would have sent you pictures of Strawberry."

She shook her head. "We didn't exactly part as friends."

The boy looked at her in disbelief. "My mom used to say he isn't your friend. He's your dad. That's why, even when he's sad, I should know that he loves me."

"He may have been my dad, too, but the man I left was a mean-mouthed—" She stopped herself, forcing the anger from her tone. "Sorry. Old habits. Look, Cory, I'm glad he was a decent enough dad to you. But my memories aren't the same as yours."

"Was he mean to you?"

"Never. At least, not until I left Wyoming. Then, it was as if I'd fallen off a cliff. I never heard from him again. I was just cut out of his life."

The uncomfortable silence was there again, like a wall between them.

Jake was relieved when Cory asked him, "How much longer before we reach your house?"

Jake pointed. "Keep an eye up ahead."

As they came up over a ridge, Jake smiled at the sight of the sprawling house in the distance. They drove under the arch with the huge C burned into the wood, along with the words DEVIL'S WILDERNESS.

Cory read the words aloud. "Is that the name of your ranch?"

"Yeah." Jake's tone warmed. "When my grandfather, Big Jim, first saw this place, he thought it was the rawest, toughest landscape he'd ever encountered. The devil's own wilderness. And the name stuck."

Meg turned to look at Jake. "You call your grandfather Big Jim?"

"That's his name."

"Did your grandfather raise you?"

"As much as my father, I'd say. My father's name is Cole, by the way. And my brothers and I call him Pa."

"And your mom?" Cory asked.

"Gone." Jake's grin faded. "She disappeared without a trace when I was a kid."

"What do you mean—disappeared?" Though it was Cory who spoke, Jake saw Meg's interest sharpen.

"She was here one day, and then gone. And through the years, there's never been a single clue as to where she went, or why."

Meg nodded slowly. "I seem to remember hearing my parents talking about it. But it was so long ago, I have only vague memories. It must be horrible to not know what happened."

"Yeah. It's a b—" Jake shot a quick glance at Cory

and added lamely, "It's a bear, not knowing. It became the new reality in the Conway household. The elephant in the living room that everybody circled, but nobody acknowledged."

Cory was watching him carefully. "You keep an elephant in your living room?"

That had Jake's frown turning into a grin. "Thanks, Cory." He tousled the boy's hair. "I needed that."

The boy turned from Jake to Meg, who was also grinning. "I don't understand."

"I'll explain it to you later," Jake said. "For now, I'd like to welcome both of you to my home."

He drove along the curving ribbon of driveway that showed off the front of the gray, three-story structure made of wood and stone, nestled in the foothills of the majestic Tetons. The sprawling house looked as though it had always been here. As though it had sprung up with the very mountains themselves.

On the long front porch sat an assortment of sturdy outdoor furniture, including two hand-hewn wooden rockers.

Jake pointed them out. "Big Jim made those by hand more than fifty years ago. He and his bride, Clementine, spent many a summer evening watching the steady parade of wildlife that crossed their property."

"Is Clementine still alive?" Meg asked.

"She's buried up on that hill." As Meg and Cory swiveled their heads, he added, "And she's as alive as ever in Big Jim's mind. He still consults her on every issue, and drops by often for a visit, or to tell her about his day."

Driving around to the back of the house, Jake continued on toward one of the barns. He turned off the engine

and walked around to open the passenger door for Meg
and Cory.

The three of them walked to the horse trailer, and Jake
lowered the ramp to allow Cory to lead the colt out into
the sunshine.

The limp, Jake noted, was no better.

"Let's get Shadow settled in." He led the way inside a
cavernous barn.

He paused to hold the door while Cory led the colt into
a stall filled with fresh straw and a trough brimming with
cool water.

The colt took a long, noisy drink.

Jake pointed to a bin just inside the barn door. "You'd
better fetch him some oats, son. After that ride, Shadow's
bound to be as hungry as he is thirsty."

The boy raced off and returned with a scoop of oats
that he dumped into an empty feed box.

When the stall door was secured, the three of them
watched as the colt began to eat.

Cory turned to Jake. "How'd you know he was hungry?"

"A calculated guess. Traveling always makes me hungry. How about you?"

The boy smiled. "Yeah."

"Good. That will make Phoebe and Ela happy."

"Why?"

"Because they like nothing better than to feed a hungry
boy. They've had years of experience."

As they made their way from across the floor of the barn
Cory asked, "Do you bring lots of sick animals here?"

"Some. Right now I've got Randy Morton's golden
Lab here." Jake paused at the dog's pen to run a hand
over her back and was rewarded with a lick from her

lolling tongue. "Honey's expecting pups any day now, and Randy had to leave town on business, so I agreed to keep her here and keep an eye on her until Randy gets back. That way we'll know Honey is in a safe shelter when her time comes."

Cory petted the pretty Lab. "Do you think she'll have them today while we're here?"

Jake could hear the excitement in Cory's voice. "I doubt it." He led the way from the barn. "But it's only a matter of days. Maybe you'll get to see them."

At his words, the boy fairly skipped up the steps toward the back door of the house.

"I think," Jake said in an aside to Meg, "I've just found something that excites him even more than the thought of good food."

Instead of the smile he was expecting, Jake noticed Meg's frown as she chewed on her lower lip. A sure sign that her nerves had returned.

"Hey. You're among friends here. Nobody's going to bite you." He touched a hand to hers. Just a touch, but he felt a sudden spark. A rush of heat that had nothing to do with the weather.

He glanced over to see the way her eyes went wide.

He'd never thought of himself as a mind reader, but he'd become very good at reading people's expressions. From the look on Meg Stanford's face, he was pretty certain that she'd just felt the same shock.

And wasn't at all happy about it.

She kept her tone low so Cory wouldn't overhear. "I seem to recall overhearing my father talking about your family when I was a kid. From the things he said, I figured there was no love lost between our families."

"Yesterday's news." Jake deliberately put a hand under her elbow, forcing himself to absorb yet another spark. "Whatever happened in the past will stay there. Now relax and enjoy a friendly visit with your neighbors."

Before she could respond he pushed open the door and led the way through the spotless mudroom and into the kitchen, where the chorus of voices told him that the entire Conway family had already assembled for lunch.

CHAPTER FOUR

"Well, boyo." Big Jim was the first to spot Jake. Setting aside his coffee he crossed the room to offer a smile to the woman and boy who stood slightly behind his grandson. "Who've we got here?"

"Big Jim, this is Meg and Cory Stanford."

"Nice to meet both of you. I'm sorry for your loss." Big Jim offered each a handshake before returning his attention to Meg. "Last time I saw you, you were about this lad's age."

Meg smiled. "My mother and I left Wyoming when I was ten."

Jake turned to include his father in the introductions. "Meg and Cory, this is my pa, Cole Conway."

As he shook their hands Cole said, "I'm sorry you had to come home for such a sad occasion."

"Thank you."

Jake continued the introductions. "This is my brother,

Quinn, and his wife, Cheyenne, and my brother Josh and his bride, Sierra."

Each in turn offered a few words of sympathy.

"And the two women who are the queens of their domain, and manage to feed us while keeping us in our place, are Phoebe and Ela."

Meg returned the smiles of the two older women. "I'm sorry to barge in on you like this at mealtime."

"You aren't barging," Phoebe insisted. "Jake called us to say you were coming. And even if he hadn't, he knows we always cook enough to feed an army."

Phoebe pointed to a tray on the counter, containing frosty glasses of lemonade. "Please help yourselves to something to drink. Lunch is just about ready."

When neither of his guests made a move to help themselves, Jake picked up two glasses and held them out. Cory and Meg each accepted one from his hand with a smile of thanks.

Cole set aside his empty glass. "Have you set a day for the funeral?"

"I spoke with Reverend Cornell at the Paintbrush Church, and he suggested I wait until Monday, since he had a wedding to perform today."

"Thibault Baxter's granddaughter," Phoebe put in. "Only eighteen, but her boyfriend enlisted and has only a couple of days before he's assigned overseas. She's borrowing her best friend's gown, since they had no time to plan anything on such short notice."

Big Jim shot their housekeeper a grin. "Been talking to Flora, have you?"

"Of course. Where else would I learn all this?" Phoebe's cheeks reddened before she bent to the oven.

Within minutes the two women had filled platters with fried chicken, roasted potatoes, and a basket of Ela's corn bread. In the middle of the lazy Susan they placed an enormous salad and a stack of salad bowls.

"Lunch is ready," Phoebe called.

The family needed no coaxing as they circled the table and began to take their places.

Jake held a chair for Meg and indicated one to her left for Cory. When they were seated, Jake took a chair to the right of Meg.

As they began filling salad bowls and passing platters, they all seemed to be talking at once.

"That garden's looking mighty fine, Phoebe."

The housekeeper smiled. "Thanks to Jake, who came to my rescue and tilled all the soil."

Quinn nudged Josh. "There he goes again. Kissing Phoebe's—" at a narrowed look from Big Jim he said quickly "—hand, hoping to earn points."

"Or a bigger slice of her strawberry pie," Josh added.

"Correct on both counts," Jake said smugly. To Meg he whispered loudly, "It pays to be the youngest. You watch your elders and learn all the tricks of the trade."

He winked at Cory, and the boy couldn't hold back a grin.

"I was up in the hills yesterday." Quinn held the salad while his wife filled her bowl. "Actually, Cheyenne and I were up there together trailing our pack…"

Cory's head came up sharply. "Pack?"

"Wolf pack," Quinn explained.

"You have a wolf pack?" Cory's eyes were as big as saucers.

"They don't know they're mine," Quinn laughed.

"My big brother is a naturalist, when he isn't ranching," Jake said. "He's been studying the life cycle of wolves for years. And I know this is hard to believe, but he was able to find a woman who's as crazy as he is. So the two of them actually hike into the hills and observe a pack of wolves while the wolves hunt and eat and sleep and do all kinds of ordinary wolf things, which Quinn and Cheyenne record and share with other naturalists." In a stage whisper Jake added, "Or, as we like to call them, other crazy wolf people."

That had everyone laughing while Cory stared at Quinn with a look that ranged from admiration to astonishment.

Quinn winked at the boy. "Jake's just jealous because I won't let him go along to doctor the wolves. If my little brother had his way, he'd have the barn filled with all kinds of sick critters that would have to be confined or they'd end up eating him and our livestock as soon as they were healed."

"Not that he hasn't tried that a number of times," Josh said with a laugh. "Oh, Cory, the stories we could tell about Jake."

The little boy grinned as the conversation drifted to the herds and the rangeland.

Quinn nodded toward the window. "Cheyenne and I found the herds looking fat and sleek up in the hills. I think the rangeland is the greenest I've ever seen."

Big Jim was smiling. "Lots of snow this past winter and the spring rains gave us just what we needed. This may be one of our best years ever." He glanced down the table at Meg. "How about your herds? Have you had a chance to look them over?"

Meg flushed. "No. Sorry. I've been wrestling with my father's paperwork, or rather, the jumbled mess he called his paperwork."

Cole arched a brow. "That doesn't sound like the Porter Stanford I knew. He may have been cantankerous, but he was a stickler for rules and order. One time we needed to produce a deed for a tract of land that had come under question by the court, and he was able to produce it before our law firm could find our copy." Cole glanced at his father, seated at the head of the table. "Do you remember that?"

Big Jim chuckled. "How could I forget? I was the one who'd questioned the ownership of the parcel. I was sure it was part of our holdings, and when I took the issue to Judge Bolton, he ordered me to produce proof. While I was still describing the parcel to my lawyer, Porter was already in the courtroom with his copy of the deed."

Meg nodded. "Funny. I'd forgotten how often he'd say, in that stern voice, 'A place for everything and everything in its place, girl. Nobody around here is allowed to suffer from dropsy.'"

Cory turned wide eyes to his sister. "He said that to you, too?"

Meg sighed. "Oh yeah. It's all coming back to me."

"What's dropsy?" Sierra asked.

"Dropping things on the floor or counter, or bed or table, instead of putting them away in a cupboard or closet or drawer." Meg shook her head. "My biggest offense in his eyes was dropping my coat and scarf and mittens by the back door. He would stand at the foot of the stairs and order me to come down at once and hang up my things where they belonged."

"Sounds like Big Jim in the equipment barn." Josh glanced at his brothers for confirmation. "Every truck, every tractor, has to be parked just so. And no matter how small the tool, everything has to be returned to the proper shelf, or we hear about it." He helped himself to a hunk of corn bread. "Remember the time Jake left the old green tractor out in the north field?"

Jake gave a mock shudder. "It was just my luck that Big Jim was flying in that very evening and saw the empty tractor sitting there unattended."

Quinn picked up the thread of the story. "Big Jim came charging into the house like a wounded bear demanding to know which of his damned fool grandsons had lost his mind and abandoned a tractor without bothering to clean it up and return it to the barn."

Phoebe gave a laugh and continued the story. "And I had just returned from a terrifying drive all the way to town to Dr. Walton's clinic and back with Jake's poor face swollen up three times its normal size after he'd unknowingly driven that tractor into a hornet's nest."

Big Jim started laughing as the memory washed over him. "I took one look at poor Jake, who looked like one of those actors in a horror show, and then saw the way Phoebe was ready to go to war for her boy, and decided I'd better hightail it out of the house until tempers cooled. I spent the next two hours driving the tractor back to the barn and cleaning it up. By the time I came in, the house was quiet, everyone had gone to bed, and I was left to eat a cold meal and face an even colder reception the next morning."

"As I recall," Jake added with a laugh, "I still got the lecture about returning equipment to the barn, and an added lecture about keeping an eye on the unknown dangers lurking all around us."

"Which didn't help where you were concerned," Cole added dryly. "Of all my sons, you seemed the most likely to step on a nest of snakes, or stumble into a cave and wake a sleeping bear."

Cory's eyes went wide. "You woke a bear?"

Jake grinned. "Only once. And he was just a little cub."

"Sleeping next to his mother, who as I recall," Quinn said, "weighed more than that tractor."

Josh roared with laughter. "I don't think I've ever seen you run that fast, bro."

"I managed to outrun the bear, didn't I?" Jake asked.

"Barely. And only because she was still groggy from hibernation."

The rest of the family joined in the laughter.

As the talk continued swirling around them, Meg sat back, listening to the easy banter among these family members. It was obvious that they enjoyed one another's company. And for all their teasing about their grandfather's strict rules, they had real affection for him. It was something that had been sadly lacking in her own family while growing up. Bickering between her parents had become a way of life, until it had become impossible to carry on a simple conversation.

Phoebe began cutting slices of an enormous chocolate layer cake. "Our dessert today is compliments of Otis Fanning's niece, Amy Jo. She drove all the way over here today, hoping to deliver it personally to her uncle's favorite veterinarian, Dr. Jake." Her eyes danced. "Imagine her disappointment to learn that Jake wasn't home. Which means, of course, that she'll probably have to devise a reason to bake something equally extravagant next week."

"Another admirer, bro?" Quinn nudged his wife. "How old is this one?"

"Apparently old enough to drive," Josh put in with a laugh.

Jake joined their laughter. "Amy Jo's eighteen, and heading off to college in the fall."

"They keep getting younger and younger." Josh turned to Sierra. "How old was the one who brought the rhubarb pie last week?"

"Fifteen. But that didn't count," Sierra said with a straight face. "I think coming here was her mama's idea."

That had everyone laughing.

Jake shook his head. "As I've said, it's my curse. I can't help it if the entire population of Paintbrush worships at my feet."

"A fifteen-year-old?" Quinn said in feigned surprise. "And her mother?"

"You're just jealous because I get the best gifts. But don't despair, bro." Jake winked at Cory. "That ninety-two-year-old naturalist out in California offered to send you her recipe for trail mix."

That had everyone howling.

While Meg watched, Ela paused beside Cory's place at the table and held out the plate of cake slices. When he started to reach for the smallest piece, the old woman gave a quick shake of her head. He quickly lowered his hand to his lap. Without a word the old woman used silver tongs to drop two big slices on his plate. When he shot her a look of surprise, her wrinkled, parchment face relaxed into a wide smile before she moved on.

Meg marveled at the fact that those two had communicated without using a single word. Yet here she was, a lawyer accustomed to using words to persuade a jury of strangers, and she seemed utterly incapable of getting through to this solemn little boy.

She glanced at Jake as he enjoyed his dessert. He obviously reveled in his role of ladies' man. She wasn't surprised. Hadn't he caught her eye at their very first meeting?

Big Jim eyed Meg over the rim of his cup. "You and Cory planning on running your father's ranch?"

Meg looked startled. "I haven't even considered such a thing."

The old man set down his cup. "Just what are you planning on doing with it?"

Meg could feel the tension returning to a spot between her shoulders. It happened every time she allowed herself to think about what she had to deal with. A huge, neglected ranch, and a half brother who was a stranger to her. Of the two, the boy was a much bigger challenge than the ranch. Though he'd revealed very little, it was obvious that Cory was scared and hurt by the losses he'd endured in his young life. The thought of transplanting him from everything that was familiar and comforting to a strange new life in a big city hurt her as much as she knew it would hurt him. But, for now, she couldn't think of any other solution.

As for the ranch, she swallowed hard before saying, "I thought I'd auction off the herds and equipment first. I had a representative from an auction house come by yesterday to look over our things and estimate their worth. And then I thought I'd put everything, including the land and buildings, up for sale."

Jake caught the look of consternation in Cory's eyes. He kept his tone deliberately soft. "Have you signed a contract with the auction house?"

"Not yet. I have another company asking to be allowed to compete with the first bid before I make my decision."

"Since you've only been home for a day, why not give it some time before you sign any contracts?"

"I'm running on a very short timetable. I have to get back to my job."

"What do you do, Meg?" Cheyenne asked.

"I'm a lawyer with Howe-Kettering in Washington, D.C."

Sierra shot her an admiring glance. "That's about as big as it gets." She turned to the others. "Howe-Kettering was involved in the murder trial of that senator's daughter who went missing. Two years later her remains were identified at a remote campsite in Nevada. Everybody thought the wealthy businessman who was the senator's biggest donor would walk because he seemed to have an airtight alibi. But some young hotshot lawyer dropped a bombshell during the trial that had him breaking down and confessing on live television."

Cheyenne nodded. "I saw that." She turned to peer intently at Meg, when the light suddenly dawned. "Oh, wow. *You* were that hotshot lawyer."

Meg smiled. "It was a very satisfying moment."

Quinn started chuckling. Seeing the questioning looks of the others he said, "I think Meg's story trumps Jake's."

"No question about it." Jake put a hand over Meg's. "Sleeping bears and mad hornets don't hold a candle to putting a murderer away for good."

Meg very carefully removed her hand and clenched it in her lap. "Actually, he's appealing the conviction."

"After a public admission of guilt?" Sierra couldn't hide her shock.

"He's claiming temporary insanity."

"Do you think he has a chance of winning the appeal?"

Meg lifted both palms up. "When you're dealing with a jury, there's no telling what the outcome will be."

"That's a lot like life, isn't it?" Big Jim sat back, watching Meg and Cory. "One day you're up, the next you're down. A big win can turn into a huge loss. But the good thing is, the next day it all starts over, and just when you think you've lost everything, you find a hidden treasure."

Cole studied the stingy slice of cake that Phoebe had placed on his plate. "Here's my treasure."

He took a bite and slowly chewed and swallowed before explaining. "Now that I'm on a restricted diet, I've learned to appreciate the little nuggets of real gold in my life. Having this woman watching out for me is one of them."

He and Phoebe exchanged looks, and the housekeeper found herself blushing at his unexpected admission.

As Phoebe circled the table refilling coffee cups, she lay a hand on Cole's shoulder. He reached up and closed his big hand over hers.

While the talk drifted to ranch chores, Jake shifted and whispered, "Heart attack. Phoebe watches out for him like a she-bear."

Meg nodded in understanding.

As Jake's shoulder brushed Meg's, the quick jolt of heat slid down his spine.

There was no denying what he felt each time they made the slightest contact. A purely sexual tug that was both pleasant and unsettling. And from the way she reacted each time they touched, he was convinced that she felt it, too. Why else would she have the need to draw away so abruptly?

Hearing Meg reply to Sierra's question, and watching Cory shyly smile at Ela, Jake was glad that he'd brought Meg and Cory home for a meal. His family had a way of getting people to relax and open up about themselves.

Like the fact that Meg and Cory had more in common than they'd first thought. They shared similar memories about a father who was now gone. Good, bad, or indifferent, they were memories that nobody else could share. They both had a love for horses. And they were both alone, with no other family members left to offer comfort.

He wondered how long it would take them both to figure out that they might be more alike than either of them cared to admit.

In the next instant he wondered why it should matter to him at all. Meg and Cory were, after all, neighbors who would probably be gone in a matter of days, without leaving a forwarding address. They wouldn't give him or his family a second thought.

Still, while they were here, they were dealing with some pretty heavy issues. It wasn't in his nature to turn his back on a neighbor as long as he could be any help at all.

One area where he could certainly lend a hand was with the colt. He'd see to it that Shadow was healthy enough to withstand whatever came next. If Meg sold all the ranch stock, the colt stood a better chance of landing in a good home if that leg mended perfectly.

The thought of separating Cory from his colt wasn't a pleasant one. Both the boy and horse would suffer from the separation. Hopefully, since Meg had gone through a similar separation as a child, she would be sympathetic to the pain her little brother would endure.

Little brother.

That had Jake sitting back with a grin. Until yesterday, Meg hadn't even known about Cory. Now she was going to have to deal with not only the loss of a father but the addition of a stranger in her life.

He shot a glance at his own father, busy talking ranch chores with Big Jim, and found himself wondering how he would feel if he learned that Cole had kept secrets from his family. Secrets that would impact them for the rest of their lives.

That wasn't a place Jake cared to visit in his mind. There already was a huge mystery in their lives. One that had never been resolved, and left a gaping wound that continued to fester.

Maybe, he thought, every family had secrets. But he doubted that many of them could compete with the mystery that had plagued the Conway family for two decades.

In the meantime, he would give as much attention as he could to Meg and Cory.

It didn't hurt, he thought with a devilish grin, that Meg Stanford was as beautiful as she was complicated.

There was nothing Jake loved more than the challenge of a gorgeous, fascinating woman.

CHAPTER FIVE

Big Jim smiled at Meg. "I hope your father's messy papers can be cleared up quickly."

"His papers are the least of my problems." Meg sat back, feeling stronger now that she'd enjoyed that excellent meal. "I woke up this morning to discover an awful mess because there had been an intruder at the ranch while Cory and I were asleep."

She realized, by the sudden, shocking silence, that she had everyone's attention. "Sorry. I didn't mean to drop a bombshell after such a lovely lunch."

Cole frowned. "How much damage was done?"

She gripped her hands together in her lap. "The windows were broken and the tires slashed on my rental car, and papers were scattered all over the floor of my father's office."

Big Jim's eyes narrowed. "Was anything stolen?"

Meg shrugged. "Without knowing what my father had,

it's impossible to tell. Chief Fletcher suggested that I talk to Judge Bolton to see if he has a current copy of my father's will, since I couldn't find a copy in my father's office."

Cole nodded. "Kirby Bolton was a good friend of your father's. If anyone would know what he had and what may have been taken, it's him."

Big Jim asked, "Have you phoned the car rental agency?"

Meg shook her head.

"I suggest you call them and explain what happened. Their vehicles are all insured. They can send someone out with a tow truck to pick up the damaged car and deliver a new one. Living so far from town, you can't get by without some wheels."

Meg smiled. "You're right. Thanks for reminding me." She scrolled through her cell phone until she located the number for the car rental agency.

Within minutes she had explained the situation to someone there and hung up with a smile. "They said they'll have someone take care of it as soon as possible."

Big Jim said firmly, "And this time, you need to lock your rental car in the barn at night."

Cheyenne glanced at Sierra. "Personally, I wouldn't want to stay there at night, knowing someone could do this again. What's to stop an intruder from coming back?"

Meg shuddered. "Chief Fletcher suggested that whoever did this may have already found what they were looking for, and won't bother returning."

"Maybe." Phoebe arched a brow. "And maybe not." She focused on Meg. "We have plenty of room here for you and Cory. Why don't you consider staying here?"

Caught off guard by her kindness, Meg chewed on her lip. "I really appreciate the offer, Phoebe, but I'm not comfortable leaving my father's ranch vacant and vulnerable to thieves. If it were known that nobody was there, the intruder could return and take as long as he pleases to go through my father's files. Besides..." She glanced at Jake before saying, "I really need to see this through. I'll feel better about myself if I stay put rather than run away and hide. But Cory is another matter." She turned to the boy. "Maybe you ought to consider bunking here. That way you could see Shadow whenever you wanted."

The boy's eyes clouded with confusion before he ducked his head. His hands, held stiffly in his lap, clenched and unclenched with nerves.

Jake could practically read the boy's dilemma. On the one hand, he'd just been offered a way out. He could remain here with his colt, and nobody would blame him. On the other hand, he would be abandoning Meg if he left her alone.

Obviously uncomfortable being the center of attention, Cory's voice was little more than a mumble. "I'll go home with you."

If Meg was relieved, she tried not to show it. With a gentle smile she said, "Okay."

Big Jim pushed away from the table and got to his feet. "I've got to get back to my chores." He offered a handshake to Meg and then to Cory. "It was good meeting both of you. I hope you'll come back."

"Thank you." Meg felt a welling of gratitude for the comfort of this large and loving family. Whatever issues had been between them and her father had apparently been put aside, and for that she was thankful. As she offered her hand to the others she added, "I can't thank you enough for your hospitality. I'm feeling a lot less alone now than I did at this time yesterday."

"That's what neighbors are for." Cole gave her a wide smile. "You need anything at all, you just let us know."

After thanking Phoebe and Ela for the meal, Meg turned to Jake. "We'd better get back now."

He nodded. "We'll make a stop in the barn first, and see how Shadow is settling in."

Before they could leave, Ela handed Meg a brown bag. "What's this?"

The old woman grinned, showing a gap where a tooth had been. "Some cold roast chicken and corn bread. Enough for dinner tonight and breakfast in the morning for you and the boy."

Meg felt an unexpected rush of tears and blinked them away. "Thank you. That's very kind."

The old woman put a gnarled hand on Cory's shoulder. "You're a good boy. You watch out for your sister."

Cory ducked his head, avoiding that dark, piercing gaze that seemed able to see clear through to a person's heart.

Jake kissed Ela's withered cheek. "I hope you saved some corn bread for me."

"You had enough." But her words were softened with a smile.

"I'll never have enough." He chuckled as he led the way to the barn.

Inside, the colt lifted its head in greeting the moment Cory stepped into the stall.

"Hey. How do you like it here?" the boy whispered.

As if in reply, Shadow tossed his head and gave a soft whinny.

"That's good." Cory looped an arm around the colt's neck and pressed his face close. "I have to leave you here. But only for a couple of days. As soon as your leg heals, you'll be going home with me."

Standing outside the stall, Meg and Jake watched in silence.

"'Bye, Shadow." Cory ran a hand along the colt's mane. "See you tomorrow."

The three of them walked from the barn and climbed into the truck.

As Jake drove along the curving driveway, Meg lowered the window and breathed deeply. "I'd forgotten how fresh and clean and dry the air is here in Wyoming. By now in D.C. there's so much humidity, I always feel like I'm breathing underwater."

Jake laughed. "I didn't notice you breathing in like this when we were in the barn."

She joined his laughter. "You're right. Funny. You never forget the smell of a barn. But after the first few hours back here, I felt as though I'd never left. Some of the memories are slowly returning, but so many others washed over me in waves so fast and furious I could hardly absorb all of them."

She fell silent and turned to look out the window, leaving Jake to wonder whether the memories had been pleasant or unpleasant.

Probably, he thought, a mixture of both. She'd left with her mother under a dark cloud of sadness. That wasn't something that would be easily overcome. But surely there were plenty of happy memories from her childhood to make up for the pain.

When they reached the Stanford ranch, they caught

sight of a tow truck in the driveway, and a man was busy securing the damaged car behind the truck.

Jake pulled up alongside and the man hurried over.

Meg spoke through the open window. "That was quick."

"Yes, ma'am. Miss Stanford?"

"Yes. I'm Meg Stanford."

He handed over a sheaf of documents. "I'll need your signature on these. I've left you a new rental car, but the same make and model as the other."

"Thank you."

Jake waited while Meg and Cory stepped out of the truck.

"I'll drive to the barn and unhitch your horse trailer. Then I'd better tend to a couple of ranchers. Like my father said, if there's anything you need, anything at all, you call me. Day or night."

Meg nodded. "Thanks for everything, Jake. I really appreciate this." She lifted the big bag to indicate the food Ela had packed. "And this."

He shot her a grin before turning to Cory. "You keep an eye out for your sister, son."

"Yeah." Cory ducked his head.

"And Cory?"

When the boy lifted his head, Jake added, "I'll call in the morning and give you a report on how Shadow got through the night. And then, if you'd like, I'll come by and pick you up so you can have a visit with him in the barn. If your colt's strong enough, I'll have you take him for a few laps around the corral."

The boy nodded and turned away.

Jake drove to the barn and unhitched the horse trailer

before driving past the ranch house. In the rearview mirror he watched as the mechanic cleaned his hands on a towel before climbing up to the seat of the tow truck.

Satisfied that Meg had a means of transportation and enough food to see her and Cory through the night, Jake picked up his cell phone and called the first rancher on his long list of patients in need of his care.

He'd put off his own schedule long enough. Now it was time to get to work. From the list of calls on his cell phone, he'd be lucky to get home before midnight.

Meg stashed the brown bag in the refrigerator and watched as Cory wandered out to the barn.

Was he working out there, mucking stalls, or was he just hoping to put as much distance between them as possible? Did he resent her in his house? After all, in the years he'd lived here, he'd never had to share it with anyone except his mother and father. And now both were gone, and he was probably feeling so alone.

Jake had suggested that she ought to know what the boy was going through, but in truth, she didn't have a clue. What could she possibly have in common with an aloof little kid who could barely stand to be in the same room with her?

How would he adjust to living in a big city? Even with a haircut and new clothes, she couldn't imagine Cory adjusting to living in her posh town house, attending a private school in D.C. while she worked. And what would she possibly do with him on the weekends, when she put in another twenty or more hours on the high-profile cases the firm handed her?

It would be a lonely, unsatisfying life for a little boy

who'd grown up wild and free here in Wyoming. She knew that only too well.

Still, what choice did she have? She'd made a life for herself in D.C. Was she supposed to just walk away from all the hard work she'd put into her career to care for a kid she hadn't even known about a week ago?

So many worries. And another headache beginning to throb at her temples.

She walked through the house, pausing to study the dusty photographs. On a cluttered mantel she found several framed pictures of her father with his third wife and Cory.

Meg wiped away the dust to study their faces. Her father, looking so much older than she'd remembered. And his wife looking like a schoolgirl in faded denims and skinny shirt. She'd been a pretty little thing. Pale, dark-haired. She looked so proud holding the baby.

What in heaven's name had her father been thinking, to marry again and have a kid? At his age. He should have been more responsible than this. Setting the photo aside, Meg climbed the stairs to her father's bedroom and began pulling things from his closet. The least she could do was to box up his clothing for a local charity.

As she worked, she came across a photo album on a top shelf. After wiping away the layers of dust, she opened it to find, on the very first page, a picture of her father and mother holding a baby and looking so proud and happy. The caption *My Meggy* had been written in her father's distinctive scroll.

Meg dropped down on the edge of the bed and began flipping through the pages. Here was a small framed picture of her with her father and mother when she'd been about five. She'd been bundled in a snowsuit, barely able to move her arms or legs with all that bulk, and the three of them were standing beside a giant snowman. The sight of them had her laughing aloud. Her father had jokingly held up his fingers like devil's horns behind his wife, who was, as always, frowning.

Meg had forgotten what a prankster her father had been. When he wasn't giving orders like a drill sergeant, which he confessed to doing only because he wanted to drill into her the importance of being orderly, he was constantly playing jokes or doing pratfalls to make her laugh. It had been his most endearing quality.

A few pages further along she found a photo of her and her father with her beloved Strawberry. Meg looked at the little girl, eyes dancing, smile so wide it would have lit up the entire sky, and her father, his arm around her shoulders, looking for all the world like a superhero.

He had been her hero that day.

She'd loved him so much. And loved that pony almost as much.

The thought had her smiling as she continued flipping through the pages and staring hungrily at her childhood unfolding before her. So many memories, and all of them forgotten until now.

How could she have forgotten the way her father had allowed her to drive the tractor—with him seated alongside, of course—while they rolled across the fields? Or the fact that on the first snowfall of her ninth year, he'd hitched a team to an old-fashioned sleigh and had taken her on a sleigh ride across the pasture? Oh, how she'd loved that feeling of skimming across the frozen land, their laughter ringing in the frosty air.

There was a picture of the two of them taking a flying leap into the creek that ran through the high meadow. It had been their favorite pastime on sultry summer days.

And another photo of them at a bonfire, roasting marshmallows. Meg could close her eyes and still taste the sticky, melted confection fresh from the fire. Her father had always saved the last one for her.

Nearly an hour later, when she closed the cover of the album, she sat on the edge of her father's bed and wiped away the tears that had welled up and caught her by complete surprise.

Not that she was feeling nostalgic, she reminded herself. It was just that she'd forgotten more than she remembered. Such sweet, innocent times. Before the anger, the bickering, the finger-pointing. Before she'd been wrenched from the only home she'd ever known to start a new and bewildering life in a big city, among strangers.

Needing to be busy, Meg returned to the closet. There were other albums, of other wives, but she had no interest in looking at the pictures. Maybe another day. For now, for this short time, she wanted nothing that would distract her from the pleasant images that were playing through her mind.

She was surprised to hear footsteps on the stairs. She peered into the hallway to find Cory walking toward his bedroom.

He turned. Seeing her he called, "'Night."

"Good night? We never had supper."

"I'm not hungry. It's late." He moved on down the hall.

"Yeah. Okay. Good night, Cory." She glanced at the window and realized that the sun had set long ago and darkness was already creeping across the landscape.

An hour later, as she made ready for bed, the pleasant feelings remained.

She made her way down the stairs to lock the doors. While she was there, she made herself a cup of tea before turning out the lights and heading for her bedroom.

Jake's sound sleep was shattered by the ringing of his phone. He rolled over and thought about ignoring the persistent ring. He'd spent hours tending to lame horses, pregnant mares, and even Flora's ancient cat, who finally coughed up enough meat loaf to kill the average kitty.

Flora had been mortified. "If you ever tell my customers what made Nippers sick, Jake Conway, I'll put arsenic in your soup."

"Yeah. I guess it might have a few of your regulars refusing to try your famous meat loaf if they heard what it did to old Nippers."

"It wasn't the meat loaf. It was his overeating. I should have named him Piggers."

The two of them laughed together before Flora sent Jake on his way with half a homemade apple pie, which he'd managed to polish off before reaching home well past midnight.

And now some fool cat had probably gotten itself sick again. Or maybe up a tree.

He was so weary. He would just—

The phone rang yet again, and swearing, he made a grab for it. "Yeah?"

For a moment there was only silence.

"Hello," he barked. "This is Jake Conway."

"Jake?" The frantic, whispered voice on the other end had him sitting up on the edge of the bed.

"Cory? What's wrong?"

"I heard a sound and looked out my window. There's someone out there."

Jake ran a hand over his face, suddenly wide awake. "Where are you?"

"Upstairs. In my room."

"All right. Now listen to me, Cory." Jake was already up and moving about his room, searching for the clothes he'd tossed aside...had it been only an hour ago? "Go to your sister's room and wake her. Tell her I want the two of you to stay in her room until I get there. And you may want to put something heavy against the door so it can't be forced open. Do you understand?"

"Yeah."

"Don't open that door to anyone but me, son."

"I won't."

Jake fumbled into his clothes and boots and slipped his phone into his shirt pocket.

Downstairs he raced to his father's big office and removed a rifle and handgun from a locked cabinet, along with a pouch of ammunition.

He was out the door and on the road within minutes. As his truck ate up the miles, he dialed a number and waited until he heard a voice that sounded as weary as his own.

"Police Chief Everett Fletcher here."

"Everett. Jake Conway." In a few terse sentences he explained about the phone call, and his destination.

"You want me out there, Jake?"

"I'll check it out and report in. If you don't hear from me within the hour, I'd appreciate some backup."

"You got it, Jake. You stay safe now."

Jake's tone was pure ice. "Count on it."

CHAPTER SIX

"Meg. Hey, Meg."

At the sound of Cory's frantic whispers, and his hands shoving roughly against her shoulder, Meg jerked awake and sat up in the darkness. "What—?"

At the sound of her voice a small hand clamped over her mouth. "Shh. There's someone out there. Don't let him hear you."

"An intruder?" She sat up, struggling to untangle herself from the blanket.

"I saw him out my window."

"A man? You saw a man?"

The boy nodded. "Jake said to wake you."

"Jake?" Her sleep-fogged brain couldn't seem to wrap around the boy's words. "Jake's here, too?"

"I called him."

"We're alone here with the intruder?" Now she was up

and rushing to the window. "Where is he? I don't see anyone. Are you sure you saw someone out there?"

"I'm sure. I know what I saw."

Meg looked around the room. "I need a weapon. Something I can use to defend us." Spotting the curtains, she pulled down the round wooden rod, testing its weight.

Seeing what she intended, Cory caught her arm. "No. Jake said we should stay here in your room until he comes."

"What if he doesn't come?"

"He said he would." The boy raced across the room and leaned his thin shoulder against the dresser. "Jake said we should block the door so the intruder can't get in."

It was on the tip of her tongue to argue, but against her better judgment Meg moved to the other edge of the dresser. Together, pushing, shoving with all their might, they managed to position the heavy dresser against the door.

Then, hearts pounding, faces intent, the two of them pressed their ears to the door, waiting for whatever danger lay just beyond.

Meg crossed to the night table and flipped open her phone, dialing the police chief's number. In a breathy voice she said, "It's Meg Stanford here. Cory spotted an intruder."

"Yes, ma'am. Jake Conway already alerted me. Are you and the boy all right?"

"We're okay for now. We're up in my room."

"That's good. You stay there. Jake's on his way. When he gets there, he'll report in."

Meg clutched her phone, wondering why the knowledge that Jake was coming gave her a measure of comfort. Still, her heart continued racing like a runaway train.

The agony of having to wait, without knowing who was out there or what he was doing, had her breathing hard and fast. Each minute felt like an eternity.

Jake drove like a madman. As though the very devil himself was after him. When he reached the gravel road that led to the Stanford ranch, he cut the lights on his truck. No sense telegraphing to the intruder that he was coming.

As he approached the house, all his senses went on high alert.

He hoped to hell the guy was still around. After the night he'd put in, Jake was feeling mean and itching for a good knock-down, drag-out fight. He couldn't think of a more worthy opponent than the creep who had trashed Meg's car and her father's office.

As he rounded the corner of the house he saw a sudden movement on the porch. Jake snatched up his rifle and was out of his truck in an instant. He could just make out a man's figure leaping over the porch railing and racing hell-bent toward the barn.

"Stop right there or you're a dead man."

The figure never even paused as it rounded the corner of the first barn and continued on, with Jake in hot pursuit.

The man ahead changed directions and suddenly veered away from the second barn in the distance, choosing instead to plunge headlong into the dense woods.

At the edge of the woods Jake paused to listen. There was no thrashing around. No snapping of twigs or crunching of footsteps. Except for the sounds of night birds and insects, there was no way of knowing where the man had gone. He could be far ahead, racing toward freedom, or hiding nearby with his own weapon, hoping to ambush his pursuer.

With a string of muttered curses, Jake turned and made his way back to the ranch house.

When he climbed the steps to the porch, he found a glass pane shattered and the back door ajar, and could see the pry marks where the intruder had used a heavy bar to force the door open. In his haste, the intruder had dropped the pry bar before fleeing.

Stepping inside, Jake threw on the lights and stepped carefully around the shards of broken glass lying on the kitchen floor. He threw on more lights as he moved through the house and up the stairs to the second-floor bedrooms.

Moving along the upper hallway he called out loudly, "Meg. Cory. It's Jake Conway. I don't know which room you're in, but it's safe to come out now."

Up ahead he could hear the sound of something heavy scraping across the floor before a door was thrown open and two frightened faces peered at him.

"You came," Cory shouted.

"Of course I did. I told you I would." Jake looked beyond the boy to the young woman who had a hand to her throat, as though forcing herself to breathe in and out. "Are you both okay?"

Meg nodded. "We're fine now that you're here. I was so befuddled by sleep, all I could think of was running downstairs until Cory said we had to barricade the door."

"If you'd gone down, you would have run right into the arms of your intruder."

"Did you see who it was?"

Jake shook his head. "It was too dark. And I had already cut my headlights, hoping to catch him by surprise. But he heard me coming and made a run for it. I chased him until he disappeared in the woods. Without a flashlight, I didn't have a chance of catching him there."

"How did he get here?" Meg stepped closer, now that she knew the intruder was gone. "Did he leave a vehicle behind?"

Jake tried not to stare at the way she was dressed—or rather, barely dressed. The sight of all that pale, smooth flesh had his throat going dry as dust. "I wish he had. Then he'd be easy to track." He shook his head. "I don't know how he got here. Maybe he left a vehicle a couple of miles from here and hiked in, so you wouldn't hear the sound of his engine."

Meg's glance settled on the rifle held at Jake's side. "Would you have used that?"

"Hell yes." To keep from staring at that sexy little bit of silk she was wearing, he turned away.

Cory trailed behind, while Meg retreated to her room and stepped out a minute later wrapped modestly in her father's oversize cowhide duster, which fell to her toes.

Jake led the way to the stairs and down to the main floor. Once there he turned to Meg. "I guess you'd better start checking to see if he took anything with him, though I'm pretty sure that I caught him on the way in instead of the way out."

Meg moved woodenly through the rooms but could find nothing out of place. When they reached her father's office, Jake paused in the doorway while she and Cory walked around, inspecting drawers and cabinets.

Cory was wearing flannel pajama bottoms and the same dirty T-shirt he'd been wearing all day.

Meg's feet, the only things now visible beneath her cover-up, were bare, the polished nails a pretty shade of hot pink. The sight of them, so out of place beneath the rough cowhide, had Jake smiling.

After a thorough check, Meg looked up with a shrug of her shoulders. "I can't see anything out of the ordinary."

Jake arched a brow. "This room looks a whole lot cleaner than the last time I was in here."

She smiled. "I guess I've inherited my father's neat gene. I couldn't rest until I'd cleaned up all the mess. I went through hundreds of documents before filing them in their proper order."

"You do good work, ma'am." Jake's lips curved into a grin.

"Thanks." Meg glanced at Cory, who stood across the room, staring out the darkened window. "After I managed to get my brain in gear, I phoned Chief Fletcher to report what Cory had heard. The chief told me that you were on your way." She couldn't help smiling. "He made it sound like having Jake Conway coming here was the next best thing to having the cavalry leading the charge."

"Remind me to thank Everett next time I see him." Jake's smile grew. "I guess I'd better let him know what we found."

He flipped his phone from his shirt pocket and dialed the police chief. At the sound of the chief's deep voice he said, "Everett? Jake. I saw the intruder, but barely. Under six feet tall, thin, and runs like a damned gazelle, which tells me he's either an athlete or a hell of a lot younger than me. I lost him in the woods." Jake listened. "No vehicle here. Could be parked on a road somewhere for a quick escape." He listened again before saying, "Meg can't determine if anything's missing. No. They're both fine." He paused. "No need. I'm not going anywhere now. I'm staying put." He saw Meg's head come up sharply and added, "Right. I'll see you in the morning."

He dropped the cell phone in his pocket before saying, "Why don't the two of you go on back up to bed? I'm going to hang here until Chief Fletcher comes by in the morning."

Cory's eyes grew round. "If you're staying the night, does that mean you think the bad guy will be back?"

Jake turned to study the boy. "I don't know. What do you think he'll do?"

Cory flushed and avoided looking at Jake.

Meg crossed her arms over her chest and chewed on her lower lip. "I hate having you feel as though you have to give up your own comfort for our sake. But..." She glanced at Cory, then at Jake. "But I'm grateful that you're willing to stay. Right now I'm feeling so jumpy, I doubt I'll be able to settle down enough to get a minute's sleep."

She walked over to where Cory stood. When she started to reach out for him he shrank back. She dropped her hand to her side and kept her tone low and even. "Why don't you go on up to bed now, Cory?"

He nodded and started toward the door, eager to escape her.

"And Cory..."

The boy paused to glance at her.

"I haven't had a chance to clear my mind until now. I'm so grateful that you heard the intruder and had the presence of mind to call Jake before you woke me. I don't know what I'd have done if I'd been alone tonight. But I doubt it would have ended so peacefully. Thank you."

The boy's eyes went wide. His lips curved into a half smile. "You're welcome."

And then he was gone, running out of the room and up the stairs. Minutes later they heard the sound of his bedroom door closing and the creak of his bed.

Meg listened in silence, chewing on her lower lip, a little frown line between her brows. Seeing Jake watching her, she turned away. "I don't know about you, but I could use some coffee."

As she headed toward the kitchen, Jake followed. "Sounds good."

She busied herself at the counter, measuring coffee and water, turning on the coffeemaker. Minutes later the wonderful aroma of coffee brewing filled the room.

Meg removed some of Ela's corn bread from the refrigerator and dug out a jar of strawberry preserves.

"Here." She shoved a plate and knife toward Jake. "Help yourself to some of this while I pour us each a cup."

"Thanks." He set aside his rifle in a corner of the room before walking to the table and slathering the preserves on several slices. He set the plate in the center of the table, so they could share.

When Meg returned with the coffee, they sat on either side of the ancient table, eating and drinking in silence.

Jake could feel his nerves begin to settle, and he watched as the color returned to Meg's cheeks. "Feeling better?"

She nodded. "I have to confess. When Cory came flying into my room and woke me from a sound sleep, I couldn't make any sense out of what he was saying. It was all babble in my brain. But when he insisted that we barricade ourselves in my bedroom until you arrived, I felt this tremendous sense of relief."

She shook her head. "It isn't like me to be timid, or to want someone to fight my battles. I've always been able to stand up for myself. But ever since I got here I've had this uneasy sense that I've fallen into a rabbit hole and landed in another universe."

That had Jake smiling. "I know this isn't Washington, D.C. But it isn't some alien landscape, either. You lived here until you were ten. I'm sure after you give yourself some time, you'll feel better about things."

"I doubt I have enough time for that. I have a career I've put on hold. Clients who expect me to be ready to do battle for them in court. And here I am playing big sister to a kid who hates me, and trying to sort through an inheritance that I don't deserve."

"Now how do you figure that?"

She sighed. "You don't know how ugly things were when my mother and I left here. She told me that my father had disinherited me. That I was no longer his daughter. I was so hurt, I wouldn't even take his phone calls the few times he tried to talk to me. And as the years dragged on, he quit calling and I was relieved. That way I didn't have to hate myself so much. I figured he hated me enough for both of us."

"Hey." Jake reached across the table and put a hand over hers. "Quit beating yourself up. You were ten. What ten-year-old knows how to deal with issues like divorce and parents who can't stand each other?"

She glanced at their joined hands before withdrawing

hers and clenching it in her lap. "Thanks. But it's all spilled milk now. And with my father gone, I can't make it right after all these years."

"Maybe not." Jake lowered his voice. "But at least you can understand what Cory is going through."

"I'm afraid you're wrong." She nodded toward the door. "You saw him. He freezes up around me."

"You're a stranger. Another adult who will be making decisions about his future. Can you blame him?"

Before she could answer, Jake added, "And remember this. He didn't freeze up when it counted. He woke you, barricaded your door, and kept you safe until I got here. I'd say that counts for more than his knee-jerk reaction when you try to play nice."

Meg sighed again. "Maybe you're right. I don't know. Right now, right this minute, I don't know anything except that I don't feel safe here. Somebody wants something, and if he would just let me know what it is that he's so desperate to find, maybe I'd just give it to him and we could all get on with our lives in peace."

Jake sat back and digested her words.

She looked over at him. "You're quiet."

"Just thinking."

"Want to share?"

He shrugged. "Not yet. Maybe later." He shoved back his chair. "Why don't you go up to bed?"

"I'm too wired. Would you like to sleep on the sofa?"

He shook his head. "I think I'll take a turn around the yard."

"In the dark?"

"Yeah." He grinned. "Don't worry. I'm not going to duck out and leave you and Cory all alone."

"I wasn't thinking that. I was worrying that the intruder could be out there right now, watching us. If he sees you coming out in the dark, he might try something desperate."

Jake picked up his rifle and cradled it in his arms. "If he's dumb enough or desperate enough to be hanging around, he'll find more than he bargained for."

Meg watched as he strode out the door. She listened to the sound of his booted feet on the porch steps.

And then silence settled over the house as she poured herself another cup of coffee and made her way to her father's office. If she couldn't sleep, she would take comfort in work.

Jake dug a flashlight out of his truck and made his way in the darkness to the barn. He tried the door and was pleased to find it padlocked. Apparently Meg had taken Big Jim's advice to heart and had locked the rental car inside. A good thing, as she probably would have had to deal with more slashed tires, or even more serious damage, had she left it out in the open.

He played the light over the door and noted the pry marks. Apparently the intruder had spent some time trying to break into the barn before moving on to the house. That would explain why he wasn't inside when Jake arrived.

Jake cursed his timing. He would have found it extremely satisfying to find this thug inside, where he could have confronted him face-to-face. Not to mention the satisfaction he'd have enjoyed by beating him senseless.

He circled the barn before walking back to the house. Along the way he thought again about the vandalism.

This was no random act. The intruder seemed focused and determined.

The question was…why?

What could he hope to gain by breaking into a dead man's house? According to Everett Fletcher, and repeated by all the gossip swirling around town, Porter Stanford's will had been properly drawn up and filed with Judge Bolton. Porter wasn't known to keep large sums of money in the house. He wasn't a collector of valuable coins or jewelry. So what could the motive possibly be?

Jake had a theory that he intended to run by Chief Fletcher before he spoke of it to Meg. There was no sense adding to her burden until he'd given it more thought.

Grim-faced, he climbed the steps and let himself in the back door.

CHAPTER SEVEN

Jake made his way along the hallway toward Porter's office. Finding the door open he paused to study Meg, seated at her father's desk and reading a document. Every so often she would stop to scribble a notation in the margin before dropping the pen and reading more.

She'd coaxed a fire on the hearth to chase the night chill. Flames leaped and danced, casting her lovely face in light and shadow. A face that was a study in concentration, her eyes steady, her lips pursed in a most enticing way.

Her slender frame was swallowed up in her father's bulky, faded cowhide coat. Her bare feet tapped a steady rhythm to some inner music. In the glow of the lamplight her hair, tangled from sleep, gleamed like fire, and he found himself itching to touch it.

She looked up at that moment and caught him staring.

A hint of color flooded her cheeks. "I didn't hear you come in."

"Sorry. I didn't mean to startle you."

She set aside the document. "There's coffee."

"I've had enough." He crossed the room and ran a hand along the rustic slab of hardwood that served as a mantel over the fireplace. Like every other article of furniture in the house it was littered with framed photographs layered in dust. Apparently nothing had been cleaned since the death of Cory's mother months ago.

Her tone betrayed nerves. "Any sign of our intruder?"

Jake turned, leaning a hip against the massive stone surround and crossing his arms over his chest. "He must have tried to break into the barn before starting on the house. He left pry marks in the wood. I'm glad you padlocked the door."

"Thanks to your grandfather." She caught the pensive look on his face. "Is there something else?"

He shrugged. "Just trying to get into the mind of an intruder. Why the interest in your car? It's a rental."

She gave a shake of her head. "I don't have a clue."

He prowled the room, pausing to study an assortment of rocks that spilled over a round wooden table, and a beautifully crafted saddle slung carelessly over a bench in the corner.

"You said that your father didn't collect anything of value."

"Not that I know of. Why?"

Again that shrug. "Just looking for a motive."

She smiled. "Now you sound like a prosecutor."

His smile came quickly. "Anyone in particular?"

"I've come up against some of the best."

"And won, I bet."

Her smile widened. "Some of the time. I pride myself on winning."

"Did your father follow your criminal law career?"

Her smile was gone in an instant, leaving Jake to regret his question. But it was too late to take it back.

"I never heard from him. I doubt he had time, considering the number of women in his life." Her tone lowered with sarcasm. "With his track record, you have to wonder why he kept bothering to marry them."

Jake winked. "Maybe he thought the third time was the charm."

That had Meg chuckling, unable to hold on to her anger. "I never thought of that."

"Or maybe he was beginning to figure out where he'd gone wrong, and decided just once to make things right."

She snorted. "He had a funny way of showing it. My mother told me that his second wife walked away with a fortune after enduring only a couple of years of his nasty temper. I can't imagine what he thought he'd learned from that mess that would have him taking a third wife, and a mere girl at that."

Jake wandered across the room and dropped down into a deep, upholstered chair. "Maybe he was lonely and looking for someone to fill the void."

"Whatever." She tossed aside the document and began tapping the pen on the desktop. "I don't really care what he was thinking. Right now, my only concern is dealing with the mess he left behind."

"Are you talking about the ranch? Or Cory?"

She gave a deep sigh. "Both. I hate the thought of auctioning off all the things my father loved. This land. The cattle. Even his tools and equipment in the barns. But I don't see that I have any choice. As for Cory, I keep trying to imagine him in D.C. with me and…" Her words trailed off with a sad little shrug.

Jake nodded. "I can see where it might seem like a mountain to climb." He smiled. "Speaking of mountains…Did I tell you that my brother Josh is an expert climber? He's the one the rangers call on whenever they can't locate a lost hiker in the Tetons."

She gave him a steady look. "That's fascinating. I'm impressed. Your family is pretty unique. But I don't see what it has to do with me."

"Just thinking out loud. The thing is that Josh claims that when he's got a dangerous climb ahead of him, he does the same thing we all do every time we have to go somewhere."

Instead of asking the logical question, she merely raised an eyebrow.

Jake's smile grew. "One step at a time."

"Gee, thanks for those words of wisdom."

He chuckled. "What I'm getting at is this: You have a father to bury, a will to be read. You have a working ranch, and all that goes with it. You have a little brother, a stranger to you, who knows no other life than ranching. And you hope to deal with all of this in a week. As a bright young lawyer, just what advice would you give to a client facing those issues?"

She dropped the pen and steepled her hands atop the desk.

Jake could see the wheels turning in her clever mind.

"The first part is certainly straightforward enough. My

client should bury her father and request a copy of the legal will."

Jake could see Meg digging deeper.

"After that I'd tell my client to have at least two legal assessments of the value of the estate, and weigh that against the latest profit-and-loss statements filed by the deceased on his annual IRS statement. I'd determine the current market value of the cattle, the equipment, the contents of the barns, and any crops that might be grown and harvested annually. Deduct the cost of maintaining and operating said ranch against the money it earns, and it's an easy decision whether it's worth more sold or retained."

Her voice was growing stronger with every sentence, and Jake could now glimpse just how effective she would be as a legal advisor.

"And finally, I'd have my investigative team do a complete background check on the newly acquired brother and his mother's family, to see if there are other blood relatives involved. That would give her a clearer picture of not only the boy's past, but of his future going forward with or without her."

"And the deadline?"

"Ah. The deadline." Meg laughed. "Very good, Dr. Conway. As we both know, the deadline is self-imposed. Therefore, my client ought to step back from that timetable and decide to move at a pace that will allow her to process all the information available and make her decisions based on what is prudent rather than what is expedient."

Jake nodded in appreciation. "You have a remarkable mind, counselor. It's fun to watch you in action."

Meg flushed. "I guess I got carried away."

"Don't apologize. I think your advice was dead on." He stood and pressed a hand to the small of his back. "Now, if you don't mind, I'll pour myself another cup of coffee. It's going to be a long night." He walked to the door and paused to look back. "Would you like a cup?"

"No, thanks." She glanced at the document lying atop the desk. "I think I've strained my eyes and my brain enough for tonight. Maybe I'll just catch a little rest over there on the sofa."

Jake walked to the kitchen and poured himself a cup of coffee. As he drank it, he stood at the window and stared at the stars in the predawn sky.

At least now Meg was thinking more clearly. A ranch of this size couldn't be dismantled and sold off piece by piece within a matter of weeks. Nor should it be, even if it were a possibility. As the owner, Meg needed to evaluate just what she had and what it was worth, not only in dollar value, but in sentiment, as well.

Hopefully, after giving it careful thought, she would begin to realize that the time spent here would offer her the best opportunity to make peace with her childhood.

And maybe, he thought, Cory could help her see, through his eyes, just what she had once loved and lost.

He drained his cup and set it in the sink before turning out the kitchen light and climbing the stairs. He moved along the darkened hallway until he came to a closed door. Opening it gently, he crossed to the bed. In the moonlight spilling through the window he studied the sleeping boy.

Cory lay on his stomach, one arm curled over his head, the other tucked under his chest. One foot dangled over the edge of the mattress.

On the night table beside his bed was a Louisville Slugger.

Jake picked up the scarred, old wooden baseball bat, noting the initials *P S* carved into the handle. A smile lit his eyes. Porter had given his son a treasure from his own childhood.

Jake's smile faded when it occurred to him that Cory had placed the bat within reach, if he should have a need for it during the night. It was no longer just a father's treasured memento. It was the son's protection, should the intruder break in again and make it up the stairs.

Jake felt an overwhelming sense of fury at the stranger who had stolen this boy's sense of security. Even in his father's home, in his very bed, Cory didn't feel safe.

Jake eased the boy's foot onto the mattress before drawing the covers over him.

Cory shifted and sighed, and Jake brushed a lock of hair from his eyes before turning away.

He closed the door as quietly as he'd opened it, before heading down the stairs.

Meg settled herself on the sofa before drawing a faded afghan over her bare feet.

She'd forgotten how cool the nights were here in Wyoming. Back in D.C. the daytime temperature was unbearable in spring and summer, and even the nighttime couldn't cool the hot, muggy air.

She hunched deeper into her father's coat and was startled by the sudden realization that she could smell him in its folds. He'd no doubt worn this only days ago, and the scent of him lingered, tugging at her heart, thrusting her back to the days when Porter Stanford had been the most important person in her young life.

So big and strong and handsome. A tough, take-no-prisoners cowboy who ran herd over the people in his life with the same sense of purpose as he did his cattle.

In Porter's world there were no gray areas. Only black and white. Whether it was a sick animal that had to be treated to a strong dose of medicine quickly and humanely, or a little girl wailing over a portion of barbed-wire fencing that had imbedded itself in her thigh, he reacted without hesitation.

She moved aside the cowhide to touch a finger to the scar on her thigh. She winced as she thought about how fiercely her father had reacted in her moment of pain and panic. It had been her tenth birthday, and she had begged her father to allow her to ride with him and the wranglers, instead of being forced to remain with her mother, who was nursing one of her headaches. Strawberry had thrown her from the saddle directly onto a section of fencing that one of the wranglers had just torn down behind the barn. She'd let out a terrible wail, and when Porter had recognized the seriousness of the situation, he'd reacted without a second thought. He'd cut away the section of fence, plucked the wire, barb and all, from her tender flesh. He'd then tied a bandana around her thigh and cradled her in his arms before climbing into the saddle of his big red gelding and racing to the barn, where he'd transferred his daughter to his truck and drove like a madman all the way to the clinic in Paintbrush. Old Dr. Walton had stitched the wound and administered a tetanus shot before congratulating Porter on his quick actions. But when they had returned to the ranch, Virginia, who had heard about the accident from one of the wranglers, was beside herself with fury that he'd left her home to pace and worry, not knowing just how seriously hurt her daughter had been.

Porter had carried Meg up to bed, no doubt hoping to spare her. But the argument soon reached such a fever pitch, their voices could be clearly overheard by the girl.

Meg closed her eyes, reliving the scene in her mind.

The fight escalated in direct proportion to Virginia's sense of outrage. Her mother had found fault with every-thing Porter believed in. He was, according to Virginia, allowing their daughter to grow up wild and free on the ranch. Meg's latest accident only served to reinforce her mother's belief that it was time for their daughter to at-tend the girls' school back east that had been Virginia's alma mater. At least there the girl would learn some re-finements.

Their ugly words, hurled in a blaze of fury, had left an indelible mark on Meg's soul. As always, Meg had been the centerpiece of their battle.

Maybe it was being back here where it had all hap-pened. Maybe it was simple exhaustion. Whatever the reason, Meg found herself suddenly sobbing uncontrol-lably.

Jake had every intention of leaving Meg to her privacy, hoping she might catch a few hours' sleep in her father's office. But when he heard the muffled sound of her cry-ing, he hurried inside and dropped down on the edge of the sofa.

"Hey. It's going to be all right."

The deep timbre of his voice, so like her father's, had Meg crying even harder.

Alarmed, Jake's arms came around her and he gathered her close. Against her temple he whispered, "Go ahead then. Just cry your heart out, Meg. You'll feel better."

Now that the floodgates had been opened, there was no stopping her. She wept as though her heart was broken. The front of Jake's shirt was damp, and still she cried until there were no tears left.

Finally, pulling herself together, she pushed away from his arms and sat back against the cushions.

Jake reached into his pocket and retrieved a handkerchief. She accepted it and blew her nose, wiped her eyes, and then looked away in embarrassment. "I'm sorry. I feel like an idiot."

"Don't. You have every right to cry. You've not only lost your father, but your homecoming has certainly been anything but welcoming."

She blinked back fresh tears. "Thanks." She knotted the handkerchief in her hands. "I didn't even cry when I'd heard about my father's sudden death. I never cry."

At his expression she managed a wry smile. "Well, hardly ever." She looked toward the fireplace. "I happened to remember an incident from my childhood, and it triggered all kinds of other memories."

He settled himself beside her on the sofa. "Why don't you tell me about it?"

She shrugged. "I took a nasty spill from my horse into a nest of barbed wire."

"Ouch."

"Yeah." She nodded. "I still have the scar." She moved aside her father's coat to show him the white, puckered skin on her thigh.

Such a shapely thigh. At the sight of it, his throat tightened, and he mentally cursed himself for thinking about such things at a time like this.

"That's pretty impressive. I think it tops mine." To keep things light he rolled back his sleeve to show her the scar on his left arm above the elbow.

Meg touched a hand to the spot and was startled by the ripple of muscle. "Barbed wire?"

"Shattered wooden fence post. Split open by a storm. I was riding an ornery mustang to win a bet from my brothers and landed headfirst. Doc Walton had to pick out the splinters one by one."

"Ow."

"Yeah." Jake nodded. "That was the least of my pain. When I got home, Pa and Big Jim were waiting in the barn. I couldn't sit in the saddle for a week."

Meg's tears were forgotten as she burst into laughter. "They punished you for riding a mustang?"

"Well, it wasn't the first time I'd been threatened with murder and mayhem if I went near that mustang." He shook his head. "But there's just something in my nature that makes it impossible for me to resist doing exactly what I've been told I can't do."

"A maverick, are you?"

"Yeah. I'm thinking we're kindred spirits." He studied her lips, so close to his. For the space of a heartbeat he paused, as though considering the consequences. Then he lowered his face to hers.

The kiss was soft and unexpectedly sweet. Little more than a whisper of mouth to mouth. But as their lips brushed, Jake was forced to absorb a quick, hard punch to the heart that had him closing his hands around her arms, as though to draw her away. Instead of pushing her back, he found himself wanting more. So much more.

He drew her even closer as his mouth moved over hers with a thoroughness that had them both sighing.

Though he'd meant to comfort her, there was nothing sweet or gentle about what they were sharing. Now it was all sizzle and spark. Hot need and a sharp, desperate flare that had them both frantic as they held on to the kiss and to each other until, with a sudden, quick intake of breath, they moved apart.

Jake's lungs were straining as he saw green eyes that were fixed on him with such focus that he couldn't look away. Nor did he want to. He could, he realized, happily drown in those liquid emerald depths.

He cupped her chin in his big hand and tipped up her face. His voice was rough with need. "Mind if I try that again?"

She looked as dazed as he felt.

Her lengthening silence was all the invitation he needed.

He lowered his face and took his time, kissing her long and slow and deep, enjoying the sizzling curl of desire that snaked along his spine.

Hadn't he known those pouty lips were made for kissing?

He took his time, drinking in the sweet taste of her, allowing the pleasure to pour through his system like a straight shot of fine Irish whiskey.

When at last he lifted his head, his lips curved into a smile of pure male appreciation.

"Sorry for that rough first attempt. Too needy, I guess. I'd been thinking about kissing you, but I hadn't planned on doing it quite so soon. I guess it was seeing that scar.

It's like we're kindred souls. Both of us bearing the scars of our childhood."

"Or baring them," she said with a throaty laugh. "As in *baring all*. I realized, just as I'd shown you my scar, that I'd revealed a bit too much flesh."

"Now, ma'am," he said in his best drawl, "I believe I speak for all cowboys when I tell you there's no such thing as a bit too much flesh."

Her laughter grew until he joined her.

"Oh, Jake. Thanks. I needed that."

"My pleasure, ma'am."

She drew the cowhide around her and got to her feet. "I think it's time I made a fresh pot of coffee."

"I'll second that. Right about now I could use some caffeine."

She started down the hallway, with Jake trailing behind. Her voice betrayed nerves that were close to the surface. "I think we're much better off in the kitchen, where we can keep the width of the table between us."

"Spoilsport."

Jake was still laughing as Meg switched on the light and began measuring coffee into the pot.

He tucked his hands in his pockets. Hands, he noted, that weren't quite steady.

He'd kissed dozens of women. Hundreds, if truth be told. But at the moment he couldn't recall a single one of them.

There was danger here, he cautioned himself. Meg Stanford was turning out to be a whole lot more fascinating than he'd first thought. Not just a tasty treat, but the whole candy store. And darned if he wasn't feeling like a kid with a fistful of dollars and eager to taste to his heart's content.

CHAPTER EIGHT

As she measured water and poured it into the machine, Meg was grateful to have something to do. Her hands were still trembling. Her entire body felt lighter than air. She was floating, and yet grounded.

She could feel Jake's cool gaze boring into her back. It was a most unsettling feeling. Not that it wasn't pleasant having him here. She was grateful for his company. And the security of his rifle, if truth be told.

But that kiss...

Well, that was another matter entirely. She'd certainly resolved her curiosity about how it would feel to kiss this cowboy. It had been amazing. In all honesty, she'd felt the earth move. A once-in-a-lifetime event. The only trouble was, now that she'd kissed him, she'd really like to do it again.

And again.

Not a very wise thing, under the circumstances.

As the coffee began perking, she had a sudden urge to laugh out loud. With her system already so jittery, she wondered what another jolt of caffeine would do to her.

She needed to get out of the room and clear her head before she started acting like a schoolgirl with her first crush. "I think I'll go up and check on Cory."

Jake straddled a kitchen chair. "I just checked him out a while ago. Sound asleep."

"You... checked on him?"

He nodded. "I just wanted to make sure he was able to get back to sleep after all the excitement." He lowered his voice. "You ought to know that he's keeping a baseball bat next to his bed."

She looked crestfallen as she dropped down in a chair, tapping a finger on the tabletop. "A baseball bat? For protection?"

"Yeah."

She brought a hand to her mouth. "Oh, that poor kid. He's been so quiet. I assumed it meant he wasn't feeling all that threatened by what's happened. But now..." Her words trailed off.

Jake's eyes narrowed. "I'd love to get my hands on the creep who's causing all this trouble."

She looked up. "Did my father have any enemies? Did he owe somebody a big debt?"

Jake shook his head. "I'm not the one to ask. I barely knew Porter. He kept to himself. I'd say Kirby Bolton was probably the one closest to him. And only because he was your father's lawyer. But if there are any unpaid debts, Kirby would know."

She nodded. "I have an appointment to meet Judge Bolton Monday, after the funeral." She sighed. "He apologized for asking me to wait so long, but he wasn't able to clear his docket until then."

Jake could hear the weariness in her tone. Everything, it would seem, was conspiring against her. She'd given herself a week to settle her father's estate, and that amount of time would barely give her a chance to bury her father and meet with his lawyer, with only three days left to deal with everything else. Add that to all the surprises she'd faced since coming here, and it was no wonder she was feeling so stressed.

When the coffee was ready she started to stand.

He reached out a hand to stop her. "You've done enough. I'll take care of it." He filled two cups and set one in front of her before sitting down across from her.

"Careful." She smiled her thanks. "I could get used to being taken care of."

"I get the impression you're good at taking care of yourself."

She looked down at the tabletop. "I guess I am. I learned it the hard way."

Jake stretched out his long legs. "If you feel like talking, I have all the time in the world to listen."

She took a long sip of coffee and felt it warm her. "I told you about my fall into the barbed wire. It was, for my mother, the latest in a string of issues that she and my father couldn't seem to resolve. They had a terrible fight, and afterward Dad stormed out of the house and up to the hills, where he bunked with the wranglers for a week or more."

She looked over at Jake. "Did you ever hear your parents fight?"

He shook his head. "I barely remember my mother."

Meg flushed. "Sorry. I keep forgetting."

She drank her coffee in silence before saying, "By the time my father returned, I'd already forgotten what had sent him away. I was just so happy to see him back with us, I guess I stuck to him like Velcro, which only infuriated my mother more. My father remained unapologetic, and my mother called him a cruel and inhuman monster. I've often thought that the two of them had this terrible need to keep opening old wounds that simply couldn't heal, until finally, at least in my mother's mind, there was no solution except the obvious one."

"Just like that? Couldn't they have tried something less drastic than divorce?"

"You mean like counseling? That would have been too sensible and slow for two such volatile people." Meg shook her head. "Looking back at all their ugly scenes, I can't recall a single instance when the fight wasn't about me. About something real or imagined that my dad and I had done together that had ended badly. Either I'd fallen, or I'd gotten sick eating something while I was up in the hills with the wranglers, or I got sunburned, or I didn't get enough sleep. To my mother it was proof that I would have a better life in the city, far from my father's interference."

"And so you relocated as far away from here as possible."

Meg nodded. "I had no idea what a big city really was. The closest thing to a city I had ever visited was Jackson Hole."

At Jake's snort of laughter she nodded. "It's the truth. I'd visited Jackson Hole several times with my folks, and thought that's what my mother meant. It had never occurred to me that we would relocate thousands of miles across the country, in a city so large and teeming with people, it seemed to be on another planet."

"That had to be a tough adjustment."

She gave a dry, mirthless laugh. "You have no idea. From a sprawling ranch to a town house in a city filled with cars and people and noise, and then I was sent to a private boarding school with girls whose only thoughts seemed to be fixated on the boys who attended the all-boys' school nearby."

His gaze swept her from head to toe. "I bet those boys took notice of the new redhead on campus."

That had Meg chuckling, in spite of her anger. "I was the youngest, most naive ten-year-old ever. I only thought about the horse I'd left behind, and riding up to the high country with my dad and the wranglers. Two short years later, by the age of twelve, I was learning the ropes and getting my share of whistles from boys."

"Uh-huh." He winked. "Was your mother happier in D.C.?"

"Much happier. A year later she married Philip, one of the partners in the law firm that handled her divorce, and she finally got the life she wanted. Which meant that my world changed yet again. I was met at school on Friday afternoons by a uniformed chauffeur and whisked away to an exotic home in the rolling Virginia countryside. I met my stepfather's wealthy, international guests at country-club dinner dances. After high school I attended an exclusive women's college and then law school at Georgetown. When I graduated, I was invited to join my stepfather's firm."

Jake grinned. "I guess it's a tough job, but somebody's got to do it."

She returned his smile. "I'm not complaining. It became a smooth ride once I decided to stop fighting my mother. But that only happened because I realized that without her, I'd have no one."

"What about your father?"

Meg ran her finger around and around the lip of her cup. "When we first settled in D.C., I used to wait for his calls. They never came. I was too hurt and angry to talk about what I was feeling. But my mother knew. She said that in time I'd get over being mad at my father and just put that old part of my life away."

"Why were you mad at Porter?"

She looked up, as though surprised by Jake's question. "In my mind, he had always been my champion. Whenever my parents waged a tug-of-war over me, he always won because I absolutely adored him. He should have fought to keep me with him. Instead, he just let me go. I figured the reason he didn't fight for me was because he blamed me for the divorce. After all, every fight was about me." She shrugged. "After a while, when I accepted that he was never going to call or come for me, I realized I had no one to hate but myself."

"Okay. I get that you were mad at Porter. But why were you mad at yourself?"

"If I hadn't been so determined to spend all my time with my father, completely ignoring my mother, maybe my parents would have stayed together."

"That's a child speaking. I hope, now that you're an adult, you've let go of all that foolish guilt and accepted the fact that some people just can't live together."

She sighed.

Jake tried another subject. "You said your mother passed away. What happened?"

"My mother and stepfather died together more than three years ago. Their boat was hit by a storm off the coast of Mexico. The craft flipped, and their bodies washed ashore a week or so later."

"I'm sorry, Meg."

She gave him a troubled smile. "Life happens. I've learned to deal with it. Of course, with Philip dead, I've had to push myself harder at the firm."

"And why is that?"

Again that shrug. "I've always had the nagging feeling that I was only accepted into the firm because of Philip, and not because of my ability. I guess I need to prove to all of them that I'm worthy."

"Do you need to prove that to them? Or to yourself?"

At Jake's question she looked away before saying softly, "You're quick, Conway. Yeah, I guess I have a lot to prove to myself."

"Are you guys having breakfast without me?"

At Cory's voice they both looked over at the boy standing in the doorway, looking sleepy-eyed and confused.

Meg turned toward the window, where the morning sunlight was already creeping into the room. "I can't believe it's morning already."

Cory glanced at their cups. "You're not having breakfast?"

"Not yet." Jake shot the boy a wide grin. "But now that you've reminded me, I think I'm ready for some of Ela's flapjacks. How about you?"

Cory's eyes widened. "With warm maple syrup?"

"I see you didn't forget. Yeah." Jake got to his feet. "Why don't the two of you shower and dress, and we'll ask Chief Fletcher to join us for breakfast at my place."

Cory was already turning away. "I can be ready in five minutes."

"Hold on." Jake waited until the boy turned back. "First you'd better ask your sister if it's all right with her."

Cory looked at Meg, his smile replaced by a frown.

His swift change of mood wasn't lost on her. She sighed. "Okay. Ela's flapjacks sound good to me, too."

Cory turned away and raced up the stairs.

When he was gone, Meg picked up their empty cups and carried them to the sink. As she washed them her voice sounded weary. "Why do I get the feeling that Cory always expects me to poke a hole in his balloon?"

Jake picked up a dish towel and dried the cups and saucers before reaching over her head to set them in the cupboard. "Maybe that's the way it's always happened to him before."

"Do you think he's been conditioned to expect the worst from adults?"

Seeing her concern, Jake touched a finger to the tip of her nose. "I think you're reading entirely too much into his reaction. The kid's scared. Give him a reason to trust you."

"Thank you, Dr. Conway." Despite the sarcasm, she didn't move or pull back, and it occurred to Jake that it would be an easy matter to lower his face to hers and kiss her again.

He wanted to. Intended to. And yet, he didn't. Instead, very deliberately he lowered his hand to his side and took a step back.

Meg took the towel from his hand and draped it over the edge of the sink. "Okay. Time to shower. I won't be long."

* * *

Alone in the kitchen, Jake stared into space. All he'd done was touch a finger to Meg's nose, but the reaction had been the same as before. Heat had spread all the way up his arm, along with this incredible urge to ravish her.

If he'd hoped that kissing her would quench the fire, he'd been dead wrong. All that the kiss had done was whet his appetite for more. He could still taste her, all sweet and tart at the same time, and sexy as sin. And feel the way she'd melted into him, with that little purr of pleasure. That had been his undoing. Maybe if she'd resisted, even a bit, he could have at least tried to do the noble thing. But the way she'd returned his kiss, with such reckless, what-the-hell abandon, he couldn't have held back if he'd wanted to.

Not that he was complaining. The trouble was, now that he knew just how willing she was, he couldn't wait to get her alone and kiss her again. Not a hurried, quick-on-the-trigger kiss, but the slow, leisurely kind that could open up all sorts of possibilities.

After that, he'd just see where it led them.

He pulled out his cell phone and called the chief before alerting Ela and Phoebe that they would be welcoming three guests for breakfast. Then he turned to the window as morning light spilled across the Tetons. It was a sight that never failed to stir his senses.

A smile touched the corners of his mouth. Not that his senses needed stirring at the moment. They'd already been heightened by what he'd shared with the intriguing Meg Stanford.

The taste of her was still on his lips. And the thought of her all warm and willing had his fingertips tingling and his blood surging.

Needing to be busy, he picked up his rifle and made a slow turn around the property, circling the barns and the corrals until he spied Meg and Cory on the porch. By the time he'd walked to his truck they were both settled inside.

He stashed his rifle before turning the key in the ignition. Taking note of the drops of water in Cory's shaggy hair, as well as the clean shirt and jeans, he shot the boy a wide grin. "You clean up good."

The boy flushed.

He looked beyond Cory to wink at Meg. "Same goes."

"Gee. Thanks."

"No. Thank you. You smell good."

Like Cory, she flushed. "Lavender body wash."

Jake nudged the boy. "Your sister smells like a city girl, don't you think?"

"Yeah." Cory ducked his head, giving Jake the perfect opportunity to stare at Meg over the boy's head.

She was wearing another pair of new denims and a sheer blouse that had a row of buttons clear down the front. It would have looked all prim and proper except that it was tied at the midriff, exposing a tiny bit of pale, smooth flesh.

Jake had to swallow hard and struggle to keep his eyes on the road.

Maybe it was a good thing that Cory was sitting between them. If they'd been alone, there was no telling just what he might have done.

One thing was certain. Come hell or high water, he was going to taste Meg Stanford's lips again. And next time, there would be a whole lot more than a stingy kiss.

Right now, with the windows down and the cool morning breeze filling the cab of his truck, he was so hot just thinking about her he could set off fireworks without even lighting a fuse.

There hadn't been a female to cause this sort of spontaneous combustion since Cammi Stillwater, and that didn't count since they'd only been thirteen, and he'd cut his lip on her braces, and his brothers had teased him mercilessly for weeks afterward.

Cammi was just a distant memory, but the woman causing all the high drama this morning was right here in the flesh. He shot Meg a sideways glance. And so far, the flesh he'd seen was enough to sweep the memory of every other female from his mind forever.

CHAPTER NINE

"Well, boyo." Big Jim looked up from his coffee as Jake led Meg and Cory into the kitchen. "You're up and out early this morning, aren't you?"

The entire family had already gathered for breakfast after morning chores and were busy helping themselves to juice and coffee while Phoebe and Ela filled platters with eggs, sausage, and steaming stacks of flapjacks.

Jake kissed old Ela's cheek before responding. "Actually, I spent the night at the Stanford ranch."

That had everyone looking up in sudden silence.

It was Meg who added, "Cory called Jake when he heard someone trying to break in."

"Again?" Cole Conway set aside his coffee to look from Meg to his son. "I hope you caught the son of a . . . gun," he added lamely with a glance toward Cory.

"He got away in the woods."

Big Jim frowned. "Did you get a good look at him?"

"Too dark." Jake handed glasses of orange juice to Cory and Meg before snagging one for himself. "But he had to be young and healthy to run that fast."

"Did he get anything?" Quinn asked.

"He didn't have time. It looks like he tried to break into the barn first. There were pry marks around the door."

Meg turned to Big Jim. "Thanks to your advice, I'd padlocked my car inside."

"Good girl," the old man muttered.

"By the time I got there, he was on the porch and trying to force the back door. I killed my headlights, but he heard me coming and stayed one step ahead of me. A few more minutes, though, he'd have been inside the house and free to do whatever he came there to do."

Big Jim studied Cory, who had drained his juice in one long swallow. "And you had the presence of mind to call Jake. That was quick thinking, boyo."

Cory flushed and bowed his head. "Jake told me to have his number on speed dial in case I needed him. When I saw someone moving outside that was the first thing I thought of."

Meg picked up the thread of the story. "I was sound asleep, and I never heard a thing until Cory came rushing into my room and told me there was an intruder, that Jake was on his way and we had to barricade the door to my room. In truth, without Cory there, I'd have probably done something foolish. My first impulse was to rush down the stairs and confront him."

"Your first impulse could have gotten you killed," Josh said with a glance toward his wife, Sierra. "Especially if the intruder was armed."

"Exactly." Big Jim pounded a fist on the countertop for

emphasis. "You always have to figure the other guy has the advantage, since he has the element of surprise on his side. Even without a weapon, he'd hear you coming and be prepared."

"Thank heaven I didn't have to deal with any of that." Meg let out a long sigh. "Cory and I just stayed locked in my room until Jake called out to us." She shook her head. "That was the longest wait of my life."

Cole looked at his youngest son. "I thought I heard you come in around midnight."

Jake gave a short laugh. "I had a laundry list of patients last night, ending with Flora's cat."

Cole eyed him. "Did you get any sleep at all?"

Jake shrugged. "Don't worry, Pa. I'll catch up tonight." He glanced out the window in time to see the police chief's car pulling up. "Here's Everett now. I asked him to join us here."

Jake walked through the mudroom and held the door open for the chief. "Just in time. We're about to eat."

Everett Fletcher was grinning as he greeted the others. "I'm always on time when I'm invited to share a meal with the Conways."

While he was greeting the others as they took their places around the table, Jake tugged on a lock of Cory's hair. "Did you see those flapjacks?"

The boy nodded.

"See that big old gravy boat?" Jake pointed to the serving bowl in the middle of the lazy Susan. "That's Ela's warm maple syrup. You don't want to miss that."

When the platter of pancakes was passed to Cory, the boy helped himself to two before dousing them with syrup.

After that, while the conversation swirled around him, the boy busied himself devouring every crumb. A short time later Ela paused beside him and held out the platter again. After a moment's hesitation, he helped himself to one more, which he washed down with a tall glass of ice-cold milk.

Jake glanced over and winked, and Cory shot him a grin before lowering his head. With a full stomach, he was content to allow the grown-ups around the table to talk among themselves.

"Can you think of anything at all that he could be after?" Long after they had finished with breakfast, the family lingered at the table, while Chief Fletcher took notes.

Meg shook her head. "I'm just not familiar enough with the house. It's been too many years. Nothing is the way it was all those years ago when I left."

"We know this is no random act of vandalism." Everett glanced around the table, directing his comments as much to the others as to Meg. "The rental car. The pry marks on the barn and back door of the house. And the earlier attempt to take Porter's files from his office."

Jake stretched out his long legs and set aside his coffee. "That's what has me puzzled. If an intruder was after something in Porter's files, why vandalize Meg's car?"

The chief shrugged. "I suppose, if he's mad at Porter, and he can't take it out on him now that he's dead, he just decided to take it out on his next of kin."

"Maybe." Jake furrowed his brow. "Another thing. If he wanted to steal Porter's files, why didn't he?"

"It sure looked like he tried," Everett said. "There were papers spilled all over that office."

"Yeah. But the glass doors were still locked from the inside. If he had an armload of files, it seems to me he'd have used the nearest, easiest exit."

"Maybe he wanted to go out the same way he came in," Everett said logically.

"Carrying an armload of loose papers? Do you think he'd have carried files all the way down the hall and out the kitchen door? And if he did, why wasn't there any trace of paper in the hallway? Not even one. Especially since there were papers strewn all over the office."

The chief's puzzled frown turned into a smile. "Damned if you wouldn't make a great investigator, Jake. Why didn't I think of that? So—" he sat back in his chair "—are you taking this where I think you're taking it?"

"It's just a thought. And I could be dead wrong." Jake glanced at Meg before saying, "What if the intruder isn't after anything tangible? What if our guy is sneaking around at night hoping to scare the person he considers an outsider so she'll leave as quickly as possible?"

"For what reason?" she asked.

Jake shrugged. "That's the part I haven't figured out yet. But the vandalism on your car just doesn't make any sense, unless someone wanted to send a message to the one who's driving it. The same with last night's attempted break-in. He wanted to get into the barn. I doubt there's anything of value in there right now, except your rental car. The herds are up in the high country. The tools and vehicles are stored in the other, bigger barn, which wasn't touched. He wanted to get at that rental car. A rental car that's insured, so it doesn't really hurt anyone but the insurance company. Again, all of this seems to point to the fact that he wants to scare the driver."

Meg gave a wry smile. "He succeeded."

That relieved some of the tension, and had everyone around the table chuckling.

She leaned forward, her hands folded on the tabletop. "So, if he frightens me, and manages to scare me into leaving town, what does he gain? My father is still dead. His ranch and holdings will no doubt still belong to me. To me and to Cory," she added, glancing at the boy beside her.

He stared hard at the table, clearly uncomfortable with the nature of the conversation swirling around him.

As if sensing his discomfort, old Ela paused beside his chair and lay a gnarled hand on his shoulder.

His head jerked up. Seeing her, he lowered his gaze, but not before he managed to give her a weak smile.

The chief began musing aloud. "All right. Let's say our intruder wants Miss Stanford gone. And he gets what he wants. Then what? What does he hope to gain by having her out of the picture?"

Around the table, everyone fell silent.

Cheyenne glanced at Quinn. "A possible chance to buy the ranch?"

Meg shook her head. "I'm already in contact with several auction houses. He would still have to bid along with every other potential buyer."

"Could there have been some kind of verbal agreement between this intruder and Porter that wasn't honored? A debt of some sort?" Josh asked.

The chief shook his head. "Without proper documentation, he wouldn't have a leg to stand on now."

There was a collective sigh among those seated at the table as they began to run out of suggestions.

Jake looked around at his family. "What if we give him what he's hoping for?" At their puzzled expressions he added, "What if the chief should happen to mention to Flora that Meg and Cory have moved in here for a while because they don't feel safe at their place?"

"Why not take out an ad on the front page of the *Paintbrush Gazette*?" Quinn said with a laugh.

"That's too obvious. But telling Flora is the same as taking out an ad. We know our intruder will hear it loud and clear."

"And then what?" Sierra, who had been watching and listening with rapt attention, looped her arm through Josh's, as caught up in the intrigue as the others.

"Then the Conway family does what it does best." Big Jim smiled at his grandson. "It's a grand idea, boyo. If this guy's after Meg, he'll have to bring his dirty tricks here. And we'll be ready for him."

"Exactly." Jake nodded.

"It's worth a try." The chief glanced at Meg. "That is, if you're willing, Miss Stanford."

Meg was chewing on her lower lip. "I don't like the idea of having all of you involved in my troubles. Especially if this intruder decides to get even more vicious than just doing damage to a rental car. You'll all be vulnerable."

"That's what neighbors do." Cole laid a big hand over hers and squeezed.

She let out a long, slow breath. "Thank you. You're all being so kind. And honestly, I can't think of any other solution. I'm such a coward, but I know I'd never be able to sleep in my father's house another night, knowing someone was waiting for his next chance to break in."

"It's only for a few days, Miss Stanford." The chief lumbered to his feet. "At least, Jake, you've got us thinking in a new direction. I'm going to ask around town, see what I can find out." He turned to Meg. "I'll be at your father's funeral tomorrow."

"Thank you, Chief Fletcher."

"See you, Cory." When the chief dropped a hand on the boy's shoulder, Cory flinched before looking away. Everett smiled at Phoebe and Ela. "Breakfast was certainly worth the long drive, ladies. My thanks to you both."

At the back door he retrieved his wide-brimmed hat before walking out to his car.

When he was gone, Jake looked at Meg and Cory. "Why don't I drive you both back and you can pack a few things?"

"Right now?" Meg pushed back her chair and stood. "I don't see why we can't stay at my father's place for the day."

He nodded. "All right. You ought to be perfectly safe all day. Whoever is trying to scare you off is afraid to show his face. Why else would he wait until dark to make an appearance?"

Meg turned to Phoebe and Ela. "I'm sorry that we'll be making extra work for both of you."

Phoebe answered for both of them. "We're happy to make you welcome in our home." She turned to Cory. "Especially because it's been much too long since we've had a boy to fuss over."

Calling out their good-byes and thanks, Meg and Cory trailed Jake to the mudroom and out the back door. Instead of going to his truck, Jake led them toward the barn, where he spent the next hour examining Shadow's leg and injecting the colt with an antibiotic before wrapping the leg with clean dressings.

Seeing Jake's look of concern, Cory looped an arm around the colt's neck, pressing his face to the soft, velvet muzzle. "Shadow's leg is getting better, isn't it?"

Jake forced himself to smile. "I wouldn't say he's out of the woods yet, but at least the leg isn't getting any worse."

Cory murmured words of encouragement to his colt. "I have to leave you for a little while, but tonight I can spend as much time with you as I like. And maybe, if nobody minds, I'll even sleep out here with you."

Jake stood to one side, watching the play of emotions on the boy's face. It was clear that Cory loved this colt with all his heart.

As they made their way to his truck, he found himself hoping that the drugs worked their miracle as promised. If anybody deserved some good news, it was Cory Stanford. With the loss of his mother and now his father, the boy had faced enough hard times in his young life.

CHAPTER TEN

On the way to the Stanford ranch, Jake played his phone messages and found himself wondering if there were enough hours in the day to complete all the ranch visits before dark.

Meg studied him as he dropped the phone into his shirt pocket. "I'm sorry we cost you a night's sleep."

"Don't be." He gave her a smile guaranteed to melt her heart. "All in a day's work for a Wyoming veterinarian. If it weren't you, it would have been Flora's cat or Honey about to give birth to her litter."

"Those are legitimate reasons to lose sleep."

"I'd say your emergency was as legitimate as it gets."

Meg couldn't help smiling. "Cory and I can't thank you enough."

He pulled up to their ranch house. "If you'd like, I could call you when I'm finished with my last patient and pick you up on my way home."

She shook her head as she climbed down from his truck. "Cory and I will drive over to your place in my car."

"Okay. I'll see you at supper time."

She and Cory waved until he turned the truck around and headed back toward the highway.

When he was gone, Meg took a deep breath and climbed the steps to the back door. She turned to Cory, who hung back. "Coming in?"

"Naw." He kicked at the dirt. "Guess I'll do some things in the barn."

"All right. Don't forget to pack whatever you'll need for a couple of days at the Conway ranch."

He nodded before shoving his hands in his pockets and starting toward the barn.

Meg watched him walk away before turning and letting herself into the house. Despite the heat of the day she shivered. Then, squaring her shoulders, she decided to do something about the gloom of this place.

Meg looked around the great room with a sense of deep satisfaction. She'd begun by taking down all the heavy, dusty draperies that probably hadn't been cleaned in years. Now sunlight flooded the room. Because there were pull-down blinds for privacy, she had no need to return the drapes to the windows.

She'd boxed up dozens of old framed photos, labeling the top of each box so that she would know which ones she wanted to keep, and which ones Cory would want. A third box held pictures of her father with his second wife, and Meg found herself wondering if Sherry had any distant relatives who might enjoy them.

She finished with a thorough dusting of the shelves,

mantel, and faded oak floor. A smile tugged the corners of her mouth. Her father wouldn't even recognize the place.

She headed up the stairs to pack what she would need for her stay with the Conways. After that, she intended to tackle her father's room and eliminate a few dozen more boxes she'd spotted in his closet.

Meg folded yet another Western shirt, her father's trademark, and placed it in a bulging plastic bag. When she'd removed all the shirts and pants from their hangers, she started on the tall leather boots lined up on the floor of the closet.

After bagging several pairs, she caught sight of the large box stored behind them. It was a plain brown box with no markings of any kind. With a sigh she set it inside a large plastic bin into which she'd already tossed several photograph albums. These would give her something to do at the Conway ranch. Whenever she wanted to slip away from the others, she could pass the time going through old photos.

It took her the better part of the day to completely empty her father's closet. Then she tackled the dresser drawers.

She stood back to admire her handiwork. Ten plastic bags lined the hallway outside her father's room, ready to be hauled to town. She'd been assured by Reverend Cornell, pastor of the Paintbrush Church, that a group of volunteers would see that everything was clean and mended before their annual clothing drive.

As she headed toward the shower, she felt a warm glow that came from a day of hard work. She'd missed this. With her work as a trial lawyer, the days and weeks of preparation often culminated in a settlement rather than in the satisfaction of a hard-fought trial. She preferred the trial. But it was really the hard work that went into each and every case that gave her the greatest sense of satisfaction.

She had always felt that way.

As a child she'd often worked alongside her father and the wranglers, sharing the hard, dirty, muscle-straining work required for the smooth operation of a ranch. She'd never forgotten the reward of such hard work. Whether it was a clean stall or a healthy horse, bales of hay in the field, or a sturdy roof over the barn, it was instant gratification. There was always a sense that all that hard work paid off. Not to mention the glow that came from the knowledge that her father approved of her.

That approval had meant the world to her as a child.

The thought had her frowning. As always, the old doubts and hurts crept in to taunt her.

If Porter had really approved of her, he would have fought to see her. Instead, he'd let her go without a word, and he had made no attempt to have any personal contact with her through the years.

What kind of father swept his daughter out of his life, and out of his thoughts, like so much dust?

She stripped and stepped under the hot spray, wishing as always that she could wash away the sting of her father's dismissal as easily as the grime of hard work.

In her old bedroom she pulled on a pair of clean denims and a cotton blouse of apple green. She allowed her hair to air dry while she packed a few necessities in an overnight bag. Slinging it over her shoulder, she paused to pick up the plastic bin in her father's room, and then headed down the stairs and out to the barn where she'd stored the rental car.

After stashing her things in the trunk, she called out for Cory. Her voice echoed around the empty barn.

Getting no reply, she struggled against the sudden panic that lodged in her throat. She'd been so preoccupied with work in the house, she hadn't given a single thought to Cory, out here in the barn. What if the intruder had found him, alone and vulnerable, and had kidnapped him?

Or what if Cory, giving in to loneliness and fear, had run off somewhere to grieve by himself?

He was just a little kid. A frightened, very lonely little boy. There was no telling what kind of trouble he could find himself in.

Nudging aside the fear that sent a trickle of ice along her spine, she drove the car to the back door before racing inside.

Cupping her hands to her mouth she called his name as loudly as she could before running from room to room.

Minutes later his head appeared at the top of the stairs. "Yeah?"

She felt a dizzying wave of relief, and realized that her nerves were strung as tightly as violin strings. "There you are. Have you packed some things?"

"Doing it now."

"All right. I have the car outside. Let's go."

She turned away and put a hand against the door to steady herself. She was going to have to do something about this unreasonable fear. She mentally cursed the intruder who had planted this seed of distrust in her heart.

The more she thought about it, the more she was convinced that Jake was right in thinking that she had been the target of this man's wrath. For whatever reason, he wanted to frighten her.

And he had done a very good job of it.

"Come on, Cory." Meg's voice sounded shrill to her own ears, and she took several deep breaths, hoping to calm her nerves.

When she heard no response, she climbed the stairs and stepped into the boy's room. He was busy stuffing things into a backpack.

He looked up in surprise, his tone betraying his frustration. "I'm almost ready."

Meg felt a wave of remorse. Poor kid. He probably felt every bit as pressured as she did. "It's okay. Take your time. I'm not in any rush. Do you need any help?"

"No."

As Cory zipped his backpack, Meg paused to study the row of faded photos that lined his dresser top. She picked up one of a young teenage girl laughing with a scruffy youth.

"Is this your mother?"

Cory glanced over. "Yeah."

She pointed to the boy. "Who's this?"

He shrugged and looked away. "Don't know," he muttered.

"You never asked your mother who he is?"

Cory gave a shrug. "Why do you care?"

"Maybe it's her brother. Maybe you have an uncle."

"She was an orphan."

"You're sure?"

"That's what she said. She was in fos...something."

"Foster care?"

He nodded. "Yeah. That's it."

"And the boy with her? Was he in foster care, too?"

"I guess. His name is Blain. That's all I know." Cory struggled with the zipper of his backpack.

Something in his tone made Meg look at him, but the boy kept his gaze averted.

"Well." She returned the photo to his dresser top and turned away. "I guess we'd better get moving."

"I'm coming." The boy descended the stairs behind her, his backpack looped over one arm.

At the back door she paused. "Did you remember a toothbrush?"

"Yeah."

"Pajamas?"

He shrugged. "Don't need 'em. Figured I'd sleep out in the barn with Shadow."

"I don't know if the Conways will allow it."

"Then I'll sleep in my underwear." He brushed past her and stormed down the porch steps.

Meg locked the back door and followed. Once in the car she waited until he'd stowed his things and secured his seat belt.

She tried to keep things light. "I guess we won't worry about getting lost on the way to the Conway ranch. It's just over that hill, right?"

Cory shrugged and looked out the side window, shutting her out.

She turned on the radio and fiddled with the dials until she found a station playing country.

With Carrie Underwood singing, Meg put the car in gear and started along the gravel drive.

"*Right now . . .*"

As the song's lyrics rolled over her, Meg added her own in her mind.

Right now, I wish I were slow-dancing....

The image of Jake Conway came unbidden to her mind, and she could almost feel his arms around her, leading her in a slow dance around the floor of some dusty saloon.

Damn the man. One kiss and he'd managed to take over her brain just the way she'd found herself wishing he would take over her body.

There was just something about that smooth-talking, slow-walking, sexy-as-sin cowboy that had a way of jumbling all her thoughts and making her feel all hot and cold and itchy.

Yeah. Itchy.

She almost laughed out loud. That was an apt description of the way she'd been feeling ever since she'd met him.

But she was a big girl now. Old enough to know that it wasn't necessary to scratch every itch.

She would ignore the temptation to get to know Jake Conway better, even though the mere thought of him had her tingling with anticipation.

Just for a few more days to practice a little self-control. She would try to think of him as a client. One who was strictly off-limits. There had been enough of them in her career. Handsome, successful guys who figured that having a good-looking lawyer from one of the country's top firms gave them license to ply their charms in the hope of guaranteeing that she would give them her full attention, at least until the trial was successfully completed. She'd learned early on to hold such clients at arm's length without being too insulting. It took some finesse, but she'd mastered the art to such a degree, she had gained a reputation among her fellow lawyers as being tough as nails.

That was how she vowed to deal with Jake Conway while she was accepting the hospitality of his family. She was certain she could find some clever ways to keep her distance from one devilishly sexy cowboy for a few days and nights.

And then she'd get back to reality and get on with her life.

She was relieved when the Conway ranch came into view over the hill. She was actually looking forward to the teasing jokes and laughter of Jake's family. After the solemn silence of her father's house, the noise of living, breathing people would be a welcome relief.

And while she was here, she would turn the task of evading Jake's charms into an amusing distraction, to keep her from thinking about the very real danger that lay in wait for her.

CHAPTER ELEVEN

Meg parked her rental car behind a ranch truck, and she and Cory hauled their gear into the mudroom, where they found Quinn and Cheyenne just washing up from their chores.

The two were laughing easily together, and Meg found herself thinking how perfectly suited they seemed.

"Hey, Meg. Let me help you with that." Cheyenne dried her hands and hurried over to reach for the plastic bin in Meg's arms.

"Thanks." Relieved of her burden, Meg was able to take a firmer grasp of her overnight bag.

In the kitchen they found Phoebe busy at the stove. She turned with a smile of welcome.

"Phoebe, if you'd like," Cheyenne called, "I'd be happy to take Meg and Cory upstairs to the guest rooms."

"That would be great." Phoebe dried her hands on a

towel and paused to hug each of them before adding, "I'll leave you in Cheyenne's capable hands."

Meg and Cory trailed behind Cheyenne as she led them up a flight of stairs and along a hallway until she paused at a closed door. Inside, as she snapped on lights, she chatted happily.

"This will be your room, Cory." There were two twin beds, each with matching spreads in muted tans and browns, and a desk with a computer. A flat-screen television was mounted on a shelf on the wall, making it visible from the beds and desk.

As Cory dropped his backpack in the closet, Cheyenne opened another door to show him the attached bathroom.

"If there's anything you need, just let us know. If it's something a boy would want, you can bet the Conways already have it," she added with a laugh. "As you can see, they've had lots of experience with boys."

Cory couldn't hold back his smile as Cheyenne led Meg from the room.

Further along the hallway Cheyenne opened another door and stepped inside, throwing on lights while Meg simply gaped.

It wasn't just the king-sized bed with its mound of pillows and its creamy comforter, or the lovely curved desk in one corner, or the elaborate flat-screen television. Even the attached bathroom, with the huge whirlpool tub, glass-enclosed shower, and elegant square-cut basin sink couldn't compete with the view outside the floor-to-ceiling windows.

"Oh." Meg caught her breath and Cheyenne turned to see what had her gasping.

Seeing her gaze fixed on the sun setting over the Tetons, with those layers of mauve and pink and purple clouds against a golden background, Cheyenne smiled. "Yeah. It's pretty spectacular, isn't it?"

"I'd forgotten. Or maybe, because I was so young when I left here, I never fully appreciated just how glorious this view really is." Meg had a hand to her throat, and the look on her face was one of awe.

"Well, enjoy. The guest suite *and* the view," Cheyenne said with a laugh. "And when you're unpacked and settled in, come on downstairs and we'll have some time to visit before dinner."

"Thanks, Cheyenne."

When she was alone, Meg stood by the window for the longest time, just drinking in the view.

On her flight here she'd been so afraid that she had somehow magnified the beauty of this place in her mind. How could it possibly live up to her childhood memories? And yet here it was, even lovelier than she'd imagined it all these years later.

Without warning Meg found her eyes filling, and she quickly blinked and turned away.

She'd learned many years ago to keep her emotions in check. Now, after years of experience, here she was, practically blubbering over a pretty sunset.

Next, she'd be openly weeping at her father's funeral. No—there wasn't a chance of that, she thought fiercely, as she turned away and busied herself unpacking.

"Cory?" Meg knocked on the boy's door. "You in there?"

A minute later the door was opened and Cory stood framed in the doorway.

"Need any help unpacking?"

"Naw." He shook his head.

Meg wanted to peer past him to see if he'd bothered to hang his things, but he stood barring the way, and she was forced to take a step back. "I'm heading downstairs. Want to come?"

He shrugged and pulled the door closed before moving along beside her.

Meg didn't want to examine her motives too closely, but she felt like a coward for hoping the boy would join her so she wouldn't feel alone as she faced the Conway family. Not that they were intimidating, but there were so many of them. By having Cory along, she hoped to deflect some of the attention away from herself.

"Think Jake will be home yet?" By the inflection in Cory's tone, Meg could tell that he sincerely hoped so.

"It's hard to say. He's been spending so much time on our problems, the ranchers might want their share of his time today."

"Yeah." Cory frowned before stepping into the kitchen. When he caught sight of Jake talking quietly with Phoebe and Ela, his face relaxed into a smile.

"Hey." Jake looked over. "I hope you've settled in." His warm smile encompassed both Meg and Cory.

"Yes. Thanks." Meg spoke for both of them. "I can't tell you how impressed I am with the guest room. And the view of the mountains makes it really special."

Jake nodded. "Yeah. I can't think of a better sight every night before falling asleep than the view of the moon hanging over those peaks. When I was away studying, I missed it like crazy."

They looked up as Josh and Sierra came in from the mudroom.

A camera dangled from a strap around Sierra's neck. Her skin was glowing from a day in the sun.

After greeting Meg and Cory, Sierra was practically gushing. "Josh and I just got back from the high country. Jake, you should have seen the herd of mustangs. They came within a hundred yards of us, and I got some of the most amazing pictures of a mare and her foal."

"Was it the one I told you about? The palomino mare with the foal that's almost pure white?" Jake asked.

"That's the one." Sierra helped herself to a glass of lemonade from a tray. "I couldn't take my eyes off him. He's probably no more than a few months old, and already racing across the fields like the wind. I told Josh that I hope the herd stays around all summer, so that I can get enough pictures to chronicle his development from foal to colt, and then in the years to come, I could capture him as a stallion with his own herd."

Meg eyed the camera. "You're a professional?"

"Yes." Sierra took a long drink of her lemonade. "And since settling here, I've discovered a real fascination with the wildlife. It's so romantic. Cattle drives. Wildcats. Mustangs."

Meg nodded. "I can see where that would hold great appeal to a photographer. When I was Cory's age, I took it all for granted. Now, returning after such a long time away, I'm more aware than ever of what a special gift this place is."

"Exactly." Sierra's voice lowered with passion. "Every morning, when I look at those magnificent Tetons, and see the amazing wild creatures that roam freely, I'm so grateful to be here." She turned to loop an arm through Josh's. "Especially since I get to share it all with my very own cowboy."

He brushed a kiss over her upturned nose, causing Jake to give a mock shudder. "Would you guys please take that to your room?" He winked at Cory. "In the past year I've had to watch both my big, strong brothers turn into—" he made a face that had Cory snorting with laughter "—lovey-dovey, let's-settle-down-and-only-go-to-town-when-we-absolutely-have-to husbands." He turned to include Cheyenne and Quinn. "Who are you, and what have you done with my freewheeling brothers, who used to love going to the Watering Hole Saloon with me on Saturday nights hoping to raise some hell?"

That had everyone laughing just as Cole and Big Jim strolled in from the mudroom, their sleeves rolled to their elbows, hair slicked back from washing at the big sink.

Overhearing Jake's words, Cole said, "I'll take these lovey-dovey men over the crazy cowboys you're talking about."

Jake gave an exaggerated shake of his head. "You see, Cory? Old men and—" he huffed out a breath "—husbands. That's what we're stuck with around here. I may have to take you and your sister to town just to save you from becoming as boring as the rest of them."

"Who're you calling old, boyo?" Big Jim nudged Cole, and the two of them started menacingly toward Jake, flexing their muscles as they did.

"Okay. I'll take back the 'old.' But there's no denying that my two brothers have turned into doting husbands."

"We refer to ourselves," Quinn said with a laugh, "as the luckiest guys in the world."

"That's what I'm talking about, Cory." Jake gave the boy a high five.

They were still laughing as Phoebe called them to supper.

Dinner was a lively affair, with Josh and Sierra still highly animated as they described the herd of mustangs that had taken refuge in a meadow in the high country.

It was clear from Sierra's questions that she was seriously in love with the idea of using the foal she'd seen on her hike in a series of pictures chronicling the life of a mustang.

It was equally clear that Josh agreed with his wife and thought she ought to actively pursue the project.

"Even your agent loves the idea," he said.

"Yeah." Sierra's smile was radiant. "And considering how well he understands the mind of all those art lovers he deals with, I'd say that's my ticket to go full-steam ahead with it."

When the meal ended, Phoebe suggested that they take their desserts and coffee in the great room around the fireplace.

They were still talking and laughing as they pushed away from the table and walked through the open doorway toward the great room.

Jake noticed the way Cory halted in the doorway and peered around with a look of extreme caution.

Turning back, Jake paused beside him. "Something wrong?"

Meg walked up beside them in time to hear Cory whisper, "Where is it?"

"Where's what?" Jake motioned for the boy to follow him, but Cory dug in his heels and stood where he was.

"The elephant."

"Elephant?" Jake looked from Cory to Meg.

"You said there's an elephant in the living room, and promised to tell me about him."

Jake's lips twitched, and he would have burst into laughter if the boy weren't so solemn. "I guess I should have explained sooner."

"You mean he's gone?" Disappointment clouded the boy's eyes.

"I mean that 'an elephant in the living room' is a saying, not a thing." Despite the words, Jake could see that he was making no sense to the seven-year-old.

He dropped down on one knee so that his eyes were level with Cory's. "Let me see if I can make this clearer. There was this little boy. He was just about your age. And his family kept an elephant in the living room. Every day the boy had to step really carefully around that big old elephant, because it took up most of the space in the room. And one day he invited a friend from school to come home with him. The friend saw that great big elephant and said, 'Wow. You've got an elephant in your living room.' And do you know what the boy said?"

Cory shook his head.

"He said to his friend, 'Doesn't everybody have an elephant in their living room?' And his friend said, 'We had one, but we all stared it down and it got smaller and smaller until it just disappeared one day.' "

Cory looked at Jake blankly.

Very patiently Jake said, "You can live with something for so long, you think it's natural, and that everyone else has it, too. Like a dad who never plays with you because he's too old, and you never talk about it because it hurts too much. Or like a mom who disappears without a trace, and you never talk about it because it hurts too much."

Slowly, the meaning began to dawn in Cory's eyes. "So, you never really had an elephant here? But you had something that hurt."

"That's right. A very big hurt. And because it hurt so much, we all tiptoed around it."

"Like the boy tiptoed around his elephant."

"Yeah. But one day we got tired of tiptoeing and decided to face it. From that day on, it got smaller and smaller. It hasn't left yet, but at least it no longer fills up the room." Still kneeling in front of him, Jake closed his hands over Cory's shoulders and squeezed gently. "A lot of people have that elephant, and if they face it down, they'll see it begin to get smaller and smaller, until it fades away completely."

Cory was silent for a long moment as he considered Jake's words.

"So, this is like those fables my mom used to read to me." Cory looked up to meet Jake's steady gaze.

"Exactly." Jake's roguish grin returned. "You know something? You're a very smart boy, Cory."

As he got to his feet, the boy's face was wreathed in smiles.

And, Meg noted, he had not only looked Jake squarely in the eye, but hadn't flinched when he'd been touched.

It may not be much, she thought, as she followed the man and boy into the room, *but it's a whole lot more than we had when this day started.*

And it was way more than any reaction she could get from Cory, despite the fact that they were related by blood.

Of course, she thought with a trace of weariness,

maybe that was the chasm that would prove too deep for either of them to cross. They might share the same blood, but Cory saw her only as a stranger. An adult who would wield power over him, and one who could alter his future forever.

She hoped the day would come when the boy would be able to put aside his fear of her and find some small, common bond.

Until that day, she would have to be content with the fact that he was beginning to trust the Conway family. Especially Jake.

And why not? There was just something about him that inspired trust.

Of course, what she considered trust could turn out to be merely the lust simmering deep in her soul that heated up each time Jake Conway got too close.

There was no denying that this sexy cowboy was getting to her.

CHAPTER TWELVE

As the conversation began to lag, Quinn and Cheyenne were the first to take their leave. They called good night to the others before heading for their truck.

"Wait." Phoebe paused in the act of wheeling the serving cart from the great room. "You're not staying the night?"

Quinn paused. "We promised Micah we'd give him a hand with the ranch chores tomorrow, so we plan on spending the night at Cheyenne's ranch."

As they left, Jake saw the question in Meg's eyes.

"Cheyenne's the last surviving member of her family. Micah is her cook, wrangler, surrogate father, and all-around head honcho, who's been with her since she was a kid. After her marriage to Quinn, she was spending all her time racing between her ranch and ours. Since her ranch is our nearest neighbor to the south, she's been talking with Kirby Bolton about the legalities of merging her ranch with ours. Pa and Big Jim are fine with it, and they're working on combining ranch hands, as well, so the wranglers can handle the chores more efficiently."

Meg laughed. "That sounds like a very good deal for both Quinn and Cheyenne. And if I hadn't seen them together, I might be inclined to think their marriage was nothing more than a good business proposition. But nobody could fake the passionate vibes that those two give off."

Jake nodded. "Yeah. They could blind a guy with all that love glowing in their eyes."

"So, growing up in such close proximity, have they known each other for years?"

Jake laughed. "Actually, they only met when Cheyenne shot the alpha male wolf that my brother had been tracking and monitoring for years."

Meg's eyes rounded. "She shot Quinn's wolf? Tell me more."

Jake shook his head. "Sorry. I'll save that for them to tell. It's a hell of a tale."

When Josh and Sierra called out their good night to the others, Phoebe stifled a yawn. "I'll say good night, too. I'll see all of you in the morning." The housekeeper turned to Meg and Cory. "If you need anything at all—"

"They can wake me," Jake interrupted. "You've done enough for one day."

Phoebe shot him a grateful smile and blew him a kiss before saying to Meg, "See why he's my hero?"

"Just making up for all those years when I was that pesky kid who gave you so much trouble."

The warmth in her smile was genuine when she said, "You and your brothers have more than made up for the times you made my poor heart stop."

Cole and Big Jim shoved their way out of their comfortable chairs and headed toward the stairs after calling good night to their family and guests.

Meg watched them go before saying, "Your father and grandfather remind me so much of my own father when I was a girl. Larger than life and able to handle so many tough ranch chores every day it would make the average man's head spin."

Jake nodded. "They're tough, all right. And despite Pa's heart attack, I haven't seen him slow down at all."

"Can't you and your brothers make him see the danger in that kind of attitude?"

Jake laughed. "You've seen how he operates. Like a bull in a pasture. He'll go where he wants to, and the rest of the herd had better get out of his way."

Meg smiled. "That's the impression I got. Watching your father and grandfather, I can see where you and your brothers learned to do things your way."

Jake shot her one of his famous grins. "Big Jim's fond of saying that there's only one way of doing things, and that's the Conways' way."

Noting Cory's silence, Meg glanced at him. "I think it's time we went up to bed, too."

Cory shot a pleading look at Jake. "Do I have to sleep upstairs?"

Jake arched an eyebrow at him. "You don't like the room we gave you?"

"Oh, I like it fine." The boy blushed. "But I was hoping I could sleep with Shadow out in the barn. I've been missing him something awful."

"Now Cory—," Meg began.

Before she could say more Jake held up a hand. "I

know just how you feel. I can't count the number of times I slept in the barn with a sick animal." He thought a minute before saying, "If your sister doesn't object, I've got a bedroll up in my room. I'll bring it out to you. It'll be a lot more comfortable than the hay in Shadow's stall."

"But the—"

Jake and Cory turned to Meg with identical looks of hope, and whatever protest she'd been about to voice was forgotten. "I guess, as long as you think Cory will be safe..."

"I'll guarantee it." Jake gave her his most persuasive smile. "You can go along to the barn with Cory, and I'll meet you there."

As she and Cory turned away, Jake took the stairs three at a time. Minutes later he caught up with Meg and Cory just as they were stepping into Shadow's stall.

He tossed the bedroll in the corner of the stall before kneeling and running a hand along the colt's flank.

Cory leaned close to bury his face in Shadow's neck. At once the colt went perfectly still.

At the look on the boy's face, Meg felt her heart constrict, and she remembered again the pain she'd felt when she'd been forced to leave her pony, Strawberry, behind all those years ago.

It was strange to think that she'd buried those feelings so deep, she'd almost forgotten about them until her return to Wyoming.

Jake got to his feet. "I think maybe Shadow is turning a corner on this infection. Or maybe he's just happy to see you, Cory. Whatever the reason, he didn't flinch when I touched his wound. And that's a good sign."

He watched the boy and horse, both standing still and quiet, oblivious to all around them.

"You've got your cell phone?" he asked.

Cory nodded.

"Okay. I know you'll call if you need me." With a smile he stepped out of the stall.

"That's it?" Meg looked at Jake, thinking he'd give the boy a lecture on staying safe if their unknown intruder should make an appearance. Instead he merely turned away.

Seeing that he had nothing more to say to her brother, Meg followed.

As Jake latched the stall door Meg turned. "Remember, Cory. We have to be up early in the morning to make the drive into town for the funeral."

The boy looked away for a moment, but not before they could both see the pain in his eyes. His voice was little more than a whisper: "I haven't forgotten."

Meg's tone softened. "I'm sorry, Cory. But I..." Again her words trailed off as she realized there was nothing more to say. "Good night, Cory."

"'Night."

Jake raised a hand in salute, and the boy did the same.

Jake crossed to the pen where Honey was resting. He took a moment to check the golden Lab's vitals before announcing, "It won't be much longer, Honey. I know you're eager to see those pups. You're going to be such a good mama."

He ruffled her fur, latched her pen, and turned away.

As he and Meg stepped from the barn, they could hear Cory's voice, soft and muted, talking in soothing tones to the colt.

Meg turned in the darkness. "Do you really think it's safe to leave him out here all alone?"

"He's not alone. He has Shadow. You saw them together. It's love. As real and sloppy and mushy as the feelings my brothers have for their new brides."

Meg couldn't help laughing aloud. "They *are* sloppy and mushy, aren't they? But I think they're sweet."

Jake tugged on a lock of her hair. "That's only because you don't have to be around them all day long, watching them giving each other those big calf eyes."

He was laughing as he said it, and Meg could hear the warmth beneath his words.

She paused to look up at him. "I don't think you mind it half as much as you let on."

"Shhh." He touched a finger to her lips. "Don't let them know. That will have to be our little secret."

The moment he touched her he felt the strong sexual current that raced along his skin. Very carefully he drew his hand away.

Meg continued walking toward the house.

Beside her, Jake was sweating. He'd forgotten just how potent the attraction was whenever he got too close to her.

Once inside the house, they climbed the stairs to the second floor, and paused outside the closed door to the guest room.

Meg turned to Jake. "I hope we're not making a mistake by allowing Cory to sleep out there."

"I didn't mention it, but while I was fetching my bedroll I arranged for our wranglers to take a turn around the barns a couple of times during the night. On top of that, Cory has his cell phone. And then there's Honey. If our intruder managed to get past all the other barriers, that she-dog would put up such a howl, the poor guy would probably run clear to Jackson Hole without stopping."

"But Cory's so little—"

"He's not helpless." Jake tilted her face upward, studying the look in her eyes. "I think that kid is getting to you."

She looked indignant. "I just don't want to see him hurt."

"Yeah. I forgot. You want me to believe you're the original hard-hearted Hannah." His finger was tingling, and he remembered, too late, how his body reacted whenever he touched her.

He thought about fighting the feeling yet again, but he was tired of fighting it. Besides, what was the harm of one little kiss?

"Just relax. Cory will be fine." He lowered his head and brushed his mouth over hers. It was the merest whisper of mouth to mouth, but the instant their lips touched, everything changed.

He drew back, as though considering his options.

And then, as if in slow motion, his arms came around her and he dragged her against him while he savaged her mouth.

God in heaven, she tasted so good. He couldn't seem to get enough of it. His lips moved over hers, drawing out all their sweet, tart flavor.

Those lips, those soft, tempting lips, held some kind of magic. That was the only explanation for the explosion of feelings rocketing through him.

With a growl of pleasure he backed her roughly against the closed door. He had his hands in her hair, though he couldn't recall how they got there.

He lowered his mouth to the soft curve of her neck, and heard her throaty sigh. The sound of it was enough to make him dizzy with need.

She'd anchored her arms around his waist as the kiss spun on and on. The feel of her, all wrapped around him, had him sweating. His head was swimming, and he breathed in the heady fragrance of her perfume, which reminded him of a field of wildflowers. Right this minute he would happily drown in her.

He knew he had to stop, but not just yet. He wanted one more touch. One more taste.

"This is a first." He spoke the words inside her mouth as he indulged himself in another slow, lingering kiss that had his blood flowing like hot lava.

"What is?" She moved her mouth to the corner of his jaw and he thought about simply devouring her.

"Kissing a girl good night in my house instead of hers."

She laughed, but it turned into a sigh when he ran light kisses across her upturned face.

"Why don't we step inside your room and see if we can't take this to the next level?"

Meg's laughter faded. For a moment she merely lay a hand on his chest, while she sucked air into her starving lungs. Then she looked up at him. "Sorry. It's a very tempting offer. But one of us has to be sensible."

"All right. That would be me. Sensible Jake Conway, they call me. I'm happy to take charge." With that rogue smile he reached around her to open the door.

Again she put her hand on his chest. But the laughter in her eyes softened her words. "Sorry, cowboy. This lady sleeps alone."

"I'd be happy to change that, too."

She stepped through the doorway and turned to him, intending to say good night. He surprised her by leaning in close enough to run nibbling kisses from her ear to the corner of her lips.

When she looked up at him he had a dangerous grin. "I just wanted to leave you with a reminder of what might have been in case you're serious about refusing my offer," he said.

"Oh, I'm serious. And it was a very pleasant reminder of what I'm missing. But I'm sure I'll survive."

"There's more to life than mere survival, Meg. Why not take a walk on the wild side?"

She lifted a hand to his cheek. "Nice try. 'Night, Jake."

He was still grinning as the door closed.

Meg leaned against the closed door and told herself to breathe. It wasn't easy, over the wild drumming of her heart.

When she was sure her legs would carry her, she walked to the bed and dropped down on the edge, breathing in and out until her heart rate settled.

She couldn't recall the last time she'd felt this out of control. Probably not since high school, when all those hormones were working overtime, and the dreamy captain of the nearby boys' school football team had singled her out for his attentions.

It shamed her to admit that she'd been sorely tempted to drag Jake in here and take what he was offering, and to hell with the consequences. It also shamed her to admit that the only reason she'd resisted was because she couldn't do such a thing in this very household after accepting the gracious hospitality of the Conway family.

But she'd wanted to. Oh, how she'd wanted to.

She stood and walked to the floor-to-ceiling-windows to stare at the darkened outline of the Tetons. At the moment, their beauty was lost on her. She was still thinking about her puzzling reaction to Jake.

There was just something about him that got to her. If anybody had told her a week ago that she would be turned on by a tall, muscled cowboy in faded denims, and frayed plaid shirts, she'd have laughed. At Howe-Kettering she was surrounded daily by men who chased money and power and success, and dressed in thousand-dollar suits and Italian leather loafers with impossible designer names, not to mention impossible price tags.

Yet here she was, a smart, sensible, career-driven woman riding the crest of success, and the only thing on her mind was a tumble with a sexy guy who spent his days delivering foals in smelly barns and mending ranch animals of every size and shape.

And right this minute, she wished she'd given in to her inclination to invite him in and forget about everything except some crazy, mindless sex.

Except, she thought, with a guy like Jake, it just might not be so mindless. Whenever she thought she had him pegged as another brainless hunk, he surprised her by being a whole lot more.

Like the tenderness he displayed whenever he was with Cory. There was a connection there. One she didn't have. Maybe it was just a guy thing. Maybe they were just wired differently to keep women out. But she thought it was something else entirely.

She was beginning to think there was a lot more to this sexy Wyoming veterinarian than she'd first expected.

She crossed her arms over her chest and gave a long, deep sigh.

And maybe she was just trying to make something out of nothing.

Not that it mattered. In a few short days she'd be gone. And all of this would be forgotten.

Jake stripped off his shirt and tossed it in a hamper in the closet before walking to the window, where he leaned a hip against the frame and drank in the sight of the Tetons in the distance.

Usually the scene had the ability to clear his mind so that he could sort through any problem troubling him. Tonight, however, he couldn't seem to focus. Maybe, he thought, because he wasn't sure yet what the problem was.

Meg Stanford was a contradiction. On the Internet he'd located a video of the trial that had brought her to public attention. While watching it he'd been struck by how cool and calm she was in the midst of a high-profile courtroom drama being played out before scores of television cameras. She'd been interviewed after the verdict, and her courtroom strategy had been dissected by every reporter on the planet. Yet she'd remained cool and aloof, as though the drama hadn't touched her at all.

He'd thought, while watching the replay of the trial, that he'd very much like to try thawing the heart of that ice maiden.

But tonight in his arms, she'd been a very different Meg. All heat and fire and passion. And he'd have bet any amount of money that she had been as reluctant as he to walk away.

Now that he'd met the other Meg, the sexy, too-hot-to-handle Meg, he couldn't wait to see which one he'd uncover the next time he kissed her.

And he fully intended to kiss her again. As often as he could.

CHAPTER THIRTEEN

The rain started around dawn, and by the time Meg awoke, it was a steady, drenching downpour.

The perfect day for a funeral, Meg thought, as she and Cory took their seats in the front pew of the Paintbrush Church.

After his night in the barn, Cory had showered and dressed in a clean shirt and denims. Despite his attempt to tame his hair, it stuck out in wild tufts here and there, and fell below the collar of his shirt.

Meg wore one of her business suits in charcoal silk. The narrow skirt and fitted jacket may have been the perfect choice for a courtroom, but now that she was seated in the simple church, they seemed too fussy. The designer shoes with skinny red heels and cutout toes had cost a fortune. When she'd worn them in D.C. they made her feel smart and sexy, a woman who understood fashion and how to use it to her advantage. Here in Paintbrush, surrounded by men in cowboy boots and women in sensible sneakers and walking shoes, she felt foolish and frivolous.

When Reverend Cornell began the service, Meg glanced around. The entire Conway family had insisted on leaving their chores behind in order to show their support, as did the police chief, as promised.

She was pleasantly surprised by the number of strangers filling the pews of the church. Had her father touched so many lives? Meg found herself wondering if the people were here out of a fondness for Porter Stanford, or simply to satisfy their curiosity about a man who had lived his life without regard to the rules that governed the rest of them.

One cowboy, who sat in a far corner of the church, head bowed, hands folded, stirred a memory in her. She glanced at him a time or two but never caught his eye.

Still, she couldn't shake that fingers-along-the-spine feeling of being watched. She soon forgot about it, however, when the minister began the service.

Reverend Cornell, tall, balding, bespectacled, had a voice that needed no amplification. He spoke in dramatic, funereal tones about a man who had kept mostly to himself, but had often reached out to help those in the town who were most in need.

Meg sat up straighter. Was the good preacher merely stretching the truth in order to ease any grief Porter Stanford's children might be suffering? Was it possible that her father had ever cared about anyone except himself? Was there a side to the man that she'd never uncovered?

As the minister switched from his personal recollections of the deceased to talk in abstract terms about life and death, Meg allowed her mind to drift back to the years she'd struggled with her self-esteem, believing always that her parents had split because of her. Despite the fortune her mother had spent on counselors for her daughter, the seeds planted in her young mind had never been completely uprooted. She'd seen firsthand the tug-of-war between two headstrong people, vying for a child's affection and loyalty. Those memories would remain for a lifetime.

Her mother may have won the battle, taking Meg far from the home and father she loved, but in the subsequent years, Virginia had lost the war. She and her daughter had grown more and more distant as she'd struggled to balance the needs of a rebellious teenage daughter against the demands of a successful, career-driven new husband. In such a battle, it seemed inevitable that her daughter couldn't win.

Meg glanced at Cory, who was shifting uncomfortably on the hard wooden seat. Though they shared the same father, their memories of the man were very different.

In that instant the boy looked up, and their gazes met and held. Meg was stunned at the pain in his eyes. Without thinking she draped an arm around his shoulders and drew him closer.

At her touch he stiffened, and seconds later, feeling awkward and completely out of her element, she removed her arm and clutched her hands tightly in her lap. It would seem that no matter what she did, it was the wrong thing, at least in Cory's eyes.

Reverend Cornell walked toward the casket, and the first chords of an old familiar hymn were played on an organ.

The minister beckoned them forward, and Meg and

Cory got to their feet and stood beside him. As the funeral director rolled the casket down the aisle, Meg and Cory trailed slowly behind.

Though she kept her head lowered, Meg was aware of Everett Fletcher standing stiffly in a pew, and behind him the Conway family. Big Jim and Cole, with old Ela and Phoebe beside them. Quinn and Cheyenne, and Josh and Sierra.

And then there was Jake. She tried not to look at him, but her eyes betrayed her, going wide, meeting his. In that quick glance she saw a look of understanding, and though she didn't want to probe her already fragile feelings too deeply, she felt a wave of extreme gratitude that he was there and that he understood what she was going through.

She glanced around for the cowboy who'd snagged her attention earlier, but he was nowhere to be seen.

As the others in the church fell into step behind them, they paraded out of the church and up the hill to the cemetery. The funeral director's assistant handed her an umbrella, and she and Cory huddled beneath it as they followed the casket to the freshly dug gravesite.

Meg noted the shiny new grave marker beside the open hole. It bore the legend ARABELLA STANFORD. WIFE. MOTHER. Other than those simple words, there was nothing more. Neither her date of birth nor her date of death were included. Maybe her father had intended to add more and had simply failed to follow through. At any rate, his name would soon be added to the stone, and the two who had been recently united in life would also be united in death.

And wasn't life strange? she thought.

There was no time to puzzle over it as the small crowd

began gathering around the minister, who read from a book. When the final prayer was concluded, Reverend Cornell walked to Meg and Cory and said a few words.

Meg's years of courtroom training took over, and though she didn't have a clue as to what the minister had said, she mouthed platitudes, thanking him for offering comfort during this difficult time.

He smiled and walked away, and only then did Meg realize that Cory was silently weeping.

She felt completely helpless against his tears. Should she put her arm around him and risk having him pull away again?

Even while that thought was swirling through her mind, she felt movement beside her and saw that Jake had come forward to wrap his big arms around the boy.

"It's all right to cry, Cory," he said against the boy's temple. "I've done it a time or two myself. That's what we do when our hearts are broken."

Without a word Cory leaned into him, and the flood of tears that he'd been so valiantly fighting were unleashed like a raging river, soaking the front of Jake's already wet shirt.

While Jake held the boy, two cemetery workers began lowering the casket into the ground. A few friends and neighbors came forward to toss a shovelful of mud on the lowered casket and to offer their condolences to Meg. Several of them touched a hand to Cory's head before making their way down the hill toward their waiting vehicles.

A glance around told Meg that she and Cory were alone, except for the Conway family. The rest had already drifted away, back to their jobs or homes.

The Conway family had very kindly waited until everyone had left before coming forward to speak to Meg.

Jake touched a hand to her arm. "My family would like to say good-bye. They have to get back to the ranch."

"Of course." She managed a smile as she extended her hand to Big Jim, and then to each of the others. "Thank you all so much for being here. Cory and I are grateful for your support."

As they spoke their words of sympathy and walked away, Big Jim held back. He laid a hand on Cory's shoulder. "It's hard, saying good-bye to the ones who gave us life. If you ever find yourself in trouble, I hope you know that you can still talk to your daddy, just the way you did when he was walking this earth. The way I see it, death doesn't mean the end of life. It's just that we can't see those who've passed over. But they can still see and hear us, and they still care about us."

The boy stared hard at the toe of his boot.

Big Jim drew Meg close for a quick, hard hug. "You stay strong."

She took in a deep breath. "I will. Thank you."

He stepped back and walked away until he caught up with the rest of his family.

Meg turned to Jake, who had offered Cory his handkerchief. "Thank you." She was surprised to hear the tremor in her voice. Oh, sweet heaven. She prayed she wouldn't embarrass herself by weeping.

"I'll wait for you at the church door."

"There's no need—"

He held up a hand. "Kirby Bolton said he'll meet with you in his office. It's right next door to the courthouse. When you're ready, I'll drive you there."

She nodded.

He walked away, leaving her alone with Cory, who was staring at the workers. An older man drove a front-end loader, dropping mounds of mud until the gaping hole in the ground was filled. A second worker used a rake and shovel to smooth the soggy earth. Nearby lay a neat roll of sod, which would no doubt soon cover the spot until it blended perfectly with the other gravesites, completely obliterating the fresh grave.

"Dad didn't like the dark."

Meg turned to the little boy, wondering what to say.

Cory's chin jutted. "He'd sit up real late in the night. And whenever I came downstairs, he always had all the lights on in all the rooms. I asked him why, and he said he didn't like the dark."

"I guess that's true for a lot of us."

"But now they've covered him." Cory blinked hard, and Meg prayed that he wouldn't start crying again. She didn't think she could bear it if he did.

She thought quickly, needing something to say. "You know our dad isn't there."

Cory looked up at her. "He's not?"

She shook her head, trying desperately to remember whatever childhood thoughts she'd ever had about death and dying. "That's just his old, worn-out body there. But his soul, his spirit, is already in heaven."

Cory seemed intrigued. "Mom talked about heaven a lot."

"Well, then. There you are. What did she say about it?"

"That there's no pain there. It's filled with happy, peaceful souls. And angels. She liked thinking about angels. She said she wasn't afraid of going to heaven to be with angels."

Meg felt an unexpected jolt of gratitude toward the young woman she'd never met. "Your mom was right. And now our dad's joined her there. And there's no pain. No anger. Just light and peace."

Though she'd intended her words to soothe a troubled boy, she found her own heart feeling lighter, as well. Did she really believe what she was saying? She wasn't sure. But right now, she needed some hope to cling to as desperately as Cory did.

"Did Dad bring you here a lot to visit your mom's grave?"

He shook his head. "Dad didn't leave the ranch much after she—"

Seeing his lips tremble, Meg had a need to fill the awkward silence. "Anytime you'd like to come here and visit, you let me know."

"I will." The boy beside her took in a long, deep breath before turning away.

As she followed suit, she felt his hand sneak into hers. Warmth speared through her, and for the first time since waking hours ago, the iron band around her heart seemed to have loosened ever so slightly.

Keeping the umbrella over their heads, she laced her fingers with Cory's and led the way down the hill.

True to his word, Jake stood waiting for them.

With quiet authority, he helped them into his truck and drove along Main Street to the courthouse.

Meg and Cory sat on either side of Judge Kirby Bolton's desk in his small, cramped chambers.

Stepping from the courtroom in his judicial robes, he looked every inch a wise magistrate. Dark, lively eyes were magnified by the thick, wire-rimmed glasses that added to his air of importance. Meg was startled to see that he was actually no more than five and a half feet tall, and thin as a stick.

Once he was seated behind his desk, he became once again a force to be reckoned with. He folded his hands atop his desk and studied the woman and boy with obvious interest.

"I'm sorry for your loss. Especially you, Cory. I know how much your father meant to you, son." His deep, theatrical voice resonated in the small room, causing Meg and Cory to sit up straighter. Despite the stern-eyed gaze and forceful tone, there was a softness in his eyes when he directed his words to Cory. "I hope you know that I'll do anything I can to make this an easy transition. But nothing can take the place of a father."

Cory nodded before lowering his head.

"I've been Porter's legal advisor for more than forty years. There are few surprises in his will. He was a very straightforward man. He wanted the fruits of his labor to be given over to those who would appreciate the sacrifices he's made for a lifetime." Kirby Bolton peered at the two of them. "Despite the fact that Porter liked the ladies and enjoyed living the good life, he worked as hard as he played. As he was fond of saying, nothing was given to him. He had to earn every penny the hard way."

The judge opened a file and studied the top page. "There are no debts on your father's estate. He saw to it that all taxes were paid in a timely manner. He recorded every wage that he paid to his wranglers. Whenever possible, he did business with locals. He saw it as his duty to keep his money circulating in the community in which he lived. And he hoped that his heirs would do the same."

Meg's chin jutted slightly, but she held her silence.

Kirby began to read from the will. "Two of my three wives received generous settlements at the time of our divorce and therefore are not entitled to any portion of my estate. My first ex-wife, Virginia, and my third wife, Arabella, rest her soul, predeceased me. Neither Virginia nor Arabella had extended family. Therefore, there are no other claimants to my estate but my two children, my daughter, Meghan, and my son, Cory. I desire that my estate be divided equally between them, with Cory's portion held in trust until he reaches the age of majority, with my trusted friend and legal counsel, Judge Kirby Bolton, as executor. I charge my heirs to see to it that the ranch and all its holdings, including the wranglers, the herds, the vehicles, and ranch implements continue to operate as they always have, as a working ranch."

Meg clenched her teeth and fisted her hands in her lap, the only sign of her agitation. It would appear that Porter Stanford had hoped to dictate even from the grave.

Kirby Bolton looked over his spectacles. "Are there any questions?"

Meg tapped a finger on the arm of her chair. "I'd appreciate your clarification on a point of law."

The judge raised his brows. "Of course. Your reputation as a criminal lawyer has preceded you. I certainly respect your knowledge of the law. What would you like to know?"

"Regarding the ranch...the estate," she corrected.

"Was my father merely stating his preference, or are these terms legal and binding? In other words, do I have the right to dispose of the ranch and everything on it as I see fit?"

Judge Bolton folded his hands. "Your father had very strong ideas about how his estate should be handled after his death. Having said that, I would add that he was stating his preference; therefore it would not be legally binding in a court of law. His heirs have the right to dispose of the estate in any manner they happen to choose. I would warn you, however, that I have been appointed executor for Cory's portion of the estate until he reaches the age of majority, and I have been charged with the duty to see to it that his best interest is being served. Since I would cast my vote in his stead, I would have to be persuaded that anything that veers from Porter's stated preference is in the best interest of Cory's future."

Meg's eyes narrowed. "His best interest meaning that you believe he should be raised here, on our father's ranch?"

"I didn't say that. I'm certainly open to suggestions as to where and how Cory should grow into manhood."

Meg studied the judge. "Do you plan on taking physical custody of Cory?"

Kirby Bolton smiled. "This was discussed at some length with Porter, when he dictated the latest version of his last will and testament, shortly after Arabella died. He wanted assurance that Cory would be taken care of, both physically and psychologically. We both agreed that it would be in the boy's best interest if he could live with family." Kirby Bolton gave her a long, appraising look before glancing down at the papers on his desk. "In the event that isn't possible, I will oversee his physical care and education until he reaches the age of eighteen."

Meg could feel Cory looking over at her, but she kept her gaze averted, wondering at the strange rush of emotions. She ought to feel relief that her father had given her an out clause. Wasn't that what she'd wanted? Why then, this feeling of dejection? Was it because her father had already decided that she would be unwilling to take on the responsibility of a half brother? Had he already written her off as too selfish, too self-centered, to care more about a seven-year-old boy than she did about her precious career, her freedom, her comfort?

Her temper flared.

How dare her long-absent father judge her and label her?

Or would it be more honest to admit that she was the one judging her own selfish motives?

She shot the judge a challenging look. "Have you heard about the vandalism that occurred at my father's ranch?"

Kirby nodded. "Police Chief Fletcher came by to ask if Porter had any enemies that I knew about. I'll tell you what I told him. Every man probably acquires a few enemies over the course of his lifetime, especially a man like Porter, who lived life to the fullest. I'm sure he stepped on his share of toes over the years. Irate husbands. Unhappy businessmen who felt that he'd taken advantage of them. And probably more than a few pretty women who hoped they could be the next Mrs. Stanford. But I don't know of anyone who would want to break into his home or to vandalize his daughter's vehicle. Along with enjoying the good life, Porter looked out for the folks in this town. Despite what his ex-wives may have thought of him, he was a good man."

Meg stared hard at her hands to keep from letting this man see the depth of her feelings. Right now, she wasn't in the mood to hear about her father's success, when she was achingly aware of his many failures.

She looked up and realized the judge was speaking to them both.

"Porter was, however, withdrawn since the death of Arabella. The day before his death, when I ran into him as he was leaving the bank, he seemed depressed. I attributed it to the sense of loneliness and self-imposed isolation. Instead of getting better, he seemed to be getting much worse. When I asked him about it, he said he was trying to stay focused on what was best for his boy." He turned to Cory. "I hope you'll always remember how much your father loved you, son."

His tone changed from observant to businesslike. "I've enclosed a copy of your father's will, along with whatever information about his estate that I had in my file." Standing, he came around the desk and handed a large manila folder to Meg. "Because of your knowledge of the law, I'm sure you'll want to go over everything carefully. If you have any questions, please feel free to call me." He indicated his card, stapled to the corner of the folder. "Speaking of the law..." He seemed to think about what he was about to say before charging ahead. "If you should decide to stay here, our town has a desperate need for good legal counsel."

"Isn't that what you do?"

He shook his head. "I'm juggling too many balls and finding that I can't keep them all in the air. I was a lawyer before I became a judge. Now I'm a full-time judge, and a part-time lawyer to those in need, but I can't really give my clients the time they deserve. This town needs a smart, compassionate expert. They need a Meghan Stanford. They would welcome you with open arms. And so would I."

His gaze met Meg's. In his eyes she thought she saw kindness and understanding. "Your father was a friend. We didn't hunt together, or play poker, or do any of the things most friends do together. But I considered him a man of his word. He knew it was the same for me. I gave him my word, as his friend, as his lawyer, that I'd do whatever necessary to see that his wishes were carried out." He offered his hand. "I'd like to be your friend, too, Miss Stanford."

"Meg," she corrected.

"Meg." He smiled. "And I'm Kirby. You should know that your father followed your famous trial, and he was as proud as a peacock."

She fought to keep the pain from her voice. "It's too bad he didn't bother to let me know how he felt."

"He didn't want to intrude on the life you'd made for yourself." When Meg said nothing, he added, "If I can do anything to ease this transition, please don't hesitate to ask."

"Thank you. And thank you for contacting me so quickly about my father's death." Meg stood and waited until Cory shook the judge's hand.

Kirby Bolton dropped an arm around Cory's shoulders. "I know you miss your father and mother, son. I hope you can trust that both your sister and I will do everything in our power to ease your pain."

The boy nodded.

Meg headed for the door. She couldn't wait to get out of this place. Her father's words were still rolling around in her mind, challenging all the neat, tidy plans she'd already put into motion.

She felt as though she could barely breathe.

CHAPTER FOURTEEN

As Meg and Cory walked from Judge Bolton's office, Jake stepped from his truck, which was parked at the curb. He took one look at Meg's face and turned to Cory, dropping an arm around the boy's shoulders.

"You have to be starving. Neither of you ate a thing this morning, and dinner will be over by the time we get back to the ranch."

Cory shot a glance at Meg. "I guess I could eat something."

"Good." Jake squeezed his shoulder. "So could I. How about stopping at Flora's Diner for some supper before heading back?"

Meg nodded. "I'm not sure I could eat a thing, but I could really use some strong, hot coffee."

"Flora's place is just down the street, but with all this rain, I'll drive." He paused to hold open the door to his truck.

When they were seated, he walked to the driver's side and climbed in. Within minutes they were stopping in front of the diner with its gaudy pink and purple letters. They made a dash through the rain and stepped into the tiny restaurant, where a crowd had already gathered.

"Looks like we'll have to sit at the counter." Jake indicated the long counter with its round, shiny red stools.

Framed behind the pass-through window was Flora, the eighty-something owner and cook, flipping burgers, lifting fries from vats of hot grease, slathering thick slices of home-baked bread with mayo, mustard, or ketchup, as she turned out more than a dozen different sandwiches, and all of it done while she kept an eye on every customer who walked through the front door.

Her white hair was held back in a hair net that resembled a spider's web. Her familiar white dress and apron bore the smudges of the many meals she'd prepared since putting them on early this morning.

Her daughter, sixty-year-old Dora, moved between the tables and the counter, tending to everyone and everything with an efficiency that made her mother proud. The two plump women, as wide as they were tall, were fixtures in the town of Paintbrush, and everyone agreed that they fully expected to see them still here, and still working, twenty years down the road.

"Well, well. Look who's here." Flora's face was beaming. "Jake Conway. And with a pretty woman, I see. Not that I'm surprised. I'm guessing there isn't a beautiful female for a hundred miles around that hasn't been part of your herd."

"Herd?" Meg arched a brow.

"Don't mind Flora. That's just her way of teasing."

"Uh-huh." Meg watched as the old woman waddled out from behind the kitchen to grab Jake by the shoulders and plant a big, wet kiss on his mouth.

"Now my day is complete," Flora said with a deep rumble of laughter.

"Mine, too." Jake framed her face and kissed her again, much to her delight. "I needed your sunshine on a gloomy day like this."

"Oh, you." She slapped his chest and stepped back behind the counter before glancing at Cory. "Aren't you Porter Stanford's boy?"

Jake answered for him. "Flora, this is Cory Stanford."

Flora leaned over the counter to touch a hand to his cheek. "I heard that the funeral was this morning. I'm sorry, sweet boy. Your pa was a good man."

Cory lowered his head and stared hard at the counter.

"And this is Porter's daughter, Meg Stanford."

At Jake's words Flora studied Meg and Cory. "Of course. Now that you say that, I can see for myself, though I should have known right away by that pretty red hair." The old woman extended her hand. "My apologies on your loss, Meg. You and your daddy used to come in here when you were a little girl."

Meg nodded. "I remember. I never dreamed you'd still be here."

"You mean still alive, don't you?" Flora cackled at her own joke. "That's what everybody says. But I'm still standing. So's my daughter, Dora." She turned to include the woman who had walked up to take their orders. "Dora, do you remember Porter's daughter, Meg?"

Dora nodded. "I sure do. Every time you came in, even before you ordered, Ma would start making an extra-thick chocolate shake and a burger with no onions."

Meg knew her jaw had dropped, but she couldn't hide her surprise. "You remember that from all those years ago?"

Dora shrugged. "I'm getting more and more like Ma. It's easier to remember things from years ago than from yesterday. But you were easy. Whenever you came in here with your pa, the two of you always ordered the same things, with no exceptions. And you'd ooh and ahh over those chocolate shakes like you'd just died and gone to heaven."

Meg laughed. "Now that you mention it, I think it's exactly what I need right now." She turned to Cory. "Want to try one?"

He looked surprised before giving a nod of his head. "Okay."

"Two chocolate shakes," Meg said. "Extra thick. And I'll have a burger with no onions." Again she glanced at Cory. "Want to give the burger a try?"

He nodded.

"Coming right up." Dora turned to Jake. "The special today is slow-cooked roast beef on Ma's sourdough."

Jake brought Dora's hand to his lips. "You had me at slow-cooked roast beef."

She was giggling like a girl as she turned away and filled three glasses with water.

Jake turned to Meg. "I thought all you wanted was strong, hot coffee."

"That was before Dora reminded me of that burger and shake."

Jake leaned past Meg to say in a loud whisper to Cory,

"That's why this place is always so crowded. Those two women know how to make you hungry even when you're not."

All three were laughing as they waited for their lunch.

Meg leaned back, thinking how good it was to be able to laugh again. Back at the cemetery, and later in the judge's office, she'd felt as though she was carrying the weight of the world on her shoulders. Right now, right this minute, she was remembering how it had felt to be eight years old, and sitting at this very counter next to her dad, nibbling a juicy burger and slurping a thick chocolate shake, without a single worry in the world.

When their order was ready, Flora carried the tray to the counter herself instead of serving their plates to Dora by way of the pass-through. As she handed them around she peered at Meg and Cory.

"Your daddy had a reputation in this town for being a hard-nosed, no-nonsense rancher, and he was that." She leaned closer, so that she couldn't be overheard by everyone in the place. "But anybody who found themselves dealing with private misery knew they could always count on Porter to lend a hand."

Meg shot her a puzzled look. "Private misery?"

Flora shrugged. "A rancher who couldn't pay his taxes might find a note from the county saying his bill had been paid by a mysterious benefactor. A girl in trouble—" Flora shot a quick glance at Cory and was careful with her choice of words "—in need of somebody to pay for a doctor to deliver her baby, or maybe help her relocate to a new place for a fresh start, would find an envelope with cash or a bus ticket."

"And you think my father—?"

"I don't think. I know." Her tone lowered, softened. "Let me tell you what I know. When I was younger, I used to spend all my time making plans. Oh, the grand plans I made. And then one day, while I was busy making my plans, life happened. My husband died, leaving me with a baby, a ranch I couldn't run, and a pile of debts. I was in here, cooking and crying on old Harding Pool's shoulder, when he told me I could have his diner if I could come up with fifty thousand dollars so that he could retire to Florida to be with his granddaughter. He may as well have asked for the moon. I didn't have two dimes to rub together. All I had was a failing ranch. But the next day, out of the blue, a very young, very brash, and handsome man offered me fifty thousand dollars for my ranch."

Meg shook her head and turned to Jake, who looked every bit as surprised as she felt. "I don't understand."

"I didn't, either. But that same handsome, brash young cowboy had been the only customer in the diner the day before, when I'd been spilling my troubles to Harding. And within a week that same handsome, brash young cowboy brought me a check for fifty thousand dollars, which I then signed over to Harding Pool in exchange for the deed to this diner."

"So a cowboy you'd never met before changed your life?"

Flora nodded. "He took my failing ranch off my hands, gave me a chance to raise my baby while earning a living, and never told a single soul. And neither did I."

Meg's jaw dropped. "Wait a minute. Are you talking about—?"

Flora laughed and patted her hand. "I am. That brash

cowboy was your daddy. And that old ranch, that had become hardscrabble and neglected, thrived under his care. Just like this old diner has thrived under mine."

Meg shook her head in wonder. "He never said a word."

"That's just like your daddy. He never told anybody about all the nice things he did. But I hear things." Flora smiled. "I know my reputation for spreading news. It's true. Every bit of it. But I also know when to keep a secret. And your daddy knew that if he asked, I'd carry his secrets to the grave. And so I have. I'll continue to keep quiet about most of the things I know about him until I meet my Maker. But I just figured his children ought to know there was more to Porter Stanford than the face he showed this town. That man knew what heartbreak felt like. He knew what it meant to be alone, and desperate for comfort. He knew that his hair-trigger temper in his younger days contributed to his problems and got him in more trouble than he could shake a stick at. But he learned from his mistakes. Instead of wallowing in misery, he put on a good show, strutting like a peacock, courting the ladies, spending his money like a drunken cowboy after roundup, and pretending that nothing mattered except a good time. But underneath, he had a heart of gold. A heart that was broken too many times to count."

She put a plump hand beneath Cory's chin and lifted his face so that the shy boy was forced to meet her eyes. "And the things he was most proud of in his whole life were his two children. He felt that he'd failed the first, and that he'd been given a chance to make amends with the second. And that's the truth."

Meg and Cory were so startled, the two of them merely stared at her in stunned silence.

As she started to turn away Meg grabbed her hand. "Wait. Flora."

The woman turned.

Meg swallowed, wondering how to put into words all that she was feeling. Instead, all she could manage was "Thank you."

Flora's eyes softened. "You're welcome, honey. I hope you'll stick around long enough to get to know the town and the people your daddy loved."

"I..." Meg glanced sideways toward Cory. "I don't know what I'll be doing. I was planning on being gone by the end of the week. Now, I guess I'll just take it a day at a time."

"And that's the way it ought to be, honey. A day at a time." Flora turned. "Now I'd better get back to my grill. I've got a lot of hungry customers to take care of."

"Well?" Jake watched as Meg polished off her burger and took the last few sips of the shake. "Was it as good as you remembered?"

"Better." She sighed. "I haven't had a lunch like this in years."

"Yeah. Poor thing. Having to make do with spinach salad and sparkling water while you go over a million points of the law with your clients. I can imagine that those fifty-dollar lunches in the big city could be pretty boring."

Meg laughed. "If you're trying to goad me into an argument, I'm afraid you'll have to wait until I'm feeling lean and mean. Right now I'm feeling so mellow, I doubt there's anything you could say or do that would even tempt me to rise to the bait."

"Quick, Cory." Jake winked at the little boy. "If you've done anything really rotten lately, this is the time to confess, while your sister can't work up the energy to get mad at you."

The boy managed a grin before returning his attention to his milkshake.

Dora walked over to slide the bill across the counter to Jake. "How was Ma's roast beef sandwich?"

He put a finger to his lips. "Don't breathe a word of this to Phoebe, but it may have been the best I've ever tasted."

Dora was cackling as she turned to the pass-through and shouted, "Better watch out, Ma. Phoebe Hogan might come gunning for you."

"What did I do this time?" the old woman called.

"Won Jake's heart with your slow-cooked roast beef."

"It gets 'em every time," Flora said with a laugh. She peered at Meg as she added, "Cowboys are so easy to please. Good cookin', good lovin', and they're yours forever." As an afterthought she said, "No charge for the advice, counselor."

Meg chuckled. "Thanks. I'll keep it in mind. But I doubt I'll be around here long enough to add a cowboy to my conquests."

Flora looked from Meg to Jake. "Oh, I'd say it wouldn't take you much time at all for that cowboy next to you. He looks primed and ready."

She was still laughing at her own joke as Jake paid the bill and led the way toward the door.

As he held it open for Meg and Cory he turned and

winked at the old woman. "You're a sly one, Flora."

"I'll take that as a compliment, Jake."

"That's how I meant it. By the way, thanks for the history lesson. You've certainly altered my perception of Porter Stanford."

With a grin he strolled out and climbed into his truck, where Meg and Cory were already settled.

"I can drive you back to the church to pick up your car, or we can leave it there and you can ride home with me. Your call, Meg."

She thought a minute before saying, "I'll follow you back to your place in my car." She turned to Cory. "Want to stay with Jake, or ride back with me?"

The boy shrugged. "I'll ride with Jake."

So much for building a bond with her half brother, Meg thought. Aloud she merely said, "Okay. I guess we know who won that popularity contest."

All she could manage on the ride back to church was a weak smile.

CHAPTER FIFTEEN

Jake parked the truck at the back door of the ranch house. As he climbed out he called to Cory, "Want to check on Shadow?"

The boy nodded.

Jake turned to Meg, who'd parked behind them and was just climbing out of her car. "How about you?"

She shook her head. "I think I'll go upstairs."

"Okay."

She watched as Jake led the way to the barn, with Cory following.

As she stepped from the mudroom to the kitchen, she was relieved to find it empty. She wasn't in the mood for conversation. In fact, today's events had left her in a strange, thoughtful mood.

She'd begun the day with a mixture of sadness and anger, both directed toward her father. Sadness at his dying, and anger at him for letting her down. In her mind he'd failed her as a father and the fierce protector she'd thought him to be.

The things she'd learned from Flora only added to her pain. If he was the kind, considerate neighbor Flora had described, how could he have been so unconcerned about his own daughter? It didn't make any sense.

In her room she tossed the manila envelope on the desk without giving it another look. She wasn't ready to tackle her father's will yet. She would save it for another time.

She kicked off her high heels and stripped away the business suit and silk shirt, replacing them with boxer shorts and a clingy tank top. Barefoot, she opened the closet door and began methodically hanging her clothes.

Spying the unmarked cardboard box from her father's closet, she picked it up and carried it across the room. Ignoring the desktop, she set it down in front of the floor-to-ceiling windows and their view of the sun setting over the distant Tetons.

She turned on all the lights in the room before sitting cross-legged in front of the box. She pried off the top and peered inside.

It was filled to the brim with envelopes.

Picking up the first, she was surprised to note that it was addressed to her in her father's scrawl.

How was that possible? She'd never seen it before. The envelope was still sealed. She knew she'd never received a letter from her father. And then she saw, in her mother's distinct script, the words *Return to sender*.

Meg read the date it had been mailed. 2005.

She began sifting through the rest, noting the dates. The deeper she dug into the pile, the earlier the dates, until she found the oldest ones dated the same year that she'd left Wyoming for Washington, D.C.

She tore open the oldest envelope and hungrily began to read the letter inside, addressed to *My Dear Darling Little Meggy*:

> *Now that you're no longer here, all the light has gone out of my world. I can't stand to do any of the things we used to do together. They just aren't fun anymore. I'll be counting the hours until you come back to visit...*

Meg's eyes filled and the words became a blur. The more she read, the more her eyes swam until she could no longer blink away the tears.

She hurried to the bathroom to fetch a box of tissues. Then, while she alternately wiped her eyes and tore open letter after letter, she sat on the floor and read a father's heart-wrenching outpourings of love for the daughter he'd been denied.

Cory wrapped his arms around Shadow's neck and buried his face in the colt's soft, silky mane while Jake examined the wound.

The boy's words were muffled. "You think he's healing?"

"Yep. Healing nicely. The antibiotic is doing the job."

"That's good." Cory looked over as Jake got to his feet. "Think I could spend the night out here again?"

"I don't see why not. As long as you keep your cell phone handy." Jake nodded toward the sleeping bag hanging over the side of the stall. "Need any help with that?"

"Naw. I can handle it."

"Okay then." Jake stepped from the stall and moved to the spot where a very pregnant golden Lab lay watching him.

He bent down and did a quick examination before running his hand over her head. "Those pups will be here soon, Honey. Very soon now."

The Lab licked his hand, causing him to smile. "I know. The calm before the storm. Hang tough, Honey."

At the door of the barn he turned to see Cory spreading his sleeping bag in Shadow's stall. "'Night, Cory."

"Yeah. 'Night."

Outside, Jake latched the barn door. Before making his way to the house he plucked his cell phone from his pocket and called the bunkhouse to ask one of the wranglers, who would be making rounds of the outbuildings after dark, to keep an eye on Cory in the barn.

Satisfied that the boy would be safe, he turned toward the house. Seeing most of the windows dark in the upper rooms, he knew that the family had already retired for the night.

Time for him to do the same. It had been a strange day. But an enlightening one.

Like the rest of the folks in Paintbrush, he and his family had always thought of Porter Stanford as nothing more than a brash, unprincipled hothead. Flora's revelations had caught him by complete surprise. But that was nothing compared with Meg's reaction.

He'd seen the disbelief in her eyes, and the gradual pleasure as Flora had told them of Porter's kindness to strangers. Jake sincerely hoped it helped ease some of the pain he'd seen in her eyes after leaving the cemetery, and later, the anger after leaving Kirby Bolton's office. It could certainly go a long way toward softening her attitude about her father.

If he'd found the day strange, how much more emotional had it been for Meg and Cory? Though the boy and the woman had found ways of keeping their emotions under tight control, a day like this would be a staggering overload of highs and lows for anyone.

He was pretty certain the boy would sleep for hours after the emotional day he'd put in.

As Jake walked silently along the upper hallway he was surprised to see the light filtering out from beneath Meg's door, signaling that she was still awake. He was about to walk on when he heard a sound that had him stopping in his tracks.

He backed up and listened outside her door.

Sobs. Unmistakable, hard, gut-wrenching sobs were coming from within Meg's bedroom.

Though her grief was none of his business, he couldn't simply walk away. Not when she was so alone and in obvious pain.

"Hey now." Jake pushed open the door and stepped into the room.

Seeing Meg on the floor, surrounded by so much paper, stunned him into silence. This wasn't at all what he'd expected to see. He'd imagined her lying facedown on her bed, or maybe pounding a fist on the wall.

When he found his voice, he waved a hand. "What's all this?"

"Letters." The word was little more than a strangled whisper.

"Whose letters?"

"Mine." She started weeping again. "From..." Her lips quivered. "...my father."

"I thought you never heard from him."

"I didn't." She wadded a tissue in her hand and pressed it to her eyes. "Thanks to my mother."

"I don't understand."

"Look." She held up a fistful of envelopes.

Jake studied the handwriting, and then the very neat script directing them to be returned. He then stared pointedly at the box. "How long did this go on?"

"Apparently all the years I've been away. The early letters told me how much..." She had to stop and swallow before she could say, "...how much he loved and missed me." Tears streamed from her eyes to run in rivers down her cheeks. "Oh, Jake. He never abandoned me. And he never gave up the hope that I'd come back. And I...broke his heart."

"Shhh." He dropped to his knees beside her and gathered her into his arms.

She crumpled against him, sobbing openly against his chest, until his shirt was soaked with her tears.

"How could she...?" The words were muffled against his chest. "How could a mother be so cruel?"

He pressed his lips to the top of her head. "You said she was angry. Hell hath no fury."

"But this was wrong. So wrong."

"Yes, it was. But now, finally, you know."

"When it's too late." She pushed away from him, her eyes blazing. "He's gone, Jake. My father's gone, and I can't ever get those years back. I can never get that love back."

As the finality of it struck her, the anger rose up, threatening to choke her. "How I hate her for what she did.

Because of her, I never really got to know my own father."

"Hey now." Jake reached out a hand to her but she drew back, her eyes flaring with white-hot fury.

He kept his tone low and even. "Maybe she thought you were too young and she would spare you from being a pawn in an ugly tug-of-war."

"Too young? What right did she have to make my decisions for me? Did she think a kid had no rights? I'll never forgive her for this, Jake. Never."

She got to her feet and began to pace, the anger that was seething inside her propelling her to move. "I had the right to know my own father. To spend time with him. To laugh with him. To fight with him if I wanted to. To make my own decision about where I wanted to live. And because of her selfishness, I was denied a life that she knew I wanted more than anything. A life here in Wyoming with my father. And now..." She paused, looked out at the darkened outline of the mountains. "...now he's gone and I can never get him back. I can never get back that life I wanted."

Her own words had her eyes filling again. The tears ran down her cheeks, and this time she didn't bother to wipe them away.

Jake stood by feeling helpless. It was obvious that she was exhausted. And so grief-stricken there was nothing he could possibly say that would give her comfort.

When her tears turned to hard, choking sobs, she flung herself into his arms. "Oh, Jake."

He gathered her close and held her until the tears had run their course, then handed her his handkerchief.

After wiping her eyes she handed it back to him. Then, without a word, she wrapped her arms around his waist and touched her cheek to his. "Thank you."

"For what?"

"Just..." She shrugged. "For listening. For being here. Today has been such an overload. The man I wanted to hate has turned into somebody I don't even know. He sounds...broken. The woman I trusted has turned into someone who betrayed me. I'm so—" she gave another shrug of trembling shoulders "—lost. I can't believe any of this. Today, I've learned so much about my father. All the truths as I've known them for most of my life have been turned on their heads. All of a sudden, I don't know what or who to believe anymore."

He took a step back and gently touched her face. "Give yourself some time, Meg. Don't rush to judge either of your parents."

When she opened her mouth to protest he pressed a finger to her lips. "Look, you said yourself you're on overload. You've buried your father, and now in a sense you've resurrected him."

He saw her eyes go wide with understanding. "I *have* resurrected him, haven't I? I've learned so many new things about him today, thanks to Flora, and now, to all these letters. Thank heaven he saved them, or I'd have never known."

"Exactly. So take things a day at a time until you've given yourself the chance to sort it all out."

She dragged in a deep breath and lifted shining eyes to his. "When did you get so smart, Dr. Conway?"

He gave her one of those rogue smiles. "Aw, shucks, ma'am. Part of my job as a local vet is to dispense wisdom along with all those miracle drugs."

She went very still. "What about aid and comfort?"

He was aware of the subtle change in her and fought to keep things light. "It comes with the territory."

"That's good to know." She caressed his cheek. "I'm in need of your aid and comfort right now, Jake."

There was no mistaking her meaning. She'd made herself perfectly clear. If her words weren't enough, the look in her eyes, all soft and inviting, spoke volumes.

He absorbed the quick sexual jolt and kept his eyes steady on hers. "I'm all about aid and comfort, ma'am. But right now, you might want to think about getting some sleep. After the day you put in, you have to be exhausted."

"Just the opposite." Her hand curved around the back of his head, drawing him fractionally closer. "I don't think I've ever felt more alert, more alive. Right now, right this minute, I'm feeling like...like I'm electrically charged."

"Yeah." His heart jolted. "I know that feeling."

He lowered his head at the same moment that she lifted hers. Their mouths met in a kiss so hot, so hungry, it caught them both by surprise.

Sparks flew between them, causing even the air in the room to feel superheated.

His hands were in her hair as he backed her against the wall and kissed her long and slow and deep.

With their bodies pressed firmly, their mouths hungry and demanding, the kiss spun on and on. Their sighs turned into little moans of pleasure. Their breathing became labored. Their greedy hands and mouths moved on one another, avid, eager. Taking. Giving.

Dazed, and almost blind with need, their bodies straining and grinding in open invitation, they edged closer to the bed, eager to feed the hunger that was driving them, just as Meg's door was unceremoniously thrown open and a voice jittery with nerves called, "Jake."

Two heads came up sharply. Two figures, still wrapped around one another, froze at the sight of Cory standing in the doorway, so out of breath he could barely get the words out over his heaving chest.

"Jake. Hurry. Something's wrong with Honey."

"Wrong?" Jake continued holding onto Meg's shoulders, afraid to let go for fear of stumbling like a drunk.

"She's making weird noises and panting really hard. I think maybe she's dying. You've got to come, Jake."

Jake sucked in a long, deep breath, struggling to clear his befuddled mind. Very carefully he lowered his arms to his sides and took a step away from Meg, who was staring at Cory as though he were completely addled.

Despite his frustration at this turn of events, Jake managed a weak smile as the light dawned.

"It's okay, Cory. Honey's not dying. Looks like her time has finally come. She's about to have her puppies." He closed a hand over Meg's shoulder and squeezed, feeling all the tension that was still spiraling through her. "You'll never know how sorry I am, but it looks like I'm needed in the barn."

With a last, lingering look at her pouting lips, he turned and followed the boy from the room, closing the door softly behind him.

CHAPTER SIXTEEN

I went to your room first," Cory said with a hint of accusation. "When I didn't find you there, I got really scared. I thought maybe you were off to someone's ranch because of an emergency. You know. To doctor somebody else's animals. Then I heard your voice in Meg's room."

How much had the kid seen? And how much did he understand? Jake struggled to remember how much he'd known when he was seven. Not a whole lot, especially when it came to men and women.

"Yeah. Sorry." And he meant it. But not the way it sounded. Even now, racing toward the barn, Jake's heart was still back there with Meg. He was damned sorry about the timing of this emergency.

She'd been amazing.

They'd come so close. A step away from paradise.

He shook off his frustration. No sense mourning his

loss now. Reality had reared its head, and he had no choice but to deal with it.

"I think you're wrong about Honey." Cory's legs were pumping as he sprinted toward the barn, with Jake lengthening his strides to keep up. "She was panting really, really hard. Like she was getting ready to climb out of her pen and take off running as far as she could. I latched the door so she couldn't get loose."

"That was smart. But trust me." Jake reached around the boy to pull open the barn door and throw on a series of overhead lights. "The sounds you heard are all normal when a mother is about to give birth."

As they raced toward the dog's pen they were greeted by a chorus of faint squeaks and tiny yips.

Honey lay contentedly licking six small bundles of pale fluff that were stumbling blindly around her.

At the sight of them, Cory stopped dead in his tracks.

Beside him, Jake bent down to run his hand along the new mother's head and across her back. "Well, just look at what you've done. All by yourself, without a bit of help."

At the sound of his voice Honey looked up at him before returning her attention to her babies.

Meg charged headlong into the barn, still buttoning the plaid shirt over her tank top; she hadn't bothered to tuck it into the denims she'd pulled on over her boxers.

Seeing Cory and Jake kneeling on either side of the dog's pen, she came to a halt and dropped to her knees beside Cory. Then all she could do was stare in delight and absolute amazement at the sight of Honey and her pups. "Oh, look at them," she cooed.

Caught up in the moment, she hugged Cory fiercely,

saying against his cheek, "Oh, aren't they just the sweet-
est things?"

The boy turned startled eyes to her. At once she lowered her arm, allowing him to draw away.

"How about their proud mama?" Jake was watching
Meg and Cory while petting Honey's head. "Six babies,
all born in record time, and all of them perfect."

As Honey continued licking her newborns, they were
finding their way to her side, where they hungrily began
feasting.

One tiny pup seemed stymied by a small dip in the
blanket beneath them. Each time he tried to climb over
the gap, he flopped onto his back. After wriggling around
and around, he righted himself and struggled to climb
over it again, only to flip backward yet again.

His antics had the three of them laughing until Jake
took pity on the poor little thing, lifting him up and placing him beside his mother.

Honey licked the puppy before closing her eyes and
stretching out, allowing all six puppies to nurse.

Jake pulled out his cell phone and snapped several
pictures. With a glance at Meg and Cory he explained,
"I think Randy deserves a chance to see what he's
missing."

"When will he be home?" Cory asked.

"Not for another week. By then, these babies will be
running their poor mama ragged," Jake said with a laugh.

A minute later he heard the beep signaling a text, and
read aloud the message from Randy Morton: " 'Good for
Honey. What a trooper. Wish I could be there. Thanks for
standing in for me.' "

Jake winked at Cory. "Do you realize that if you hadn't

been here with Shadow, we would have completely missed Honey's big event until morning?"

The boy's eyes were shining. "Then I'm glad I was here. I mean, I didn't do anything, but it's nice to be able to share this with her."

"I can tell that Honey liked having you here, too. As the days go by, she'll welcome an occasional distraction so she can catch her breath. Those six are going to be a handful for their sweet mother. So, whenever you want to hold them, I doubt she'll complain."

"You mean it? I can hold them and Honey won't mind?"

"Sure. Just give them some time to get their bearings, and to give their proud mama time to lavish a lot of love on them."

Jake motioned toward the dog, whose eyes were now open, keeping watch on her babies as they began to curl up around her, their yipping falling silent as, replete, content, exhausted from their big event, they began to nod off.

He again touched a hand to the dog's head. "I knew you would be a great mama, Honey."

She licked his hand before turning her head to look at Cory.

The boy caught his breath. "Do you see how she's looking at me?"

Jake nodded. "I think that means she likes you and she's glad you're here."

"Really?" Cory reached out a tentative hand and brushed it over the golden Lab's head. As she had with Jake, she licked the boy's hand, bringing a wide smile to his lips.

It was, Jake realized, the first time he'd ever seen the boy completely, utterly happy, unhampered by all the drama that had been apparent in his life these last few days.

"If you two want to get some sleep, I'll stay here and take care of a few things."

Cory shook his head. "I'm not tired. I'd like to help."

Meg nodded. "Me, too."

"Okay. Time to clean up here and give Honey and her babies some fresh bedding." Jake got to his feet and crossed the barn. He wheeled a cart over and removed the soiled hay, replacing it with fresh, clean hay. Then, from a row of shelves he chose several clean, folded blankets.

He motioned toward the pen. "If you two will take hold of the edge of that blanket, and pull it toward you, I'll slip these underneath."

With Meg and Cory tugging the damp blanket aside, Jake managed to replace it with a several fresh ones, barely disturbing Honey and her puppies. He bundled the soiled blanket into a plastic bag before laying out a supply of fresh food and water for Honey.

"Very efficient, Dr. Conway." Meg gave a nod of approval at the spotless pen.

"It just takes a little planning."

"I'm betting you've done this a time or two."

He chuckled. "More like a dozen times or two."

As the puppies snuggled close to their mother, Cory leaned his arms on the side of the pen, staring transfixed at them.

Jake touched a hand to his shoulder. "You may as well get some sleep now. They'll probably rest for a few hours before they start pestering Honey again."

Cory shook his head. "Is it okay if I just stay here and watch them? I won't bother them at all. But I'm not tired and I like looking at them."

Jake shot him a smile. "They won't be bothered by having some company. You take as long as you want."

He turned to Meg. "You ready to go up to bed?"

She couldn't seem to tear her gaze from the serene mama and her pups. "Not just yet. If you don't mind, I think I'll stay here awhile with Cory."

Jake saw the look of surprise on the boy's face, before the look turned to one of pleasure as Cory turned to stare at Meg.

The two shared shy smiles before returning their attention to Honey.

Watching them, Jake couldn't help smiling himself. "Okay, then. Guess I'll head up to bed alone."

He shot a final look at Meg and Cory, wearing identical looks of pleasure and satisfaction as they knelt side by side watching every tiny movement, no matter how insignificant, of Honey and her puppies.

Meg turned to Cory to whisper, "Have you thought of any names?"

Cory shrugged. "Not really. Except for that little one there."

"The smallest one?"

"Yeah." Cory laughed as the runt of the litter began nudging his litter mate aside to snuggle closer to its mother. "He's Trouble. At least that's what I'm calling him in my mind."

Meg was chuckling. "Oh, Cory, that's perfect."

As Jake made his way from the barn to the darkened house, he felt a flicker of hope. Could it be that a dog and her puppies might possibly be the first crack in that thick, impenetrable wall between Meg and Cory?

If so, he thought, the miracle of birth wouldn't be the only miracle that happened this night. An even bigger one might be the discovery that a brother and sister had finally found some common ground on which to build a future.

Meg and Cory had been watching Honey and her puppies for more than an hour.

"This is better than TV," the boy said softly.

"Yeah. I'm so glad we're here." Meg touched a finger to one of the puppies, enjoying the downy softness.

"I'm glad Jake was here." The boy yawned. "I was really scared."

"I would've been scared, too."

"You would?"

Meg nodded. "I've never seen puppies being born. I would have felt completely helpless."

"Jake knew just what to do."

"You like Jake, don't you?"

Cory shrugged. "He's really smart. About animals and stuff."

"Yeah." Meg leaned back, keeping one eye on Honey and her puppies while she finished buttoning her shirt. She'd dressed so quickly, she couldn't even recall putting on her sneakers.

Cory had gone very still, and Meg could see that he was fighting to stay awake. Without a word she entered Shadow's stall and carried the sleeping bag over to Honey's pen.

When she had it laid out, she nudged Cory to lie on

it. When he didn't protest, she knew she'd done the right thing.

Minutes later she zipped it, and he curled on his side, sound asleep.

She thought about going up to her room, but decided that this was the perfect time and place for some heavy-duty thinking.

She'd learned so much about a father she'd thought she already knew. But in truth, she hadn't known Porter Stanford at all. The man his lawyer had described, and the man that Flora had praised to the heavens, was a complete stranger. The loving, emotion-filled letters he'd written to his long-absent daughter were heart-breakingly honest.

She'd spent a lifetime blaming him for every pain, every childhood misery, as though he'd been some evil sorcerer.

Now, she thought, it was time for some soul-searching. And time for some painful decisions.

She'd come here four short days ago thinking she could dispose of the ranch, land, and livestock in a week, and return to the life she'd made for herself in D.C. Now, having reconnected with her former life, she needed to re-think her original timetable.

What had Jake said that first night? It was a self-imposed deadline. There was no good reason why she couldn't change it.

Of course, that would require some risk. She would have to request a leave of absence from the law firm. It wasn't something she was looking forward to doing. She'd been given some high-profile cases, and the firm wouldn't be happy about passing all that work off to the partners—to say nothing of the clients, who expected their money's worth in defense.

Still, she needed to take whatever time necessary in order to make the best decision possible, not only for her own future, but also for Cory's.

Cory. She glanced at the boy asleep alongside Honey's pen. He was a strange little kid. Much more comfortable, it would seem, in the company of animals than people. Still, she had to try to get through to him. She needed to know what it was he wanted going forward.

She remembered all the disturbing emotions of being yanked unceremoniously from the only life she'd known, to find her way among strangers in a strange new setting. Adults had made decisions that affected the quality of her life. It wasn't something she wanted to put Cory through, if it could be avoided. And knowing that Judge Kirby Bolton had volunteered to be the boy's guardian lifted some of the burden from her shoulders. Still, it would be nice to hear from Cory himself just what he wanted.

But what did *she* want? She might have come here thinking that all she wanted was to dispose of the ranch and return to the life she'd made for herself. Now, everything had changed. And all because of the letters her father had written, letters that confirmed what the people who knew him best had told her.

Knowledge is power. It had been her father's favorite saying when she'd been a little girl. Now, those words had taken on a new meaning.

While the boy and dogs slept, Meg paced the length of the barn and back, mulling the decisions she was facing.

One of the decisions she'd been avoiding was what to do with her father's ranch.

Her ranch.

She paused as the thought struck with all the forced of a thunderbolt. For the longest time she'd thought of the ranch as her father's. Since relocating to a new place and new life, she'd divorced herself from the land she'd always loved. But now, it was hers. And she was, by heaven, going to get to know it intimately before making any decisions about its future.

She continued pacing. With each step she felt her resolve firming, and her spine stiffening. She'd been forced, early in life, to stand up for herself. Since coming back to Wyoming she'd turned into some weak, weepy female she didn't recognize, leaning on neighbors, and especially Jake, for comfort and strength. It was time to morph back into the Meg Stanford she'd always been. No stranger was going to scare her off her land. And no law firm was going to guilt her into returning to the city unless she was ready to make that decision for herself.

She paused beside Honey's pen and watched the dog, her puppies around her.

Some things, she thought, were just natural and right. Birth. Death. And a deep and abiding love for the land.

She took her cell phone from her pocket and shot off an e-mail to her law firm.

Feeling at peace with her decision, Meg dropped to her knees and listened to the soft sounds of the night. Cattle lowed. A lone coyote howled his mournful cry. And beside her, Cory snored softly.

As was her custom, Ela awoke at dawn and made her trek to the chicken coop at the rear of the barn to collect fresh eggs. With her basket full, she was returning to the house when she heard voices coming from inside the barn.

Curious, she opened the door, surprised to see all the lights on inside.

Cory and Meg looked up as the old woman approached.

"Look, Ela. Look what Honey's got." Cory was on his feet, as eager as a proud papa showing off Honey's puppies. "There are six of them."

"I see." Ela set aside her basket and knelt down for a better look. "Did you see them being born?"

"Almost. I heard her panting and ran to get Jake. By the time we got here, they were all born, and she was licking them clean."

Ela glanced over the boy's head to smile at Meg. "And you woke your sister to share the good news with her."

"I didn't mean to, but Jake wasn't in his room, and when I heard him in Meg's room I just..." His voice trailed off as he was suddenly reminded of the scene he'd witnessed when he'd burst into Meg's room. Jake and Meg were standing awfully close together, and he thought maybe they'd been kissing.

"Anyway"—he shoved aside the vision and forced himself to concentrate on his good news—"when Jake figured it was safe to leave Honey with her babies, I asked if I could stay, and Meg decided to stay with me. So here we are."

If Ela saw the discomfort in Meg's eyes by what the boy had just revealed, she didn't let on. She stood and picked up her basket of eggs. "You have an hour or more before breakfast will be ready. I am sure, as I tell the others your good news, that you will have many visitors admiring Honey's babies."

Before walking away she paused to stare at the two of them. "My people believe that to witness new life on the very day that marked the end of a life is a very rare and special gift indeed, for it is the way of things. Each life must have a beginning and an end. It is a good sign that the two of you were here to share in this very special time together."

When she was gone, Cory and Meg fell silent, lost in their own private thoughts. It was obvious that her words had touched a chord in each of them.

It didn't take long for the news of Honey's litter to spread to the rest of the family. All of them came streaming out of the house and into the barn for their first glimpse of Honey and her babies.

"Will you look at that?" Cole said.

Cole and Big Jim stood beside Honey's pen. Both men were smiling broadly.

"We had to come as soon as Ela told us the news." Big Jim bent to pet Honey's head, while Cole ran a finger over the downy back of one of the pups.

"Oh, how precious." Cheyenne let go of Quinn's hand and dropped to her knees beside the pen, while Sierra, standing with Josh, lifted her ever-present camera to record the scene.

Phoebe hurried out with a dish of cooked rice and ground beef. "For energy," she explained as she offered it to Honey, who began wolfing it down. "Our new mama will need all the strength she can get, feeding six hungry babies."

The family gathered around, cooing over the puppies and praising Honey, and all the while asking questions of

Cory, who was only too happy to relate the story, time and again, to each of them.

Cole looked around. "Where's Jake? Shouldn't our vet be here?"

"He was here in the night. When he was sure they were all right, he went up to bed."

"Why didn't you go too, son?" Big Jim asked.

Cory shrugged. "I wanted to stay here and just look at them"

"I can see why." Cole glanced at Meg, kneeling beside Cory. "Have you been out here all night, too?"

She nodded. "After seeing these babies, I was too keyed up to think about sleep."

"I don't blame you." Sierra pointed to two of the puppies tumbling over a third, and the three of them stuck on their backs, legs all tangled, doing their best to get untangled and back on their feet.

While everyone roared with laughter, she snapped picture after picture.

"Look at this one." Cheyenne pointed out the smallest, trying to nudge his way between two bigger puppies.

"That's Trouble," Cory said.

Quinn arched a brow. "Is that his name or his reputation?"

"Both," Cory said with an air of importance. "He spent the whole night fighting the others for a spot near Honey. Every time he wakes up, he causes trouble."

Big Jim winked at the boy. "I think since you've been here from the beginning, you have a right to name him, son. And now, I'd better get to my chores, or the rest of you will be eating breakfast without me."

"Same here," Josh said, as he turned away and picked up a pitchfork.

One by one the others drifted away to see to their chores, leaving Cory and Meg alone.

She dropped a hand on Cory's shoulder. "Maybe you and I ought to lend a hand with those chores. After all, we don't want to be unwelcome guests, do we?"

With a laugh Cory followed Meg to help himself to a pitchfork from one of the hooks along the wall of the barn.

For the next hour they mucked stalls and listened to the teasing conversations of Quinn and Josh and their wives.

When the chores were complete, and the others were heading toward the house, Meg turned to Cory. "I think we'd better go inside and grab a shower."

Cory was reluctant to leave the pups for even a little while. "Do I have to?"

Meg gave a negligent shrug of her shoulders. "I'll leave it up to you. But I'd hate to have you miss out on Phoebe's really great breakfast."

As she turned away, Cory got to his feet and started after her.

At her look of surprise he shot her a grin. "I guess I don't mind taking a little time to eat."

She ruffled his shaggy hair. "Smart boy. Especially since Honey and those babies aren't going anywhere, and you can be back here within the hour."

CHAPTER SEVENTEEN

By the time everyone had gathered for breakfast, Jake was just stepping into the mudroom after a visit to the barn. He washed at the big sink before taking his place at the table.

"Did you see Honey?" Cory asked.

Jake nodded. "Sure thing. She's looking well rested. I think, after we eat, I'll start examining her babies and recording their vitals for Randy. Would you like to be my assistant?"

Cory's eyes went wide and his mouth opened and closed several times before he was able to make a sound. "You mean it?"

"Of course. I figure if you're going to lend a hand, you may as well get used to handling the puppies."

The boy ducked his head, but not before the others saw the smile of pure pleasure alight in his eyes.

Jake glanced past Cory to Meg. "You want to lend a hand, too?"

"I'm happy to." She chose her words carefully. "Afterward, I'll be leaving. I've decided that it's time I return to my own place."

Everyone turned to look at her.

Big Jim set aside his coffee. "What about the intruder? Have you had some news from Chief Fletcher?"

"No news. I figure the intruder has had more than enough time to break in and help himself to whatever he can find. But his time's up. I've made up my mind. I'm going home."

Cole's eyes narrowed. "I suppose you're in a hurry to meet with the auction houses?"

"Not yet. First I'm planning on riding up to the hills to meet with Yancy Jessup and see how my herds are doing."

Jake sat back, sipping his coffee and wondering if the rest of his family had caught the changes yet. It had suddenly become Meg's ranch. Meg's herd.

Interesting, he thought. As was the change in her tone. There was a thread of steel that hadn't been there yesterday.

"If you don't mind waiting—" he nodded toward the barn "—as soon as we're through examining Honey's pups, I'll go along. That is, if you'd like some company riding to the high country."

"Thanks, Jake. I appreciate that." She turned to the others. "I'm so grateful for your hospitality. I don't know what Cory and I would have done without all of you and this wonderful safety net."

Big Jim closed a hand over hers. "You just remember

that we're here for you. Whatever you need, don't be afraid to ask."

"Thank you, Big Jim. That means the world to me."

As the family began to shove away from the table, each of them took a moment to wish her well before heading out to tackle their daily chores.

Meg followed Jake and Cory to the barn.

"Three males and three females." Jake handed Cory the last of the puppies.

The boy set the squirming, wriggling ball of fluff down in the pen, while Jake finished recording the weight, length, and gender of each pup on his computer.

As always, Honey took the time to lick this last puppy as it stumbled to her side to nurse.

Meg stood beside Jake, watching as his fingers flew over the keys. "So many details."

Jake looked over. "Yeah. But at least now I only have to jot it down once, and my computer does the rest. Randy will get an e-mail with all the information before he even gets home."

"Veterinary medicine in the twenty-first century," Meg said with a shake of her head.

"You bet. And if I run up against a problem I've never seen before, I can do my research on the Internet and probably find a dozen similar cases on which to base a diagnosis." Jake closed the lid on his computer before turning away. "Time to head out of here. Why don't you two pack up, while I get my truck out of the other barn?"

As Meg started away, Cory held back.

Seeing it, Jake paused. "Something wrong?"

The boy shrugged. "Do I have to go?"

Hearing him, Meg stopped with her hand on the barn door. "I thought you'd be happy to be going home."

He stared hard at the toe of his worn boot. "Shadow's here. And Honey. They need me."

Meg bit her lip. "Yeah. I guess they do."

His head came up sharply. "But if you need me more than they do, I can go with you."

She retraced her steps and paused beside him. Touching a hand to his shoulder she said softly, "I'd love for you to be there with me, Cory. Comfortably settled into your own room, in your own bed. But I understand that Shadow and Honey are important to you. If Jake doesn't object, maybe you could stay here a day or so until Shadow is ready to come back. And maybe, by then, Honey will be going home, too."

He brightened. "You don't mind?"

"Of course not." She brushed the shaggy hair from his face and was pleased that he didn't pull away. "I guess I'll see you in a couple of days."

"Yeah. See you."

Meg walked from the barn, aware that both Cory and Jake were watching. Squaring her shoulders, she let herself into the house and climbed the stairs to her room to fetch her belongings. While she packed, she thought about Cory. She wished she knew how to reach him. Though she understood his attachment to Shadow and Honey, she sensed that part of his reluctance to go home was his shaky relationship with her.

It saddened her that he felt more comfortable here with strangers than at home with her. But she was at a loss as to how to turn the situation around. For now she would try to be patient and hope that the situation would improve with time.

Half an hour later Meg walked downstairs to find Phoebe and Ela waiting. She hugged each of them in turn. "I can't thank you enough for all your hospitality."

Phoebe spoke for both of them. "We loved having you. We hope you'll come back soon."

"I just hope I can survive one night alone," Meg said with a laugh. "If you hear someone pounding on the door in the middle of the night, you'll know that I lost my nerve."

Phoebe looked around. "Where's Cory?"

"He asked if he could stay, since his two BFFs at the moment, Shadow and Honey, are still here. I hope you don't mind—I told him I'd be fine without him."

"Of course he's welcome to stay. And you will be fine." Ela's dark, piercing eyes bore into hers. "You are a strong woman. As for the boy, we will see that he is kept safe."

"I know you will. Thank you."

Ela and Phoebe picked up several linen-wrapped packages from the counter. "Corn bread," Ela explained.

"And chicken, and green beans from the garden," Phoebe added. "If you're riding to the high country, you won't have time to fix yourself something to eat."

"We made enough for two," Ela said. Though she remained serious, there was a twinkle of humor in her eyes. "But since the boy is staying here, you may have to persuade Jake to eat the boy's share."

The two women shared a knowing look before Phoebe held the door and said, "We'll carry these out to your car."

Jake was waiting beside one of the ranch trucks, to

which he'd hitched a horse trailer bearing two horses. "I'll follow you back, Meg, and we can ride up to the hills together."

He took the parcels from Ela and Phoebe and loaded them on the passenger seat of Meg's car while she settled herself behind the wheel.

Cory walked from the barn leading Shadow.

Jake cupped his hands to his mouth. "Be sure to walk him slowly around the corral at least three times. I want you to watch for any sign of limping."

"I will." The boy waved to Meg.

She waved back.

As Jake started toward his truck she called to him. "That was clever of Cory."

He looked over. "What was?"

"Bringing Shadow out as I was leaving. It gave him an excuse to not get close enough to be hugged."

Jake threw back his head and laughed. "I hadn't thought of that, but yeah, I guess he's thinking that he managed to dodge a bullet." He shot her a sideways glance. "Of course, when he gets a little older, he'll be just as sneaky about trying to get all the hugs he can from a pretty woman."

Meg was smiling as she started the ignition and eased the rental car along the curving driveway, feeling the breeze on her face, enjoying the view of the lovely countryside. And most of all, enjoying the view of the cowboy driving his truck behind her, his arm stretched out along the open window, his dark hair ruffled by the wind.

He'd called her a pretty woman. Not that she'd been fishing for compliments, but it made her extraordinarily happy to know that Jake Conway thought she was pretty.

As she followed the lane to her house, Meg took the time to really see it.

After spending time at the Conway ranch, she realized that her ranch looked sad and neglected by comparison. The yard was nothing more than a weed patch. The garden needed plowing. The porch steps were sagging. The house and barns hadn't seen a coat of paint in years.

Cosmetic, she told herself. It was nothing that couldn't be fixed with enough love and attention.

And didn't she wish she could say the same about herself?

She brushed aside the gloomy thoughts that began gathering in her mind as she came to a stop and stepped out of the car. No matter how sad the ranch looked or how many things were in disrepair, she needed to cling to the decisions she'd reached during the small hours of the morning.

She wouldn't commit to staying here. But she would definitely take as much time as necessary to make an informed decision.

Jake climbed down from his truck and hefted her suitcase and the food parcels from her car.

Meg hurried up the steps and tested the door, pleased to find it still locked. She quickly unlocked it and held it open, allowing Jake to precede her into the kitchen, where he deposited her things.

"Thanks, Jake."

He gave her a smile. "Want me to check the rooms while you wait here?"

She shook her head. "That's not necessary. Since the door hadn't been forced, I'm feeling confident that our intruder hasn't been around."

"Okay." He gave her a long look. "You may want to bring along a jacket. The temperature in the high country will be a lot cooler than here."

"I have something up in my room."

"While you find it, I'll saddle the horses."

"Thanks."

He surprised her by leaning close and brushing a quick kiss over her cheek.

She looked up at him and found him grinning from ear to ear.

"Just a reminder that I'm hoping for a rain check on what we started last night."

She couldn't help laughing. "Before we were so rudely interrupted."

"Yeah. Honey's timing was really off."

"Maybe it was fate."

He shot her a look. "What's that supposed to mean?"

She shrugged. "We almost crossed a line."

He gave her his most endearing smile. "A line I hope we most certainly cross very soon."

"Oh, you." She gave him a shove toward the door. "Go. Saddle those horses while I go find my jacket."

"I'd be willing to forego my work if you'd do the same."

She held the door open. "Not on your life, cowboy."

He brushed past her and paused to whisper, "That wasn't my final offer. I'll check again later to see if you've changed your mind."

He strolled out the door and down the steps.

Watching him through the window, Meg took in a deep breath. There was just something about Jake Conway that turned her brain to mush and undermined all her firm resolutions. But now that she'd had time to think, she'd come to one more conclusion. Last night, with her emotions on overload, she'd wanted, more than anything, to lose herself in the passion Jake was offering. And what a passion. Even now, just thinking about the way he made her feel, she absorbed a quick rush of heat all the way to her toes.

Today was a new day. Her mind was clear. She had rediscovered her iron will. She was a woman on a mission.

As she raced up the stairs and found a denim jacket in the closet, she played in her mind a litany that had carried her through a painful childhood and a challenging path to her chosen career. *I am strong, smart, and capable.*

She would take the time she needed to determine just what she had here before making any decisions about the future.

She checked her cell phone and found half a dozen e-mails from the law firm, all reminding her of her duty to their clients. The last one, from the firm's senior partner, demanded her immediate response. She took a deep breath and sent an affirmation that though she understood his concern and the needs of the firm, her own needs and those of her family had to come first.

Promising a more detailed message later, she tucked the phone away and dashed down the stairs, picturing in her mind the flurry of staff meetings and the exchange of phone calls and e-mails as the firm pondered the extended absence of one of its lead trial lawyers.

* * *

"Oh, Jake." As their horses crested a hill, Meg looked around with a look of absolute wonder. "My dad and I used to ride up here when the herds were summering in the high country. One night he let me sleep up here, under the stars. I felt so grown up and special."

Jake chuckled. "I did the same thing. I guess I was six or seven the first time Pa let me come with him and my brothers. I stayed up half the night listening to the old wranglers talking about what it was like in Big Jim's day, with nothing but a campfire and a horse-drawn chuck wagon."

He pointed to the sea of black in the distance. "There's your herd."

Meg caught her breath at the size. "How many do you think I have?"

He shrugged. "A couple thousand, I'd guess."

"Thousand?" She blinked. "When I left, there were a few hundred."

"How long have you been gone?"

She laughed. "Too long, apparently." She nudged her horse into a trot. "Come on. I want a closer look."

"How do, ma'am." The lanky cowboy urged his horse closer and touched the brim of his hat before looking beyond Meg to Jake. "You folks looking for Yancy?"

"Yes. Is he here?"

"Over that hill, ma'am."

"Thank you." Meg followed the wrangler's direction and reined in her mount when she came up over a ridge to find the old foreman on foot, checking a stray.

Keeping hold of his horse's reins, he looked up.

"Yancy, I'm Meg Stanford."

"Ma'am." He whipped his wide-brimmed hat from his head in a courtly gesture. "Thank you for your call. As I said, I'm sorry as I can be at the loss of your daddy."

"Thank you, Yancy." At his sweet, formal words, Meg absorbed a sudden, wrenching pain around her heart and had to swallow hard.

She indicated Jake riding up beside her. "This is—"

"Jake Conway," the old cowboy said. "Good to see you again, Jake. I hear you're a vet now."

"That's right." Jake climbed from his horse to shake the older man's hand.

"I'm not surprised. According to Big Jim, you were always hauling home some wounded critter or other, and always mending their injuries without regard for your own hide."

Jake laughed. "That about sums up my childhood, Yancy."

The old cowboy turned to Meg, his eyes squinting against the sun. "Rumor has it that you're about to auction off the ranch and all the cattle, ma'am."

"That was my original plan, Yancy. Now that I'm here, I'm not so sure."

His brows shot up, the only indication that he'd been caught by surprise.

"Tell me, Yancy, are the cattle healthy?"

"Some of the healthiest herds I've tended. We had a warm spring, and that helped to make this calving season easier than ever."

"If I were to stay on here through the summer, could I count on you to see the herd through to the end of the season?"

He nodded. "Yes'm. That was my promise to your daddy."

"When do you and the wranglers get paid?"

"Your daddy paid us half up front. The rest comes after roundup."

Meg looked toward the bunkhouse in the distance. "Do you have enough supplies to see you through the season?"

He gave her a gentle smile. "No need to worry about us. Your daddy saw to everything at the start of the spring. Matt Fender's our cook, and he makes the hottest chili in Wyoming. Of course, if you ever feel like sending along a couple of cases of longnecks, we won't refuse them, ma'am."

Meg laughed. "I'll put that on my list, Yancy." She leaned down to offer her handshake. "I want to thank you for staying, even though my father is gone now."

"I gave your daddy my word that I'd see the herd through the season. And that's what I intend to do, Miss Stanford."

"It's Meg. And I'm grateful, Yancy."

He hauled himself into the saddle of his spotted mustang. As Meg and Jake were turning their horses, he waved his hat, looking for all the world, Meg thought, like one of those cowboys on the cover of a magazine about the Old West.

Jake pulled his mount alongside Meg's. "Feeling better now that you've seen the herd?"

She nodded. "Yancy says they're healthy. I'm going to take him at his word."

Jake caught her hand. "Yancy's one of the good guys. If he says something, you can take it to the bank. Your dad made a wise choice for ranch foreman."

She glanced at their joined hands and wondered at the way her heart stirred.

Maybe it was being back in the high country again, where she'd once felt on top of the world. Or maybe it was merely the fact that she was finally taking baby steps toward being in charge of her life again. Whatever the reason, she shot him a challenging look before firmly withdrawing her hand.

"Let's race."

He was grinning. "Where to?"

She shrugged. "Back to the house, of course. Last one there gets to make supper."

Without a backward glance she gave her horse its head and they went racing across the high meadow, with Jake's mount in hot pursuit.

Oh, she thought as she leaned low in the saddle, it felt so good to be back in the place that had owned her heart all those years ago. A place of such incredible beauty, it clogged her throat and brought tears to her eyes.

Maybe it wasn't home yet. But it was as close to heaven as she'd ever been.

CHAPTER EIGHTEEN

Their race ended long before the ranch house came into view. One minute Meg's horse was far ahead of Jake's, the next, her mount stumbled, sending Meg sailing through the air to land with a thud in the tall grass. By the time Jake reached her side she'd managed to get to her feet, where she stood rubbing her sore backside.

He slid from the saddle. "You all right?"

She managed a laugh. "I'm sure I'll pay for this tomorrow. For now, the only thing hurt is my pride." She walked over to catch the dangling reins of her horse, busy nibbling grass. "I guess I'm not as good a rider as I used to be."

"You looked damned fine to me. Until that spill, you were the clear winner."

She looked up at the saddle, then at the ranch house in the distance. "I'm not sure I'm ready to climb back on my horse and take any more punishment."

Jake grabbed his horse's reins and moved along beside her. "It's not that far. Let's walk for a while."

She gave him a grateful smile. "Thanks."

They walked in silence for a bit before Jake asked, "So what happened to Meg Stanford between yesterday and today?"

She shrugged. "I'm not sure. I guess it goes back to that challenge you issued, about the arbitrary deadline I'd set for myself. Last night I had time for some soul-searching. I decided that I didn't much like the person I'd become."

"What's wrong with her?" Jake matched his steps to hers as they moved through the tall grass.

"When I left here as a girl, I stopped trusting the people who were in charge and decided to take control of my own life. I studied hard, played by the rules, and made myself fit into the new life I'd been thrust into. I thought I'd done a good job. I stopped feeling sorry for myself and started planning my future. It didn't hurt that my stepfather had some very influential friends that made my climb a lot easier. And I never looked back."

"And now?"

She sighed. "Now, I'm being forced to question everything I'd been told. I don't have the answers yet. I'll probably need lots of time to figure things out. But I've decided that the old Meg, who came here with a chip on her shoulder, needs to be buried along with the father she never really knew. I don't have a clue what the new Meg will be like, but I'm willing to give her time to figure it out and reveal herself to me. For instance, I'd almost forgotten what it felt like to ride a horse at a full gallop across a meadow filled with wildflowers. Or—" she bent

to pluck a tall stem of grass and chew on it before looking at him "—to taste a blade of grass. Who knows what
almost-forgotten thing from my childhood I'll rediscover
tomorrow?"

Jake grinned before nodding toward the barns looming
in the distance. "I'm no fortune-teller, but I'll be willing
to bet that one of those things will be mucking out the
stalls." He pretended to test the muscle of her upper arm.
"Think you're up to it?"

She shot him a sideways look. "You think I'm some
weak, prissy city girl, don't you? Let me remind you that
I was mucking stalls before I could read." She pulled herself up into the saddle before wincing in pain.

Jake followed suit before he threw back his head and
laughed. "And I'll remind you of this tomorrow when
both your arms and aching back complain as loudly as
your backside."

They were both laughing as they urged their horses toward the house.

Both Meg and Jake studied with interest the sleek car
with the tinted windows that was parked beside Jake's
truck.

As they approached, the driver's side door opened, and
a beautifully dressed man wearing tailored slacks, a white
shirt and tie, and mirrored sunglasses stepped out.

"Noah." Meg reined in her mount and stared in stunned
surprise.

"That's not exactly the greeting I was expecting." He
looked from Meg to Jake.

"Sorry. I'm just caught off guard." She waved a hand in
Jake's direction. "Noah Kettering, this is Jake Conway."

"Conway." The man gave Jake a dismissive look before returning his attention to Meg.

She slid from the saddle. "What are you doing here?"

"I might ask you the same thing. When you left, you said you'd be back by the end of the week. Then the firm received your e-mail requesting a leave of absence. You can't be serious."

"I wouldn't have sent it if I hadn't meant it. I've decided that I need some time here."

"Time *here?*" He looked at the house and outbuildings, which were nearly swallowed up by the sea of rangeland that stretched for miles in all directions. "What about the firm's time? What about our clients?"

"I was hoping you and the other partners could handle them in my absence."

He whipped off his sunglasses, revealing pale blue eyes as cold as chips of ice. "Just like that? You're expecting our valued clients to start over with a new lawyer who isn't familiar with their cases? And what about those of us in the firm who are already overburdened with our own clients?" His words were as frosty as his eyes.

Jake took the reins of Meg's horse from her hand. "While you two talk, I'll see to the horses."

"Thanks, Jake." Meg nodded absently, her attention riveted on the man beside her.

Jake led both horses toward a corral, where he unsaddled them and turned them loose before filling a trough with feed and water.

While he worked he studied the man with fair, razor-cut hair and a face like a male model. Though Noah Kettering had shed his suit jacket, the shirt was custom-made, as were the pants and shoes. The watch at his wrist cost more than the rental car he'd driven here. And the fact that he'd flown thousands of miles across the country as soon as he'd heard from Meg told Jake that she must mean a great deal to Noah Kettering of the firm Howe-Kettering.

Why was he surprised? Meg was smart and ambitious and beautiful. She would be an asset to any man's firm. Or to his personal life. And judging by the chill in Noah Kettering's eyes, he wanted her firmly back in place. This didn't appear to be strictly business with Kettering. This was personal.

Though Jake couldn't hear everything that was said, he could hear bits and pieces.

Noah's voice, low with drama. "My father...terribly disappointed."

"I'm sorry. Your father...my champion at the firm."

"What about...I feel?"

Jake watched as Meg lay a hand on Noah's sleeve. "Please don't think this is about you, Noah. I'm doing this for me. I need time here."

"Is there no way to change your mind?"

Her chin came up. "You know me well enough to know that I'd have never sent that e-mail if I hadn't thought this through."

Noah clenched his hands at his sides before looking around. "Is there some place we can go for dinner and a quiet place to talk? I really need a drink."

"The nearest town is a hundred miles from here."

"Unbelievable. That's where I left the firm's plane. I had it stocked with your favorite wine and that seafood salad from Nino's that you love, in the hope that I could persuade you to return with me."

"Thank you, Noah. That was very kind of you."

"I wasn't being kind. I was being practical. Something you've apparently forgotten. What you're doing here is—" he looked with contempt at the dusty yard, the shabby ranch house, before his gaze swung back to her, noting her wind-blown hair, her grass-stained denims "—completely insane."

"I'm sure it seems that way to you. In fact, a day or so ago, I'd have agreed with you." Her voice lowered. Softened. "Why don't you come inside and I'll make some coffee?"

"Do you have anything stronger?"

She smiled. "There may be a few longneck beers left over from my father's stash. As I recall, he used to enjoy a cold beer on a hot day."

"Sorry. Not my style. And this isn't yours. At least it wasn't the style of the Meghan Stanford I knew." Noah sighed and replaced his sunglasses, hiding his eyes from view. "I really can't spare any more time. I left the office in such a hurry, I carried at least a hundred documents that will require my attention on the flight home. A flight I fully expected you to be taking with me."

"I'm sorry I've disappointed you, Noah."

"I'm not the only one who's disappointed. Think about my father." He gave a sigh of disgust. "You'll let me know when you've made a decision to return to civilization?"

"You'll be the first one I contact."

He managed a thin smile. "I guess I'll have to take some small satisfaction in that. Good luck, Meg. I hope..." He glanced toward Jake before finishing. "...I hope you come to your senses sooner rather than later. The firm needs you. And I..." He leaned close and pressed a lingering kiss to her lips before turning away to settle himself behind the wheel of the car. "...I need you, too. But I like to think I'm a patient man."

"You are. And I'm grateful." Meg leaned in the open window. "Thanks for coming all this way, Noah."

"It was Dad's idea. In fact, he insisted."

"Thank your father for me. Safe flight."

She stood watching as he drove along the curving driveway, leaving a trail of dust in his wake. When the car was out of sight she turned to see Jake leaning against the corral, his arms crossed over his chest.

She was grateful that he'd given her some space. She turned away, her gaze sweeping the landscape, her foot tapping.

Finally, she took in a long, deep breath and crossed the distance between them. "I'm sure you have questions. Can we talk in a little while?"

He shrugged. "If you'd rather."

"Thanks. If you're hungry, Ela and Phoebe sent chicken and corn bread."

He followed her up the steps of the porch. As she unlocked the door and stepped inside, he remarked casually, "I didn't hear you invite Noah to stay for supper."

"He's not a chicken-and-corn-bread kind of guy."

Jake chuckled. "Too bad. His loss. I guess that means more for me."

"If I don't eat it all first." Relieved that Jake was willing to give her time to clear her mind, she washed her hands at the sink and began removing the bags of food from the refrigerator, while Jake set the table.

"Milk or coffee?" Meg asked.

"Both, as long as you have both."

"I do." She measured coffee and filled the maker with water before fetching two frosty glasses of milk.

When everything was ready, they took their places across from each other. As they ate, Jake tried to gauge Meg's mood while he waited for her to fill in the blanks. She took her time, feeding an appetite sharpened by the hours spent in the high country.

At last, when the meal was finished, and they were sipping strong, hot coffee, she began to talk haltingly.

"Noah is the son of Cyrus Kettering, the senior partner of Howe-Kettering. He's being groomed to replace Cyrus when he retires."

"And you're being groomed to be the wife of the new senior partner."

"I know how it looks, but..." She sighed. "It isn't something we've talked about exactly. Mostly, when we have time away from work, we talk about our latest clients, and our strategy for winning our next trial. It's an extremely high-energy world, and that leaves little time for small talk or romance. But he's made it plain that we'd make an unbeatable team. His father makes it equally plain that he approves. It was Cyrus who interviewed me, at my stepfather's request, and Cyrus who gave me my first assignment with the firm, and who has personally watched my star ascend."

"And you owe him."

She nodded. "Big-time."

"Enough to marry his son?"

When she said nothing in her defense, Jake studied her over the rim of his cup. "So he sent his top gun out here to bring you back to the fold."

Meg nodded. "Something like that. I think Cyrus was

not only sending a message to me, but he was also asking me a question. Just how important is all of this to me? And now he has my answer, and I have his. Though he doesn't like it, he has no choice but to grant me this time, or he risks losing me."

"What about your risk?"

She sighed. "It's huge. Cyrus could decide to bring in a replacement. The city is full of hotshot legal eagles who would die to have a chance at my job."

"That's the business risk. What about the personal risk?"

She shook her head. "What Noah and I have is a mutual love of our chosen careers. We've never actually talked about a commitment." She kept her eyes on the tabletop, avoiding Jake's gaze. "I'm sure a lot of people slide into an arrangement because of a shared interest."

"Slide into marriage? What about love? Passion? Romance?"

She gave a short laugh. "A nice thought. In my world, there isn't time."

"That's a pretty harsh world you're living in." He reached over to press his hand over hers. Cold, he realized. "Maybe some people settle. You don't strike me as someone who'd settle for less than having it all."

"I thought I had it all." She sighed again, long and deep. "Now I'm not sure about anything. In the dark of the night, watching Cory asleep in the barn and seeing Honey with her puppies, I felt so sure. Staying here until I figured things out seemed like the right thing."

"And now?"

She gave him a wan smile and withdrew her hand from his to clench it tightly in her lap. "I'm sure I'll have to fight a lot of demons, but for now, I'm doing the only thing I can." She drained her cup. "And it's not some big, noble gesture. It's purely selfish. I'm doing this for myself. So that whether I stay or go, I'll be satisfied that I took the time to think it through. One step at a time."

Jake crossed to the sink and filled it with hot water before gathering the dishes. Meg removed a clean linen cloth from a drawer and dried. When the dishes had been put away and the table wiped down, Meg set mugs, coffee, cream, and sugar on a tray and led the way to her father's old office.

While Meg filled their mugs, Jake piled logs and kindling on the grate and started a fire to chase away the chill of the night.

As they settled themselves in front of the fire, Meg sipped her coffee and smiled. "It's hard to believe that the nights are still cool enough for a fire. Back in D.C. I'd be cranking up the air in my town house."

"Do you miss it?"

She thought about his question before forming a response. "Funny. I don't, so far. I have friends there, of course. Guys from the office who are always willing to talk shop over a quick dinner. And friends from boarding school who are often in the city for a day of shopping, or a weekend. I'm comfortable enough with them that I can call, even at the last minute, if I find myself with a free evening and a chance to enjoy a leisurely dinner." She glanced at him. "Maybe, if I stay long enough, I'll miss the city and all it has to offer. But right now all of this is so new and yet so familiar, I'm beginning to feel that I never really left." She shook her head. "I can't believe what a difference a day makes."

"Yesterday was a tough one for both you and Cory."

She nodded. "And so enlightening. It was like having a switch thrown, and suddenly I was bathed in so much light it was blinding. I couldn't seem to take it all in. I didn't know if I'd been blinded, or blindsided, but I was definitely overwhelmed."

"Either way, you're dealing with it."

"I hope Cory is." She turned to him. "How do you read Cory, Jake?"

"He's scared. He's lost his anchor. I'd guess that after his mom died, the only secure thing he had left was his father. And now that anchor's gone, too. Any kid would be scared and angry."

"I don't know. Sometimes I think—" she searched for the proper words "—he's carrying a heavy load of guilt."

"Don't you think it's natural for a kid to feel guilty because he's alive and his parents are dead?"

"Maybe." She sipped her coffee. "I just wish I could get him to open up to me."

"Give him time, Meg. If last night was any indication, he's come a long way from that mute kid you confronted when you first arrived."

Meg laughed. "You're right. I'd forgotten just how alarmed I'd been, thinking he couldn't speak." She got to her feet and set her empty mug on the tray. "There's another cup of coffee left. Want it?"

Jake shook his head. "I've had enough." He crossed the space that separated them and set his cup down before taking her hand. "If you'd like, I'd be more than happy to keep you company here tonight."

Her smile was quick and easy. "I just bet you would.

That's very generous of you, but I need to prove that I can take care of myself."

"You don't have to do this alone, Meg."

"I do." She picked up the tray and started toward the kitchen.

Jake followed. "If you really plan on being alone, I could lend you my rifle. It's in my truck."

She shook her head as she set the tray aside on the kitchen counter. "I've never even handled a rifle. If an intruder broke in, I'd probably blow a hole in the wall, or shoot myself in the foot. And wouldn't that have everyone in Flora's Diner laughing at the silly city girl?"

Jake couldn't stop the grin that curved his lips. "Yeah. You've got a point. You'd be the talk of the town. But I wish you'd let me stay. I could sleep in your dad's office, if you'd like."

"Nice try, cowboy. But since I've decided to be perfectly honest, I have to admit that if you were anywhere in this house tonight, we'd find a way to get together. And it wouldn't be just for warmth."

"Now you're talking." That sexy smile widened.

"That's why you're going back to your ranch. And I'm going to prove to myself that I can survive the night by myself."

His smile faded. "Keep your cell phone charged and by your side."

"I will." She held open the back door.

"It probably wouldn't hurt to leave the outside porch lights on."

"All right." She touched the switch, flooding the area with light.

He paused. "I don't like this, Meg. I should stay."

"I don't like it either. But you're going."

He paused and brushed a quick, hard kiss to her mouth. They were both startled by the sparks that sizzled between them.

She put a hand to his chest and looked up at him. "Don't make this any more difficult than it already is, Jake. Go."

He stepped out the door and made it down the steps before turning. "I could—"

"Good night, Jake. And thanks for everything."

He folded his arms over his chest. "I'm not leaving until you close the door and lock it. And for good measure, wedge the back of the chair under the handle."

She did as he asked. When she waved from the window, he turned and walked to his truck. She was still waving as he drove away.

She looked, he thought, like a scared kid putting on a brave face before boarding the bus on the first day of school.

It was killing him to drive away and leave her. But she'd probably kill him if he stayed.

CHAPTER NINETEEN

Jake parked the truck behind the darkened ranch house and let himself into the barn. At this late hour, he'd expected the building to be dark, but all the lights were on.

Cory was leaning on the low rail of Honey's pen, watching her and her puppies while they dozed. The boy looked up in surprise. "You're not staying with Meg?"

Jake shook his head. "She wants to prove that she can take care of herself."

"But..." Cory looked genuinely alarmed. "She shouldn't be alone."

"If there's one thing I've learned, it's that there's no use fighting a female once she sets her mind to something. Especially that female. Your sister is one tough cookie." Jake's laughter faded as he studied the boy more closely, seeing the real terror in his eyes.

He put a hand on Cory's shoulder. "Hey. What's this all about?"

Cory turned away, avoiding his touch. "Nothing. She just shouldn't be alone is all."

"Do you know something I don't?" Jake struggled to keep his tone deliberately casual and nonthreatening, but it wasn't easy when Cory was so obviously unnerved.

The little boy avoided him, walking into Shadow's stall and shaking out the bedroll hanging over the railing. He seemed to be shaking it as hard as he could. Almost as if, Jake thought, he was shaking the very devil out of it.

Jake heard the ping of a text message and pulled his cell phone from his pocket. Seeing nothing, he glanced over at Cory. "That must have been your phone."

Without looking Cory shook his head. "Who'd be texting me?"

"I don't know. Why don't you check?"

The boy removed his cell phone from his pocket and turned away, blocking Jake's view. Then he returned it to his pocket with a shrug. "Like I said. Nothing."

Jake's eyes narrowed. He knew what he'd heard. Knew also that the boy was hiding something from him. But short of calling Cory a liar, he didn't see much that he could do about it.

"I guess I'll go up to bed then, unless you'd like some company." Jake backed away, hoping Cory might relent and share whatever was bothering him.

Instead, the boy kept his back to him, looping an arm around the colt's neck.

"All right then," Jake called. "If you ever feel like talking, I'm always ready to listen. 'Night, Cory."

"'Night."

Jake studied the boy's rigid back as he closed the barn door and latched it.

As he made his way toward the house by the light of the moon, Jake wrestled with the idea of going back and confronting Cory.

Though the boy denied knowing anything, Jake was more convinced than ever that Cory Stanford knew a whole lot more than he was admitting to.

And just what he knew could be the key to solving the mystery of who was intruding on Meg's private life. And why.

Meg had all the lights in the house turned on. The windows of the ranch house were ablaze. To help keep her spirits up, she added another log to the fireplace. The warmth of the fire added a layer of comfort. Cory's baseball bat at the side of her desk added an extra layer of safety. She realized it wasn't much of a defense, but just knowing she had something handy to swing at an intruder gave her courage.

She was dressed in a pair of comfortable flannel pajama bottoms and a soft tee. Her hair was held back with a rubber band.

Because she was too nervous and keyed up to sleep, she decided to tackle some of her father's files. She spent the next hours going over his financial ledgers, noting the cost of feed and grain for the herds, the cost of maintenance on the house and outbuildings, and the detailed list of wranglers employed to tend the herds and their payments. Her father's meticulous bookkeeping would certainly make it easier for Meg to plan for the final payments to the wranglers at the end of round-up. Whether she was still here, or whether she was back in D.C. in her town house after directing Kirby to make the payments out of the estate, at least she would have a handle on the expenses.

Meg studied her father's scrawl, methodically marking the date, the check number, and the amount of each transaction. It was shocking to think that he'd made these entries just days ago. And now he was gone.

She struggled to put the thought out of her mind. It was too painful to think that if she'd only come here for a visit a week ago, she would have been able to sit down with her father and catch up on his life. She could have told him about all the things she'd accomplished, and the life she'd made for herself. Maybe they could have put aside their differences to share a laugh or a hug.

Could have.

Would have.

Should have.

She tossed her head, as if to dispel the thoughts crowding her mind. There was absolutely no point in playing the guilt game. There wasn't a chance on earth that she'd have paid a call on her father a week ago, or a year ago. All the hurt and anger of the past would have to stay in the past. There would never be an opportunity to make it right.

Now she needed to plan for her future. Hers and Cory's.

As her finger moved down the page, she came across the last entry. It wasn't like the others. Perhaps, Meg thought, because her father had been already feeling too weak or too sick. Had he had some warning about an impending heart attack? A warning that he chose to ignore?

The last line in the ledger showed a date and an amount. The handwriting was so shaky, the zeroes ran together. It could have been one hundred or one thousand. There was no check number, but since it was so close to her father's passing, Meg was left to assume it had either been paid in cash, or her father had forgotten to register the check. Once she received the bank records, she could match the checks to this page and find out the details.

There was no name. Just some scrawled initials that appeared to be a *P* or a *B*, along with a *T* or an *I*.

Odd, she thought, and made a mental note to phone Kirby Bolton in the morning and ask him about it.

As she closed the ledger, she could feel her eyelids growing heavy. After the day she'd put in, with hours in the saddle riding to the high country and back, her body was beginning to protest. Like it or not, she was going to have to give in to sleep.

At the moment, it seemed too much effort to even climb the stairs to bed.

She crossed the room and lay down on the sofa, pulling the faded afghan over her.

She was asleep instantly.

Morning sunlight was just climbing over the peaks of the Tetons and slanting through the floor-to-ceiling sliding windows of the office, waking Meg from a sound sleep.

She sat up, brushing hair from her eyes. As she tossed aside the afghan and got to her feet she was feeling more than a little bit smug. She'd made it through the night without any incident, and had actually managed to sleep.

This reinforced her conviction that she'd made the right decision. It was time to get on with her life, without taking advantage of the kindness of her neighbors. She was, after all, an independent woman with a successful career. Just because some nutcase had trashed her car and property didn't mean she couldn't spend a few nights alone at her ranch without calling in the troops.

She padded barefoot along the hallway toward the kitchen. She would start the coffeemaker, and then head upstairs to shower and dress.

As she stepped into the kitchen, she glanced out the window and came to a halt.

A familiar truck was parked outside.

She removed the chair from beneath the doorknob, throwing open the back door before running down the steps. Peering in the truck's window, she saw Jake behind the wheel, the driver's seat tilted back as far as it would go, his long legs stretched out in front of him, his chest rising and falling in a steady rhythm. His hat was pulled low over his face, his rifle on the passenger seat beside him, presumably where he could grab it in a hurry.

For a moment she merely drank in the sight of him. She felt a rush of such mixed emotions, she had to swallow hard as she studied the open shirt beneath the denim jacket, revealing the mat of dark hair on his chest. More dark stubble covered his cheeks and chin, adding to the rogue look that she found so appealing.

Her hero. Her champion. He'd stayed the night, even though she'd ordered him to leave.

As though sensing her presence, he woke.

She saw the way his dark eyes widened at the sight of her, before his lips curved into that wonderful, sexy smile.

"'Morning." He lowered the window. His gaze moved slowly over her, from her bare feet to her sleep-tossed hair. "Don't you look fetching this morning."

"I might say the same."

He opened the truck door and stepped out, holding the rifle loosely in one hand.

Meg arched a brow. "Expecting trouble?"

"I'm always prepared."

"Like a Boy Scout." She smiled. "Okay, Conway. What's this about? I assume you spent the night here?"

"I did." He stretched his arms above his head, causing his shirt to pull away from his faded jeans, showing a flat, hard stomach.

Meg's heart slammed against her ribs and beat a steady tattoo.

He nodded toward the porch. "Come on. I'd rather talk inside, over coffee." He held the door and followed her inside. "You did make coffee, didn't you?"

"I was just about to when I spotted your truck." She crossed to the kitchen counter and began measuring coffee and water into the coffeemaker. "There's corn bread in the fridge. Ela didn't want me to go hungry."

"Bless Ela." Jake set his rifle by the door and began rummaging through the refrigerator, bringing a plate of corn bread and a jar of strawberry preserves to the table.

A short time later Meg and Jake sat on opposite sides of the table, sipping coffee and nibbling corn bread.

"Okay." Meg studied Jake over the rim of her cup. "Let's talk. Why are you acting like my bodyguard?"

He took his time, wolfing down two slices of corn bread and washing them down with coffee before answering. "When I got back to my place, Cory was still awake. And he seemed alarmed that I wasn't staying the night with you."

"I told you I'd be fine."

"Yeah. And that would have been enough for me, except that I found Cory's reaction strange."

"In what way?"

He shook his head and stretched out his long legs. "I can't quite put my finger on it. But something about his behavior last night was off. He was jumpy. And then there's that text he got."

"Who would be texting Cory?"

"That's exactly the excuse he gave me when he denied that he'd received a text. But I know what I heard, and it wasn't coming from my phone. Since there were only the two of us in the barn at the time, it had to be someone texting Cory. But who? And why? Especially at that hour of the night."

"So, Cory gets a text message and you decide to sleep outside my place all night?"

He grinned. "Yeah. Crazy, isn't it? But I figured it's better to be safe than sorry."

"And it was all for nothing."

"How do you know that?"

She stared at him. "It's morning, and there was no intruder."

"Unless your intruder spotted my truck and turned tail to run away."

Meg's smile faded. "But how can we be sure?"

Jake shook his head. "We can't. That's why you just may have to agree to let me be your bodyguard for a while."

She shoved away from the table. "Not on your life."

"And why not?" He remained sitting, his smile still in place.

"Because you have a life to live. And so do I."

"We're neighbors, Meg. I can easily stay here at night and get home in plenty of time to lend a hand with the chores and see to my veterinary patients."

"No. You don't understand." She leaned her palms on the tabletop and fixed him with a steady gaze. "I need to face down my fears and deal with my life as it is now. And I need to do it alone."

"And you will. But I'll just hang around at night and see that you're safe."

"Safe?" Her eyes flashed. "We both know what's going to happen if you stay here at night."

"Oh. That." He gave a low chuckle. "We'll treat this like our own private Vegas. What happens at the Stanford ranch stays at the Stanford ranch."

"This isn't Vegas. And I'm not having some mindless sex with my hot cowboy neighbor."

His head came up, and he latched onto the only thing that caught his attention. "You think I'm hot?"

"I think you're pushing your luck, Jake. Now go home. I have things to do."

As she turned away, he saw the way she pressed a hand to the small of her back.

"All those hours in the saddle can play hell with your muscles, can't they? Sure you wouldn't like a massage before you shower?"

She shot a look over her shoulder. "Thanks for playing bodyguard during the night. I really do appreciate it. In fact, I'm very touched by it. But now, just go home, cowboy."

"Sure thing." He drained his coffee and got to his feet. "By the way, I'll be driving into town later. If you'd like to hitch a ride, I'll be happy to pick you up."

When she didn't reply he added, "I'm going to try to persuade Cory to go along. I'm hoping to pry some information out of him. You might want to give it some thought."

She paused halfway up the stairs. Turned slowly as she mulled his words. "All right. Call me when you're leaving and I'll be ready to join you."

"I could join you in that shower right now."

"Don't push your luck. I told you I'd go with you to town. That's all you're getting from me."

"For now." Jake whistled as he let himself out and made his way to his truck.

CHAPTER TWENTY

Josh looked up from the stall he was mucking as Jake strolled in. "Hey, bro. Nice of you to join us."

"Were you looking after somebody's sick cow?" Quinn, working alongside Josh, leaned his arms on the handle of his pitchfork.

"Not this time." Jake picked up a pitchfork and joined in, tossing a load of straw into the wagon being pulled by Cory, who hadn't spoken a word.

"I'll be heading to Paintbrush after breakfast." Jake paused to turn to Cory. "Along the way I promised to pick up your sister. Want to join us?"

The boy's head came up sharply. "You talked to her? She's all right?"

"Why wouldn't she be?"

Jake watched as Cory averted his head to mumble, "You know why. That guy."

"The intruder?"

Cory nodded.

"So you think he's still around?"

The boy shrugged his thin shoulders, but refused to look at Jake.

"Why is he targeting Meg?"

Silence greeted his question.

Jake decided to take Cory into his confidence. "After our talk out here last night, I figured you were right. So I slept outside your ranch in my truck, playing body-guard."

"You did?" Cory turned to look at him. "Did anybody come around?"

"Not that I could see. I figure if anybody tried, they'd spot my truck and take off before I had a chance to catch them." He looked pointedly at the boy. "So what do you think? Has this intruder skipped town, or is he just laying low?"

Cory looked away. "How should I know?"

With a sigh Jake decided to enlist his brothers into turning the conversation to something light. "Who decided to assign chores this morning?"

Josh straightened. "I did. Why?"

"'Cause I noticed that you gave Cory my old dirty job." He grinned at the boy. "My brothers always used to grab the pitchforks first so I'd be stuck with the honey wagon."

"Honey wagon?" Cory stared at the smelly pile of straw mixed with manure. As the light dawned, he couldn't help the smile that tugged at the corners of his mouth. "Is that what you call this?"

"It suits, don't you agree?"

Cory started laughing. "How old were you when you stopped hauling the honey wagon?"

"About your age. That's when it dawned on me that if I got out to the barn before my brothers, I could muck and one of them would have to haul."

"That's just what we wanted you to think, little brother." Quinn nudged Josh, and the two of them laughed. "That way, we got to sleep in an extra half hour while you were out here being so smart."

"Oh yeah?" Jake nudged Cory. "Is that why I finished my chores in the barn a half hour earlier and was the first one to the breakfast table?"

Josh shot a look at Quinn. "I never thought about that. Did you?"

Quinn shook his head. "And guess who always got the biggest slice of Ela's corn bread?"

The two men nodded in unison, while Cory and Jake shared a grin.

Jake pointed to the row of pitchforks hanging on hooks along the wall of the barn. "Help yourself to one of those, Cory, and we'll get this work done in half the time. Then we can head on inside and let Ela spoil us."

The boy matched his movements to Jake's, forking wet hay, tossing it over the side of the wagon, then bending to lift another pile. When they were finished, Jake led the way toward the house. Once inside, he paused to roll his sleeves and wash at the big sink in the mudroom. Cory did the same. When Jake filled his big hands with water and used it to slick back his hair, Cory followed suit.

As Jake and Cory sauntered into the kitchen, Jake paused to sniff the air. "I smell corn bread."

Cory nodded. "Me, too."

Ela turned. "I saved you a big piece, Jake."

"I thank you." He brushed a kiss to her cheek.

Smiling, she turned to the boy. "I saved you an even bigger piece."

He lifted himself on tiptoe to kiss her withered cheek. Then, realizing his boldness, his face turned every shade of red.

The old woman touched a hand to his face. "Such a good boy."

Jake helped himself to a glass of orange juice before settling himself at the table, where Cole and Big Jim were waiting.

Cory did the same, settling himself beside Jake, just as Quinn and Josh walked into the room.

"What took you so long, boyo?" Big Jim called to Josh. "You and Quinn are holding up my breakfast."

"Don't blame them, Big Jim." Jake winked at Cory. "Now that they're old married men, they just move slower."

"Old married men?" Cheyenne and Sierra exchanged glances while Cory had to cover his mouth with his hand because he couldn't stop giggling.

As the family shared a meal, Jake couldn't help noticing the new lighthearted mood that seemed to have enveloped Cory Stanford. Maybe the boy was coming out of the fog of grief that had surrounded him. If so, it was obvious that playing bodyguard to Meg had something to do with the sudden change.

"Time to head to town." Jake led the way to the mudroom, where he plucked a wide-brimmed Stetson from a hook by the back door. Glancing at Cory, he paused to consider. "You don't have a hat?"

Cory shook his head.

"Try this one on." Jake removed a smaller version of his hat. "This used to be mine before I outgrew it."

Cory ran the hat around and around in his hands, noting the sweat stains, the grass stains, the stains from past rains and snows. He noticed something shiny stuck in the hatband. "What's this?" He held up a sharp blue-and-gold veined stone.

"Hey, my lucky stone." Jake accepted it from his hand and turned it over and over, holding it up to the light.

"Why is it lucky?"

Jake shrugged. "Darned if I can remember now. But I always called it my lucky stone. You want it?"

"You mean it?" Cory studied the stone before placing it back in the band. When he set the hat on his head, he caught a glimpse of himself in the window.

His brows shot up. "You sure you want me to have it?"

"I'm sure."

As Jake started out the door, Cory stood a little taller as he followed him to the truck.

Meg stepped out the door before the truck came to a stop. It was clear that she'd been watching for them.

"Hey. 'Morning, Cory." She took note of his hat as he stepped out to allow her to sit in the middle.

"'Morning." He hauled himself up beside her and closed the door before fastening his seat belt.

Jake closed a big hand over hers before putting the truck in gear and heading back toward the highway. He adjusted his sunglasses. "Cory and I beat Quinn and Josh at our barn chores this morning."

"Was it a contest?" Meg asked.

Jake shrugged. "When you've got older brothers, all of life is a contest. Isn't that right, Cory?"

The boy nodded.

Meg smiled. "I wouldn't know. I never had an older sibling." She took in a breath and decided to follow Jake's lighthearted lead. "But now I have a younger brother." She stared pointedly at Cory. "I like your hat. Where'd you get it?"

"It's one of Jake's." His smile glowed.

Meg shot a sideways glance at Jake. "I guess every cowboy's got to have a hat."

"You bet. It's the law here in Wyoming."

All three of them laughed.

Meg watched the passing scenery. "How long do you intend to stay in town?"

"I'm just picking up a few supplies. But I can stay as long as I please. Do you need to go somewhere?"

"Just to Judge Bolton's office. I called ahead for an appointment. It shouldn't take me long."

As they drove along the main street, Jake pulled up in front of the courthouse. "Why don't you go ahead and take care of your business with Kirby. I'll head on over to Homer's Grain and Seed and be back to pick you up in an hour."

Jake turned to Cory. "You want to go with Meg or stay with me?"

"I'll stay with you." Cory stepped out and held the door for Meg.

"No surprise," she said with a laugh.

Minutes later the truck was rolling toward the paint and hardware store at the end of the street.

* * *

Meg watched as Kirby Bolton, fresh from a morning court session, removed his judicial robes and pulled on a suit jacket before taking a seat behind his desk.

"Now, Meg, what can I do for you?"

She leaned forward in her chair. "Last night I spent some time going over my father's ledgers. I have a question about what I believe was his last payout. It was dated the day before his death, but it doesn't follow the same pattern as the others, although it could be because he was already suffering the heart attack that later took his life."

The judge studied her with interest. "What makes you think that?"

"His handwriting was really shaky. Barely legible. And he didn't record a check number."

"Maybe he paid in cash."

"That thought crossed my mind. But why? Wouldn't it have been simpler for him to mail a check than to withdraw cash from the bank and then pay his bill?"

"It was his custom to keep some cash at home to pay small bills."

"I couldn't tell if the amount he wrote was a hundred dollars or a thousand."

Kirby smiled. "Porter was full of contradictions. He may have considered a thousand dollars his mad money. But I can't think of anything worth a thousand dollars that he'd have purchased lately. I'm sure it was probably more like a hundred. Maybe even ten dollars."

Meg returned his smile, hoping he was right. "I guess the simplest way to check this out would be to see his latest bank receipts."

Kirby nodded. "I'll call Roxanne over at the bank, and

ask her to have your father's bank records available when you get there."

Meg got to her feet. "Thank you, Judge."

"It's Kirby." He offered his hand.

She accepted his handshake. "Thank you, Kirby."

He looked up at her before withdrawing his hand. "Any more problems with that mysterious intruder?"

"No. And I spent the night alone at the ranch, just to prove that I wasn't going to be intimidated."

"Good for you, Meg."

She flushed. "What I didn't know was that Jake Conway spent the night in his truck parked alongside my back porch. I'm sure if the intruder planned any trouble, the sight of Jake would have sent him running."

Kirby threw back his head and roared with laughter. "Good for Jake. I know one thing. There aren't many in this town who'd be willing to stand up to him. If I ever found myself in a knock-down, drag-out brawl, I'd want Jake Conway watching my back."

Meg thought about the judge's words as she left his office and crossed the narrow street to the Paintbrush Bank, where a smiling young woman greeted her.

"Miss Stanford, I'm Roxanne Fisher. Judge Bolton asked that I have your father's latest deposit and withdrawal records ready. If you'll follow me."

Meg was led into one of the glass-walled offices.

Roxanne pointed to the desk. "I think that's everything you need, but if you have any questions, please let me know."

The young woman closed the door behind her and left Meg with photocopies of the latest checks cashed and a record of all her father's deposits and withdrawals for the past month.

By the time Meg left the bank, she had checked every amount against her father's handwritten ledger. All the checks had been accounted for. That served as further proof that the amount in question must have been paid in cash. And he had made a withdrawal of exactly a thousand dollars on the day he died.

She felt more frustrated than ever. Because of his barely legible record, she had no way of knowing the recipient or the reason for the payment.

It was probably of no consequence whatever. But the fact that it appeared to be for a very significant amount, and it was one of her father's last acts before his death, made it feel important in Meg's eyes. She had a sudden yearning to learn everything she could about the father she'd been denied.

Meg stepped out of the little shop called Odds N Ends. The words of the sign had always made her smile, even when she was just a girl.

It read: IF WE DON'T HAVE IT, YOU DON'T NEED IT.

Of course, they'd had everything she needed. She held a shopping bag brimming with fresh underthings, a pair of simple, lightweight pajamas, a couple of T-shirts, as well as toothpaste and shampoo, since she'd brought only sample sizes, thinking she'd be here for a week.

Jake's truck rolled to a stop at the curb, and he lowered the window to call, "Hey, pretty lady. You need a ride?"

She laughed as she walked up to the truck. "Thanks. I'm awfully picky. I only accept rides from handsome strangers."

Jake gave an exaggerated nudge with his elbow to Cory's ribs. "Hear that? She thinks we're handsome."

Cory was grinning as he opened the door and stepped out to allow Meg to climb in.

Jake glanced at the shopping bag. "Find what you were looking for?"

She nodded. "I wasn't planning on staying this long. I needed a few things. As for what I was looking for at Kirby Bolton's office, I wasn't as lucky. He sent me to the bank, but there's no record of a check. That means that my father paid in cash. Since the bank shows a withdrawal of a thousand dollars, I know the amount, but not the recipient."

Jake whistled. "A thousand's not petty cash."

Meg nodded her agreement.

Jake pointed up the street. "How about some lunch at Flora's Diner before we head back? Lifting all those sacks gave me an appetite."

Meg glanced over her shoulder at the back of the truck filled with grain sacks. She had a quick image of Jake, muscles straining, as he hoisted each sack before tossing it neatly in the bed of the truck.

His arm muscles were clearly visible beneath the rolled sleeves of his shirt. "I think I could eat something." Meg turned. "How about you, Cory?"

The boy shrugged. "I guess."

"It's settled." Jake put the truck in gear, and they rolled along the main street until they parked in front of the diner.

The lunch crowd was already inside, filling every table. That left only the stools at the counter. Jake led the way, and he and Meg and Cory perched on the shiny red stools and breathed in the wonderful aroma of onions on the grill, and the pungent smell of ground beef simmering in spices, prominently featured on Flora's sign listing the specials of the day.

Flora looked up from her grill behind the pass-through and shot Jake a wide smile as she emerged, wiping her hands on her wide, white apron. "Hey, handsome. You and the world-famous counselor are turning into regulars."

"World-famous?" Jake chuckled. "Where'd you hear that juicy gossip?"

"Oh, I hear things. A little bit here, a little bit there. Word around town is that Porter Stanford's daughter turned herself into a first-class, bona fide celebrity lawyer." She leaned her elbows on the counter to peer directly at Meg. "Wouldn't your daddy have loved knowing his little girl put a murderer behind bars?"

Before Meg could respond she added, "And wouldn't he love seeing his daughter and son hanging out together here in Paintbrush?"

With a laugh she tousled Cory's shaggy hair. "Too bad you didn't get your daddy's red hair like Meg here. But I've always thought you looked more like your mama than your daddy."

The boy blushed clear to the tips of his ears.

Flora turned away to say to Jake, "Our special today is my red-hot chili. Want to give it a try?"

"Why not?" He winked at Meg. "Want to take a walk on the wild side?"

She shook her head. "Not a chance. I'm having my usual. Burger and chocolate shake."

Jake looked across Meg to Cory. "You going to risk Flora's red-hot chili? Or wimp out with a burger and shake?"

The boy shrugged. "I'll have what Meg's having."

Flora shot a grin at Jake. "I could have told you. Blood's thicker than water."

"What does that mean?" the boy asked.

"It means that nine times out of ten, family will choose to stand with family over friends. Or," Jake added with a grin, "it could mean that you and Meg, coming from the same bloodline, share the same taste buds."

While Flora disappeared behind the pass-through to begin making their lunch, Cory ducked his head and stared hard at the old plastic menu.

Dora waddled over and set down three glasses of water. "Anything else to drink here?"

"Coffee," Jake said. "Thanks, Dora."

A short time later he dug into his bowl of chili while Meg and Cory enjoyed their hamburgers and chocolate shakes.

By the time they finished, the lunch crowd had thinned considerably, with only a couple of stragglers left at a few of the tables.

Flora came out from behind her grill to help herself to a tall glass of ice water. Wiping her forehead with the hem of her apron she paused at the counter.

"The talk around town is that you've put a halt to any auctions. Does that mean you're thinking of running the ranch yourself, counselor?"

Meg laughed. "I've only been here a couple of days, and already the gossip has me pegged as a world-famous lawyer and a magician."

Flora arched a brow. "Magician?"

"I'd need to be a magician to take over my father's ranch by myself."

Flora shook her head. "Oh, I don't know. You've got Yancy Jessup wrangling your herds. They don't come better. And you've got the Conway family right next door." She added in a stage whisper, "From the looks of Jake here, he could be roped, hog-tied, and branded without putting up much of a fight. He'd make a fine addition to your holdings."

Meg and Jake joined Flora in the good-natured laughter.

Before Flora could walk away Meg caught her hand. "The last time I was in here, you mentioned how my father often paid someone's bill, or surprised someone who needed help. Did you happen to hear of such a thing just before he died?"

Flora considered the question before shaking her head. "Sorry. I haven't heard of a thing lately. Why?"

Meg swallowed her disappointment. Flora had been her last resort. "Dad recorded a sum of money in his ledger on the day before his death. There was no check written on that date, so it must have been a cash payment, and I was hoping he did it for someone here in town who could confirm the payment."

"He didn't record the name of the person he paid?"

Meg nodded. "Actually, he wrote some initials. But his writing is so shaky, it isn't legible." She shrugged. "It isn't really important. Being a lawyer, I guess I just have this need to have all the loose ends tied up."

"If I hear about of anybody in town who received a helping hand from a mysterious benefactor around the time of your daddy's passing, I'll be sure to let you know."

"Thanks, Flora." Meg smiled as the old woman returned to her grill.

While Jake paid the bill, Meg glanced toward Cory, but the boy was busy setting aside his half-eaten burger.

"You didn't like it?" she asked.

He avoided her eyes. "Not hungry, I guess."

Meg touched a hand to his forehead, pretending to check for a fever. "Well, you don't feel too hot. But I've never heard of a seven-year-old who couldn't devour a burger and shake in half the time it takes to make one, unless he's coming down with something. I think I'd better keep an eye on you."

Even her attempt to make a joke didn't bring a smile to his lips.

He slid from his stool and followed Jake and Meg from the diner.

CHAPTER TWENTY-ONE

As they headed home from town, Jake regaled Meg with stories of his childhood that made her laugh so hard her sides hurt.

She wiped tears of laughter from her eyes and, when she looked at Cory, she realized he hadn't heard a word of Jake's story.

"Something wrong?" she asked.

The boy's head came up sharply. "Nothing."

"You sure?"

He gave a shrug without bothering to respond.

When the truck came to a stop at Meg's back door, she looked over at Jake. "That was the fastest ride ever." She touched a hand to his arm. "I love your stories about your childhood here. But I have to say that it only serves to reinforce my belief that I would have loved growing up here with my father."

Jake closed a hand over hers. "Don't play that game,

Meg. We don't get to choose our childhood." He glanced past her to where Cory remained silent and aloof, his face turned away from the two of them, staring out the side window. "Some of us are dealt a tougher hand than others. But we all get to choose how we'll live our lives going forward as adults."

"Thanks for that reminder." Meg smiled. "This adult still has a lot of work to do. Now to get started." She motioned toward the door. "Cory, we're home."

Instead of opening the door he looked past her. "Can I go home with you, Jake? Shadow and Honey and her puppies need me."

Jake shook his head. "That's not my call, Cory. You'd better ask your sister."

Meg didn't wait for Cory to plead his case. "I know you're happy at the Conway ranch, and it's fine with me if you stay there, as long as they don't object."

Jake gave a quick shake of his head. "You know we're all fine with it."

With a visible sigh of relief Cory opened the truck door and climbed down, holding the door for Meg.

She paused beside the little boy who was trying to look so grown up in his cowboy hat. "Will I see you tomorrow?"

"Sure." He climbed back into the truck and fastened his seat belt without meeting her eyes.

As they began moving along the driveway he turned to Jake. "You planning on spending the night out here again?"

Jake studied him. "You think I should?"

Cory looked away quickly. With his head firmly turned aside he muttered, "Yeah."

"Okay. If you say so." Jake was grinning. "Although the final word will have to come from Meg."

Not that it mattered whether or not she approved. Wild horses couldn't keep him away, he thought.

Now, more than ever, Cory's behavior convinced him that the boy was keeping secrets. And until Cory opened up and spilled what he knew, there was no way Jake was going to allow Meg to be alone. Not tonight, nor any other night.

Of course, if she happened to relent and invite him inside, they just might find themselves in a whole lot of a very different kind of trouble.

A man could always hope.

Meg climbed the steps to the attic. When she'd been a girl, this place had been her playroom in winter, when the snow was too deep for her to make it to the barns and outbuildings.

She shoved open the door and played her flashlight around the gloom, illuminating a tangle of cobwebs and a floor littered with dusty boxes and plastic bags.

She spied the chain dangling from a bare lightbulb and yanked it, flooding the space with light. Pleased that the old light still worked, she set aside her flashlight and crawled through the assorted clutter.

She opened albums that contained photos of her father when he was a boy, and set them aside to look at in her leisure. She hoped she'd find some time to show them to Cory, as well. He deserved a chance to see his father as he'd been when he was young and strong and reckless. Maybe there would come a day when she and Cory could go through these and actually share a few laughs together.

There'd been so little laughter in the boy's life. If she thought her own childhood dysfunctional, Cory's was even more so. A mother who was little more than a child herself, and a father too old to do the things most fathers took for granted.

At least she'd had her father when he'd been at the height of his strength and ambition. He'd been her big, strong, brave protector.

She opened a dusty wooden box and found a few feminine trinkets inside. A girl's hairbrush with butterflies on the plastic handle. A cheap bracelet with a rose that dangled from a small metal clip. A faded photograph of a man and woman standing very close together, while the man held a little girl in his arms. As Meg held the photo to the light, she could see the resemblance between the girl in the picture and Cory. The same smile. The same small, upturned nose. And the same scruffy brown hair.

Of course. This had to be Cory's mother.

Meg set aside the box of trinkets and moved on to another, larger box. This contained a child's spiral notebook. Inside, the pages were filled with letters of the alphabet, and the name Hazel Godfrey carefully printed at the top of each page.

Since the name was unfamiliar to Meg, she was about to ignore the box until she caught a photograph of Cory's mother half hidden beneath some old school papers. In the picture, the girl couldn't have been much older than Cory was now, and the name Hazel had been crossed out, replaced by the carefully printed name Arabella.

Intrigued, Meg began removing papers and notebooks from the box, and discovered that many of them bore the name Hazel Godfrey, while many more had been crossed out or erased, and replaced with the name Arabella.

There were pictures of the girl with other adults. Men and women, and occasionally other children. None of them bore any identification. And in all of them, the girl was unsmiling, often with her face turned away, as though distancing herself from the others in the pictures.

Cory had said that his mother grew up in the foster-care system. That might explain the unidentified photos of families, and the little girl who looked as though she never belonged.

Meg's heart went out to this stranger. This girl named either Hazel or Arabella. Or perhaps both. Could it be that Hazel Godfrey had changed her own name in order to give herself a new identity?

Whatever her background, she had apparently cared enough about these meager belongings to keep them.

Meg set the box aside with the other things, and continued opening yet more boxes, and examining the contents.

In one long box she found a carefully preserved wedding gown layered with blue tissue. Had it been her mother's, she wondered, or had it belonged to one of her father's other wives? She supposed there were wedding photos somewhere that would identify the bride who'd worn this particular gown. Not that it mattered. She had no use for it, and she doubted anyone else would, either. She set it aside and moved on to other boxes, and other family mementoes.

Several hours later, she gathered the things that interested her and placed them in a single big box before turning out the light and descending the stairs.

In the kitchen she made a pot of coffee and began going through the items in the box. Though she wasn't certain the things she'd collected belonged to Cory's mother, she was convinced enough in her own mind to add them to the pile of things she thought he might want to look at.

When she'd sorted through everything, she carried an armload of photo albums and memorabilia up the stairs to Cory's bedroom.

After setting them on his bed she turned and was about to leave when the framed photograph on his dresser snagged her attention.

Cory had said it was a picture of his mother and the boy named Blain.

As she studied the gawky teenage boy, Meg had a sudden flash of recognition. The cowboy who'd been sitting in the back of church the day of her father's funeral. Though she couldn't be absolutely certain, she felt strongly that he'd been the one. His face was older and tougher, and his body leaner.

His seat had been vacant by the time the service ended, and she'd all but forgotten him until now.

But she hadn't forgotten that feeling of being watched during the funeral service. That fingers-up-the-spine tingle that had been distracting while Reverend Cornell had been speaking.

She picked up the photo and started down the stairs. Tomorrow, when she saw Cory, she intended to ask a few more pointed questions about his mother and Blain. And this time she intended to get some answers.

The day had been a long and busy one.

As Jake was leaving for Meg's ranch, he motioned for his grandfather to follow him to the mudroom.

"What's up, boyo?" Big Jim leaned against the open doorway. "Where're you headed at this time of night?"

"I'm going to Meg's. I'm not comfortable with her being alone there."

"I don't blame you, boyo. She talks a good game, but a city girl so far from civilization, with no one close by that she can turn to in an emergency, is probably spending her nights shaking in her boots."

"I wonder if you could keep an eye on Cory."

"Sure thing. Is he spending the night in the barn again?"

Jake nodded. "The boy's troubled, Big Jim."

"He has a right to be. Both his parents gone, and a stranger his only kin. If that's not enough, there's someone out there who seems bent on destruction. That'd be enough to keep anybody awake nights, let alone a seven-year-old."

Big Jim dropped an arm around his grandson's shoulders. "Don't worry, boyo. I'll keep watch over the lad. I've been meaning to stop by and see how Honey and her puppies are getting along." He paused. "Now about you spending nights at the Stanford ranch..." He gave Jake a sharp-eyed look. "Just keep in mind that you're there to protect the lass."

"I will, Big Jim."

As he plucked his hat from a hook by the door, the old man cleared his throat, causing Jake to turn back.

"You were right about one thing, boyo." The old man grinned. "Meg Stanford is just about the prettiest redhead this town has ever seen."

Jake's smile grew. "I thought that might have slipped past you."

"I'm not that old yet, boyo."

His rumble of laughter followed Jake all the way out the door to his truck.

"Jake's riding shotgun again tonight, Clemmy." Big Jim stood with his hand on the headstone in the small plot of land just beyond the barns. It was a pretty place, with the summer breeze whispering through the trees, and a stone bench set to one side, so that Big Jim could sit and visit. Surrounding the tall grave marker were five smaller ones, decorating the graves of the five sons Clementine Conway had given birth to and then buried before each had reached a first birthday.

Big Jim came here almost daily to chat with his Clemmy and fill her in on the latest news regarding the family. Besides sharing news, he often left a plate of her favorite food or dessert, even though he knew it would draw the wild creatures to this spot. It pleased him to think that even the animals paused here to pay their respects.

"The boy's falling hard, Clemmy. I'm not sure he knows it yet, nor does she. But when I see them together, I see us." He chuckled. "We were just as young and randy, and just as brick stupid about love. But it was the real thing, darlin', and I thank heaven every day for you."

A small figure stepped out of the shadows and peered at Big Jim as though he'd just sprouted two heads. "Who're you talking to?"

Big Jim looked over to see Cory walking toward him. "My wife, Clementine." He patted the headstone. "I buried her and my five sons here many years ago."

"And you talk to her?"

"I do, boyo. Just about every evening."

The boy's eyes grew round. "What do you tell her?"

"How my day went. Anything that's bothering me. All the good—and bad—things that happened. All the things I shared with her when she was alive."

"Why?"

Big Jim motioned toward the stone bench, and Cory followed him over. When they were both settled Big Jim looked toward the headstone. "I shared everything with Clemmy when she was living, and it just makes me happy to share things with her now. In my eyes, she's never been gone. She's just...not visible to others."

"Do you see her?"

Big Jim nodded. "In my mind, she hasn't changed a bit. She's still the prettiest girl in all of Wyoming. And the best thing is, she never grows older." He studied the little boy. "How about you, boyo? Can you see your mama in your mind?"

Cory nodded.

"Can you still hear the sound of her voice?"

Cory stared down at the ground and swallowed. "Yeah."

"In my day, we said 'yes, sir.'" Big Jim laid a hand on the boy's shoulder. "I bet your mama told you that."

"Yeah...yes, sir."

Big Jim smiled. "Women are God's special gifts to us, boyo. They deserve to be cherished. Oh, I know they're strong and capable and willing to do whatever they have to do to take care of us. But men, good men, recognize that they also need to be taken care of and treated like the treasures they are. We always have to put their safety ahead of our own." He stared at the head-stones. "Women are responsible for life, and they have this deep core of goodness and reason that they pass on to each generation. Sometimes, when we find ourselves in trouble, or we feel like doing foolish things, we need to listen to their voices in our heads, telling us to do the right thing."

Cory looked over. "You mean our conscience?"

Big Jim arched a brow. "That's a mighty big word for a little boy."

"Jake talked about it."

"Did he now?"

"Uh-huh. And my mama talked about it, too."

Big Jim smiled. "That's good, boyo. As you go through life, always listen to your conscience. You do that, you won't go wrong. As long as you do things for the right reasons, they'll work out."

The old man got slowly to his feet and the boy did the same.

As they passed the headstones, Big Jim paused and rubbed a big hand over the edge of the tallest one. "Good night, Clemmy. I'll see you tomorrow."

As they walked away, the old man set his hat on his head, and Cory followed suit.

Big Jim paused. "Is that Jake's old hat?"

Cory nodded. "Jake said I could have it."

"Did he now? You must be pretty special, boyo. Jake loved that hat. His ma brought it back from a trip to Jackson Hole, and after she gave it to him, I don't think he ever took it off. Not even to sleep. His pa would sneak into Jake's bedroom after he was asleep and hook it on the bedpost. Jake would wake up in the morning and have that hat on before coming down to breakfast."

At his words, Cory walked a little taller, the smile on

his face dazzling. When they approached the barn, Cory paused and turned toward the door.

"You spending the night with your colt, boyo?"

"Yeah...yes, sir."

Big Jim smiled broadly. "Sleep tight then. And listen to your mama's voice in your head, boyo. You do that, you'll never go wrong."

With a thoughtful look, Cory let himself into the barn.

Jake turned out the lights when he hit the driveway leading to Meg's ranch. If the intruder was watching from the safety of the woods, there was no point in broadcasting his arrival.

Up ahead, the house was ablaze with lights. The sight of all those windows gleaming in the darkness brought a grin to his lips. Meg talked a good game, and he had no doubt that she wanted to prove to herself that she could bravely handle these problems without asking for help. But she wasn't about to do battle in darkness.

He brought his truck close to the back porch before turning off the ignition.

Setting his rifle beside him, he touched the button that lowered the back of his seat until he was reclining. He pulled his hat over his face to blot out the glare of the porch light and settled in for another uncomfortable night.

Not that it mattered. After the day he'd put in, first with Meg and Cory in town, and then seeing to the needs of half a dozen nearby ranchers—with everything from an injured horse that had required surgery to a herd of cattle that would have to be quarantined until the cause of their fever could be identified—Jake knew he could fall asleep anywhere. Even standing in a corner of a barn, with nothing but the rough boards of a stall for support.

It was his last thought before sleep claimed him.

Meg shed her filthy denims and tee and stood under the warm spray of the shower, scrubbing the cobwebs that had snagged in her hair. Wrapped in a towel, she made her way to her room and pulled on a pair of boxer shorts and a cami before blowing her hair dry.

The photo albums of her father in his younger days were neatly stacked on her dresser. She'd gone over every page, giving herself time to drink in the sight of him when he'd been a wild, reckless youth, in search of his destiny. It pleased her so much to see something of the man she barely knew. It was yet another side of the Porter Stanford that had been denied her.

She looked at photos of her father and mother together. The gown she'd found upstairs had been her mother's. The smiling faces peering at her from the albums had warmed her heart.

She descended the stairs and headed for the kitchen. Tea, and the last of Ela's corn bread, would be just the thing to take with her to her father's office. Though she was tempted to sleep in her own bed, she wanted to be downstairs in case the nighttime visitor decided to pay a call.

She thought about Cory's baseball bat residing on her father's desk. She hoped she wouldn't need to use it.

As she stepped into the kitchen, she caught sight of the truck's outline parked alongside the porch. Her hand leaped to her throat before she recognized it as Jake's.

It took her several deep drafts of air before her breathing returned to normal, along with her heart rate.

She filled the kettle and set it on the stove.

Then, because she couldn't bear the thought of Jake sleeping in his truck another night for her sake, she yanked open the back door and marched outside.

Jake was having a weird dream. Meg had followed Flora's cat, Nippers, into the diner's cooler and had somehow become trapped inside, and nobody could find the key. Flora was pacing back and forth from her kitchen to the counter and back again, worried that poor Meg and Nippers had already frozen to death because nobody could get to them.

Jake kicked in the door, only to find a second, stronger steel door barring his way. With Flora weeping and wailing, Jake started pounding on the door, asking Meg to knock if she could hear him.

He heard the faint knocking, and felt a wild surge of relief. She was alive.

Cory came racing up and handed Jake a key, which unlocked the door. Meg fell into his arms, and they embraced. But before he could carry her out of the cooler, the knocking started again.

Louder.

Then louder still.

He jerked awake and shoved his hat away from his face.

It took his sleep-fogged brain a moment to register the fact that Meg was standing outside his truck, tapping loudly on the window.

He opened the door and gaped at the sight that greeted him. Meg's hair was long and loose, spilling around a face devoid of makeup. She was barefoot, and wearing only a pair of boxers and a skinny little camisole that hugged every dip and curve of her body. Such lovely dips and curves, he thought with a sexy grin. Who would have ever guessed that the brainy lawyer hid such a luscious body under those very proper business suits he'd seen in the videos of the trial?

He actually had to shake his head to be certain he wasn't still dreaming. Was this Meg or a vision?

As if to answer his silent question, the vision shimmered and spoke.

"I said, why don't you come inside? I've got the kettle on, and I think there's still some of Ela's corn bread."

He snatched up his rifle and followed the vision up the steps and into the house.

Heaven help him. If he was still dreaming, he never wanted to wake up.

CHAPTER TWENTY-TWO

The shrill whistling of the teakettle greeted them as they stepped into the kitchen. Meg yanked it off the burner and set it aside.

"Tea or coffee?"

Jake blinked at her terse question. "Coffee."

"Fine." Meg started to measure coffee, but in her agitation she spilled it all over the counter. She tossed it aside in disgust and turned on him with a frown. "Jake Conway. You can't keep this up."

"What—?"

Before he could say a word she was across the room, jabbing a finger into his chest. "You can't do ranch chores and take care of other people's animals all day, and then spend all night in your truck watching over me like some avenging angel. Look at you." She paused to study him, from the lean denims to the plaid shirt with the sleeves rolled to the elbows. His eyes were still heavy-lidded from sleep, his lips curved in that killer smile that always destroyed her.

A jolt of pure lust slammed into her. Without realizing it, her voice softened. As did her eyes. "I mean, just look at you, Jake. You're practically dead on your feet. What am I going to do with you?"

"Point me toward a bed?"

Her anger deflated on a deep sigh. "Take your pick. There are three bedrooms upstairs, and all of them empty."

"Which one are you sleeping in?"

She nodded toward the doorway. "I plan on staying in the office."

"Okay." He draped an arm around her shoulders and shot her his sexiest smile. "I can manage that."

Her whole body tingled from his touch, but she was determined to ignore it. "I sleep alone."

"Fair enough. But it's what we can do before you fall asleep that takes two."

"Nice line, Conway. But it's not working."

"I must be losing my touch." He kept his arm around her shoulders as he inched her along the hallway. Once inside her office he paused to set his rifle in the corner of the room. When he straightened, he put both hands on her shoulders and turned her to face him. "How about a quick good-night kiss before I pass out?"

Her lips curved in the slightest hint of a smile. "You're good, Conway. And very clever. But I'm not falling for any of your tired lines."

"I forgot." He slapped a hand to his forehead. "You're that jaded, big-city lawyer who's heard it all before. Let's see if I can come up with something new and unusual."

His hand snaked out, catching her by surprise. "How about this?"

Before she could form a response he dragged her close and kissed her long and slow and deep.

It wasn't just a kiss. It was an invasion of all her senses. She couldn't think when he was kissing her like this. Couldn't seem to make her mind function at all. Her brain cells were slowly turning to mush.

The kiss softened to an invitation she couldn't refuse. She had no choice but to return it with an invitation of her own.

Jake drew her fractionally closer, changed the angle of his head, and kissed her again, all the while backing her across the room until they abruptly bumped into the wall.

As they slowly surfaced, he plunged his fingers into her hair, combing it back and staring deeply into her eyes. Eyes that looked as dazed as he felt.

"Conway—"

"I know. Too rough. I'm sor—"

She pressed a finger to his lips. "Jake, I'm trying to tell you—"

"I know. I need to head upstairs. Just give me a min—"

She framed his face with her hands and forced him to look at her. "Shut up and kiss me, cowboy."

"But—"

"Right now."

"Yes, ma'am." He gathered her into his arms and kissed her until they were both breathless. And then, for good measure, he kissed her again, slowly, thoroughly, pouring himself into it with such intensity that she was actually vibrating with need.

With her lithe body pressed to his, he could feel her in every part of himself. All the blood seemed to drain from his head to pool in a certain portion of his anatomy with throbbing insistence. And still the kiss spun on and on as they practically crawled inside one another's skin.

"I love kissing you, Jake," she managed to breathe inside his mouth.

"You call that a kiss? I can do better." To prove it, he ran nibbling kisses down her throat and buried his lips in the sensitive little hollow at the base of it before trailing hot, wet kisses across her shoulder to the tiny strap of her camisole.

With his teeth he drew the strap down her arm before moving his mouth ever so slowly across her collarbone to the other side to do the same.

The cami slipped free, baring her breasts.

When Jake cupped them in his palms, she made a sound like a half sob before arching her neck to give him easier access.

"Meg, you're so beautiful." His mouth followed his hands to caress, to kiss, to nibble and tease, until she felt her knees go weak.

She was frantic to touch him the way he was touching her. She reached a hand to the buttons of his shirt and nearly shredded it in her haste to tear it away.

With a laugh he pulled it over his head and tossed it aside before kicking off one boot and then the other. She had her hands at his waist and was about to help him out of his jeans when he managed it by himself.

She suddenly stopped and simply stared.

He had the body of a Greek god. All lean, hard muscles honed by a lifetime of ranch work. He was so sexy, so unbelievably gorgeous, he quite simply took her breath away.

She stood perfectly still as his hands moved over her, stripping aside her boxers and camisole, and dropping them at her feet.

Despite the sexy grin that curved his lips, his eyes were narrowed on her with such intensity, she couldn't help shivering.

"There's a sofa across—"

"Too far." He reached for her and dragged her against him.

"But the floor—"

"—will have to do." He was on fire. Every part of his body burned for her, and he knew that he had to touch her, taste her, take her, right this minute, or simply go mad.

His hands weren't quite steady as they framed her face before claiming her lips. His fingers tangled in her hair as he drew her head back and nearly devoured her with his kisses.

Meg's arms encircled his neck. She was as eager, as hungry, as he. With her hands in his hair, her fingers massaging his scalp, he could feel her little moans of pleasure as her body arched toward his, urging him to take her.

It was all the invitation he needed.

He lifted her, wrapping her legs around him, driving her back against the wall.

His hands moved over her at will now, savoring all that hot, firm flesh that was his for the taking. And he took, with a need that staggered him, feasting on the curve of her jaw, the soft, sweet column of her throat, and lower, to the full roundness of her breasts. He nibbled and suckled until she cried out and begged for release. He brought his hand between their bodies and found her, hot and wet, and brought her to the first crest. With her breath coming in hard, short gasps, he gave her no time to recover as he took her up and over yet again. And still he held back, keeping his own release just out of reach until he knew he could wait no longer. The beast inside him was fighting to be free.

There was no gentleness, no tenderness, in him as he drove himself into her. She responded with the same wild, primitive need, her body taking him in, closing around him, driving him half mad with desire.

They took each other on a frantic climb, and an even more desperate ride across the heavens.

When they reached the very edge of the world, they seemed to hang suspended in space until at last their bodies convulsed in a shattering climax that had them clinging together, their breathing harsh and ragged, their bodies slick with sheen.

Jake pressed his forehead to Meg's and fought to quiet his strangled breathing, his wildly beating heart.

As his world slowly settled, he continued holding her against him. He was grateful for the wall behind her. Without it, they might have slid to the floor.

"Sorry I was so rough."

She placed a palm to his cheek. "Were you?" She managed a dry laugh. "I guess we were both too greedy to take our time."

"If you'll give me a do-over, I promise next time I'll be slow and tender. You deserve that, Meg."

"A do-over?"

"Um-hmm." He nibbled her lips. "Slow and tender. Promise."

She pressed her mouth to his ear and almost purred. "I guess I could be persuaded. Would you like to start now, or do you need time to recharge your engine?"

He threw back his head and laughed. Oh, she was such a delightful surprise. If he'd expected haughty recriminations, or words of regret about their out-of-control lusty romp, he was oh so wrong. "Baby, my engine is always charged and ready. So if you've got the time, I've definitely got the energy."

"I don't know." She brushed a lock of dark hair from his forehead and allowed her hand to linger on his cheek. "I really liked you hot and fast. It was what we both needed. But now that we've fed the hard edge of hunger, I guess I'd be willing to see just how a cowboy does it when he's feeling all slow and mellow."

"Why, ma'am," he said in his best lazy drawl, "you're just full of surprises tonight. I do believe I can do slow and mellow, and any other way that you'd like it."

She was laughing as he carried her across the room and lowered her to the sofa. And then, before she could say a word, he dropped feather-light kisses over her face, her neck, her collarbone, before dipping lower to tease her already sensitized breasts ever so softly with the tip of his tongue.

When he moved lower, to the soft skin of her stomach and thighs, she found herself falling back against the cushions, too steeped in pleasure to do more than purr little murmurs of appreciation.

With soft sighs and tender kisses, as though he had all the time in the world, he took her away from all the cares and worries that had plagued her these last days, from all that was familiar, to a place so sweet, so rich in sensual delight, all she could do was try to follow where he led.

It was a journey neither of them would ever forget.

"What's this?" Meg awoke to find Jake, wearing nothing but his denims unsnapped and riding low on his hips, sitting on the edge of the sofa, holding a steaming mug of coffee.

"The coffee you promised me hours ago."

With a laugh she sat up and tossed aside the afghan, only to find herself naked. "I seem to have lost my clothes."

"I had the same problem. Some damned clothes gnome must have come sneaking in while we were otherwise occupied. There were clothes scattered everywhere. It looked like some kind of war was fought in here."

Still laughing, she said, "Really? Who won?"

He gave her a knowing smile. "I don't know about you, but I woke up feeling like a winner."

"Same goes for me." She picked up his shirt from the arm of the sofa where he'd just tossed it and slipped it on before reaching for his coffee. "Are you going to share?"

"You bet." He watched as she took a long, soothing drink. "After what you so generously shared with me, I figured it was only fair that I make the coffee and share it."

She handed back the mug. "How long have I been asleep?"

"A couple of hours. It's almost three in the morning."

"I don't think I've slept this soundly since I got here. So, thank you."

"It's my pleasure, ma'am." He set aside the coffee and took her hand in his. "Speaking of pleasure..." He kept his eyes steady on hers. "So far we've tried fast and slow, passionate and gentle. Is there anything else you'd care to do while I'm here to serve you?"

Meg gave a delighted laugh. "There is one thing we haven't tried yet."

"Name it and it's yours."

Her laughter grew. "We haven't yet shared a bed."

"A bed? Now there's a novelty."

She was still laughing as he scooped her up and headed for the stairs.

"Your wish is my command, ma'am."

He kicked in the door to her bedroom and carried her across to the bed where he deposited her gently before shucking his jeans and lying beside her.

"Hold me, Jake." Meg curled into his arms and wrapped herself around him.

"You feel so good here, Meg. So right." He brushed kisses across her forehead, over her cheeks, to the tip of her nose, to the corner of her mouth, and finally to her waiting lips.

"I have to admit, Jake. You feel just right, too." Meg sighed and returned his kisses, softly at first, and then growing more urgent, more heated, as her body began responding to the touch of his hands, the press of his body against hers.

As though a switch had been thrown, they went from slow and easy to avid and hungry in an instant.

They came together in a firestorm of passion.

Meg lay in Jake's arms and watched the first blush of morning light begin to color the sky outside the window.

She felt slightly dazed by the intensity of their love-making.

She'd known, of course, that sooner or later she would give in to the temptation to taste the forbidden fruit this cowboy had been so blatantly offering since they first met. What she hadn't expected was how he would make her feel.

Special. Cherished.

She knew she was fooling herself, thinking that this was anything more than a romp in the hay with a notorious ladies' man. Everyone from Flora and Dora at the diner, to his own sisters-in-law, teased him unmercifully about his attraction to women. Maybe he'd simply perfected the art of seduction, and she would end up being just another of his one-night stands.

She knew she shouldn't be fooled by his aw-shucks-ma'am act. But the truth was, she found him charming, funny, and downright irresistible. And if she was being a fool, at least for now she would revel in it.

She'd never felt this good. Never. And right now, she felt like shouting it to the rooftops.

Jake Conway was the world's greatest lover. And she wanted to store up all the loving he was willing to give, so that on long, cold, lonely nights back in her town house, working on the latest earth-shattering trial that would demand every ounce of her energy, she could revisit this night in her mind, and enjoy once again the special way he'd made her feel all night.

She knew better than to believe in happily-ever-after. But if she couldn't have forever, at least for now she would treasure the special way this cowboy made her feel.

She saw his eyes open and fasten on her. Until now she hadn't noticed that his eyes were the color of dark chocolate, and there was always a glint of humor in them. Up close, she could see herself reflected in them, and it made her throat ache with unexpected need.

"'Morning, gorgeous redhead."

"'Morning, sexy cowboy."

He touched a finger to her mouth. "I hope I have something to do with that smile."

"You have everything to do with it."

"Good." He stretched, before wrapping his arms around her and dragging her closer. "Let's find another reason to smile."

She offered her mouth like a banquet and shivered at the thought of what was to come. "I thought you'd never ask."

CHAPTER TWENTY-THREE

Meg and Jake stepped from the shower together, looking thoroughly sated, and began to towel themselves.

With the towel draped around her, Meg sat on the edge of the bed and began running a comb through her wet hair.

"Let me do that." Jake tied his towel around his waist before taking the comb from her hand and combing it through the thick red tresses.

He gave a murmur of approval. "Even wet, your hair feels like silk."

Meg wondered if he knew how purely sensual it felt to have him combing her hair. It wasn't something she'd ever let a man do before, and though they'd shared the most intimate acts during the night, this wasn't something she'd have expected a rough rancher like Jake to want to share.

Then again, Jake Conway wasn't like any man she'd

ever known. He was full of surprises. Silly and irreverent, he constantly made her laugh. But he was also thoughtful and bright and respectful, in his own unique way.

Unique. It was the singular word she would use to describe Jake. A one-of-a-kind man who had come into her life when she'd least expected him. He was tough, as only a Wyoming rancher could be. In a fight, she would definitely want him on her side. But she'd watched him connect with Cory in a way that showed him to be compassionate and tender. Two traits she'd never have expected from a guy who looked like Jake.

She was sorry they couldn't have met under more ordinary, relaxed circumstances. Maybe then they could have moved along at a slow, leisurely pace, and actually built a relationship. As things stood now, the turmoil of her current situation made it impossible for her to think beyond today.

She was so deep in thought, she wasn't aware of the sigh that escaped her lips.

Hearing it, Jake set aside the comb and moved his hands to her shoulders, where he kneaded and massaged the tight knots of tension he could feel there.

She dipped her head forward, allowing the warmth of his touch to seep into her bones. "Oh, that's nice."

"Speaking of nice..." His hands moved seductively down her back. He glanced at the tangled bed linens. "There's still time..."

Meg laughed and got to her feet. "Conway, you're insatiable."

He stood and drew her back against him, pressing his mouth to her ear. "Are you saying that's a bad thing?"

She shivered and turned into his arms, lifting a finger

to his lips. "Not at all. In fact, it's a very good thing. But right now, we need to get dressed and think about morning chores."

"Am I hearing right? Who are you, and what have you done with Meg Stanford, Washington's toughest trial lawyer? Is this really you, talking about mucking stalls and riding the range? Have you suddenly become a serious rancher?"

She grinned. "Maybe it's contagious and I caught this ranching bug from you."

"Go ahead. Lay the blame on me. I've got broad shoulders."

She ran a hand up his arm and across his shoulder. "Yes, you do. Very broad shoulders. And the most glorious muscles."

He pretended to flex them. "I take it you approve?"

"I certainly do. Ranch chores apparently do very good things for a body."

"Yours is already perfect." He wrapped his arms around her. "Come to bed and I'll make you forget all about ranch chores."

She sighed before pushing away. "You're getting way too sure of yourself, cowboy." She walked to the closet and pulled out a pair of denims and a simple cotton shirt. "I don't know about you, but I'm going to get dressed. I have tons of work to see to."

"Spoilsport. I think I liked the old Meg better." With a laugh he trudged down the stairs to retrieve his clothes.

When he returned, he was dressed, and Meg was just slipping her feet into sneakers.

"If you'd like we could—" At the ringing of his cell

phone, Jake paused to remove it from his shirt pocket. Seeing the caller's identification, he grinned as he said, "Hey, Big Jim. I was just going to suggest that Meg and I head over for—"

His voice faded and he listened in silence before saying, "I'll check right now."

At Meg's questioning look he said, "Cory and Shadow aren't in the barn. Big Jim figures they're probably riding over here. I'm going to check outside."

"I'll go along."

As they descended the stairs Meg was chewing on her lower lip. "I know Cory's just a kid, and a troubled one at that, but he should have let your family know he was leaving. It isn't right to just saddle up and go."

"Yeah. You might want to have a little talk with him." Jake threw open the back door and started down the steps. "I'll check the barn."

While he was gone, Meg circled around the ranch house, checking for any sign of Cory and his pony.

Seeing Jake returning alone she ran up to him. When she got close enough, she could see the frown on his face. "He's not here?"

Jake shook his head. "But he could be on his way. Big Jim said nobody saw him leave, so they don't know how long he's been gone."

Meg dug out her cell phone and punched in her brother's number. After half a dozen rings she looked over at Jake. "No answer. Now what?"

Jake shrugged. "I guess we'd better wait here for a while and see if he shows up."

Meg was gripping her hands together tightly. "And if he doesn't?"

"Hey now." Jake closed a hand over hers. "Let's not borrow trouble. He's a kid. They do dumb, careless things."

She nodded. "I know. But why would he take off without telling anybody?"

"We'll deal with that later. For now, I'll let my family know that we're going to hang here for a while longer and wait for him to join us."

They waited more than an hour.

To pass the time, Jake suggested they clean Shadow's stall and have it ready with grain and water.

When they'd finished, they took a turn around the house and even walked to the high meadow, but there was no sign of Cory. Jake phoned his ranch to see if the boy had returned.

He and his grandfather exchanged a quick conversation before Jake dropped his phone into his pocket and said to Meg, "No sign of him there, either. Big Jim thinks it's time to call Everett Fletcher."

He saw fear dart into her eyes as she put a hand on his arm. "Are you thinking something bad has happened to him? Do you think he's been kidnapped?"

"I didn't say that." He caught her hand in his and led her toward his truck. "But Big Jim thinks we shouldn't waste any more time. Even if Cory's just off for a joyride with Shadow, it's better to be safe than sorry. I told my grandfather I agree with him. He's phoning the police chief."

The ride to the Conway ranch was the longest of Meg's life. She and Jake sat in complete silence, but it was clear that their minds were twisting and turning around the fact that a seven-year-old boy wasn't where he ought to be.

She refused to allow herself to think the word *missing*. It was too ominous. And even more so, when she thought about the fact that the Conway family had been living with that word for a lifetime.

Jake and Meg pulled up just as Everett Fletcher stepped from his police vehicle. They were met by the entire family, who spilled out onto the back porch as soon as they arrived.

"Okay." Chief Fletcher had his notebook in hand. "Give it to me from the beginning. What do you know for certain?"

"I walked with Cory to the barn last night." Big Jim's tone was rough with emotion. "He saw me at Clemmy's grave, and we spent a few minutes there before I headed up to the house and he went inside the barn."

"What did the two of you talk about?" Everett said.

Big Jim pursed his lips. "Death. Talking to those who have left this world. Our conscience. I admired Jake's hat that he'd given to the boy. Just...things."

"Did he say anything about leaving?"

Big Jim shook his head sadly. "Not a thing. We said good night, and I went up to the house. On my way there I asked Manning in the bunkhouse to check on him. He claims he saw the boy shortly after midnight, asleep in his bedroll in Shadow's stall. Honey and her puppies were asleep as well. No sign of any trouble at all."

The old man's tone deepened with anger. "This morning, the stall was empty. Cory and his colt gone. Honey and the puppies had been fed and watered, so I know he saw to his chores before taking off. Nobody heard Honey barking, so we don't think any strangers were involved in this."

Chief Fletcher turned to Meg. "Your ranch is the nearest neighbor. Any sign of the boy?"

She shook her head, fighting a sudden welling of tears. "My place is miles from here. Chief, he's only seven."

"But he grew up here. He knows the countryside." Jake kept an arm around her shoulders while he added, "Before leaving, we checked the barns and pastures, Everett. No sign of him or Shadow. We waited an hour before heading here. That was plenty of time for a horse to cover the distance."

"Where would he go?" Meg asked. "And why?"

"All right now. Let's not get ahead of ourselves." The police chief tucked away his notebook. "He may be gone, but we don't know that he's in any danger. After all, it appears that he left of his own free will, and that means we ought to assume he and his colt are safe, for the moment."

He turned. "Let's start in the barn. I'd like to see the stall, have a look around, just to be sure there aren't signs of a forced entry."

Everyone trooped after him.

Clayton Manning, the wrangler who had checked on Cory, was summoned to give his statement to the chief. He repeated what had already been told by Cole.

Everett listened before asking, "And you checked again around five this morning?"

"Yes, sir. I saw that the stall was empty, and the boy and his horse were gone. Just then Big Jim came walking in, and I told him what I'd found. It was Big Jim who noticed that Honey's food and water had been taken care of, so we figured the boy hadn't been gone very long."

Big Jim added, "The water was still cold from the faucet."

Clayton Manning nodded. "Big Jim had me scour the west pasture, while he took the east, with Josh and Quinn taking the north and south."

"And none of you found a thing?"

Jake stalked over to the stall and noted that the bedroll still lay where the boy had left it. He idly picked it up to toss over the rail when he heard something fall into the hay. As he rummaged around, he found Cory's cell phone.

His shout had the others racing over to gather around.

"See if he had any incoming or outgoing calls," Everett Fletcher ordered.

Jake scrolled through and held it up for the police chief to read.

"A text," he announced. He read it aloud.

One hour. Or else

The chief snatched the phone and noted the number of the person who'd sent the text. Then he removed his own cell phone from his pocket.

His tone was crisp and businesslike as he spoke. "Everett Fletcher here, up in Paintbrush. We have a possible incident on the Conway ranch. I'd appreciate some information on a cell phone number, and possibly some backup."

He walked some distance away, speaking into the phone in crisp tones.

When he hung up he returned to where the others were standing together. "We can count on help from the state police. They're checking now on the number where the text message originated."

He paused to place a beefy hand on Meg's shoulder. "We're going to find your little brother, Miss Stanford. You just keep on holding a good thought."

"I'll try. Thank you, Chief."

While the others began following him from the barn, Meg remained behind, biting her lip while deep in thought.

Reaching for her cell phone, she called a number on her speed dial.

"Raven? Meg Stanford here. I have an important case that needs your expertise. How many operatives can you spare?"

She listened, then gave him what little information she had before ringing off.

Minutes later, looking grim and thoughtful, she joined the others.

It was a somber group that gathered around the kitchen table.

Even after the time they had already put in combing the pastures for Cory, they had no appetites. Phoebe's omelets lay untouched. Even Ela's corn bread failed to entice them.

Meg sipped strong, hot coffee and brooded. "The tone of that text was way too frightening. 'One hour or else.' Why would Cory agree to meet someone who was threatening harm?"

"Because he's a scared kid who doesn't know who to trust." Jake closed a hand over hers.

"Are you saying that he'd go to someone who threatened him, but he wouldn't confide in his own sister?"

Jake touched a finger to her lips. "I'm saying that we don't know the nature of this threat. Maybe Cory thought doing what he was told was better than the alternative."

"Why couldn't he have opened up to someone? If not to me, then to someone here? Can't he tell the difference between someone who loves him and someone who means him harm?"

Jake's tone was unusually gentle. "Would any of us have known the difference at the age of seven?"

The others around the table remained silent.

Meg shook her head. "But why? What would make a little boy go to the very person who was threatening him?"

The others shrugged.

"Desperation?" Sierra pushed aside her plate. "Before coming here and finding out what family and love really mean, I trusted someone who threatened me."

Beside her, Josh closed a hand over hers and the two of them stared into one another's eyes.

"I trusted someone, too." Cheyenne's voice was hushed. "Someone who looked normal and even insinuated himself into my family. But he turned out to be evil and twisted."

Meg looked at the two young women with new respect. "And you both survived."

Cheyenne nodded. "And so will Cory. You'll see, Meg. This family doesn't give up on people. We'll all fight to get him back and to keep him safe."

Meg felt those damned tears again and had to blink hard to hold them at bay.

"Thank you. That means the world to me." She cleared

her throat of the lump that was threatening to choke her. "I phoned the detective agency in D.C. that our firm often uses on special, hard-to-resolve cases. They're considered the best in the business. They're sending a couple of operatives via private plane."

Cole arched a brow. "That has to be pretty pricey."

"I don't care about their fee." Meg glanced around at the others. "They're worth every cent. I've never known them to fail when we needed quick, efficient information on impossible situations."

Big Jim looked at her. "You don't trust Chief Fletcher and the state boys?"

"I *do* trust them, Big Jim. But they have to play by certain rules. I've learned, when dealing with criminal cases, that while the authorities' hands are tied, private detective agencies are free to gather intelligence without those legal restraints. That can make a huge difference, since criminals never play by the rules."

"You've got a point, young lady." Big Jim drained his coffee and shoved away from the table. "I think as we go about our chores, we should keep our eyes and ears open. And maybe, if we're lucky, we won't need the police or private detectives. Maybe Cory will just come back to us before the day is over."

"From your lips, Dad." Cole paused to squeeze Meg's shoulder. Leaning close he murmured, "Just remember that all of us here know what you're going through, Meg. We've been where you are now."

At his quiet words, the first tears slid from beneath her lids and rolled down her cheek.

Mortified, she brushed it aside and took several deep, calming breaths. She was not going to dissolve into a puddle of helplessness. Not while Cory was somewhere out there, in need of her strength.

Not when she was with a family that had seen someone they loved disappear without a trace. A strong, determined family that continued to survive and stand tall despite their unspeakable heartache.

How could she do less?

CHAPTER TWENTY-FOUR

Meg saw Jake field a phone call and shake his head before pausing to nod. As she walked closer she could hear him.

"Of course I'll come right over, Mel. Don't you worry."

He glanced at her before saying, "Sorry. A rancher with an emergency. I'm the only vet in the area, and he's worried sick."

"You have to go, Jake." She caught his hand. "Life doesn't stop just because we have something awful happening." She took a breath. "I'm sure you and your family had to learn that painful fact the hard way."

"Yeah." He gave her a smile. "Thanks for understanding. I won't be gone long. As soon as I get back, I'll join Pa and Big Jim and my brothers out in the pastures."

She matched her steps to his as he started toward his

truck. "I'm not staying here, Jake. You can drop me at my ranch."

"I don't think you ought to be there alone."

"I'll be fine." She glanced at her watch. "Raven said the plane will be putting down shortly. He and his operatives will be at my ranch in the next hour or two. That will give me time to ride up to the high country and talk to Yancy."

"He already said there's no trace of Cory up there."

"I know. But he may know something we've overlooked. He's been my dad's foreman for a while now."

Jake nodded. "You're right. Okay. I'll let my family know we're leaving."

A short time later, as Jake pulled his truck alongside the porch at Meg's ranch, he called, "Keep your phone close. Call me the minute you hear anything."

"I will."

He watched her climb the porch steps before putting the truck in gear. He knew she was right. Life didn't stop during times of trouble. He had a job to do, and he had no choice but to leave her. But that didn't mean he had to like it.

Yancy Jessup saw Meg's horse approaching and rode across the field to meet her. In his eyes was a look of understanding.

He lifted his hat in a courtly greeting. "Any word on Cory, ma'am?"

"Nothing. I was hoping you might have thought of something that we've overlooked."

The old cowboy shook his head sadly. "Sorry, ma'am. I don't claim to know much about the lad. He stuck close to his ma and Porter. Struck me as a good boy, though. Not one to go off and leave folks worried about his whereabouts."

"That's my thinking, too, Yancy. I hope you and your wranglers will keep an eye out for him. He..." Her voice trembled slightly and she was forced to swallow before saying, "He's had a lot of things happen to him in his young life. He's a very special little boy."

"Yes, ma'am. He is. We'll be extra careful to watch for him. And you know I'll call you if I should see or hear anything at all."

"Thanks, Yancy."

She rode home with the weight of the world heavy on her shoulders.

Will Raven had been a Navy SEAL, and the majority of his operatives had been Special Ops or Secret Service. Now working in the private sector, they had mastered the art of following a trail that was all but invisible to most professionals. No clue was too small or insignificant to ignore. Raven often boasted that when he finished with a suspect, he and his men would know the suspect better than his own mother did.

These private detectives had become, out of necessity, masters of disguise. In the city, they blended in with all the other professionals, clad in nondescript business suits and mirrored sunglasses.

Today they wore faded denims and plaid shirts and dusty boots, faces unshaven, giving them the look of wranglers fresh off the range.

Meg wasn't fooled by the clothes or the laid-back poses. While she and Raven talked quietly in the kitchen, there was a sharp-eyed look to his companions as they moved around the property and buildings that told her they were already committing every inch of her ranch to memory.

"Is this the boy?" Raven studied the framed photo Meg was holding out to him.

"This is the most recent photo of Cory. Sierra Conway is a professional photographer. She took it yesterday morning, in the barn."

It showed Cory, flushed and happy, surrounded by Honey and her puppies. In his hands was Trouble, the runt of the litter.

Raven removed his cell phone and snapped a picture of the photo before sending it to his operatives' phones.

"And this," Meg added, "was in Cory's room. It's a picture of his mother."

"Who's the boy with her?" Raven asked.

"A boy named Blain that Cory claims was in the foster-care system with her."

Raven followed the same routine, snapping a picture of the photo and sending it to the phones of all his operatives before he looked up. "Okay. Tell me about this."

Meg glanced at the photo of Cory's mother and Blain when they'd been two young, scruffy teens. "I don't know where they're from. Cory never said. He may not even know where his mother was born, or where she grew up. Apparently these two were traveling together when they arrived in Paintbrush, hoping to find work."

"How long ago was that?"

"I'm guessing it was eight years ago. My father's second wife had died, and shortly after that he hired Arabella to clean his house. Sometime after that he married her and Cory was born. Cory's seven now."

"So, the kid's mother and this guy in the picture were drifters?"

Meg shrugged. "I really don't know anything about them." She handed Raven the spiral notebooks. "I believe these belonged to Cory's mother. As you study them you'll notice that she's often signed the papers as Hazel Godfrey, but in most instances, that name is crossed out and replaced with Arabella."

"Sounds like Hazel Godfrey decided to reinvent herself."

Meg nodded. "That's what I think, too. But I have no clue about this Blain. Except..."

"Except what?" Raven's tone sharpened.

"I think he was in the back of the church during my father's funeral. I can't be certain. By the time the service ended, the pew was empty. But it's just a feeling I have."

"Okay. It stands to reason that he'd know your father, if the girl he'd been traveling with worked for Porter and later married him. Could he be related to our mysterious Hazel-slash-Arabella?"

"Cory said she had no relatives. But then, I don't know how reliable he is. He's just a kid."

"A kid who left the safety of a ranch before daylight and hasn't been heard from since."

Meg clutched her hands together at her waist.

Seeing it, Raven gave her a reassuring smile. "We're going to find him, Meg. And then we're going to get to the bottom of all of this."

"I know you will, Raven. You've never let me down before."

"That was business. All you had to lose before was a verdict in a trial. I understand the difference. This time it's personal. You have a whole lot more riding on the outcome. So just remember this: whoever persuaded the kid to leave doesn't have any idea of the powerful enemies he's just made. My team and I play for keeps."

Meg let out a long, deep sigh. "Thanks, Raven."

"Now let's talk about your father. I want to know his friends, his enemies, his life as others knew him, and especially his secrets."

Over coffee the two talked for more than an hour. During that time, Raven made an occasional notation in an e-mail, which he would immediately send to his operatives.

At last he stood. "Since your ranch was the target of a vandal, I'd like you to accept the hospitality of the Conway family for a little while longer."

"Why? What do you have in mind?" Meg asked.

"I'd like to use your place as a sting, in the hope of drawing our vandal out. I'll have one of my operatives drive you to the Conway ranch, so that your rental car can remain here, parked in the barn. I'll have a red-haired female moving around the house both day and night, in case our vandal is watching from somewhere nearby."

"You don't think binoculars will point out the difference between me and one of your operatives?"

Raven merely smiled. "You know better than to question our work, Meg. We're good at what we do."

She sighed. "Yes, you are. And you're right. I realize that this is different from every other time. I have a lot more at stake." She could feel the tremor returning to her voice and struggled to remain calm. "He's just a little boy, Raven. A scared little boy."

Determined to hold herself together she unclenched

her hands and turned away abruptly. "Let me pack and I'll be ready to leave in half an hour."

"Good girl."

He watched her climb the stairs before starting yet another e-mail to his people in the field.

When Jake returned from a nearby ranch, he was surprised to find Meg in the kitchen, surrounded by Sierra and Cheyenne, Phoebe and Ela. It was obvious from the tea cups and the plate of chocolate chip cookies fresh from the oven that the women had spent some time talking and bonding.

Jake's eyes lit with pleasure. "Hey, you. I didn't see your car."

She couldn't hide the pleasure she felt just seeing him. "Raven...William Raven, the head of the detective agency I've hired, wanted me to leave it at my ranch, in the hope of luring the vandal out of hiding."

"Good. I hope it works." He studied her face, seeing the worry and the weariness she couldn't hide. He wanted to hold her. Needed to. Instead, he had to satisfy himself with a touch of his hand to her cheek. "No word yet on Cory?"

"None." The single word nearly stuck in her throat. All through the long, endless day, she'd been on a roller coaster of emotions. Each time the phone rang, or someone came to the door, she'd felt a surge of hope, expecting to be told Cory had been found. And with each disappointment, she'd experienced a terrible hollow emptiness.

Her only salvation had been listening to the fascinating stories told by Jake's sisters-in-law, who had faced down their own demons recently. Cheyenne had recounted her threat at the hands of a sociopath who had been like a brother to her. Sierra then talked about the stalker who had tried to carry out an elaborate plan to steal her away to a foreign country.

As a trial lawyer, Meg had thought she'd heard everything. Betrayal. Embezzlement. Grand theft. Murder. But always before, the victims had been clients. These women had become her friends and most loyal supporters, and it helped tremendously just knowing that she wasn't alone.

"Well, you're in the company of some pretty strong women here." Jake winked at old Ela, whose face softened as she returned his smile.

"Yes, I am. I can't believe the things they've been through."

Jake helped himself to a warm, sticky cookie, before brushing a kiss over Phoebe's cheek. "Now that was worth coming home to. And so is this." He surprised even himself by leaning down to kiss Meg's cheek, as well. He didn't care who was watching. "Now I'd better shower and change. I smell like a barnyard."

As he walked away whistling, the others had gone completely silent.

Meg touched a hand to her cheek and wondered at the strange feeling of peace that came over her. As though, oddly, she'd come home. Silly, she knew. Home was thousands of miles away from here.

Still, as Phoebe poured more tea, and the women resumed their chatter, the feeling persisted.

While her whole world was in turmoil, and her fear for Cory a raw and palpable wound, a sense of calm came over her, as softly, as gently as the touch of a butterfly's wings.

She pictured Cory in her mind, riding up in time to join them for dinner. He would lead Shadow to his stall, take time to admire Honey and her pups, before joining them at the table to help himself to a big slice of Ela's corn bread.

He has to come back. Please, heaven, she thought fiercely. She didn't know what she would do if that scruffy little boy didn't come back and give her a chance to show him that she could be a real sister to him.

She wasn't even aware of the big, wet tears that were rolling down her cheeks, until the others gathered around her to gently hold her in the circle of their embrace.

CHAPTER TWENTY-FIVE

About time you got here, kid." Blain Turner stepped from the shelter of a stand of evergreens and caught the reins of Cory's colt before hauling the boy from the saddle.

Seeing him, Shadow's ears flattened, and the colt sidestepped quickly away.

Blain tugged roughly on the reins, and Cory reached out to soothe and quiet the colt.

"Did you tell anybody you were coming?"

"No." Cory swallowed hard. His erratic heartbeat could be seen beneath the thin T-shirt he wore with his dirty denims. Beneath Jake's hat his hair stuck out in wild tufts, and it was plain that he'd been forced to move quickly.

"Just so you don't try any funny business, hand over your phone." Blain held out his hand.

Cory reached into his pocket, before his eyes took on a wild, deer-in-the-headlights look. "I guess I . . . lost it."

Blain swore. "You'd better know the cell phone number of that sister of yours."

Cory swallowed. "I do."

Blain pulled out his own phone and held it in his hand. "Tell me the number. And be quick about it."

"What do you want with her? You said if I came you wouldn't bother her anymore."

"Shut up and give me her number."

"No. You said—"

Blain's hand shot out, slapping the boy so hard his head snapped to one side. "Give me her number, or next time it'll be your colt here. And you know what I can do to him."

"You said you wouldn't hurt him again."

"That's up to you. If you do as you're told, I'll leave your horse alone. If not..." He shrugged.

With his arm around Shadow's neck, Cory spoke the numbers. Blain punched them into his own phone's menu before tucking it back in his pocket.

"Let's go." Pulling himself into the saddle of his borrowed mare, he grabbed hold of the colt's reins, just to ensure that Cory couldn't turn tail and bolt.

Cory climbed on Shadow's back and was forced to hold on to the saddle horn while Blain urged both horses to move.

As they melted into the woods, Blain kept a firm hold on the kid's reins as his mind raced ahead to the next step in his plan. He considered himself an expert on always having a plan while being on the run.

It had started when he was twelve, living on the mean streets of Detroit, and found himself in juvenile detention for the first time. Over the next six years he'd been in and out of foster care, and had spent so many months in everything from military-style camps to lockups that he'd been labeled incorrigible. His rap sheet was longer than his arm and leg put together. Everything from petty larceny to breaking and entering to carjacking. By the time he'd aged out of the foster-care system he'd graduated to armed robbery, and he knew that his next offense would land him in prison. He was cagey enough to know that he needed a fresh start.

The fifteen-year-old runaway he'd met in juvenile detention was just the ticket. Hazel hated her abusive foster father enough to offer the use of his car if Blain would take her along. Three weeks and dozens of gas station and party store robberies later, they'd landed in Wyoming, ready for a fresh start.

Keeping a firm hold on the colt's reins, Blain turned his horse away from the ranch house in the distance and headed into the high country.

The shed was concealed in a cluster of evergreens, and far enough from the rangeland that no one ever came by. It had been closed up for years now, and though the roof was sagging and the floor rotting, it was sturdy enough to imprison one little boy and his colt.

When they halted, Cory turned wide eyes toward the man. "You said we were going away."

"And we are. After I take care of some business."

Cory swallowed. "You said if I came alone you'd let Shadow go. He knows the way back to the barn."

"Which is why I can't turn him loose yet. If he returned without you, we'd have the whole town out searching for you, wouldn't we? And we wouldn't want that."

"But you said—"

"Shut up." His hand shot out, catching Cory on the side of the jaw.

Inside the shed Blain Turner tied the boy's wrists and ankles, and then he led Shadow inside and hobbled the colt.

He nodded toward the door. "I won't be back until I have what I want. Until then, if you have to pee, you'll just have to wet yourself." His lips peeled back in a sneer. "Probably won't be the first time." His smile dissolved into a feral, steely-eyed look he'd perfected years ago when facing guys twice his size. "And just remember. If I find out you tried to be a hero, I'll slice you up and feed you to the wolves. And your sister, too."

"You said you wouldn't hurt her."

"That's up to her. She does what I tell her, or she'll be joining you."

"But you said—"

"I lied." Blain threw back his head and laughed. "Got that, kid? I lied. And you bought into it."

He forced the door shut and braced a tree limb against it. Then he mounted his horse and rode away.

He'd come across this hiding place while working briefly for Porter Stanford. This was where he'd kept his stash, and whenever he could slip away, he'd spend hours getting high. The pay for wrangling a herd had been fair enough, he supposed. The working conditions good, if you liked living up in the hills with nothing but cattle to talk to. But once he'd persuaded old Stanford to hire Hazel to clean his house, the pay had been considerably better.

At first she'd manage to filch a pair of gold cuff links

and a tie tack that had brought a bonus at the loan shack in Crawford, a town two hundred miles from here. Twice she'd even found money the old coot had stashed in his kitchen drawer. But when she'd suffered guilt for stealing from an old guy who was nice to her, Blain had a better idea. Instead of settling for a few pieces of ratty jewelry or petty cash, she could have it all, if she played her cards right.

As Porter's wife, she would have access to Stanford's bank account. Even a stock portfolio, if the old geezer invested in stocks. And an entire ranch. Acres and acres of Wyoming rangeland, complete with herds of brown gold, which was what the hicks around here called their cattle. Herds of them, as far as the eye could see.

And all she had to do was agree to marry Porter Stanford.

It took some heavy-duty "persuading." Of course, Blain had to make sure that none of the bruises were visible on her face or arms, or Porter might have become suspicious. But in the end, she went along with it. And, as he'd promised, she became the person she'd always wanted to be. A respectable lady. Mrs. Arabella Stanford.

For a while it was so easy. Fifty dollars here, a hundred there. Enough drugs to keep Blain high and happy. The old man was so crazy in love with his new bride, he never even bothered to check his bank statements. But then, gradually, it all changed.

She said she liked the old guy. He was the first person who had ever been kind to her. And then there was the coming baby. The old man was elated. He acted like a proud peacock, strutting around, being extra generous to her. She decided she didn't want her old life anymore.

Or her old friend.

She stopped meeting Blain. Said she was sick. Then she stopped giving him money. Said the old guy was finding errors in the bank statements and getting suspicious.

Blain let it slide until the brat was born. Then he found her alone one day out behind the barn and let her know that she either got him money or he'd go to Stanford and let him know the truth about her.

He'd told her she'd just have to lie to her husband about the bruises. Tell him she'd slipped and fallen. Whatever it took. But at least the money started again. Just like he'd figured.

It started at a hundred a week. Then two hundred.

And then she'd up and died.

By then he'd lost his job with Stanford. No surprise. Once old Yancy Jessup had taken over as foreman, Blain found himself out in the cold. So he got a job fixing ranch equipment on the Mercer place, about fifty miles from here. But the lure of easy money kept calling to him.

There had to be a way. For weeks after Arabella died, he'd been mulling over the idea. Then one night, after getting liquored up, he decided he'd go right to the source.

And like he thought, after what he'd had to say, the old guy caved.

A thousand dollars. Just like that. Jackpot.

Stanford had said it would be a one-time payment, but Blain knew he'd back down. The old man would keep on paying because he couldn't afford not to.

And now the golden goose had died.

But it didn't have to be the end of the rainbow. The kid was his ticket to the big pot of gold. Time for the sister to step up. Unless she wanted to see the golden goose sacrificed for her greed. Because Blain Turner had an ace in the hole. And he wasn't afraid to use it.

He headed toward the ranch house in the distance. He'd watch and wait. And when the time was right, and Stanford's daughter had worked herself up into a frenzy of worry, he'd strike like a rattler.

"What do you have for me, Raven?" Meg gripped the phone like a lifeline.

"We have a couple of solid leads, Meg."

"Tell me."

"It's too soon. I'd rather wait until I have something concrete. But I can say that you were right about the boy in the photograph. His name is Blain Turner. Twenty-six. He aged out of the Michigan foster-care system at eighteen and took off for parts unknown. Hazel Godfrey was a fifteen-year-old runaway. I don't know anything more than that yet. But they both spent time in juvie. We're trying to find out if they were ever there at the same time."

"Why would he want to lure Cory away?"

"I don't have that answer yet, Meg. But it's only a matter of time."

"Time." Meg paced to the window of her room at the Conway ranch and stared out at the sun setting behind the peaks of the Tetons in the distance. "With each hour Cory is away, the clock is ticking. He's only seven, Raven. He could be lying somewhere, bleeding." Her imagination had been working overtime ever since this morning. "I've worked on too many criminal trials to fool myself into believing there aren't evil people out there, just waiting to prey on helpless little kids."

"Stop tormenting yourself, Meg. Just hold a good thought, and let us do our jobs. We'll get this bastard. I promise you."

"More than that, I want Cory safe. And you can't promise me that, Raven."

"No, I can't. But I give you my word, I'll do everything in my power to find him, Meg."

She gave a long, deep sigh. "I know you will, Raven. Has there been any activity at my ranch?"

"Nothing yet. I have a female operative inside, and several more watching from a distance. So far, nobody has come close. But it's early. I still think whoever lured Cory away will try to make contact."

When he rang off, Meg stood by the window, her hands folded as if in prayer. *Hang on, Cory,* she thought fervently. *Don't lose hope.*

Now, if only she could take her own advice.

Jake returned from his rounds, tired and sweaty and desperate for a shower and a cold beer. But first he wanted to find Meg and hear firsthand what she'd learned about Cory.

Just as he was stepping down from his truck Everett Fletcher pulled up behind him and climbed out of his police vehicle.

"Got any news, Everett?"

The police chief shook his head. "Some. I wish I had more. Is Meg inside?"

Jake nodded and led the way.

Meg was standing in the kitchen, talking softly with his family, when he and Everett walked in. At the sight of the chief all conversation ceased.

Meg stopped in midsentence to hurry over. "Do you have some news, Chief?"

"We've run a trace on your father's third wife. Judge Bolton said that Porter had asked him to file the necessary papers to legally change her name from Hazel to Arabella. Kirby's files show that her name had been Hazel Godfrey. She'd presented all the necessary documents before their marriage, but a check on them now shows they were very good fakes. The date of birth had been altered, because she'd been ineligible to be legally married in Wyoming without parental consent. Kirby had no reason to believe they weren't authentic, and he performed the ceremony in his chambers. The records we've uncovered show her to be fifteen at the time of the marriage to your father."

"Fifteen." Meg's breath came out in a long huff of disapproval.

"Kirby thinks that Porter actually believed her when she'd told him she was eighteen. He'd even joked at the time that he couldn't decide whether to marry her or adopt her. But Kirby said that all joking aside, Porter was obviously in love with the girl. It may have been a May-December affair, but they both seemed happy with the arrangement."

Meg drew inward, letting all these facts play through her mind. There was so much to take in.

Later, Phoebe announced that dinner was ready and invited the chief to stay and join them, and he accepted.

While the others filled their plates with roast beef, mashed potatoes, and garden vegetables, Meg moved the food around her plate, and sipped great quantities of tea, hoping to soothe her jangled nerves. How could she pos-

sibly think about food when Cory was out there somewhere, alone and afraid?

Sensing her nerves, Jake closed a hand over hers and
squeezed. She glanced over and caught his gentle smile.
Though she tried, she couldn't return his smile. Her heart
was too heavy.

She lowered her head, afraid that at any moment she
would break down and embarrass herself by weeping.

Cory wanted to cry. He'd figured that if he just came as
he'd been ordered, Blain would take him away, and that
would be the end of it. In his heart, the boy had thought it
was the right thing to do.

Meg would be safe. That was all he cared about anymore. He was sick of the lies. Sick of the threats. Sick of
all the death and pain and misery that seemed to surround
him like a dark cloud. He'd thought he could make it all
go away.

But Blain had promised, and now he saw that it had
been a lie.

It was all just a big mess. And it was his fault. All
he'd wanted was to make things better, and all he'd done
was make things worse. All of a sudden it didn't seem to
matter that everybody would know the awful truth. Something even worse was going to happen now. Blain was
still planning on hurting Meg.

The ropes that were burning into his wrists and ankles,
and the fact that poor Shadow was hobbled and miserable, didn't matter as much as the fact that it had all been
for nothing.

He thought about all the things Jake and Big Jim had
told him about following his conscience. But they were

wrong. Look what had happened. And all because he'd done what he thought was the right thing. But it was all wrong, and it was all his fault.

One big tear slipped from the corner of his eye, and he couldn't even wipe it away. It rolled down his cheek and dampened the front of his shirt.

He looked at Jake's hat, lying in the straw beside him.

He wanted Jake right now. He had a sense that if Jake were here, everything would be all right.

He felt a sense of guilt because he wanted Jake even more than he wanted his own dad or mom. But maybe it was only because they were dead and couldn't help him. Jake was big and strong and alive, and if only he were here...

He sniffled, wishing he could wipe his nose.

Oh, Mom, he thought. *I've let Jake down. Let Meg down. Let Big Jim down. I've let you and Dad down.*

He felt like the lowest creature in the world, lower than a worm, for all the trouble he'd caused.

And all because he'd wanted to do the right thing.

CHAPTER TWENTY-SIX

As he had often in the past, Blain Turner sat in the fork of the tall tree, which afforded him a clear view of the Stanford ranch house. Hidden as it was in the shadows of the forest surrounding it, he was able to see without being seen.

He'd been watching the woman inside now for more than an hour. She was sitting at the table with her back to the window, occasionally lifting a cup to her mouth.

Blain felt a tingle of apprehension. Why was she alone? Especially now that she knew the kid was missing? It didn't make sense. Where was Jake Conway? Out searching for the kid?

Blain decided to test the waters. He needed to keep her busy at the back door while he slipped around to the front and forced his way inside.

He composed a text.

Go to back door for a note from your brother

When he hit send, he waited to see her reaction.

The woman continued drinking her coffee. As far as he could see, she hadn't reacted to the delivery of a text to her phone in any way.

Meg was sitting in the great room of the Conway ranch, where the others were doing their best to keep her mind off her troubles. She loved them for it, even though her mind kept wandering to Cory. Where was he? Was he alone? Afraid? Hurt?

Big Jim was relating an amusing incident from his past.

"...driving the herd down from the high country when..."

She heard the ping announcing a text on her phone and snatched it up. When she read the text she let out a gasp.

Big Jim stopped talking. Everyone looked over as she read the message aloud.

"This text says, 'Go to back door for a note from your brother.'"

"That's good—," Cole started to say.

"Oh. No." Meg covered her mouth with her hand before quickly dialing Raven. As the others gathered around she put the phone on speaker so they could hear.

"Raven, the kidnapper has sent me a text. I'm supposed to go to the back door for a note from Cory. But I'm not there."

Raven's tone was firm. "This could be a trick, since none of my operatives reported seeing anyone near your ranch house, Meg. But just in case he's serious, text him back saying you'll need a minute to comply. I'll phone my decoy right now and advise her to go to the back door. If this guy tries to force his way inside, my operatives will be ready for him."

Meg sucked in a quick breath before texting:

Will do. Give me a minute.

Then she looked around at the others, seeing the concern on all their faces.

She sighed. "Please say a prayer that this is all a trick and they manage to catch him."

Jake closed a hand over hers and squeezed.

After receiving the text, Blain saw the woman answer her phone and nod her head before setting the phone aside. She sat a few moments before getting up from the table and moving away from the window. Scant seconds later the back door opened and the woman stood framed in the porch light, looking around for the promised note.

Blain tensed. The timing was all wrong. A woman frantic for news of a kidnapped kid didn't behave like this. She'd have been at the door in the blink of an eye.

He lifted his binoculars and studied the woman's face. She had red hair and was slim and young. But that was where the similarity ended. This woman, clad in simple denims, wasn't the pretty woman he'd observed in the past. This one was taller. And definitely not a knockout beauty.

Not Meg Sanford, but someone standing in for her in a sting.

He knew a thing or two about how cops worked.

With the high-powered binoculars he began scanning the area around the ranch until he located a man lying in the grass at the top of a hill overlooking the house. Scanning further he spotted a figure crouched beside the barn. Circling back he spied yet a third man at the base of a tree, nearly lost in the shadows.

Satisfied that he hadn't been spotted, he slid silently from his hiding place in the tree and slipped away into the surrounding woods.

As he made his getaway he felt the hot bile of fury rising to his throat.

Who did they think they were dealing with? Some half-baked amateur?

He'd show them. All of them. And especially the high-and-mighty Meg Stanford. Hotshot, famous trial lawyer, was she? When he was through with her, she'd be reduced to begging for both the kid's life and her own miserable life.

"Meg. Raven here."

Meg and the others had waited for what seemed an eternity for some sort of report. In reality it had only been a half hour or so. But the agony of not knowing had them all pacing.

Now they gathered around her phone to hear what he had to say.

"There was no note outside the door. Not that we expected one. We think he was probably watching the house and wanted to shake things up a bit."

"He managed to do that, Raven." Meg's voice was trembling slightly. "Do you think he noticed that the woman wasn't me?"

"Hard to say. If he was the cowboy at your father's funeral, he had a good look at your face."

"What do we do now?"

"He's holding the cards. We just wait to see what he does next."

"You're sure we'll hear from him?"

"He has Cory. He wants something in exchange. I have no doubt he'll contact you. Let me know the minute you hear from him."

She ended the connection and was just about to set down her phone when she heard the ping of an arriving text.

She stared at the words in horror.

It read:

You think you're so smart. You've just signed the kid's
death warrant.

Meg let out a cry before dialing Raven to read him the text. As she did, the Conway family let out a collective gasp.

Jake closed a hand over her shoulder and felt her tremble.

She drew in a breath before saying, "You realize that the decoy you set up has gone horribly wrong."

"Now, Meg, don't panic."

"Raven, your plan just collapsed. Now tell me what Plan B is."

He sighed. "I have people searching for the boy."

"Not good enough, Raven. This text mentions Cory's death. I don't believe this guy is just playing us."

"I don't think so, either. But you have to be patient, Meg."

"No." She bit off the word and took several deep breaths before saying, "You can afford to be patient. You're the professional. But we're talking about my little brother, Raven. I want you to step back from this and let me try my way."

"Tell me what that would be."

"I'm going to text this person and tell him I'll do whatever he asks. No more decoys. No tricks."

Raven's tone held a note of resignation. "That's what he expects to hear."

"Then you agree with me?"

"I'll agree that you should react the way he expects you to. If you text him saying you'll do whatever he asks, he'll demand money, and lots of it. And he'll demand that you meet him alone, with no police."

"I'm willing to do that."

"I'm sure you are. As I said before, for you, this is personal. But you pay me to stay one step ahead of the bad guys. And in this case, you have to listen to me, Meg. You go off thinking you can rush in where angels fear to tread, you could ruin everything. Do you understand?"

Meg swallowed. "I understand."

"Good. Text our guy and let him know that you're willing to hear his demands, once he proves that Cory is alive and well. Then call me with his response."

Raven rang off, and Meg looked around at the others. "It never occurred to me that Cory could already be—"

"Don't go there, Meg." Jake's eyes were as hard as

flint. "He's fine. I know he is. But Raven's job is to think of every angle. Now send the text."

Nudging aside the nagging fears that swept over her, she composed a short text and read it aloud to the others: "I'll do whatever you ask as soon as you prove that Cory is safe."

They nodded their approval as she pushed send.

Seconds later came the kidnapper's text:

You'll get proof in an hour.

Jake turned to his father and grandfather. "It sounds to me as though he isn't with Cory."

"Right you are, boyo." Big Jim swore softly. "He needs an hour to use his blasted phone to take a photo. That tells me he's stashed the boy somewhere. And since he had the boy riding out of here alone, it can't be too far. I'm betting it's either on our land or on Meg's."

The others nodded.

Meg was already dialing Raven. At his terse greeting she read him the text.

He muttered an oath. "That has to mean he doesn't have the boy with him." There was a pause before he said, "I'll have my men fan out. Maybe they can spot him heading toward a hiding place."

Jake reached for Meg's phone and she handed it over.

"Raven, this is Jake Conway. We believe he has to have Cory somewhere on either our rangeland or Meg's. Anything else would take him a lot longer than an hour to reach."

They could hear the rustle of paper at Raven's end of the phone. "My thinking, too, Jake. I'm looking at an overlay of the properties. The trouble is, it's so vast. And he could have stashed the kid anywhere."

"Not just anywhere," Jake corrected. "If you'll bring your map here, we can point out the places where our herds are grazing. He wouldn't want to take a chance on having his hideout discovered by our wranglers. So that will eliminate a lot of property."

Raven's voice was brisk. "I'm on my way."

By the time Raven arrived, followed by Everett Fletcher, Phoebe and Ela had made fresh coffee, and the kitchen smelled of sugar and cinnamon from the sweet cinnamon rolls they'd baked in order to stay busy. Even now, they were cleaning, scrubbing, to keep from wringing their hands.

The family gathered around the kitchen table, where Raven spread his maps of the countryside. With Magic Markers they carefully circled all the areas used for spring and summer grazing. They were still marking off sections of land when Meg's phone announced an incoming text.

The room went deathly silent as they gathered around.

Her phone's small screen filled with the image of Cory, hog-tied, lying in a nest of filthy straw. His colt could be seen, cruelly hobbled, behind him. Neither the boy nor the horse could move much more than their heads.

Meg's eyes filled with tears. "How can he do this? What kind of monster is he?"

While Jake placed his big hands on her shoulders, Raven faced her. "He's desperate, Meg. Desperate for money. And he'll do whatever it takes to get it."

Seconds later a text appeared:

Ten thousand dollars. Small bills. I'll tell you where
and when.

Raven's lips thinned. "Bingo." He nodded toward
Meg's phone. "Text him back that you'll need to arrange
this through the bank at Paintbrush tomorrow morning."

When she'd sent the text she looked up. "I wish I could
go into town right now and settle this. I don't care about
the money. I'll gladly give it to him if he'll free Cory."

"Of course you will. He's counting on that. But listen
to me, Meg." Raven's voice was eerily calm. "Once he
has what he wants, he'll need something else, as well."

She met Raven's eyes. "What's that?"

"He'll need to walk away from this without facing the
authorities. He wants to walk free. And that means elimi-
nating any witnesses who can identify him."

"I'll give him my word—"

"Not good enough, Meg. He'll want a money-back
guarantee. And there's only one way of getting that."

She blinked, before dropping her face into her hands
and softly weeping.

Raven looked around at the family standing shoulder
to shoulder, ready to do battle for Meg and Cory.

"We need to come up with a plan. Nothing elaborate.
Just something that will lead us to Cory in time to save
him."

Cole said grimly, "Big Jim and I can take up our plane at
first light. It's the easiest way to cover a lot of ground and
maybe catch a glimpse of this guy and his hiding place."

Quinn kept an arm around his wife as he said,
"Cheyenne and I are trackers. We'll hit the rangeland at
dawn and see if this guy left any sort of trail."

Josh and Sierra nodded. Josh said, "We can do the same. If we can climb the Tetons, we can certainly hike the hills around here without any trouble. We'll divide up the rangelands with Quinn and Cheyenne, and stay in touch by phone."

"That's all good." Raven looked at Meg. "But this guy's going to want you to come alone."

"I'll do it."

Raven nodded. "I know you want to, Meg. But first, there's the money he's demanded. A guy like him will want to watch, to see that you actually go to town and withdraw cash from your father's account. He doesn't want to open a suitcase filled with shredded paper."

He glanced at the police chief. "Which means that we ask the state boys to help us keep a watch out for this guy. I've already sent his photo to all my operatives, but the fact is, that picture is eight years old. By now he's probably changed his appearance. He might have grown his hair long, or grown a beard. If he's been working in the area, he's probably bulked up considerably. I had one of our artists do a couple of sketches suggesting how he might look now. I'll have her send them to the state police, as well."

Everett Fletcher nodded. "They can have plainclothes detectives all over the bank and town tomorrow. If necessary they can even act as bank tellers."

Raven shook his head. "This guy is probably familiar with the bank tellers. We'll want everything to look as normal as possible." He glanced at the clock on the wall. "We have time enough to set this up. I know it's foolish to suggest that any of you get some sleep. So I'll just suggest that you do whatever you can to calm your nerves until morning. I'm heading back to town to go over some details with my operatives and the state police."

Everett nodded. "I'm going with you."

The police chief turned to Meg. "I know the hours will crawl by until morning. But hold on to the thought that all of us are here for you, Meg. We're going to bring Cory home safe and sound."

"Thank you, Chief Fletcher. Thank you, Raven."

The two men nodded before taking their leave.

Phoebe put her arms around Meg and hugged her fiercely. "I know you don't want to hear this, but I think you should go upstairs and take a long bath and then try to rest. If you could fall asleep for even an hour, it will turn off the painful images in your mind."

"Thanks, Pheobe." She managed a weak smile. "I can't imagine not thinking about Cory. He's all I can think of. But I'll try to do as you suggest."

Jake caught her hand. "I'll walk with you."

She called good night to the others before allowing him to lead her up the stairs to her room.

Outside the door he drew her close for a hard embrace. "Do you want me to stay with you?"

She shook her head. "Thanks, Jake. But I think Phoebe's right. I'm going to try to just get through the night. I need to be alone for awhile."

He tilted her face up and kissed her. Then for good measure, he kissed her again. "I wish I could do something to make this easier."

"You and your family have been wonderful, Jake." She touched a hand to his cheek. "I've never known a family like yours before. I'm just so grateful for all of you."

He watched her walk away and shut the bedroom door.

A part of him wanted, more than anything, to stay the night with her and offer her whatever comfort he could. But another part of him wanted, needed, the release of hard, physical work.

He headed for the barn, determined to have it sparkling by morning.

As Phoebe had suggested, Meg took a long bath. Then, too agitated to lie down, she dressed in denims and a simple tee, pulled her hair back in a ponytail and made her way downstairs, hoping a cup of tea would help settle her nerves.

She was relieved to find the kitchen deserted. After setting the kettle on the stove she rummaged through cupboards until she located Phoebe's tea. Though there was every kind imaginable, she opted for plain black tea.

When the kettle whistled she began to fill her cup just as Cole stepped in from the mudroom.

"Can't sleep, Meg?"

She shook her head. "I'm too jumpy to even settle. I feel like I want to run across the pastures shouting Cory's name."

"I'd go with you if I thought it would help." He looked over her shoulder. "What're you drinking?"

"Plain old tea. Would you like some?"

"Yeah."

She filled his cup and handed it to him before sitting down at the table.

He dropped down into a chair across from her and spooned sugar into his tea. Without looking up he said, "The time crawls by. You look at the clock and want to scream because only a minute has passed since the last time you checked. And your whole life lies before you in tatters, everything you ever wanted is broken, and all you can do is endure."

"How do you endure?" She looked over at him.

"You just—" he shook his head "—do whatever you have to. Work until you drop. Lie awake in fear that if you sleep, the dreams will be even worse than the things you're imagining. And your mind never lets you forget. There's not a day, not a night, not a minute, that you aren't reminded that there must be something more you can do."

"Oh, Cole." She shoved away and circled the table.

He stood and caught her in a hard hug as she wrapped her arms around his waist and buried her face against his chest.

His cowhide jacket reminded her of her father's. He smelled of horses and leather and earth, all the things that she'd always loved about her father.

For one small moment in time she felt that her father had come back to comfort her.

"I can't stand thinking about Cory out there in the dark." Her words were muffled against his jacket.

"I know."

"How did you bear it?"

"I did it badly. I was too rough on my boys. Distanced myself from my own father. Avoided my neighbors. And I worked until I couldn't stand another minute. And still I raged against the doubts and fears and uncertainty."

He continued holding her until the tears stopped. When at last she pushed free of his arms he handed her his handkerchief. She wiped her eyes and blew her nose and sat down beside him, needing to feel him close.

"It's only been a day, and I feel like I'm going to explode. But it's been years for you."

"Twenty-five years, two months, and sixteen days."

Meg stared at him in absolute disbelief. "Oh, Cole." She caught his hand between both of hers. "How do you go on every day?"

"I have no choice. In the early days, when the pain was so bad, I thought about taking my life. But I had three motherless little boys to think about, and a father who had already buried five sons. How could I add to their pain? My own pain was nothing compared to theirs. So I moved ahead, day after day, hoping, praying, that the pain would ease."

"Did it?"

He shrugged and looked down at their joined hands. "Some days I can go for hours without thinking about Seraphine. Other days she's on my mind as soon as I wake, and she hovers there all day. As the years have passed, I no longer think of her as suffering, and that's a real comfort. I've convinced myself that wherever she is, it's a place that gives her peace. Otherwise, she'd have returned to me."

He patted her hand. "My dad always says that life hands the toughest assignments to the strongest among us. He claims that heaven knows which of us can carry the load, and which of us will bend or break. And he ought to know. Big Jim is the strongest man I know. He had to be, to bury a wife and five little babies and carry on with me just scant weeks old. But with Ela's help, he raised me. And when Seraphine went missing, how could I do less for my boys?"

Meg felt the tears threatening again. She shook her

head. "I don't think I have your strength, Cole. I'm not like you and Big Jim."

He lifted a hand to her cheek. "Trust me, Meg Stanford. You come from strong stock. You'll get through this. You'll do what you have to, and you'll get Cory back safe and sound."

She sniffed. "Thanks for talking about Seraphine, Cole. I know it had to be hard to do. But I need to remember that other people have gone through much worse things than this and survived."

He gave her a sad, haunted smile. "I'm glad I could help. And the truth is, talking about Seraphine didn't hurt as much as I'd expected. If anything, it just reminded me that I've been living in the past too long. The people who care about me have been patient, but it's time for me to step out of the shadows."

He leaned close and brushed a kiss on her cheek before heading toward the stairs.

When she was alone Meg looked toward the mudroom to see Jake standing there. From the looks of him, he'd been there long enough to overhear everything his father had said.

He walked closer and took her hand, helping her to her feet.

"You heard?"

He nodded. "I'm glad he was able to talk to you about her. I think it helped him as much as it helped you."

She sighed. "You have an amazing father."

"Yes, I do. And you are an amazing woman. Now come with me to bed."

They walked up the stairs to her room together.

CHAPTER TWENTY-SEVEN

The entire family was up and moving long before dawn, and it was plain that none of them had spent much time sleeping.

Meg and Jake came downstairs to find Phoebe and Ela hard at work in the kitchen.

Phoebe turned to Meg. "Did you sleep?"

Meg shook her head.

"There's coffee." Phoebe indicated a tray of mugs on the counter.

While Jake was pouring coffee he said, "I thought I heard Pa and Big Jim talking."

At that moment Quinn and Cheyenne came in from the mudroom. Overhearing Jake's remark, Quinn said, "They're in the barn running a check on the plane before takeoff."

Josh and Sierra came downstairs arm in arm. Sierra hurried over to hug Meg. "I'm sure the night seemed endless."

Meg nodded and accepted a mug of coffee from Jake.

Minutes later they heard the crunch of tires and the sound of an engine, and looked out to see Raven and Everett Fletcher arriving in separate vehicles. The two men strode inside and greeted everyone before accepting coffee from Phoebe and Ela.

The police chief spoke first. "It's all arranged with the bank. Judge Bolton contacted the bank president. As soon as the bank opens at nine a teller will have the money ready. You'll have to go through the motions of a regular bank transaction, in case Blain is watching from somewhere nearby."

Meg nodded. "I understand."

Raven opened a backpack and began removing several items, which he laid out on the kitchen table. "The state police agreed that you need to wear a wire."

"A wire?"

"This guy isn't stupid. He was wise to our sting at your ranch. He has to assume that you've gone to the authorities. His only hope is grabbing the cash and getting away without being caught. He knows we won't move on him as long as Cory is in danger. We're assuming that he'll choose an isolated spot to have you deliver the money. A spot where we can't plant our people ahead of time. But with a wire, we get two things. First, a tracking device. We'll know where you are every step of the way. And second, a microphone. We'll be able to hear every word he says once you get within close range of him."

Jake frowned. "You're thinking of letting her go alone?"

"He'll insist on it."

"And she can refuse. She can insist that I go with her."

The police chief shook his head. "Be reasonable, Jake. The last thing this guy wants is a big, strong cowboy getting in the way. Right now he thinks he's on easy street. A kid and a woman. And he's holding all the aces. He's never going to agree to let you come."

Raven nodded. "The chief's right. Meg will have to do this alone."

When Jake opened his mouth to argue, Meg put a hand to his cheek. "I know you're worried, Jake. I'm worried, too. But I have to do whatever he demands. For Cory's sake."

She turned toward Raven. "Let's get this wire hooked up to me. The sun's coming up and Paintbrush is an hour away."

Cole and Big Jim were airborne as soon as the sky was light. They used Raven's map and grids to check off each parcel of land as they swept overhead.

While Cole handled the controls, his father focused high-powered binoculars out the windows of the cockpit.

"Such beautiful land," Big Jim remarked. "Sad to think that somebody could spoil it with something as hideous as harming a helpless boy."

"In our lifetimes we've come across our share of evil," Cole muttered.

"So we have." Big Jim lay a hand on Cole's sleeve. "But the good we've seen far outweighs the bad."

"Let's hope the good guys win today." Cole touched the wheel, and the little Cessna dipped lower as they passed over a pasture dotted with Conway cattle.

* * *

Quinn, Josh, and Jake had been assigned the task of searching the rangeland around the Conway and Stanford ranches.

Chief Fletcher pointed to the picture of Cory. "You can see the straw, and a bit of an old wooden wall behind him. That means he's in a building. A wooden structure of some sort. I don't care how big or small or how abandoned it may appear, if it's got four walls, you need to check it out."

Quinn and Cheyenne headed out on their all-terrain vehicles for the rugged hills above the tree line of the Conway's north range. Josh and Sierra opted to hike the southern range. Jake took the western ridge of Conway land that abutted the Stanford land. Because of the tall grass, he decided to go by horseback so that he could have a closer look.

After he rode only a few miles the sun had begun climbing steadily over the foothills of the Tetons, filling the rangeland with light. On any other day Jake would have paused to enjoy the beauty around him. Today, all he wanted was to hold back the sunrise and slow down the hours.

Though it weighed heavily that he couldn't be with Meg, keeping her safe, he took comfort in the thought that if he could only find Cory, they could call off this dangerous game she was being forced to play.

Meg's hands were slick with sweat, and her heart was pounding as she walked into the bank in Paintbrush.

It all looked so normal. The tellers, sitting at their windows. A smattering of men and women going in and out, some standing at tables, filling out forms, others pausing to chat with neighbors.

Looking at them, Meg couldn't tell if they were operatives playing a part, or if they were actually innocent people, unaware of the terrible drama being played out before their eyes.

A young teller removed a closed sign and beckoned Meg forward. Meg handed her the withdrawal slip that had been prepared by Judge Kirby Bolton and the young woman said softly, "I'll have to clear this with our bank president."

Meg wanted to catch her sleeve and stop her, but the teller was already walking away.

Panic gripped Meg by the throat. Had she chosen the wrong teller? Was she making a terrible mistake?

The young woman spoke to the man in the office before returning to her station. With a smile she said, "Sorry. Bank protocol when there's a withdrawal of this size. And we always follow protocol."

"Of course." Meg ordered herself to breathe.

Obviously the teller had been briefed ahead of time, and knew that she had to play this by the book.

Minutes later she counted out the money in denominations of tens and twenties as requested, and offered Meg a heavy cloth bag. "You may want to use this, since that's an awful lot of cash."

"Yes. Thank you." Meg set the bag of money inside the oversize shoulder purse Raven had provided. Hefting the purse to her shoulder, she turned away.

Though she'd been warned not to call any attention to herself, she couldn't help noting the number of men on the street outside as she stepped out of the bank. Every one of them appeared to be busy, but she felt her skin prickling at the thought that all of them were there watching and waiting.

She hadn't taken more than a couple of steps on the sidewalk before she heard the ping announcing the arrival of a text on her cell phone.

Go to your ranch. Alone.

She climbed into her rental car, which Raven had provided, and began the long drive to her ranch. Along the way she spoke, knowing Raven and the state police could hear. "I've been ordered to drive to my ranch alone. Since the message came as soon as I'd left the bank, I have to assume he was watching. I hope someone has already spotted him."

A text arrived saying:

No sign of him, but you're not alone.

Not alone? She looked in her rearview mirror, and there wasn't another car on this stretch of deserted highway. Still, she had to believe that the professionals who had planned all this knew what they were doing. Besides, Raven had more than a dozen operatives already in place around her house.

As she came up over a rise, she had to stand on her brakes to keep from hitting a line of cows slowly crossing the highway. She could see a length of fencing down and the cattle moving with deliberation, following the lead cow. There was no telling how long this delay might last.

While she waited, she sat drumming her fingers nervously on the wheel. When a hand slapped her driver's side window she nearly jumped out of her skin.

A man in a plaid shirt and dirty jeans was turned away from her, watching the movement of the cows. With one hand he motioned for her to roll down her window.

She was smiling, expecting to hear a word of apology from the wrangler about this unexpected delay. Instead, when he turned, she sucked in a breath of recognition.

Despite the scraggly beard and battered Stetson, it was Blain Turner.

"Get out of the car now. And don't forget to bring the bag."

Blain was astride a bay gelding and holding firmly to the reins of the spotted mare on which Meg rode. By the time the long line of cattle had crossed the highway, the two riders had disappeared into a thick wooded area.

Meg knew that Raven would have overheard Blain's command to step out of the car, and she was comforted by the fact that his operatives were tracking her, but she could only hope that someone had spotted the cattle and had seen her leaving on horseback.

"Where are you taking me?" She needed to keep Blain talking so Raven and the state police could get a fix on them.

"Shut up."

"You'd better be taking me to see Cory."

He turned and pointed a gun at her head. The look he gave her was so dark and menacing, she felt her heart leap to her throat. "What didn't you understand about 'shut up'?"

She fell silent and struggled to breathe. Her heart was pounding so hard she was certain Raven and his men could hear it.

They rode deep into the woods before Blain suddenly stopped and slid from the saddle.

"Are we here?" She swiveled her head, straining to see some sign of a cabin.

"Shut up." He dragged her from her horse, tore the shoulder bag from her, and lifted his hands to her shirt. Without warning he tore it open, popping the buttons as he did.

"Are you crazy—?"

As the fabric shredded and fell away, the hidden wires were revealed.

"I knew it." With a vicious oath he tore them from her and stomped them into the spongy ground.

When she tried to resist, he slapped her so hard her head snapped to one side.

"Get on your horse."

"My shirt..." She clutched wildly at the torn bits of fabric.

"You're lucky I let you keep your bra. And if you open your mouth one more time, I'll rip that off you, too."

He boosted her into the saddle and grabbed up her reins before climbing onto his own mount. As they continued on, her heart fell. She was no longer in contact with Raven and the others. She was completely on her own.

With a madman determined to leave no witnesses.

They'd been riding through the dense woods for what seemed like hours when Meg heard the drone of a plane's engine, and looked up, hoping to catch a glimpse of the Conways' Cessna. All she saw was a glint of silver through the thick foliage before the little airplane made a slow turn and flew in the opposite direction. Soon the sound of the engine had completely disappeared. For some reason, the silence seemed harder to bear now that Cole and Big Jim had flown away.

Alone, she thought desperately. She was all alone now.

She was tempted to leap from her horse and make a run for it, but she was desperate to get to Cory. The thought of that frightened little boy was all that kept her going. She needed to be strong for him.

Blain slowed their horses to a walk as they picked their way through fallen trees and rocky terrain.

Up ahead Meg spotted what appeared to be a small wood shack, no bigger than an outhouse. Her heartbeat quickened. Cory. She would see Cory. And whatever happened after that, she would focus all her attention on keeping him safe from this monster.

The thought had come to Cory when he'd finished crying. He'd been staring at Jake's old hat, and thinking about Jake, wishing he would come and save him. That was when he caught the glint of Jake's lucky stone in a stray sunbeam that had slipped through the cracks of the old shack at sunset. With a faint flicker of hope, he'd started nudging himself closer to the hat.

Even when he was close enough to touch the hat, it had taken an hour or more to work the stone from the band. At first he'd thought he would just hold it. For luck. But then the desire to escape had begun to take shape. What if he could use the sharp edge to cut through the ropes that bound him?

He'd had to figure out how to position the stone in the hay so that he could rub his ropes over and over the sharp edge. It hadn't been easy. But a tiny crack in the floor had provided just enough of an anchor to keep the stone from slipping away.

At first he'd despaired of ever cutting through the rope. But when he'd finally felt that first small bit of fiber unraveling, hope had begun blooming in his heart. This was, after all, Jake's lucky stone. How could he go wrong?

The longer he rubbed the rope against the stone, the more he cut himself. His skin burned like fire, and by the time the rope finally gave way, his poor wrists were a bloody mess. But his hands were now free and he grabbed up the stone, working the sharp edge furiously against the rope binding his ankles.

He had no idea how long he'd been working on his bonds, but he could tell, by the pitch darkness in the shack, that it was nighttime. Blain had said he'd come back after dark, but Cory decided that since Blain had lied to him once, he'd probably lied about that, too.

By the time bright morning sunlight began filtering through the cracks in the walls and roof, Cory had managed to free himself and was working furiously on the rope that hobbled poor Shadow. Though he was desperate to escape this filthy prison, he wasn't leaving without his colt.

And then there was the brace against the door.

He would worry about that when Shadow was able to stand.

Blain had heard the drone of the plane and figured it was the state police. He expected to see plenty of frantic police activity in the next couple of hours. That was why he'd moved so quickly. He needed to get the money, grab the kid, and use the woman to carry the message that unless the police kept their distance, he'd waste the kid.

That ought to stop them long enough for him to get clean away.

He'd already stashed the truck less than a mile from here. Nobody would be looking for it, since it belonged to an old rancher who never knew what hit him. As always, Blain had found the perfect mark. A bachelor with no family and hardly any visitors. The old geezer could be dead for weeks before anybody found him. And even then, they wouldn't be looking for an old stake truck when there was a newer pickup truck parked in the barn right alongside the body.

He slid from the saddle and turned to Meg, hauling her roughly from her horse. When she lost her balance and fell to her knees he grabbed a handful of her hair and yanked her upright.

With his hand digging into her shoulder he gave her a shove and she staggered ahead of him toward the shack.

The door, though still padlocked, was swinging open on one rusty hinge.

Blain swore viciously and flung the door wide, filling the space with light.

The little shed was empty. A trail of blood spilled across the floor and out the door.

CHAPTER TWENTY-EIGHT

T he little bastard!" Blain was in a full-blown fury. The look on his face had gone from incredulous to mind-numbing rage in the blink of an eye. "If he makes it home, everybody will know about this place."

Blain saw Meg look hopefully toward the door.

"Don't even think about making a dash for it." He used a booted foot to kick her backward into the dirty straw. Picking up the bloody ropes that had bound Cory he began tying her hands behind her back. When he was finished he leered at her torn shirt, revealing a lacy bra and a great deal of bare flesh. "Too bad there's no time now. But maybe later."

He saw the way she shuddered and threw back his head and laughed. "Guess you're not so high and mighty now, are you, counselor?" His laugh turned into a sneer. "You're all the same. Strip away the fancy clothes and fancy titles, and you turn into weak little crybabies."

Meg sucked in a breath as he pulled the ropes as tight as possible, determined to hurt her, before getting to his feet. But his words had strengthened her resolve to show no weakness. Though the pain of her bonds was another jolt to her already overcharged system, she refused to cry or let him see just how desperately afraid she felt.

He emptied her shoulder bag and checked the money. When he saw the pile of tens and twenties, he stuffed it back into the bag and smiled. "At least something's going right. Now we have to get out of here and fast. And since the brat managed to escape, it looks like you've just become my insurance." He gave a mirthless laugh. "That's a good one. The big-shot lawyer has just become my stay-out-of-jail card."

Jake read Raven's message, which had gone out to everyone involved in the operation.

> All contact with Meg Stanford has been severed. It can only mean the wire was discovered. She and the boy are now at the mercy of a desperate criminal. We believe Blain Turner to be armed and dangerous. Proceed with extreme caution.

Raven's words had him desperate to find Meg and Cory.

He came up over a hill, his gaze sweeping from one side of the pasture to the other. He noted the dense woods and decided to ride closer. It could hide any number of wooden structures.

Before he could follow through on his intention, he caught a blur of movement out of the corner of his eye.

Was that a horse up ahead just cresting that ridge? He urged his own mount into a gallop, and as he made it to the top of the next hill he couldn't believe his eyes.

Shadow. There was no mistaking the colt. And on his back, Cory.

He knew there was no sense shouting. The boy and horse were too far ahead to hear, and they appeared to be riding like the wind. Urging his horse even faster, he began to slowly catch up.

As he came up even with the colt he reached over and grabbed the reins. Cory looked over, pale as a ghost, and seemed about to fight until he recognized Jake.

From the other side of the hill came a flurry of horsemen, and as Jake slid from the saddle and gathered Cory into his arms, he and the boy found themselves surrounded by Meg's wranglers, with Yancy Jessup in the lead.

"Where'd the boy come from?" Yancy remained in the saddle, staring down at them in surprise.

"I just spotted him." Jake felt the boy's small body shaking with nerves, and sought to soothe him by running a hand over his head and back. "It's okay, Cory. You're safe now."

The boy continued clinging to Jake's neck as though attached by Velcro.

Gently Jake eased Cory's arms from his neck and stared down into his eyes. "Was Meg the one who freed you?"

Please, he thought, *let it be so.*

Cory shook his head, dashing any hope. "I spent all night working on my ropes. I just got free now."

"Then you haven't seen Meg?"

"Isn't she with you?"

"She's with Blain Turner."

The boy's eyes went wide with horror. "He promised not to hurt her. But he lied. He lied."

"Cory, listen to me." Jake closed his hands over the boy's upper arms, seeking to still his protest. "If Blain doesn't know that you've escaped, it stands to reason that he's taking Meg there right now. Can you take me to the place where you were being held?"

He could see the sheer terror on Cory's face, and it pained him to force the boy back to that place again. But it had to be done. And quickly.

Cory swallowed. Nodded. "It's not far."

As Jake and Cory pulled themselves into their saddles, Jake turned to Yancy. "Do you have weapons up in the hills?"

The old man nodded. "Up at the bunkhouse."

"I need you to get all you have and follow our trail."

As he wheeled his mount, Jake called his father on his cell phone.

At the sound of Cole's voice Jake said, "No time to explain. Cory escaped. He's taking me to where he was held, since I believe that's where Blain is headed with Meg." He gave his father the approximate location, then ended by saying, "Call the others. Get them here right away. Especially the state police and Raven's people."

"It's in there." Cory brought Shadow to a halt and pointed toward the dark, dense woods. From their vantage point in the sunlight the forest seemed even darker and more menacing than ever.

"Good boy. I want you to stay here with the horses. If

you spot Blain coming this way, ride as fast as you can toward Yancy and the wranglers. And make sure you take my horse along, so Blain has no way of escaping, except on foot."

Cory's eyes were wide. "But aren't you going to stop him, Jake?"

"I will. Or die trying." Jake slipped his rifle from the boot of his saddle, wishing he had a handgun. He handed Cory the hunting knife he always carried. "Keep this with you. Just in case."

He turned away and started into the woods. Within a few hundred yards he spotted the shed. As he crept closer he could see that the door was wide open. There was no sign of life.

He inched close enough to see that the shed was empty. He was too late. A wave of bitter disappointment washed over him, filling him with a sense of dread.

He was about to turn away when a sound alerted him that he wasn't alone. Taking aim with his rifle he started forward.

When Jake was halfway there Blain stepped out from behind the shed. He was holding Meg in front of him like a shield. He held a small, shiny pistol to her temple.

"Well now." Blain's voice was oddly high-pitched with excitement. "Looks like I'll get a chance to test my little ticket right here." He waved the handgun. "Toss the rifle, or—" he gave a shrill, mad laugh "—you know the drill, don't you, cowboy?"

"Don't, Jake." Meg's voice trembled. "He's lying. You can't trust him."

"If you listen to the smart counselor here, she'll get to die before your eyes." He tightened his arm around her neck, cutting off her breath. "Or you can be smart and do as you're told."

Jake saw the way Meg clawed at Blain's arm, which only caused the gunman to tighten it even more until she went limp.

Tamping down on the fury building inside him, Jake tossed his rifle.

Blain loosened his grasp, and Meg began coughing and sucking air into her starved lungs.

"Stay strong, Meg." Jake's words, spoken softly, had her lifting her head to look at him.

"Ah, now, isn't that sweet?" Blain laughed. "She'd better stay strong. She's going to need all the strength she can find. This pretty little counselor and I are heading to Canada."

Jake glanced around. "By horseback?"

"Truck," Meg said. "He claims he stashed it a mile from here."

"Where'd you get the truck?" Jake was desperate to distract Blain by getting him to talk.

"Borrowed it from a rancher who didn't have any use for it. Since he's dead." Blain couldn't help boasting. "Speaking of dead..." He gave Meg a rough shove that had her dropping to one knee. "Kick that rifle over here."

With her hands bound behind her back, Meg stumbled to her feet and kicked at the rifle.

Jake waited until Blain bent over to retrieve it. Using that moment of distraction he shoved Meg out of the way and made a dive for the gunman.

His timing was a second off. Blain's gun fired just as Jake reached for his hand.

Blood spurted from Jake's shoulder. Fighting the pain,

Jake knocked the pistol from Blain's grasp. It fell to the ground and the two rolled over and over, fighting for control of his weapon.

Cory heard the sound of the gunshot and his little body jerked in a spasm of terror. Had it been Jake's rifle discharging? Or Blain's gun?

He stood perfectly still, frozen to the spot, unable to go or to stay.

If he went into the woods and only Blain was left, he'd be walking right into a trap. But how could he stay here without knowing whether or not Jake and Meg were alive?

In the end, his worry about Meg and Jake overcame the very real terror he was experiencing at the thought of facing down Blain Turner yet again.

Tethering the horses to a nearby tree limb, he stepped into the woods and made his way toward the shed, the one place he'd hoped to never see again.

Chief Everett Fletcher was with the state police when the call came through from Big Jim Conway that Cory was safe and leading Jake to the place where he'd been held.

"Jake shouldn't go in there alone." Everett was shouting into his phone, to be heard above the sound of the police helicopter.

"You know there's no stopping him," Big Jim said. "Where are you, Chief?"

"Heading toward the south pasture. Our copter should be there in about five minutes."

"We're over the spot now, and ready to land."

"Wait for us," Everett shouted, but the line had already gone dead. Not that he'd expected Big Jim or Cole to acknowledge his order. The Conway men had always played by their own rules. Why should this time be any different?

He turned to the pilot to relay the destination. Then he leaned forward to watch as they began their descent.

After getting word from Big Jim, Quinn and Cheyenne turned their ATVs toward the pasture between Conway land and Stanford land. Along the way they picked up Josh and Sierra, and the four of them fairly flew across meadows alive with wildflowers.

It seemed incongruous that such a serene, peaceful meadow could be the setting for violence.

When they came to the spot where Cory had tethered the horses, they turned off their engines and looked around for some sign of life.

Just then the Cessna circled once and came in low and fast for a clean, easy landing in the pasture. Minutes later Cole and Big Jim came rushing toward them.

"Where's Cory?" Big Jim demanded.

"Not here." Quinn pointed to Shadow. "But his colt is here. And so is Jake's." His eyes narrowed. "I say we head into the woods and see if we can find them."

"I'm right behind you." Josh turned to Sierra. "You and Cheyenne stay here with the vehicles."

"Oh, right. Like that's going to happen." Tight-lipped, Cheyenne strode behind her husband, and Sierra followed suit. With Cole and Big Jim taking up the rear, they marched single file into the dense woods.

Minutes later, Yancy Jessup and his wranglers came

riding up, bearing weapons. They tethered their horses beside the Cessna and started into the woods.

Jake and Blain were fighting for their lives. With every bone-jarring blow, they poured themselves into it, knowing only one of them would walk away.

Both men were lean and tough from their years of ranch chores, but the wound to Jake's shoulder was taking its toll, draining his strength.

What Blain lacked in muscle he made up for in determination. He was desperate, and he knew that every minute counted. If he didn't soon break away, the authorities would catch up with him.

Aloud he shouted, "They're never taking me to jail. Never. Even if I have to die in this godforsaken wilderness, I'll fight you to the last breath, Conway."

The toes of his work boots were steel, and he knew how to use them. Launching his booted foot he kicked Jake as hard as he could in the groin. With Jake doubled over, he moved in for the kill. As he knelt in the grass and fumbled for his pistol, Jake brought his head up directly into Blain's face. The sound of bone on bone had Blain moaning in pain as his broken nose became a fountain of blood.

Jake followed that with a fist to the jaw that had Blain slumping backward.

Before Jake could grab the pistol, Blain's boot found Jake's head, opening a gash that had blood streaming down the side of his face, spilling into his eyes and blinding him.

"Stop. Don't hurt him."

Hearing Cory's voice, Jake shook his head, struggling to clear it.

"It's me you want," the boy pleaded. "If you let him live, I'll go with you. I swear I will."

Jake could barely make out the image of the little boy through the blood that was obscuring his vision. He wiped blood from his eyes. When he sat back on his heels, everything stopped swimming in front of him, and for a moment he could make out Blain's face, wearing a twisted smile.

And then he felt Blain's pistol pressed against his chest.

"Too late, brat. This cowboy's time is up."

With her hands bound behind her back, Meg watched helplessly as Jake and Blain fought like madmen. When she saw Cory break through the dense woods into the clearing, her poor heart nearly stopped.

Alive. Cory was alive. Before she could savor that knowledge, she realized that he had now come charging back into danger. He'd risked his safety for hers and Jake's.

When Blain suddenly took control of the pistol, pointing it at Jake's chest, she whirled around and held out her bound hands toward the little boy, begging him without words to free her, desperately hoping he understood.

Using Jake's hunting knife, Cory made one quick slash at the ropes.

His confidence restored, Blain gave a chilling smile. "Don't worry about the pretty counselor or the brat, cowboy. I intend to take real good care of—"

Jake watched as Blain slowly squeezed the trigger. The roar of an explosion followed, and Jake waited to feel the pain of dying.

Instead, he saw Blain turn to Meg with a look of complete astonishment, before clutching his chest and falling forward.

Jake managed to scramble out of the way, his arm dangling uselessly at his side as he slumped to the ground.

Meg and Cory fell on him, tears streaming from their faces.

"Please don't die, Jake," Cory was saying over and over. "I was trying so hard to cut through Meg's ropes, but I wasn't fast enough. It took me too long."

Jake wanted to reassure the boy that he'd done just fine, but he couldn't seem to get the words out. He could feel himself fading, and struggled to hold on.

Meg, the ropes still dangling from her wrists, was wiping the blood from his face, and kissing him over and over, while Cory just clung to him and cried.

"Hey, city girl," Jake managed. "At least you didn't shoot yourself in the foot."

Meg began laughing through her tears. And all Jake could do was lie there, somewhere between extreme pain and wild relief, while an army of people began milling around.

Someone jabbed a needle into Jake's arm and shouted for a gurney.

Everett Fletcher's voice could be heard above the din. "Turner's alive. I want him kept alive. He has a lot to answer for. Get me a stretcher. We need a medevac for this creep."

In all the chaos Cole and Big Jim were barking orders. Quinn, Josh, Cheyenne, and Sierra kept asking questions that nobody bothered to answer.

Jake caught glimpses of a whole host of strangers.

Police bagging evidence. Police photographers snapping pictures. Raven and his people talking frantically into phones. Yancy and his wranglers moving through the crowd, like extras in a movie.

Overhead helicopters hovered.

Nearby horses whinnied.

None of it mattered.

Meg was safe.

Cory was safe.

His upside-down world had righted itself.

Life didn't get much better.

CHAPTER TWENTY-NINE

Cole brought his face close to Jake's. "Meg said you've been shot. How bad is the pain?"

Jake gave his father a lopsided grin. "You ever been shot, Pa?"

His father nodded. "Once."

"You remember how it hurt?"

"Real bad, as I recall."

"That's about it."

"Okay. The state police have already alerted Doc Walton at the clinic. You can take their copter, or Big Jim and I will fly you there."

Jake turned to Cory, who hadn't let go of him since he'd dropped to the ground. "How would you like to fly to town with me?"

"You mean it? In a real airplane?"

"Yeah."

The boy's eyes went wide with excitement. "Can Meg come, too?"

Jake turned to Meg, who was busy snapping Sierra's denim jacket over her torn shirt.

When she returned to kneel beside him his eyes narrowed. "Did that bastard...hurt you?"

"There wasn't time. Thanks to you."

"Thank heaven." Jake gave her a long, appraising look before his lips split into a teasing grin. "I sort of liked the way you looked before. But I guess, with all these guys milling about, modesty is called for."

"Jake Conway." She closed a hand over his. "How can you keep making jokes at a time like this?"

"Just my nature, I guess. Besides, I'm floating. Must be that shot they gave me." He looked at their joined hands. "How're you holding up?"

"Fine." She took in a deep breath and gave a quick shake of her head. "And isn't that amazing? I mean, considering what we've been through, it's a miracle that we can smile."

"It beats crying." He nodded toward Cory. "You going to ask Meg if she'd like to go flying?"

She looked from Jake to Cory and back. "What's this about?"

"Pa's going to fly me to Dr. Walton's clinic in Paintbrush. I was hoping you and Cory would go along."

She could see the pleading look in Cory's eyes, though he didn't say a word.

She squeezed Jake's hand. "Let's see. We're miles from civilization. We've created more excitement than this sleepy place has probably seen in a while. We've got nothing better to do. I'd say it's the perfect time for a plane ride."

* * *

The familiar comfort of the Conway ranch was a soothing balm after the chaos of the crime scene, and the frantic activity in the clinic. Dr. Walton had sedated her patient before removing the bullet from his shoulder and stitching his wounds. She'd sent him home with a warning to take it easy, though she doubted Jake Conway knew the meaning of the phrase.

The family gathered in the great room after a fabulous dinner of slow-roasted beef swimming in rich gravy, whipped potatoes, fresh garden vegetables, and home-made bread. Three strawberry pies sat cooling on the counter, along with a bowl of fresh whipped cream, which they would enjoy soon with their coffee.

It was obvious that Phoebe and Ela had spent the day cooking and baking, in order to calm their nerves.

"You two fine ladies outdid yourselves." Big Jim patted his middle as he settled into his favorite chair.

Jake, swathed in dressings at his head and shoulder, reclined on the sofa in front of the fire, surrounded by pillows to cushion his injury. He'd been content to sip some chicken soup.

Cole tucked his cell phone away to announce, "Chief Fletcher and Raven are here with the report from the state police."

He walked from the room and returned minutes later with the police chief and the private detective.

Within minutes both men were given steaming cups of coffee and made comfortable before Phoebe and Ela began passing out plates of pie and whipped cream.

Cole received a sliver of pie with a mound of fresh strawberries. He opened his mouth to complain, then quickly closed it when he saw the look in Phoebe's eyes.

"Okay, Everett." Cole sat back and sipped his hated decaf. "What have you found out?"

"Our guy's going to live. And believe me, he'll do hard time, because we found the truck he'd intended to use to make his escape, about a mile from the crime scene, along a dirt road. The truck belonged to old Mule Bremmer over in Caseville. Shot dead for a measly truck."

"Mule Bremmer." Big Jim shook his head sadly. "I've known him for fifty years. A hard-working rancher."

"With no family. That's why Blain Turner targeted him. He figured he'd be in Canada before anybody noticed the old guy missing."

"Has Turner said what this is all about?" Cole asked.

The chief turned to the detective. "I think Raven can fill you in better than I can. All I have are the things our state boys have been able to uncover. But Raven's file is a lot more detailed."

Raven set aside his coffee. "As you know, Turner was in the foster-care system in Michigan at the same time as Hazel Godfrey, who later changed her name to Arabella." He glanced at Cory, who had lowered his head to avoid looking at anyone.

Old Ela crossed over to where Cory was sitting and took hold of his hand. He looked up and she smiled. "Come with me. I have a special dessert for you."

He glanced around, then allowed her to lead him to the kitchen. Once the boy was gone, the others breathed a sigh of relief.

Raven said, "Hazel Godfrey was eager to get away from an abusive foster father, and Turner was her means of escape. She gave him the keys to the foster father's car, and they drove across the country in a crime spree. As far as my operatives can determine, Hazel didn't commit the crimes. She just went along. I'm not even sure she knew just how vicious Turner could be. At least until much later."

He opened a file folder. "At that time Turner was eighteen and Hazel was fifteen. Once they got to Wyoming they did odd jobs to pay for a cheap motel room. But Turner had a problem." Raven looked up. "Drugs. And that gets to be expensive. So when he learned that a rich rancher had lost his wife, he suggested that Hazel apply for a job cleaning his house. Turner figured she could steal enough from Stanford to take care of his needs.

"But once she got the job, their relationship changed. Porter Stanford had two weaknesses. Women and folks who were down on their luck, as he'd once been. Hazel played into both his weaknesses. Seeing how thin she was, he started asking her to stay and eat dinner with him. When winter came he bought her a warm parka.

"And then one night she didn't come back to the motel room she shared with Turner. That's when Turner decided he was losing her. So he suggested that she marry Porter, so she would have access to his bank account. That worked for a while, but it all went south when she found out she was having a baby. Porter was ecstatic, and Hazel found out what it felt like to be really treasured. That's when Turner became desperate. He'd lost his access to money.

"So he came up with a new scam. He threatened to go to Porter and tell him that Hazel had only married him for his money. Then he 'persuaded' her that she'd better go along, or that abusive foster father she'd escaped would look like heaven next to what Turner had in mind for her."

Meg, who had been silent until now, gasped. "He beat her?"

"On a pretty regular basis, from what I could gather." Raven turned the page of documents. "When Hazel died, that should have been the end of it. But by then Blain Turner was deeply into drugs, and he had no credit with his drug dealers. Desperate, he showed up at Porter's house and demanded money."

"I hope my father threw him out," Meg said softly.

Raven looked at her. "That appears to have been his intention. But Blain must have said something that persuaded Porter to give him money. Porter withdrew a thousand dollars from the bank and gave it to Turner. That same day, Porter had his heart attack, and once again Turner was cheated out of a scam because of death. By the same token, we're cheated out of knowing what Turner had on Porter to get him to pay in the first place."

Cole leaned forward. "Is that why Blain broke into Porter's house the night Meg arrived? Was he looking for more money?"

Raven shook his head. "That's where it gets confusing. He had apparently targeted Meg. But why? What could he possibly have on her that would make her susceptible to his blackmail scam? Whatever he had on Porter couldn't possibly matter to his daughter." He closed his document file. "I have my people working on it. We hope to have more in the next day or two. And the state police are still interviewing Turner. We're hoping he might tell us—"

They all looked over when the door to the kitchen was shoved open and Cory paused in the doorway. Old Ela stood behind him, looking perplexed.

"Ela said I should stay in the other room and eat my cookies, but I heard what you said, and I have to tell you something." Cory looked at Jake, and then at Big Jim. "Before my mom died, Blain used to come to our house sometimes and talk to her. He had her cell phone number, and when he asked for mine, I gave it to him. I thought he was my mom's friend. After she died, I didn't see him again for a long time."

The little boy looked at Big Jim. "Do you remember when you said women have to be taken care of? No matter how strong they are?"

Big Jim nodded. "I remember, boyo."

Cory took a deep breath. "The night Blain Turner broke into the house and tossed my dad's files all over the office, he texted me to say that was how easy it would be to hurt Meg. So if I didn't want to see her hurt, I had to do what he said. But I... I didn't. And so he did it again. Once we came here, I figured he wouldn't be able to hurt Meg. But then she moved back home and I..." He forced himself to go on. "I was a coward and stayed here where I wouldn't have to see what Blain was doing."

"You're not a coward, Cory." Meg rushed to his defense. "You're just a little boy. How could you—?"

"He said I could stop him any time if I would just meet him. But I was afraid he'd take me away, 'cause that's what he'd told my dad the night he came asking for money. But then, after Big Jim said women had to be taken care of, I decided that I had to do the right thing, even though I was scared."

"You went because of me?" Meg was staring at him with a look of confusion. "I don't understand, Cory. What could he do to me?"

"He said he'd kill you, and then he'd ruin the good names of my dad and mom and you. And all because—" he sucked in a big breath before saying the words in a rush so they wouldn't hurt too much "—because I'm not Dad's son. I'm Blain's."

Everyone in the room had gone deathly silent. So silent, they could hear the ticking of the clock on the fireplace mantel.

Meg and Jake reacted at the same moment. Meg was at the boy's side, gathering him into her arms. "Hush now, Cory. You don't know that."

She led him to the sofa and Jake held out his good arm, drawing him close. Meg sat beside him, holding the boy's hand in hers.

Jake kept his tone gentle. "You already know that Blain is a liar, Cory. What makes you think he was telling the truth this time?"

The little boy swallowed hard. "I saw Blain Turner the night he came to see my dad. I was supposed to be upstairs in my room, but I was scared, because they were talking loud, and I hid in the hallway. He told my dad that if he didn't pay him a lot of money, he'd take me away and my dad wouldn't be able to stop him because..." The boy's lips began to quiver and he looked from Jake to Meg before saying, "...because I wasn't really Dad's son. My dad got real quiet, and then he agreed to pay him a lot of money, but only if he'd go away and never bother us again. Blain said he would, but he lied."

"Yes, he lied," Jake said firmly. "He's a habitual liar.

And there's no reason to believe he was telling the truth about you, either."

"None of it matters now. What he told my dad hurt him so much he died." Cory turned to Meg. "I saw him give Blain Turner the money, and right after Blain drove away, Dad sat down in his chair and died." It was the first time he'd talked about it, and the memories were so painful, the little boy burst into tears.

Meg and Jake sandwiched the little boy between them, murmuring words meant to soothe his broken heart, while the others found themselves wiping away tears of their own.

Jake handed Cory his handkerchief before glancing at Everett Fletcher. "Can we arrange a DNA test?"

The chief nodded. "I don't see why not. The court can order one. I'm sure Kirby Bolton will sign the order."

"Then request it. And get that…creep's DNA sample."

"I'm on my way." The chief drained his cup and got to his feet.

Raven tucked away his notes. "I'll be leaving, too."

Meg was on her feet. "I'll walk you out, Raven. There are some things I'd like to discuss before you leave."

When they were gone, Jake continued holding Cory close while the family gathered around them to touch his head or pat his shoulder, offering him whatever comfort they could.

When Meg returned she cleared her throat and it was plain that she'd been crying. "Cory, I think what you did was the bravest, most heroic thing I've ever seen. You risked your life to save mine."

Her tears started again and this time she didn't bother

to wipe them away. She sat down on the sofa and drew the little boy into her arms. "I don't know if you're my brother by blood, but I want you to know this. You're the little brother of my heart. And nobody is ever taking you away from me."

Phoebe lifted the edge of her apron to her eyes before turning into Cole's arms. With tears in his own eyes, he held her close while she wept silently.

Ela stood in a corner, watching with moist eyes, until she fled the room.

The others merely looked on in silence. But it was clear that all of their hearts were aching for this brave little boy, who had risked it all for a woman he hadn't even known scant weeks ago.

CHAPTER THIRTY

The Conway house was strangely silent. It was, Meg thought, a comforting silence. She had sat with Cory until he'd fallen asleep.

As she slipped into Jake's room she could see, by the light of the moon, that he was resting comfortably. The drugs Dr. Walton had sent must have done the trick.

She was about to leave when his hand reached out to hers. "Stay."

"I thought you were sleeping. I'll only stay a minute. You need your sleep."

"I'm fine. But I'd sleep better with you beside me."

She shook her head. "I'm planning on taking a long, soaking bath and then falling into bed. Alone, cowboy."

"You really know how to hurt a guy." He chuckled. "Tell me how you're doing, Meg."

She settled herself on the edge of his bed. "I don't know. It's been a crazy day and a lot to take in. I don't think it's really hit me yet that the danger is past and I can get on with my life."

"It's about time."

"Yeah." She sighed. "When I heard Blain's gun go off, and thought he'd killed you—"

He squeezed her hand. "I'm too tough to die."

"Oh, Jake." She lay down beside him and touched a hand to his bandaged head. "When I saw all that blood, I thought my poor heart would stop."

He gave her that rogue smile she'd come to love. "Are you trying to say you care about me, Ms. Stanford?"

"More than I realized."

"Do you care enough to stay in Wyoming?" He waited a beat. When she didn't respond, he said, "I don't think there's much of a need for a veterinarian in D.C. Although I suppose I could just give it all up and become your love slave."

"You'd do that for me?"

He closed his hand over hers. "I could be persuaded to sacrifice myself for your pleasure."

"If only it were that simple." She sighed. "Oh, Jake. What a mess."

"Hey. No complaining allowed. We're alive. You and Cory are safe. Right now, that's all that matters to me." He fell silent for a moment. "Those are strong drugs Doc Walton gave me. I'm drifting."

"Go to sleep." She touched her mouth to his and lingered over the kiss for long moments before getting to her feet. "I'll check on you in a couple of hours."

"Good. Maybe by then I can find something better to do with you in this bed than sleep."

He didn't even hear the door close as she walked away.

* * *

Her skin glowing from the bath, Meg wrapped herself in a bulky robe she'd found in the guest closet and descended the stairs to find Phoebe and Ela talking quietly in the kitchen.

"Don't you two ever sleep?"

Ela merely smiled. "What about you?"

"Too much on my mind." She glanced around. "Do you mind if I make tea?"

"It's made." Phoebe indicated the teapot. "Help yourself."

Meg poured a cup of tea and carried it to the table. "I hope I didn't interrupt anything."

Phoebe shook her head. "We were going over the events of the day. It's a lot to take in. How's Cory doing?"

"I waited until I was sure he was sound asleep." A light came into Meg's eyes. "I still can't get over the fact that he was willing to sacrifice himself to save me."

Ela nodded her head. "I knew the first time I saw him that he was a good boy."

"Then you're a better judge of people than I am. I thought he hated me, or at least resented me for being here. I'm ashamed of the things I was thinking."

Phoebe's tone was gentle. "Don't be too hard on yourself, Meg. We all misjudge people sometimes."

Meg sipped her tea. "Look how I misjudged my own father." She gave a dreamy smile. "If I hadn't come back to Wyoming, I'd have never known how much he loved and missed me. I would have gone through life believing the worst about him." She stared into space. "Jake said there are no accidents. Do you believe that?"

Ela said, "My people believe that the spirits of those

who have passed often remain to ease those they love during their passage in this world. Would it be so hard to believe that your father remained here to see his children united and happy in the place that he loved?"

Meg leaned over and kissed the old woman's withered cheek. "It's not hard to believe at all." She swallowed the lump in her throat. "Sorry. I'm feeling all weepy tonight."

Phoebe lay a hand over Meg's. "You've been through a lot."

"It isn't just the danger that has me on edge. It's all these feelings for—" she shrugged, embarrassed by emotions that were too close to the surface "—all these feelings for people."

"Anyone in particular?" Phoebe bit back her smile.

Meg pushed away from the table. "It's late." She drained her cup and set it in the dishwasher. "I'd better get to bed. Good night."

As she hurried away, the two women exchanged knowing smiles.

"Do you think she knows yet?" Phoebe asked softly.

Ela shook her head. "The ones caught in the confusion of true love are often the last to recognize it."

Phoebe's smile faded a bit when she realized the old woman was watching her with a shrewd look in those blackbird eyes. She tried for a casual tone. "I thought we were talking about Jake and Meg."

"You were. As for me, I have watched you and Cole deny your feelings for a lifetime."

"He's still in love with Seraphine."

"As you still love your Tim."

"That's different. I was able to bury Tim."

"Did you bury your love, as well?"

"Of course not. I'll always have a very special place in my heart for him. He was my first love."

"As Seraphine was Cole's first love. But time moves on. Hearts are capable of more than one great love."

Phoebe sighed. "You're talking to the wrong person, Ela. I don't think Cole is able to move on."

"Then you haven't seen the man I see when he looks at you. Try looking at him with your heart."

When the old woman left the kitchen, Phoebe remained alone, her thoughts a jumble of conflicting emotions.

Meg walked up the stairs, intent upon going to the guest room. Instead she walked past it and let herself into Jake's bedroom.

By the light of the moon she made her way to the bed. As she lay down beside him, his arm came around her waist, drawing her closer.

"Sorry I woke you, Jake."

"I was awake. I've been waiting for you." He kissed her long and slow and deep. "I think I've been waiting for you all my life."

"Jake Conway." Phoebe turned from the stove to see Jake, his shoulder still bandaged, dressed for chores and heading for the mudroom. "Where do you think you're going? Dr. Walton said you shouldn't tax that shoulder until she says it's completely healed."

"I'm just going to the barn to meet Randy Morton. He's back in town and heading over here to pick up Honey and her pups."

"All right. See that you don't do any heavy lifting, or

try doing any chores while you're out in the barn. Quinn and Josh have already mucked the stalls, and they said they'll be back in plenty of time to do whatever else is needed."

"You worry too much."

"Somebody has to. You never worry about yourself."

Jake pressed a kiss to Phoebe's cheek before sauntering out the door.

It had been three days since he'd been shot. Three days of pure bliss, while he'd lounged around recovering. Each day his shoulder felt stronger, and each night, when Meg came to him, the feelings he had for her grew stronger, too. The problem was, she'd started talking about going home. And he wasn't certain if home to Meg meant Washington D.C. or her father's ranch. She refused to be pinned down. She completely avoided the subject.

As expected, Cory was already in the barn, taking care of Honey and her puppies. He'd become absolutely devoted to them, and to anything that had to do with being a veterinarian.

He looked up as Jake approached. "They're already fed. And I cleaned the hay and changed the bedding in Honey's pen."

"Good boy. You're becoming a really valuable assistant, Cory."

The boy flushed with pleasure.

"Time for their last shots."

Cory reached for one puppy after the other, holding each one the way Jake had taught him, while Jake administered a shot. As each pup gave a few yips of displeasure, Cory would soothe and cuddle it before returning it to its mother, who would lick and calm it.

"I guess that's it." Jake looked up as Randy Morton appeared in the doorway. "And just in time. That was their last shot before going home."

"They're going home?" Cory looked stunned.

"Randy's here to pick them up."

"Oh." Without realizing it, Cory reached for Trouble and cradled the pup to his chest.

"Hey, Jake." Randy Morton strode to the pen and was rewarded by a tail-wagging, hand-licking welcome by Honey, who seemed to be beaming as she showed off her new family. "Well, aren't you just the prettiest new mama in the world?"

Randy got down on his knees and was instantly mobbed by tiny bundles of fluff. He laughed and rolled around with them, clearly delighted by the additions to his family.

"Randy, this is Cory Stanford. Cory, the guy being manhandled by the puppies is Randy Morton."

Randy stood and offered a handshake to the boy. "I'm sorry about your daddy, son."

Cory lowered his gaze, unsure how to respond.

Randy indicated the puppy in Cory's arms. "Is that one of Honey's pups?"

"Yes, sir. I call him Trouble."

"Does he live up to his name?"

Cory nodded. "He likes getting into everything he can. So far he's knocked over the water dish about a hundred times, emptied Honey's food dish, too, and got himself tangled up in the blanket, but I freed him."

Randy studied the boy and the pup. "He looks pretty comfortable in your arms. I'm thinking he likes you, Cory."

Cory's smile would light up the entire barn. "I like him, too."

"Well." Randy turned to Jake. "I heard about all the excitement while I was gone. It's the talk of the town. Next time we have a beer you can tell me all about it. Now I'd better get the new mama and her babies back home."

"Cory and I will give you a hand."

Randy led Honey toward his truck, with the five puppies trailing behind. Honey jumped up into the back of the truck and stepped into a large cage Randy had provided for safety during the ride to town.

Cory carried Trouble to the truck and set him up in the back beside his mother, before lifting up the others. Before he could close the cage, Trouble bounded out and leaped into Cory's arms. For long minutes the boy held the pup close until his face and neck had been bathed in puppy kisses. Finally, when Randy stood holding the tailgate, Cory was forced to return Trouble to his cage. Randy closed the truck's tailgate and turned to shake hands with Jake.

"Thanks for standing in for me, Jake."

"Any time, Randy."

"And thank you, Cory. Jake says you're the one who was with Honey when all this started."

The boy shrugged, his gaze still on the puppies.

"I won't forget it, son." Randy climbed into his truck and drove away.

Long after Jake had walked away, Cory remained by the barn door, watching until the truck was gone and even the dust of departure had blown away. Then, with a heavy heart, the boy went in search of Shadow in the corral.

* * *

It was noon, and though it was rare for the entire family to gather for lunch, it happened occasionally.

Ever since the terrifying incident with Blain Turner, the entire Conway family had been closer than ever. Big Jim referred to it as "circling the wagons." Whenever they sensed trouble, it was a natural inclination to stay close and guard one another's backs.

Phoebe and Ela were in their element, cooking and baking up a storm, and happy to see their efforts appreciated.

"Now this was worth coming home to," Quinn remarked, as he filled his bowl with Phoebe's spicy hot chili.

"Were you up at the cabin?" Sierra helped herself to chili before passing it to Josh.

Cheyenne answered for both of them. "Quinn and I are thinking of adding on to the cabin."

"Why?" Josh broke open a steaming hot roll and slathered it with butter.

Quinn shrugged. "Way too many female things cluttering my once-sparse hideaway." He looked over at Josh. "How are your house plans coming?"

Josh and Sierra exchanged knowing smiles. "We think we've found the perfect style of architecture for the bluff."

"I hope there will be lots and lots of glass," Cheyenne said. "That spectacular setting just begs for lots of windows."

Sierra nodded. "And local stone. I want it to look like it grew right out of the mountains."

Big Jim glanced at Meg, who had been strangely silent

throughout the meal. "It seems like everybody's busy making plans, Meg. What are yours?"

She shrugged. "I wish I knew. I'm still taking it a day at a time. But I do think it's time that Cory and I went home and started dealing with our future."

"You know you're welcome to stay here as long as you—"

Cole looked up at the sound of a car's engine, and the others did the same. Minutes later Everett Fletcher knocked on the door and stepped inside.

Even before he had time to greet everyone, Phoebe was on her feet and fetching another place setting at the table.

Everett lifted a hand to stop her. "I know that it seems I always time my visits to your ranch so I can sample all your fine cooking. But this time, I'm here with news that won't wait." He glanced around the table. "It's nice that you're all here, so you can hear this together." He turned to look at Cory and Meg. "The state lab has sent back the test results of your DNA."

Everyone fell silent.

Without realizing it, Meg reached out and caught Cory's hand. The boy squeezed her hand hard and stared at the tabletop, afraid to look at anyone.

Everett reached for an envelope in his breast pocket and carefully unfolded the document inside. "It says after extensive testing, they've proved that there is zero chance that you are in any way related to"—he looked over at Cory—"Blain Turner."

The little boy let out the breath he'd been holding, and Meg did the same.

Everett went on. "From the DNA provided by Meg,

and the things of Porter's that were available for testing, there is no doubt—in fact, there is a ninety-nine percent probability—that you and Meg had the same father: Porter Stanford."

Meg was crying as she enveloped Cory in a fierce hug. The others had jumped out of their chairs to gather around and embrace them.

Everett stood back, watching the celebration with a huge smile on his face. He blinked hard as he said, "You know, folks, there are days when being in law enforcement just makes me so damned proud. This is one of those days."

With handshakes all around, he grabbed the little boy by the shoulders and said, "I'm so glad I could be the bearer of good news for a change, son. Now I hope you and your sister have a good, long life together."

CHAPTER THIRTY-ONE

The celebration for Meg and Cory went on throughout the day, with Phoebe and Ela making a special dinner in their honor and, later, a gloriously decadent strawberry shortcake shared by everyone in the great room.

The following day Meg knew that she'd been putting off making any decisions about moving forward, but she couldn't seem to focus. She felt...twitchy. She couldn't seem to settle, flitting from helping Jake and his brothers in the barn to helping Phoebe and Ela in the kitchen.

When her cell phone rang, she saw Raven's name and knew that this had been what she'd been waiting for so impatiently.

She answered quickly. "Raven. Do you have news?"

"I don't know if it's what you were hoping for." He spoke in short, staccato bursts, filling her in, before adding, "How soon can you get the Conway family together?"

"I don't believe any of them are up in the high country. I think most of them are around the barns and outbuildings, so it shouldn't take any time at all to get them here."

"If you'll ask them to meet with me at the house, I can be there within the hour."

She agreed before tucking her phone away and hurrying out to the barn.

Puzzled by Meg's unexplained summons, the Conway family came from the fields, the barns, the kitchen, to assemble in the great room.

Jake hurried across the room to close a hand over Meg's shoulder. "What's wrong?"

She stood wringing her hands. "Oh, Jake, I hope I've done the right thing." She seemed to gather herself before saying, "Raven is on his way with some important information."

"I thought the DNA tests were conclusive."

"They are. But he asked that I bring everyone together before he arrived to share some news."

"News? I don't underst—" He looked up at the sound of a truck's engine, and the crunch of gravel, announcing the arrival of their guest.

When Raven walked in, he was followed by Chief Everett Fletcher.

Cole looked from one man to the other. "What's this about, Everett?"

"Raven asked me to come along in my official capacity as chief law enforcement officer of the county. For now, I'll just stand back and let him explain everything."

The chief chose a seat apart from the others, while

Raven stood in the center of the room facing the Conway family, who sat sprawled on sofas and chairs, with Josh and Sierra snuggled together on the floor at Cole's feet.

Raven began in a clear, controlled voice. "On the day Blain Turner was caught, Meg was feeling more than a little overwhelmed, and grateful just to be alive. When all the excitement ended, she asked me if I would keep my team here in Wyoming to follow a twenty-five-year-old cold case to whatever conclusion we might find. She asked me to use all my resources, and that meant several dozen operatives poring over hundreds of hours of newspaper articles, radio and TV news bites, and police and FBI files, to find out what happened to Seraphine Cramer Conway."

"You would do that for us?" Cole shot Meg a look of pure astonishment before another thought struck. "Wait. You've found her?"

He sat very straight in his chair and looked from Meg to his family, and then to Raven, before gripping his hands together tightly in his lap.

"In order to handle such a cold case, we first had to gather the facts that had been reported and verified. This is what we know for certain. Seraphine was home on the morning of her disappearance. She'd had breakfast with her husband"—Raven looked at Cole—"and her three sons." He looked directly at Quinn, Josh, and Jake. "She was in high spirits, planning to celebrate her youngest son's fifth birthday. She'd asked him what he wanted, and he'd told her he wanted balloons. Lots and lots of balloons."

Jake smiled and nodded. "I think I remember asking for them. But after all these years, I can't be certain."

"I deal only in facts." Raven passed around copies of the depositions taken in the days following Seraphine's disappearance. "According to their sworn statements, Big Jim and Cole had finished barn chores and had headed up to the north pasture to tend a herd. Ela, the family housekeeper, was busy in the kitchen. Seraphine and the three boys had gone to the playroom, and had spent more than an hour painting and coloring. When the boys grew restless and went outside to play, Seraphine remained behind. All of this has been corroborated."

He took in a breath. "What we've learned has been pieced together carefully to form a more cohesive picture of Seraphine's day. She didn't drive." He looked at Cole. "Is that correct?"

Cole nodded. "Seraphine was a city girl and a dancer. She was obsessed with dancing. She grew up in New York City, and joined a professional dance troupe at sixteen, by lying about her age." He shrugged off her lie. "She never learned to drive. Actually, she had no reason to. She took the subway everywhere she went. She said it was done all the time. She traveled by bus with the other dancers. They were never in a town or city for more than a day or two. A gypsy, she called herself."

Raven smiled. "That's the information I got, as well. But despite her tender age, her fellow dancers described her as inventive, creative, and fearless."

That had Cole chuckling. "That's my Seraphine."

Raven read from his notes. "On the day she went missing, Seraphine had it in mind to go to Paintbrush and get a dozen helium balloons."

Cole's head came up. "I never heard her say that. How would you know such a thing?"

"Hearsay evidence. I discovered it in my research."
Raven went on: "Paintbrush is an hour away by car. Impossible to walk. But Seraphine was determined to get to
Paintbrush and buy those balloons. Knowing her husband
and father-in-law were up in high country, she crossed the
hill out back and walked out to the highway. We know
this, because there was a witness. A trucker from a logging company in Canada was just passing by. The driver's
name is Sean McInnis, retired now from the Lapham
Forest Farm in Saskatchewan, Canada. Though he's over
eighty now, he's of sound mind and was willing to give
sworn testimony as to the passenger he picked up that
day."

"How could you find someone that the authorities
couldn't find?" Cole demanded. "I've never heard of this
Sean McInnis."

Raven read from his document. "We checked the
records of every known company that had regular runs
through this part of Wyoming, and the Lapham Forest
Farm was just one of dozens. But since their truck was
recorded as having passed this way on that particular day,
we checked further and found Sean McInnis. As I said, he
may be elderly now, but he was more than happy to try to
help. He said the woman gave him the name Seraphine,
an unusual name that stuck in his mind, and she was
wearing some kind of long, gypsy skirt in rainbow colors
that covered her ankles, and she had 'platinum blonde
hair that fell around the face of an angel.' He said he
would have stopped for anyone needing a ride, but it was
easy to stop for a woman that stunning."

No one spoke. No one seemed to be breathing. They
were in another place now. A place that brought with it a

sense of dread. Finally they would learn the answers to a lifetime of questions.

"Mr. McInnis said he couldn't take her all the way to Paintbrush. He explained that he could only take her as far as the turnoff that led to the new highway." Again, Raven referred to his notes. "I checked with the highway authority, and I've learned that the 'new highway,' which is now twenty-five years old, was built to replace the old road that curved over several foothills and had been the site of dozens of fatal accidents."

Because the others had gone silent, it was left to Big Jim to say, "I remember that. A lot of grumbling by folks around here about the federal government spending money on a highway that led to the same place as the old one. Once the new highway was built, the old one was abandoned and left to fall into disrepair and rot until it wasn't even navigable anymore. A lot of folks wanted to know why we needed a brand-new highway."

Everett Fletcher cleared his throat. "According to statistics, that old road was a death trap. The new highway has probably saved thousands of lives in the last twenty-five years."

Raven set aside the first page of his report and began to read from the next. "Mr. McInnis pulled over at the turnoff to let his passenger out. About that time the sky was growing dark with a coming storm. He warned his pretty passenger, but she laughed and said she loved the rain. As Mr. McInnis was pulling away, he saw a panel truck coming up behind him. Seraphine waved at the driver of the panel truck, and it slowed and then pulled over. As Mr. McInnis was driving away, he watched in his rearview mirror as Seraphine got into the truck. He couldn't recall the name on the panel truck, but he did remember that the letters were green, and there was a shamrock somewhere in the words. He remembered it for all these years only because he's of Irish descent, and his daughter had given him a big plastic shamrock for luck. A shamrock that he always kept on his dashboard."

Raven's gaze moved over the family, all of whom were staring at him intently, concentrating all their energy on him, as if to pull everything from his brain.

"I'm sorry if this seems agonizingly slow. It's just that I need to give you every detail as I've learned it. My team has been working nonstop on this since Meg first asked me to look into it."

He returned to his notes. "This was the tough link in the case. This panel truck turned out to be privately owned. It wasn't a company truck, which made it nearly impossible to track. But that shamrock turned out to be our good-luck charm. In our research, we discovered a welder by the name of Patrick Flannery who had retired after thirty-five years working with a fabricating company in Cheyenne. Flannery was a widower with no children, and on his final day he told his coworkers that he intended to drive up to Canada and spend the rest of his days fishing, hiking, and living the life of a hermit. His old panel truck was stocked with all his worldly goods, and had the words Go Irish, and a shamrock, all in green, on one side. And it was Patrick Flannery who stopped to pick up Seraphine."

Sensing that this could be very hard news for Cole, Phoebe walked up behind him, her hand gently resting on his shoulder. Jake quickly joined her. Seeing them, both

Quinn and Josh followed suit, along with their wives, with Ela joining them. Big Jim reached over to grab his son's hand.

The entire family was joined, in an effort to lend each other their strength.

"Patrick's work records describe him as always going the extra mile for friend and stranger alike. It's no surprise, then, that he stopped and offered a pretty lady a ride, even if it would take him out of his way. After all, Paintbrush wasn't that far off the beaten track. The trouble is, the old highway had been closed, and the new one had only recently opened. With Seraphine never driving, and Flannery a stranger to this part of the state, neither of them was aware of the change. We'll never know if the darkening sky was the reason that Patrick Flannery mistakenly drove past the barricade and took the old highway. We surmise that a sudden downpour may have turned the highway slick. Whatever the reason, he apparently skidded and lost control. From our records we can only deduce that his truck went over the embankment and was swallowed up in a deep gorge. We believe both he and Seraphine were probably dead on impact."

There was a collective gasp, though no one spoke.

"The authorities who were searching for Seraphine spent most of their time searching the rangeland around here, suspecting that she'd been on foot. And, of course, no one was looking for Patrick Flannery, who had no immediate family to miss him."

Raven set aside his notes. "Because the old highway was abandoned, there were perhaps a few dozen, probably no more than a hundred or so people, who passed that spot. Without a guardrail showing damage, or any sign of an accident other than skid marks that were probably washed away by the rain, no one saw even a hint of what lay deep below the highway's edge, covered by foliage in the gorge. We would have never checked there ourselves. But after learning that Seraphine had been picked up by the driver of a panel truck, my operatives decided to go over every inch of the land alongside both the old and new highways with metal detectors. Even then, they almost missed the site, because the gorge was so deep."

His tone lowered. Softened. "Once we found the remains, we sent them to a lab for positive identification. Because she didn't want to worry any of you unnecessarily, Meg managed to find intimate objects used by Seraphine, and Patrick Flannery's nephew, his only living relative, was able to send us what little he could of his uncle's things. The lab has determined that the remains are, without a doubt, Patrick Flannery and Seraphine Cramer Conway. Flannery's nephew has claimed his uncle's remains, though he'd long ago lost track of his reclusive uncle. And this—" Raven handed Cole a thick, padded envelope "—is what we were able to recover from the crash site. There was a shoe. Remnants of clothing. Seraphine's purse had decayed over the years, but a small enamel-covered notebook that had been inside a zippered pocket of the purse still bears her smeared, handwritten notes, which she'd apparently written before leaving home."

Cole withdrew the notebook with a drawing of a dancer on the enamel cover. His voice was so raw, he had to clear his throat several times before he could manage to speak. "I gave Seraphine this notebook on our first anniversary. She loved it and always carried it with her." He opened it and could almost make out a few of the handwritten words —*dozen helium balloons*.

Raven glanced at Everett. "The lab has returned the remains on which they'd run the DNA tests. Flannery's remains are on their way to his nephew in Idaho. And Chief Fletcher has Seraphine's remains in his car."

The chief nodded. "They're in a box. I know you'll treasure them, Cole." He crossed the room and had to stop and swallow the knot of emotion in his throat. "I'm sorry. I wish..." He shrugged. "I guess we all wished for something else, but at least now, finally, you know."

Cole sat holding the small enamel notebook in both hands, staring at it as though seeing the face of the woman who'd loved it so. The woman who'd owned his heart, whose memory had teased and taunted him for all these long years.

Raven glanced at Meg before saying, "I'm really sorry to be the bearer of this news. But I'm proud of my operatives. They found what the authorities hadn't found in twenty-five years. And though it isn't what we'd hoped for, the case of Seraphine Cramer Conway is now, sadly, closed."

He handed Cole the file containing all the notes before saying, "I'll see myself out."

Meg got up and hurried after him.

A short time later, after the family had shed their tears and comforted one another, they formed a solemn procession to the police chief's car. He lifted the box of remains from the backseat and handed them to Cole.

Big Jim kept his hand on Cole's shoulder as the entire

family climbed the hill and chose a spot near Clementine and her five sons for a proper burial.

It was a fine day, with the sun so bright it hurt to look at it. Quinn, Josh, and Jake had been up on the hill early that morning to dig into the rich earth beside the graves of Clementine and her five infant sons.

When Reverend Cornell arrived, the Conway family climbed the hill to watch as Cole placed a small, ornate metal box in the open grave. Inside the box were Seraphine's bones, along with a shoe, some remnants of now-faded fabric, and the lovely enamel notebook with the picture of a dancer on the cover. Cole removed the wedding band from his finger and kissed it before placing it inside.

Reverend Cornell read from a book of prayers and blessed the box before stepping back to allow Cole and his three sons to each toss a shovel of earth over the box. When it was completely covered, they patted the soil smooth and rolled a length of sod over the dirt.

Big Jim used a Bobcat to hoist the smooth marble headstone into place.

Cole ran a hand over it before reading aloud the words:

SERAPHINE CRAMER CONWAY
BELOVED WIFE
DEVOTED MOTHER
SWEET DREAMER
SHE DANCES NOW WITH THE ANGELS

As Big Jim climbed down from the Bobcat, Meg and Cory, who had remained behind the others, stepped forward. "What's this?" he said.

"Balloons." Cory glanced shyly at Meg. "We thought Jake's mom would be happy if he finally got his birthday balloons."

Cory and Meg handed Jake a blue helium-filled balloon, before passing the rest around to the others.

When everyone was holding one, Ela stepped forward and touched a hand to the headstone. "I feel Seraphine's spirit in this place." She looked upon the grave. "She is at rest now. At long last, she has come home, and she is at peace."

The family released the balloons and they lifted into the air, soaring higher and higher until they were mere specks on the horizon.

When they had completely disappeared, Ela gave a satisfied nod before turning and walking away.

Slowly, one by one, the others did the same until only Cole and his three sons remained.

By the time they all returned to the house, they seemed filled with a rare sense of peace.

Cole found Meg and dropped an arm around her shoulders. "I can never thank you enough for what you did."

Her eyes filled with tears. "I know how I suffered for those hours that Cory was missing. It made me realize how much you've suffered all these long, endless years. I couldn't bear that you should have to go on any longer, without knowing."

He kissed her cheek, and then, as had been his custom for so long, turned away, intending to go off to the barn alone.

Seeing Phoebe scrubbing the countertop, he changed course, walked to her, and gently removed the damp cloth from her hand. Caught by surprise, her head came up sharply until he bent close to whisper something.

Moments later Cole and Phoebe walked outside. Halfway up the hill he could be seen sliding an arm around her shoulders as they continued the climb, their heads bent in quiet conversation.

CHAPTER THIRTY-TWO

Meg remained at the Conway ranch for several more days. While she quietly helped with chores, her mind was working feverishly. Not wanting to intrude on the family's shock and grief, she kept her thoughts to herself as Jake's wounds mended, as tears were shed, as hearts broken for so long slowly began to heal.

On the final day of her stay at the Conway ranch, Meg gently removed the dressing at Jake's shoulder while he lay on his bed, stripped to the waist, his jeans riding low on his hips.

"No sign of infection. I think Dr. Walton will be pleased." She applied ointment before adding a fresh dressing.

Jake pillowed his head on his other arm. "Haven't you figured out by now that I'm too tough to get an infection?" As she cut a strip of gauze he studied her. "I heard you pacing through the night."

"Sorry. I didn't mean to disturb you."

He caught her hand. "You're always going to disturb me, Meg. Don't you know that by now? Tell me what's bothering you."

She sat back, refusing to meet his eyes. "Lately I've begun to feel...to feel like I'm losing myself. I don't know who I am anymore. In D.C. I was a tough trial lawyer, a career woman with no thought of settling down and taking care of anyone but myself. Here I'm a rancher with a little brother who has no one but me."

Restless, she set aside the scissors, walked to the bedroom window, and stared broodingly at the Tetons in the distance. "I need to take control of my life again. I need to face up to some tough decisions."

"Like what?" He swung his legs to the floor and sat watching her as he pulled on his shirt.

"Like where Cory and I are going to live. And what we intend to do going forward. I owe it to the firm to let them know if I'm in or out. And I owe it to Cory to give him a chance to compare life here with the kind of life he could have in the city."

"You're going to D.C.?"

She kept her face averted. "Cory and I have talked it over. It's only fair that he get a chance to look at all the options. Who knows? Maybe he'll fall in love with the big city."

Jake shoved a hand through his hair. "What about the ranch?"

"I'll be leaving it in Yancy's capable hands. He's already signed on through the rest of the season. By then I'll have a better idea of how I want to proceed going forward."

"Does going forward include you and me?"

She turned to meet his look. "You...matter to me, Jake. I'll miss you terribly." Seeing his face, as dark as a thundercloud, made her lift her chin in that way she had when dealing with unpleasant things. "But I need to do this."

"It sounds as though you've given this a lot of thought. How long before you leave."

"Today."

"Today? Isn't that awfully sudden? What about plane reservations?"

"The firm is sending its plane."

Jake's tone was sharper than usual. "Sending the big guns, I see."

Meg nodded. "As you once reminded me, I need to consider my own problems in the same way I would a client's problems. I've already taken a hard look at the life I left when I was a girl here. Now it's time to revisit the life I made for myself, so that I can decide where I should be."

"And Cory?" Jake's tone was curt.

"Whatever we decide, we'll do it together. Cory's vote will carry as much weight as mine."

"And he's okay with this?"

Meg shrugged. "I've promised him that if he's not happy in the city, we can always come back here."

"The last time you left, it took you twenty years to come back. You're running away, Meg. Just the way you did when you were a kid. Only things are different now. I'm not your father. I won't call and beg you to come back. And I won't write you hundreds of letters, either. But, like Porter, I guess all I can do is hope you figure things out before it's too late."

"Jake—" Before Meg could say more, he spun away, ending any further conversation.

Downstairs, Meg squared her shoulders, prepared to face Jake's obvious anger while she told his family of her plans. Instead, his chair at the table was vacant.

Over breakfast she told the Conway family what she'd already told Jake. Though they expressed sorrow that she and Cory were leaving, their reaction was much more accepting.

"You do what you have to, sweetheart," Big Jim said. "After all you did for us, you deserve to take as much time as you need to decide your future."

"Thank you, Big Jim."

After she and Cory went upstairs to pack their things, Big Jim glanced around at his family before turning to Cole. "That explains why Jake skipped breakfast to work in the barn. I guess he learned from watching you all these years that hard, physical work was the best release from a mind in turmoil."

Meg carried her overnight bag downstairs and paused in the kitchen to bid good-bye to the Conway family. After many emotional hugs and kisses, Meg looked around. "Where's Cory?"

"He's already packed and out in the barn with Jake," Phoebe said.

"Then I'd better get going."

Phoebe hugged her fiercely. "I'm so happy to see that you and Cory are already becoming a family."

"Thank you, Phoebe. We're working at it. And thanks so much for making us feel at home here."

"I hope you'll always consider this your second home."

Meg turned to Ela, who opened her arms wide. "You've been so good to both of us," Meg whispered against her parchment-like cheek. "And especially to Cory."

"With such a sweet boy, it is easy to be good to him. And I know you will be a loving big sister to him."

"I hope you're right. I don't have any experience at being a sister, but I guess I'll learn as I go along."

Ela handed her a heavy bag. At Meg's questioning look she laughed. "We could not send you away without food. Roast beef. Corn bread. And chocolate chip cookies for Cory to eat on the plane."

"Thank you." Meg blew them a kiss.

"Meg..." Phoebe drew her close to press a kiss to her cheek. "I hope...I hope you'll find what you need in the city. And that if you don't, you'll come back. You mean the world to all of us, and to one of us in particular."

Meg sighed. "I wish I could be in two places at once. I want to be here with Ja—with all of you. But I need to do this. The decisions I make now won't just affect me. I have to consider what's best for Cory, too."

"I know you'll make the right decisions for both of you," Phoebe whispered against her cheek.

Outside, Jake and Cory had their heads together, talking in low tones. When Meg got close, Jake took her bag from her hand and stowed it in the back of the truck.

The drive to Paintbrush, which had always seemed so long, flew by in what seemed minutes. A few minutes more and their luggage was being loaded aboard the firm's sleek private jet.

"Wow." Cory's eyes went wide with disbelief. "We're flying in that?"

"Yeah. What do you think?" Meg grinned as the boy's gaze was riveted on the smartly uniformed pilot and copilot just stepping aboard.

Cory ducked his head and caught Jake's hand. "Can I text you?"

"Every hour if you'd like."

"You'll take care of Shadow for me?"

"Like he was my own." Jake drew the boy close for a hard hug before watching him start toward the plane.

He turned to Meg. "You don't have to do this."

"I do, Jake. I wish…" She was clasping and unclasping her hands. "I wish you could go with us, but I know that's not possible."

"I'd be a fish out of water. But you…" He managed a lopsided grin. "You'll be back in your element. And who knows? If Cory's reaction to the plane is any indication, he just may find himself fitting into the big city like he was born to it."

She got up on tiptoe and gave him a quick kiss on the lips. "I won't promise to text you every day, but I will call, Jake."

He made no effort to return her kiss. "Don't make empty promises, Meg. Just… be happy."

"That's all I want. And I want it for you, too."

Before the tears could spill over, she hurried toward the plane.

Minutes later the ramp was pulled up and the door closed. With a roar the small plane taxied down the runway and then lifted into the air.

Long after it was airborne, Jake remained beside his

truck, staring at the empty sky.

Cole looked around the breakfast table. "Where's Jake?"

Phoebe looked up from the stove. "He left for the Carson ranch hours ago."

"Hours ago? It's only seven. I heard him come in after midnight. Does he ever sleep anymore?"

Phoebe glanced at Ela, and the two women wore matching looks of concern. "He's pushing himself, Cole. I should think you'd understand."

"I understand that he's going to push himself right into a sick bed. A man has to sleep."

"Not if his sleep is troubled." Ela set a platter of corn bread on the table. "Jake learned at an early age that a woman can leave and never return."

Around the table, everyone went silent.

Cole turned to his father. "Can you talk to him, Big Jim?"

"I can try. But you know only too well that a man has to work out some things for himself."

"All the same, try talking to him. If he keeps this up much longer, he's apt to drop in his tracks."

The family remained subdued. Though Jake still managed to charm half the female population of Paintbrush, a great deal of the flirtation that had been his trademark seemed to have faded away. And though he relayed only bits and pieces of the conversations he had with Cory, those pieces were enough to tell them that the boy was making a real effort to fit into Meg's life in D.C.

Meg was in a strange mood as she stepped into the foyer of her condo and kicked off her shoes. She ought to have been feeling on top of the world. It had been her input earlier in the week that had given a team of lawyers at the firm their key defense for their client. Because of it, the prosecution was seeking to cut a deal in the hottest trial of the year. And Cyrus Kettering had requested a meeting with Meg in the morning. The buzz around the firm was that she was in for a big promotion. There were even some who'd dared to use the word *partner*. It was unimaginable that a woman her age would be invited to be a partner in a firm as prestigious as Howe-Kettering. But crazier things had happened. Like the housekeeper, Theresa, who'd been heaven-sent. She'd come highly recommended by one of the lawyers in Meg's firm. Theresa had even agreed to the flexible hours Meg had required, so that until Meg's life settled down a bit, someone would always be here with Cory.

But despite all the good things that had happened in the four weeks since she'd returned, Meg couldn't seem to summon any joy in her success.

A gray-haired woman poked her head in the doorway. "I thought I heard you come in, Miss Stanford. I'm keeping your dinner warm in the oven."

"Thank you, Theresa." Meg set her laptop on a marble side table. "Where's Cory?"

"Up in his room. He and his tutor just finished their lessons."

The door to the den opened, and the young man she'd hired to prepare Cory for private school was standing in the doorway. "I heard your voice. Perfect timing. I wonder if I could have a few words with you before I go."

Meg returned his smile. "Of course. Let's talk in the den." She turned to her housekeeper. "If you'd like to leave now, I'm home for the evening, Theresa. I'll see you at seven in the morning."

"Good night, Miss Stanford."

Meg waited until the front door closed behind the older woman. In the den she indicated a pair of chairs and sat facing Zach Tracy, the brilliant young teacher that so many of her friends raved about.

Zach wore his long, sun-bleached hair tied back in a ponytail. Instead of the dress pants and shirt-and-tie look expected of a prep-school tutor, he favored skinny pants tucked into high-tops, and a wrinkled shirt over a faded tee. He'd arrived at Meg's condo carrying a skateboard under his arm, explaining that this was his summertime persona. Come autumn and the start of the school year, he would once again morph into a buttoned-down prep-school teacher.

"How are things working out with you and Cory?"

"Cool. He's a great kid."

She noted that he used *cool* or *great* in nearly every sentence. "So you think he'll be ready for private school?"

"Academically? Hey, if you hadn't told me he was homeschooled, I'd have never guessed. He's a really smart little kid."

Meg began to relax.

"But he's . . . different, you know?"

Meg's protective antenna went up. "Different? In what way?"

Zach shrugged. "When I asked him what he'd like to do for fun, he said he wasn't here to have fun. He was here to make you proud of him. He said somebody named Big Jim had said that women were to be protected. And he'd promised somebody named Jake that he would do everything he could to be a good brother." Zach shook his head. "He's a funny little kid. Calls me 'sir.' He's smart, and cool, but he's just not like any kid I've tutored before. It's like he just dropped down from another planet. Planet Old School." Zach chuckled at his little joke. "And I'm not sure just how he's going to fit in when school starts."

The young teacher got to his feet. "I just thought you ought to know. Maybe you'd like me to work on his social skills along with his academics. Speaking of social skills, I tried to tell him to ditch the cheesy cowboy hat, and you'd have thought I'd insulted his mother. You'd better let him know that he won't be able to wear it to school." He paused. "Same time tomorrow?"

Meg forced herself to smile as she walked with him to the door. "Let me think about it, Zach. I'll call you."

"No problem. If you leave the kid to me, I'll have him up to speed in no time."

When he left, Meg walked to the kitchen and filled a glass with water before looking out the window. Several boys, not much older than Cory, were laughing and shouting as they followed Zach along the sidewalk on their skateboards.

Feeling troubled, she set aside the water and climbed the stairs. She was about to knock on Cory's door when she found it ajar. Inside she could hear Cory talking to someone on the phone.

"... had supper with my tutor, Zach. He said I'm lucky to have a housekeeper who cooks. His mother was a college professor, but the only thing she knew how to cook was grilled cheese sandwiches." There was a pause before he said, "She's fine. She's working awfully hard. She said she has to make it up to the firm because of all the days she missed. She said when she clears her desk, we'll take a day to see the monuments and stuff. But I don't mind. I know she's got to work even harder now that she's got me." His voice lowered. Trembled. "How's Shadow? Does he miss me?"

Meg turned away and made her way to her own room. She didn't want Cory to see her feeling so distressed.

Inside her room she began to pace. Where had it all gone so terribly wrong? When had the joy gone out of her career? Even the tantalizing thought of being offered partnership in the firm had lost its thrill. When she was at the office, all she could think about was Cory spending his days with strangers. When she was here with him, it broke her heart to see how hard he was trying to make this all work.

She thought of Zach, trying to make Cory over into a boy who would fit in with all the other prep school boys. She tried to imagine Cory maneuvering a skateboard along the hot, crowded sidewalks, trading in Jake's old cowboy hat for a backward baseball cap. The mere thought of it had tears stinging her eyes.

And then she recalled Zach's words.

He said he wasn't here to have fun. He was here to make you proud of him...And he'd promised somebody named Jake that he would do everything he could to be a good brother.

A good brother. He was the best little brother in the world. But what kind of sister was she?

Meg dropped down on the edge of her bed and covered her face with her hands, unable to stop the sobs that tore through her.

Jake had been right about her. She'd been running away. Unable to face the truth. The loss of her father had broken something inside of her. Instead of staying and fighting to get back the life she'd been denied, she'd taken the same route her mother had taken all those years earlier. She'd run away. But this time, there would be no one to blame but herself. She might have been a little girl then, but now she was an adult, and responsible for the life of another.

Cory. The memories of her early days in the city, feeling lost and bewildered, came rushing back to her. No one had been here to ease her through that painful transition. She'd felt completely abandoned.

Did she want the same thing for her little brother?

But what was the alternative? How could she return to Wyoming, after that horrid scene with Jake?

She hadn't heard a single word from him. Not one.

By now Jake would have moved on with his life. A life that would have no place for her.

At the soft knock on her door, her head came up.

"Meg? You in there?"

"Yes." She wiped frantically at her eyes as Cory stepped into her room.

"I heard something." He walked closer to peer at her. "You crying?"

"Yeah. Blubbering like a big baby." She tried to smile, but her lips quivered. "Sorry."

"Did somebody hurt you?" His hand was on her shoulder, his eyes suddenly hot with anger.

So like another, she thought with a fresh stab of pain to her heart.

"No. It isn't like that. I'm just feeling . . . sad."

"Is it something I did? I know Zach didn't like my hat, but I thought..."

She drew him down beside her on the edge of the bed. "It isn't anything you did, Cory. It's me. I'm afraid I've made a mess of things."

"What things?"

"Everything. My life. Your life. This." She looked around, trying to see it all through his eyes. "I was hoping we could be happy here. I thought I owed it to myself and you to see if this could work."

"I'll work harder, Meg. I'll do whatever you want."

His words brought a fresh round of tears to her eyes. She sighed and pressed a kiss to the top of his head. "Ela was right, you know. You're such a good boy. But this isn't about anything you did or didn't do. This mistake is entirely mine. And I'm the only one who can fix it."

He turned trusting eyes to hers. "I don't understand."

She took in a deep breath, wondering how she would get through the meeting with Cyrus Kettering in the morning. She would be letting him down. But in the end, she had no choice.

She'd thought, after seeing Jake shot, and thinking that she'd once again lost the person who mattered most in her life, that the wisest thing was to leave before she got her heart broken again.

She'd honestly believed that by coming back to the life she'd made, she would find herself. The only problem was, the person she'd found was no wiser than that girl who'd carried a chip on her shoulder a lifetime ago.

She gathered Cory close. "Pack your things. I need...to see about the ranch. And you need a visit with Shadow."

CHAPTER THIRTY-THREE

As the family gathered around the breakfast table, Big Jim caught sight of Jake's back as he started toward the mudroom. "You think you could spare us some time, boyo?"

"Sorry. Not today." Jake reached for a slice of corn bread before moving toward the door.

"More sick cows this morning, bro?" Josh asked.

"Too many to count. And the day is just starting...." Hearing the ping of a text, Jake caught sight of the caller and read the text before looking up. "It's Cory. He and Meg are flying in. She has to meet with Kirby about ranch business. Cory says they'll be in Paintbrush at noon."

Cole and Phoebe exchanged looks. "Are they coming back for good?" Cole asked.

Jake's fingers shot over the keyboard of his phone, then read the next text. "Cory doesn't know. Apparently

Meg needs to make some decisions about the ranch. But he says she had a serious meeting with her law firm."

"That's good, isn't it?" Phoebe asked.

"Maybe. Maybe not. Cory says they're on the company jet."

Quinn shook his head. "That doesn't sound like a good thing. I don't think the company would fly an ex-employee clear across the country."

"Maybe it's part of her severance package." Sierra glanced hopefully at Josh, who squeezed her hand.

"You should go to Paintbrush and pick them up," Cheyenne said. "You need to pour on the charm so Meg will decide to stay here."

Jake started out the door. "I'm fresh out of charm. I have some things to do in the barn."

"Look, son—"

Jake kept walking. "Not now, Pa."

Before Cole could say more, Big Jim put a hand on his arm to silence him. "He'll work it out in his own way."

Cole said what the rest of them were thinking. "He'd better do it fast before he lets her get away for good."

Phoebe dropped a hand on Cole's shoulder. "If I were betting on the outcome, I'd put my money on Jake." She gave him a gentle smile. "He inherited his father's charm, and that's a very good thing. That Conway charm's been known to persuade a woman to wait a lifetime if necessary."

Her words were enough to silence anything more Cole intended to say.

Meg stared hungrily at the herds of cattle darkening the rangeland as the plane flew over the green fields. In no time it was circling the town of Paintbrush before gliding to a smooth landing. She followed Cory from the plane and saw Big Jim standing beside a ranch truck.

She felt her heart plummet. Though she had adamantly refused to admit it to herself, she'd been hoping to see Jake waiting for her.

The old man hurried forward and caught Cory in a fierce bear hug.

"Did Shadow miss me?" the boy asked.

"Almost as much as the whole family missed you." With his arm around the boy, Big Jim hugged Meg. "Welcome back."

"Thanks. I missed...all your family."

If he noticed her hesitation, he gave no indication.

"Where's Jake?" Cory asked. "I was hoping to see him here."

"Ranch chores. Vet chores. A lot of sick animals around here. You know how it is."

Meg saw the disappointment on Cory's face and hoped her own didn't give away her feelings as easily.

"Come on. I'll drive you home." Big Jim tossed their luggage in the rear of the truck before climbing behind the wheel.

"I ordered a rental car." Meg fastened her seat belt. "I have to pick it up here in town."

"Okay."

"And then I have to make a stop at the courthouse to see Kirby Bolton."

Cory looked up. "Could I go back with Big Jim, or do I have to stay with you?" Seeing Meg's surprise, he added, "I can't wait to see Shadow."

She nodded in understanding. "I don't mind picking

you up later." She glanced at their driver. "As long as it's all right with you, Big Jim."

"It's fine with me. And I know two women who can't wait to feed you, boy."

Cory beamed as they drove through town and stopped at the car rental agency.

Minutes later they waved good-bye to Meg and headed toward the highway.

Meg's meeting with Kirby Bolton went even better than she'd expected. If only, she thought as she drove the rental car along the highway, her meeting with Jake and his family could go as smoothly.

Of course, it wasn't his family she was worried about. They were all such warm, loving people. They had welcomed her when she'd been a stranger, and they would do the same now.

Jake was another matter. She hoped that she could find a way to make him understand why she'd had to leave.

Their parting had been strained. She'd recognized the pain, the anger, inside him. And though she understood it, there was no way to undo what she'd done.

"Oh, Dad," she whispered. "I've made such a mess of things."

She could almost hear Porter's voice. *One step at a time, girl. Rome wasn't built in a day.*

But it wasn't Rome she wanted to build. It was the relationship with Jake that she'd so callously shattered.

As she turned off the highway and followed the curving road to the Conway ranch, she squared her shoulders and took in several quick breaths. Parking behind a row of ranch trucks, she walked up the steps and knocked.

It was Cole who opened the door and hugged her fiercely. "Welcome back, Meg. Come on in."

She saw Cory at the table, with Ela and Phoebe seated on either side of him. Around the table sat the rest of the family, watching while he devoured a thick slice of corn bread and drank a foaming glass of milk.

Meg's heart dropped to her toes. Jake wasn't with them.

The others were on their feet, rushing over to hug her and kiss her cheeks. She found herself answering a dozen questions at once.

"Cory says you're here on ranch business." This from Quinn. "Does that mean you're turning over the control of your ranch to Kirby Bolton?"

"Don't be silly." Cheyenne shot him a look. "Do you think a smart woman like Meg needs someone else to manage her business?"

"It's hard to manage a ranch in Wyoming when you're living in Washington, D.C." This from Josh.

"Are you thinking of coming home, sweetheart?" At Big Jim's question, the others watched with intensity. Even Cory stopped eating to hear her answer.

"A few days ago I would have answered that with a question of my own. Where is home? Wyoming? D.C.?" She crossed the room and lay a hand on Cory's shoulder. "But now, after a lot of soul-searching, I think I know. Though I have a lot to learn, and a lot of years to make up for, Wyoming is the place I intend to call home."

While the others murmured words of approval, Cory stood and gave a little fist pump before wrapping his arms around her waist and giving her a fierce hug.

For a moment she was so startled, she could only stare

down at him. Then, wrapping her arms around him, she returned the hug.

He pushed free of her arms. "Are we really home to stay?"

She managed a laugh. "I wish you'd show a little enthusiasm."

That had everyone laughing with her.

"Can I go tell Jake?"

Meg's smile faded. "He's here?" She'd assumed, by his absence, that he was on a neighboring ranch.

"He's out in the barn with a sick calf."

She struggled to hide the cloud that had suddenly darkened her day. Jake was just steps away, and he hadn't even bothered to welcome her. "I guess, if you've finished your snack..."

The little boy glanced at Ela and Phoebe, who both nodded.

"But just for a minute. We'll need to head back to our place soon."

Before Meg finished speaking, he was out the door in a flash.

"Well." Cole was eyeing Meg carefully while the others fell silent. "I guess I'd better get back to my chores. Will we see you later on?"

Meg shrugged. "I'm sure you'll see me so often you'll be sick and tired of me."

"That will never happen." Cole smiled and turned away.

"We'll join you, Pa." Quinn caught Cheyenne's hand and the two hugged Meg before starting out behind Cole.

"Come on, Sierra." Josh winked. "Playtime's over."

He and his wife gave Meg quick hugs before leaving.

"I'll go with you, boyo." Big Jim squeezed her shoulder before trailing after them.

Phoebe waited until the others had gone before turning to Meg. "Do you have time for some tea?"

Meg gave a shake of her head. She needed, desperately, to be alone with her misery. "I think it's time I get Cory and head home."

Phoebe glanced at Ela, and the two women shared a knowing look before Phoebe said, "I understand. You've been through a lot, Meg. And you've had to make some life-altering decisions in a very short amount of time, without any family to lend a hand."

Meg sighed. "Oh, Phoebe. You have no idea how confusing it's been. I'm still not certain I'm making the right decisions. It's hard enough trying to decide what's best for me. But holding Cory's future in my hands is...terrifying. I want so badly to do the right thing for him."

Phoebe squeezed her hand. "Trust your instincts, Meg."

Ela nodded and lay a hand on Meg's shoulder. "More than anything, trust your heart."

Meg wanted to fall into their arms and weep. But pride wouldn't allow it. Instead, she straightened and stepped back.

"Thank you both. Now I'd better fetch Cory."

She walked out the back door and stood by her truck, cupping her hands to her mouth as she called Cory's name.

After a few minutes she sighed. He wasn't going to make this easy for her. Like it or not, she would have to go into the barn. And that meant facing Jake, who had made his feelings for her abundantly clear.

"Cory." She pulled open the barn door and stepped inside, waiting for her eyes to adjust to the gloom.

Hearing no reply she walked from stall to stall. As she rounded an open stall door a dark head came up and she found herself face-to-face with Jake, who was holding a syringe to a calf.

Her heart took a series of sharp, quick bounces at the sight of him. She'd been so afraid that she'd magnified him in her mind. That she'd turned him into a larger-than-life hero. But here he was, the same sexy cowboy who was perfectly at home in dusty boots, faded denims, and a sweat-stained shirt, sleeves rolled above the elbows to reveal arms corded with muscles.

He set aside the syringe. "Cory said you've come back to stay."

Unable to trust her voice, she simply nodded.

His eyes, she noted, were fierce. Fixed on her as though he couldn't quite believe what he was seeing.

"Well, you've made him one happy little kid."

"His happiness is important to me."

Jake nodded. "That's what happens in a family." He paused before asking, "What about your job?"

"I was offered a dream title. Partner. At one time, it would have meant the world to me. I told Cyrus that I was grateful, but I needed to leave the city and go back to my roots. The ride home on the corporate jet was his way of thanking me for all I'd contributed to the firm."

"And Noah?" Jake's voice was tight. Strained.

She shook her head. "He's already moved on to one of the new hires. She's young and bright and easily impressed by his success."

"So, you've severed all your ties?"

She nodded.

"I met with Kirby Bolton. He's asked me to take on some of his clients. Between the law and the ranch, I'll have my hands full." She managed a dry laugh. "Now, if I can just make it all pay the bills."

"You're a smart woman, Meg. You'll manage just fine." He turned away and wiped his hands on a towel before latching the stall door.

She was being dismissed. Coldly. Completely. And didn't she deserve it, after the way she'd left?

She felt the sting of tears as she looked at the rigid line of his back.

"I believe you came looking for Cory. He's out in the corral with my family."

He was giving her an excuse to escape. Her first inclination was to take it and run. She turned away.

In the blink of an eye it occurred to her that she'd been doing that for a lifetime. No more. No more running.

She was better than that.

The words that had played through her mind, first as a frightened child and later as an overwhelmed adult, taunted her.

I am strong, smart, and capable.

She squared her shoulders and turned back to face Jake.

"I need to say something."

She saw the flicker of surprise in his eyes before the wary look returned.

"You were right, Jake. I was running away. When I saw you shot, I thought I'd lost you. Something inside snapped. I figured I'd leave you before you left me. I wasn't ready to trust the feelings I had for you. Maybe it was too much too soon. I'd buried my father, acquired a little brother, and found myself head over heels in love with a guy that I figured was all wrong for me. Whatever the reason, I was running—"

He caught her roughly by the shoulders, his eyes hot and fierce. "Say that again."

She stiffened and sucked in a breath. "I said you were right. I was running away."

"Not that. The part about being head over heels in love."

"Oh." She managed to breathe. But just barely.

"Say it, Meg." His gaze challenged her. "Tell me again."

"I'm crazy in love with a cowboy, Jake." She gave a little laugh. "Can you imagine? The sophisticated, big-city lawyer lost her heart to a—"

Her words were abruptly cut off as his mouth covered hers in a kiss so hot, so hungry, it stole all her breath.

When they came up for air she stared at him with a dazed expression. "You're not mad?"

"Yes. I'm mad. More than mad. I've been over-the-edge crazy since you left. Meg, the minute you walked out of my life, left, all the things I once loved weren't fun anymore. It was like a switch had been thrown and all the sunlight went out. I realized that I didn't want to live another day without you." He shook his head. "I know that legal mind of yours would like to figure all the angles before you commit, but if you're serious about loving me, I'm asking you to just throw caution to the wind and agree to the biggest, craziest contract of your life." At her puzzled look he said softly, "I'm asking you to be my wife."

"Jake, I..." She sniffed and wiped at the tears that were rolling down her cheeks like a river. "I thought I'd hurt you too badly, and that you'd never...we'd never..."

"No speeches, counselor." When she swiped at her tears he said softly, "A simple yes or no will do."

Too choked up to speak, she simply nodded her head.

He dragged her into his arms and kissed her with a sharp hunger that caught them both by surprise.

She felt the world do a slow dip, and she wrapped her arms around his waist to anchor herself. Oh, it felt so good to be held in these strong arms once again. "I missed this, Jake. I missed you so much."

"Not half as much as I missed you."

"Oh boy!" Cory's shout of joy from the doorway of the barn had Meg and Jake looking back to see the entire family gathered around, hanging on their every word.

"It's about time the two of you figured out what's really important," Big Jim called.

"We were afraid you'd let that stubborn pride get in the way," Cole added.

Laughing, crying, Meg threw herself into their out-stretched arms.

Cole winked at his son. "That boy of mine's been moping around ever since you left, Meg."

Meg turned to him. "Oh, Jake." She was laughing through her tears. "What am I going to do with you?"

"Marry me as soon as possible," he said, dragging her close for another kiss while his family cheered, "and make me the happiest cowboy in Wyoming."

"How could I refuse such a romantic proposal?"

Phoebe, Ela, Cheyenne, and Sierra gathered around, hugging Meg, hugging Jake, hugging Cory, and wiping tears of joy from their faces.

"Just think." Phoebe turned to the women. "We get to plan another wedding."

Quinn and Josh caught Jake's arm and pulled him aside.

"You know what this means, bro." Quinn made a throat-slitting gesture. "We get treated to weeks of questions on where you'll live, and what you'll wear, and what kind of ceremony to plan."

"We can live at Meg's ranch, at least until Meg decides what she wants to do with the place. I'm sure, if you and Cheyenne could manage two ranches, we can, too."

Quinn rolled his eyes. "Is this the brother who thought love was too mushy, and insisted he was never going to cave in? How the mighty have fallen, little bro."

Jake dragged Meg into his arms for yet another kiss. "Don't listen to a word they say. I have no idea who they're talking about."

Meg wrapped her arms around his waist and looked into his eyes, the love shining so brightly it almost blinded her. Then she turned to look at his big, wonderful family. And then at the gloriously happy face of her little brother.

At the moment her heart was so full, she was afraid it might burst like a bubble.

Life, she thought, just didn't get any better than this.

While the others headed toward the house to celebrate the news, Cole caught Phoebe's hand and drew her aside.

"There are some things I need to say, Phoebe." Cole's voice, low and deep, had a catch to it as he spoke her name. "And it's taken me a long time to say them."

She glanced at their joined hands, and then up into his eyes.

"When you first came here, I was drowning in despair."

"Cole—"

He put a finger to her lips. "Let me finish. I need to say this. When you first walked into my life, I truly believed that I would never feel anything again except pain and anger and bitterness. I walked around in a cloud of self-pity. I neglected my boys, my father, my health. I couldn't see beyond my own pain. But through it all, there you were. Calm. Quiet. Efficient. Loving. Able to love all of us, and especially me when I was so undeserving of love. There were so many times when I thought my bad temper would drive you to leave us. But you stayed. And I'm so glad you did. I never believed I had the right to tell you what I was feeling. But now..." He framed her face with his big, work-worn hands and gazed into eyes that were filled with trust and something more.

"I love you, Phoebe. I've loved you for a very long time now, though I was afraid to admit it, even to myself. Somehow, I felt that I didn't have the right to such feelings. But now, with the last of my sons ready to settle down and make a life for himself, I'm free to say it out loud. If I could, I'd shout it from the rooftop. I love you, Phoebe. I know I'm not the easiest man in the world to live with, but if you'll have me, I'd be honored if you'd be my wife."

"Oh, Cole." She brushed her lips over his. "I've waited so long to hear those words. Of course I'll marry you. But let's wait to tell the family until after Jake and Meg have their special day."

"All right. We'll wait to tell them, and then we'll pay a call on Reverend Cornell. Just the two of us." He gathered her into his arms and kissed her.

"The two of us. That has a nice ring to it." She wrapped her arms around his neck and returned his kisses with all the passion she'd been holding inside.

Against her lips he muttered, "And when the snows come, and the ranch settles down into the quiet of winter, we're going to slip away to a sunny spot somewhere and lie on the beach like a couple of teenage lovers."

"It's a date. I like the way you think." She laughed. "But I'm betting we'll miss the ranch and the family so much, we'll cut our honeymoon short just to be with all of them."

"You're probably right. But we won't let them know."

They stood together, laughing, kissing, then laughing again.

Love, it seemed, was contagious, and the entire Conway family had been infected.

"Oh, Phoebe." Cole looked into her eyes. "We can finally be together. Really together."

Together. She'd waited a lifetime to heard that word. A word so sweet, it brought tears to her eyes.

EPILOGUE

Summer had turned the lush meadows to fields of tall wavy grasses. The cattle were fat and healthy, feasting on the rich grass of the high country. The days were long and hot, the nights perfumed with the fragrance of fields of wildflowers.

Meg and Jake loved the nights best of all. After the back-breaking chores and long, noisy dinners with the Conway clan, they would hurry back to Meg's ranch to tuck Cory into bed and then, while the world was hushed and cloaked in darkness, they would lie together, caught up in the wonder of their newly discovered love.

That love touched everyone who came near them, and had everyone's heart beating faster because of it. There were more secret smiles. More whispered words of endearment, not only by the soon-to-wed couple, but by Jake's brothers and their wives, as well. Even Big Jim and Cole seemed more at ease, while Phoebe and Ela delighted in the newest additions to their world. The presence of Cory reminded them of the boys they'd helped raise, and gave them glimpses of the man he would become.

Now that Cory's future was no longer in question, the little boy blossomed under all this new attention. The knowledge that he was now part of a big, affectionate family calmed his fears and had him playing and laughing like any seven-year-old boy.

Before their wedding day dawned, Meg had insisted that Jake spend the night at his place, leaving her alone with Cory. Brother and sister had sat up late, talking about the father they'd shared, and the memories Cory had of his pretty, young mother. Meg was determined to help him keep his memories alive.

"Judge Bolton was one of the few folks who knew your mother, Cory. And he told me that she'd confided in him that she'd finally found a man who treated her with love and respect. And despite their age difference, our dad loved her, too. He said he'd found his 'forever' wife."

"Is that what you're going to be, Meg? Jake's forever wife?"

She nodded. "That's the plan."

"Good." He yawned loudly, before she followed him up the stairs and tucked him in for the night. "'Cause I really want to be like Jake when I grow up."

She kissed him and felt a quick tug at her heart.

After Meg loaded their wedding clothes in her new truck, she walked out to the corral, where Cory was riding Shadow bareback.

"Time to go, Cory."

The boy slid from the pony's back and carefully

latched the gate before racing ahead to the truck. When
it came to going to the Conway ranch, Cory needed no
coaxing.

As Jake had taught him, he held the door until Meg
was settled in the driver's side, then he rounded the cab
and climbed in before fastening his seat belt.

She turned on the ignition and caught Cory watching her.

At her arched brow he asked, "You ready?"

Her smile was radiant. "I can't wait."

His smile matched hers. "Me, either."

The Conway kitchen smelled of slow-cooking roast beef
and biscuits. There was a hint of cinnamon and spice in
the air. Phoebe was busy putting the finishing touches on
the special wedding cake she had baked. Atop the chocolate cake, mounded with whipped cream frosting, she had
added a bride dressed in a prim jacket and skirt and holding an attaché case as a tribute to the fact that Meg had
opened a small law practice in town. The groom atop the
cake wore denims and was carrying a calf slung over his
shoulders. Between them was a small boy looking up at
them and smiling.

The men had taken themselves off to the hilltop, anx-
ious to leave the serious business of getting ready to the
women of the house.

Meg was upstairs with Cheyenne and Sierra. In these past
few weeks the three young women had become closer
than sisters.

At the moment the three were dressed in robes. Meg's
was a short silk kimono that fell to her knees. Cheyenne

wore a cotton wrap, while Sierra wore a long terry robe that could have easily fit someone twice her size. On her, it managed to look chic.

Meg was seated in front of a dressing table. Cheyenne stood behind her, hairbrush in hand. Sierra stood to one side, adjusting the focus of her camera.

"How about a manicure after this?" Cheyenne asked.

"I'll only ruin it when I muck stalls tomorrow."

"Am I hearing right?" Sierra lowered her camera. "Meg, you've already morphed from designer-clad city girl to practical rancher."

"I guess all that contact with Jake rubbed off on me."

The three laughed as Cheyenne unzipped the plastic cover shielding Meg's gown. "Oh. Look at this. Where did you find it?"

Meg shed her kimono and began slipping into the gown. "In the attic of my fath—of my ranch house," she corrected. "It was the gown my mother wore when she married my father. I thought it would make them both happy to see me wearing it today."

"So you've forgiven them for the past?" Cheyenne asked.

"Like Jake said, it's all in the past. I'd rather concentrate on the future."

Both Cheyenne and Sierra sighed as Meg finished dressing and turned for their approval.

The old-fashioned gown had a sweetheart neckline, and fell in a fluid column of white silk to her ankles. She wore strappy sandals on her feet. At her throat and ears were her mother's pearls.

"Oh, Meg, you look stunning," Cheyenne breathed.

"Good. I think I'd like to stun Jake."

"You don't need a gown for that," Sierra said with a laugh, as she slipped into the pretty pink dress she'd chosen to wear. "The minute that man saw you, he fell. Hard."

Meg arched a brow. "You knew?"

Sierra laughed. "We *all* knew it."

"All except Jake, of course." Cheyenne zipped the pale lemon dress Meg had helped her choose for the ceremony. "Men are always the last to know."

Meg paused to admire their dresses and accessories. Then she pulled two small jeweler's boxes from her purse and handed them to Sierra and Cheyenne.

Cheyenne studied the box. "What's this?"

"Open it and find out." Meg watched as they tore open the boxes and gaped at the simple platinum bracelets, each bearing a single jeweled charm. "Cheyenne, yours is a wolf. For obvious reasons," Meg said, as she fastened the bracelet to Cheyenne's wrist. "And Sierra, there was never any doubt that yours would be a camera."

The two young women turned their wrists this way and that, watching as the charms glinted in the sunlight.

"I love it," Cheyenne whispered, as she hugged Meg.

"I'm never taking it off," Sierra said, wrapping her arms around Meg's neck.

"I wanted something special, to let you know how grateful I am for having the two of you in my life. I feel so lucky to have you as sisters and friends."

"We're the lucky ones." Cheyenne linked her arms with Meg and Sierra. "Let's go downstairs and let Phoebe and Ela see the beautiful bride."

As they started out of the room, Meg paused to pick up a mesh bag.

"More gifts?" Sierra asked.

She merely nodded and gave them both a mysterious smile.

Big Jim stood beside Clementine's headstone, watching as the others began arriving.

Cole, carrying a box of cigars, climbed the hill with Quinn, who was holding a bottle of Irish whiskey, and Josh, who was juggling a tray with five crystal glasses.

Behind them, Jake, looking handsome in his jeans and denim jacket, had an arm around the shoulders of Cory, who sported a fresh haircut and a starched white shirt tucked neatly into his jeans.

Big Jim chuckled. "I see Ela had her way, boyo. She said she was trimming that hair and getting you into a white shirt for your sister's wedding day."

Cory merely smiled, something he'd been doing for days now.

Cole cleared his throat. His voice was solemn. "We stand here on sacred ground, to celebrate a very special occasion."

He watched while Josh filled the glasses with whiskey and handed them around.

"I'll begin," Big Jim said. He raised his glass. "Here's to Clementine and Seraphine, the brave women who made this day possible."

They turned toward the graves and took a long drink, while Big Jim and Cole ran their hands lovingly over the carved headstones.

Cole offered the second toast. "To Jake, who found himself a bride worthy of the Conway name."

They lifted their glasses and drank again.

Jake's eyes twinkled with humor. "And to Cory, who is about to become the youngest member of our family. For now, at least."

"To Cory," the others said solemnly.

Cory, getting into the spirit of the event, looked around at the tall, handsome Conway men. "Jake said when he marries my sister he'll become my brother. Does that mean that Quinn and Josh are my brothers, too?"

"That it does, boyo." Big Jim was grinning from ear to ear. "And you gain a whole big loving family, as well."

"Oh boy." Cory was beaming with pleasure.

"And in honor of the occasion I've brought a surprise." Jake unbuttoned his jacket to reveal a yellow ball of fluff.

"Trouble!" Cory's voice was high-pitched in disbelief. "Jake, where'd you get him?"

"From Randy. He said now that Trouble is old enough to be weaned, he wanted you to have him."

"You mean it? Forever?" The boy's eyes were wide with pure joy as he gathered the puppy into his arms and had his face licked over and over.

"He's all yours, Cory. But remember, his messes are also yours to clean. And with a name like Trouble, I'm guessing there will be a whole lot of messes before he's through growing up."

"You bet. Puppies are a lot like sons," Cole said with a wink.

"Can I show him to Phoebe and Ela?" Cory asked.

"I don't see why not."

The minute the words were out of Jake's mouth, the boy was flying down the hill toward the house, leaving the men to drink their whiskey and wait for the preacher and the women who would be joining them shortly.

* * *

"Oh, just look at you." Phoebe stood at the bottom of the stairs and watched as Meg descended, the silk gown swirling gracefully about her ankles. The housekeeper used the edge of her apron to wipe her eye. "You're so beautiful, you've got me all teary eyed."

Beside her, Ela folded her hands at her waist and merely smiled.

"I have something for each of you." Meg opened the mesh bag and removed two silver boxes.

Phoebe opened hers first to reveal a platinum bracelet bearing a charm depicting a mother and three sons. Two were holding to her skirts, while the third and youngest was in her arms. All three were looking at her with love and trust.

"Jake and I thought it suited you. He told me that you bought his first suit for a dance. You listened to his troubles with his dad, with his friends, with girls. You're his mother, Phoebe, even though you didn't give him life."

Phoebe's eyes filled and she found herself too overcome to do more than hug Meg before wiping her eyes with her apron.

They turned to watch Ela open her jeweler's box. Inside was a platinum bracelet with a charm depicting a woman in elaborate Arapaho dress, holding in her hands a loaf of bread.

"Bread is life," she said softly.

"That's what Jake told me. You've been here, giving Big Jim, Cole, and his sons life for as long as they can remember. You're as essential to this family as life, Ela. And we're so lucky to have you."

Deeply touched, she held out her arm while Meg affixed the bracelet around her wrist. The two embraced.

They all looked up when Cory burst into the room shouting, "Look. Look what Mr. Morton gave me. He's mine to keep. Forever."

"Trouble." Meg's smile was almost as wide as Cory's as he passed the puppy around for everyone to admire.

Hearing the sound of an engine, Phoebe dried her tears and turned toward the door. "Reverend Cornell is here. We'd better get outside for the ceremony."

With Cory running ahead, Trouble at his heels, the women held hands and started up the hill.

Halfway there, Jake was waiting, his look both fierce and tender as he got his first view of Meg. The others went ahead, leaving him alone with his bride-to-be.

"Just look at you." His words were whispered, as though spoken in a church.

She laughed. "I wasn't going to indulge in a gown, but this was my mother's, and I told myself that a girl only gets to do this once. At least if she's lucky."

"I'm the lucky one." Jake took both her hands in his and continued staring at her. "I'm afraid, Meg."

"Of marriage?"

He shook his head. "Afraid that I'm dreaming. That none of this is true. That I'll wake up and this wonderful feeling of absolute love and peace will be gone, without a trace."

Without a trace.

Her heart nearly broke for him. She touched a finger to his lips to silence him. "I'm not going anywhere, Jake. I told Cory that I'm your forever wife. And you're my forever love."

He drew her close and kissed her with the sort of reverence that had her heart tripping over itself. Then for good measure, he kissed her again, before drawing a little away and catching her hand in his.

"Let's join the preacher and make it official."

As they joined the Conway family on sacred ground, with the graves of Clementine and her five sons, and the fresh grave of Seraphine beside them, they spoke their vows.

Out of the corner of her eye Meg saw Phoebe tuck her hand through the crook of Cole's arm. The two shared a look that was so tender, so loving, so intimate, it sent a thrill through Meg's heart.

Then she was kissing her new husband, and the family surged forward to offer their hugs and kisses and heartfelt congratulations.

Above the sound of voices talking, laughing, she heard the sighing of a woman's voice. Was it Seraphine, letting her know that she was grateful for the chance to be home? Or just the sighing of the wind through the leaves?

No matter. Seraphine wasn't the only one who'd come home.

Meg thought of the woman she'd been when she'd come here, angry and bitter, determined to bury her past along with her father. Instead, she'd regained the love she'd had for this land, and had found a new love that was as shiny and bright as the sun.

It had to be the sun that had made her eyes all misty.

Meg looped her arm through Jake's, and they watched Cory chasing after Trouble, and the family descending the hill to the house and their wedding supper.

They paused to share a long, lingering kiss.

"Come on, wife." Jake kept his arm around her shoulders. "I can't wait to spend the rest of our lives together forever."

Together. Forever.

His words sent a thrill coursing along her spine.

Now weren't those just the finest words ever?

As the oldest of the Conway brothers, Quinn's only concern is protecting his family and their land. But when beautiful Cheyenne O'Brien's ranch is plagued by a series of "accidents," Quinn will risk his heart—and his very life—to keep her safe...

❧

Please turn this page
for a preview of

QUINN

Available now

Quinn framed the wolf in his long-range viewfinder and snapped off a couple of quick photos. The male's coat, thick and shaggy, was matted with snow from the blizzard that had been raging now for three days.

After Quinn had left the ranch and returned to the mountain, it had taken considerable skill to locate the pack, despite the homing device implanted in the male. Cut off from their den by the storm and with the alpha female about to give birth, the pack had hunkered down in the shelter of some rocks near the top of a nearby hill. Since there'd been no sighting of the female, Quinn was fairly certain there would be a litter of pups before morning. That would create a problem for the leader of the pack, whose hunting ground had been narrowed considerably by the unexpected spring snowstorm. The alpha male would have to provide food and shelter for his pack, and all would have to wait out the storm before returning to their den.

Quinn saw the male's attention fixed on something in the distance. Using his binoculars, Quinn studied the terrain. When he spied a small herd of deer nearly hidden in a stand of trees, he understood what had snagged the wolf's interest.

The springtime blizzard had caught all of nature by surprise, it would seem. As Quinn watched, a doe dropped her newborn into the snow and began licking it clean of afterbirth.

Sadly, the doe and her fawn, in such a vulnerable state, would be the perfect mark for a hungry pack of wolves desperate for food during their own confinement.

The male wolf took up a predator position, dropping low as he crept slowly up the hill until he reached the very peak. For a moment he remained as still as a statue, gazing into the distance.

Quinn watched, transfixed. Even though he knew this would end in the bloody death of a helpless newborn fawn, he also knew that it would mean the difference between life and death for the pack of wolves unable to go forward until their own newborns were strong enough to travel. Their strength, their survival, depended upon sustenance. The female, too weak at the moment to hunt, would trust her leader to provide fresh meat while she nursed her young.

Quinn felt again the familiar thrill as he saw the alpha male rise up and begin to run full speed across the rim of the hill. The raw power, the fierce determination of this animal, never failed to touch a chord deep inside him.

The wolf dipped below the rim of the hill and was lost from sight.

Quinn experienced a rush of annoyance. He wanted to

record the kill for his journal. But something had caused the wolf to veer off-course at the last moment. Snatching up his camera, Quinn was on his feet, racing up the hill, half-blinded by the curtain of snow that stung his face like shrapnel.

He was halfway up the hill when he heard the unmistakable sound of a rifle shot echo and reecho across the hills. It reverberated in his chest like a thunderous pulse.

Heart pounding, he ran full speed the rest of the distance.

When he came to the spot where the male had fallen, Quinn stared at the crimson snow, the beautiful body now silent and still, and felt a mingling of pain and rage rising up inside, clogging his throat, tightening a band around his heart until he had to struggle for each breath.

How dare anyone end such a magnificent life. Why?

He studied the prints left in the snow made by a single horse.

Far off in the distance, barely visible through the falling snow, was a tiny beam of light.

An isolated ranch house, it would seem.

Clouds scudded across the rising moon, leaving the countryside in near darkness.

Quinn knew that he needed to return to his campsite soon and settle in for the night or risk freezing. But he was determined to confront the rancher who had just robbed Quinn's pack of its leader. A cruel act that had not only left the vulnerable female and her newborn pups without a guardian but had also cut short the scholarly research that had consumed the past five years of Quinn's life.

With a heavy heart he turned away, knowing that by

morning scavengers would have swept the area clean of
any trace of carnage. It was the way of nature.

Even if he were so inclined, there wasn't time to dispose of the wolf's body. Quinn needed to follow the
tracks in the snow before the storm obliterated them completely. Already the surrounding countryside had fallen
under the mantle of darkness.

He returned to his campsite and began to pack up his
meager supplies. As he did so, anger rose up like bile,
burning the back of his throat and eyes.

All attempts at scholarly disinterest were swept away
in a tide of fury at the loss of the wolf Quinn had come to
love.

He could no longer hide behind a professional wall of
anonymity.

This was personal.

He needed, for his own satisfaction, to confront the
rancher who had snuffed out the life of the creature that
had consumed every minute of every day of his life for
the past five years.

As he shouldered his supplies and began the trek in
the darkness, he found his thoughts turning to his father.
There was no comparison between this despicable act and
the horrible trauma Cole had suffered at losing Seraphine.
Still, the loss was so deeply felt that it connected Quinn
to Cole Conway in a way that nothing else ever had.

Was this how Cole had felt when he'd faced the greatest loss of his life? Had he been swamped with this
helpless, hopeless sense that everything that he'd worked
for had just been swept away by some cruel whim of
fate?

Cole had been, in those early days, inconsolable. A

man so grief stricken, even the love for his children and his father, Big Jim, hadn't been able to lift him out of the depths of hell. Cole's only coping mechanism had been to throw himself into every hard, physically demanding chore he could find around the ranch, many of which would have broken a less determined man.

Right this minute, Quinn would welcome any challenge that would lift him out of his own private hell.

Quinn moved through the waist-high drifts, keeping the light of the distant ranch house always in his sight.

Someone would answer for this vicious deed.

Someone would pay.

As Quinn drew close enough to peer through the falling snow, he could make out the sprawling ranch house and, some distance away, the first of several barns and outbuildings.

He was turning toward the house when he caught the glint of light in the barn. Pausing just outside the open door, he watched the rancher forking hay into a stall, where a horse stomped, blowing and snorting, as though winding down from a hard ride. The snow that coated the rancher's parka and wide-brimmed hat was further proof that he'd just retreated from the blizzard that raged beyond these walls.

Quinn stepped inside, holding his rifle loosely at his side. It wasn't his intention to threaten the rancher, merely to confront him. But right this minute, Quinn relished the thought of a good knock-down, drag-out fight. For one tiny instant he was that helpless boy again, confronting the rancher Porter Stanford as he'd gloated over the needless deaths of a wolf and her pups. Then Quinn snapped back to the present, though the thought of that long-ago scene had his voice lowering to a growl.

"I'm tracking a wolf-hating rancher. Looks like I found him."

The figure whirled.

Quinn continued to keep his rifle pointed at the ground, though his finger tightened reflexively on the trigger when he caught the glint of metal as the rancher lifted the pitchfork in a menacing gesture.

"Who the hell do you think you are?"

Quinn blinked. The voice didn't match the image he'd had of a tough Wyoming rancher. It was obviously female. Soft. Throaty. Breathless, as though she'd been running hard.

"My name is Quinn Conway. My spread's about fifty miles east of here. And you'd be ... ?"

"Don't act coy with me. You know who I am. You're trespassing on my land. I'll give you one minute to turn tail and leave, or you'll answer to this."

Quinn realized that, though her left hand continued to hold the pitchfork aloft, her right hand had dipped into the pocket of her parka and she was holding a very small, very shiny pistol aimed at his chest.

He lifted a hand, palm up. "I didn't come here to hurt you."

"Oh, sure. That's why you burst into my barn holding a rifle?"

"I'm here to get some answers."

"Sorry. I'm fresh out." She tossed aside the pitchfork and in one quick motion pocketed the pistol and grabbed a rifle leaning against the wall. Taking careful aim, she hissed, "Now get, whoever you are. And tell Deke I have no intention of changing my mind. If he thinks he can send some bully—"

Quinn reacted so quickly she didn't have time to blink. He kicked aside her rifle, sending it flying into the air. Before it landed in the hay, he'd leaped at her, taking her down and pinning her arms and legs with such force beneath him that she was helpless to move anything except her head.

She let loose with a stream of oaths that would have withered a seasoned cowboy. That merely reinforced Quinn's determination to pin her down until her fury ran its course.

In the process, his own anger seemed to intensify. He'd come here to confront a cold-blooded wolf killer. What he'd found was a crazy woman.

"Let me up." Teeth clenched, she bucked and shuddered with impotent rage.

"Not until..." His breath was coming hard and fast and he found himself having to use every ounce of his strength to keep her pinned. In the process, he became aware of the soft curves beneath the parka, and the fresh, clean evergreen scent of her hair and clothes. "...you agree to give me some answers."

"Go to hell."

Damn her. He wanted to end this tussle, but she wasn't going to make it easy for him. And the longer he lay on top of her, the more aware he became of the woman and less of the enemy he'd come here to confront. "You're not going to cooperate?"

When she made no response, he dug in, using his size and weight to intimidate. "You shot a wolf out there on the trail. I want to know why."

"A wolf?" She stopped fighting him.

He absorbed a small measure of relief that she seemed to be relenting.

She was clearly out of breath. "What business is this of yours?"

"That wolf is my business."

He saw her eyes go wide. "This is really about the wolf?"

"What did you think it was about?"

He saw the way she was studying him beneath half-lowered lashes and realized how he must look, hair wild and tangled, his face heavily bearded from his days on the trail.

He decided to take a calculated risk. Moving quickly, he got to his feet and held out a hand.

Ignoring his offer of help, she rolled aside and got her bearings before turning to face him.

Her hand went to the pocket where she'd stowed her pistol but didn't dip inside, remaining instead where he could see it.

"Let's start over." He fought to keep the anger from his voice. "My name is Quinn Conway. I study the life cycle of wolves. I was tracking my pack when the alpha male was shot. I followed the shooter here. Now I want to know why a rancher would kill a wolf that was only hunting food for his pack."

When she held her silence, he arched a brow. "It's your turn to introduce yourself and say... 'My name is... I shot the wolf because...' "

"My name isn't important, but the wolf is. It was threatening my herd. That's what wolves do. And what smart ranchers do is shoot them before they can rip open a helpless calf."

"My wolf was stalking a herd of deer."

"Your wolf?" She eyed him suspiciously. "I didn't realize he was a pet."

"He isn't. Wasn't," Quinn corrected. "He was, in fact, the object of years of scholarly research."

"Uh-huh." She shot him a look guaranteed to freeze a man's heart at a hundred paces. "I wouldn't know anything about scholarly research, but common sense told me he was about to take out one of my calves. And I got him before he could get to my herd. Now if you don't mind..." She turned away.

Before she could reach for her rifle Quinn caught her arm. "I don't believe you. I saw the herd of deer."

She yanked herself free of his grasp. "I don't give a damn what you believe. I know what I saw."

"Prove it."

Her head came up sharply. "I don't have to prove anything to you."

"You already have. The fact that you're a liar."

Her eyes narrowed on him. "Look. I don't care what you call me. I know what I saw."

But even as she spoke, he could see the wheels turning as she cast a glance at the snow swirling in the darkness just beyond the barn. Neither of them was eager to face the blizzard. But neither of them was willing to concede that fact.

She took in a breath. "You can saddle up the mare over there."

Without another word she turned away and began saddling the big roan stallion she'd been tending.

Quinn crossed to the other stall and began saddling the spotted mare.

When both horses were saddled and ready, Quinn and the woman moved out single file, into the stinging snow and darkness of night.

Each of them was carrying a rifle.

Neither of them was willing to give an inch until this trek was over.

In Quinn's mind, it would end with this crazy woman admitting her mistake and apologizing for the wrong she'd done. Not that it would make anything right. The wolf would still be dead and his pack left without a leader. But for Quinn this was all about justice.

Once again he flashed back to that incident in his boyhood. He hadn't been able to do anything about that female wolf and her pups. But things were different now. This time, he would have the satisfaction of knowing he'd done all he could to persuade at least one angry rancher to give the wolves of this world a fighting chance to survive.

THE DISH

Where authors give you the inside scoop!

♥ ♥ ♥ ♥ ♥ ♥ ♥ ♥ ♥ ♥ ♥ ♥ ♥ ♥ ♥

From the desk of Kristen Callihan

Dear Reader,

I write books set in the Victorian era. Usually we don't see women with careers in historical romance, but one of the best things about exploring this "other" London in my Darkest London series is that my heroines can lead atypical lives.

In WINTERBLAZE, Poppy Ellis Lane is not only a quiet bookseller and loving wife, she's also part of an organization dedicated to keeping the populace of London in the dark about supernatural beasts that roam the streets—a discovery that comes as quite a shock to her husband, Police Inspector Winston Lane.

Now pregnant, Poppy Lane develops a craving for all things baked, but most especially fresh breads. Being hard-working, however, Poppy has little time or patience for complicated baking—an inclination I share! Popovers are a great compromise, as they are ridiculously easy to make and ridiculously good.

Poppy's Popovers (yields about 6 popovers)

You'll need:

- 1 cup all-purpose flour
- 2 eggs

- 1 cup milk
- 1/2 teaspoon salt

Topping (optional)

- 1/2 cup sugar
- 1 teaspoon ground cinnamon
- a dash of cayenne pepper (to taste)
- 4 tablespoons melted butter

Directions

1. Preheat oven to 450 degrees F. Spray muffin tin with nonstick spray or butter and sprinkle with flour. (I like the spray for the easy factor.)
2. In a bowl, begin to whisk eggs; add in flour, milk, and salt, and beat until it just turns smooth. Do not over-beat; your popovers will be resentful and tough if you do! Fill up each muffin cup until halfway full–the pop-overs are going to rise. (Like, a *lot*.)
3. Bake for 20 minutes at 450 degrees F, then lower oven temperature to 350 degrees F and bake 20 minutes more, until golden brown and puffy.
4. Meanwhile, for topping, mix the sugar, cinnamon, and dash of cayenne pepper—this is hot stuff and you only want a hint of it—in a shallow bowl and stir until combined. Melt butter in another bowl and set aside.
5. Remove popovers from the muffin pan, being careful not to puncture them. Then brush with melted butter and roll them in the sugar mix, shaking off the excess. Serve immediately.

Inspector Lane likes to add a dollop of raspberry jam and feed them to his wife in the comfort of their bed.

He claims they make Poppy quite agreeable...*Ahem*. You, however, might like to enjoy them with a cup of tea and a good book!

♥ ♥ ♥ ♥ ♥ ♥ ♥ ♥ ♥ ♥ ♥ ♥ ♥ ♥ ♥ ♥

From the desk of R.C. Ryan

Dear Reader,

To me there's nothing sexier than a strong, handsome hunk with a soft spot for kids and animals. That's why, in Book 3 of my Wyoming Sky series, I decided that my hero, Jake Conway, would be a veterinarian, as well as the town heartthrob. Now, who could I choose to play the love interest of a charming cowboy who has all the females from sixteen to sixty sighing? Why not a smart, cool, sophisticated, Washington, D.C. lawyer who looks, as Jake describes her, "as out of place as a prom dress at a rodeo"? Better yet, just to throw Meg Stanford even more off her stride, why not add a surprise half-brother with whom she has absolutely nothing in common?

I had such fun watching these two try every possible way to deny the attraction.

But there's so much more to their story than a hot romance. There's also the fact that someone wants to harm Meg and her little half-brother. And what about the mystery that has haunted the Conway family for twenty-five years? The disappearance of Seraphine, mother of Quinn, Josh, and Jake, chronicled in Books 1 and 2, will finally be resolved in Book 3.

In writing the stories of Quinn, Josh, and Jake, I completely lost my heart to this strong, loving family, and I confess I had mixed emotions as I wrote the final chapter.

I hope all of my readers will enjoy the journey. I guarantee you a bumpy but exhilarating ride.

Happy Reading!

R. C. Ryan

RyanLangan.com
Twitter, @RuthRyanLangan
Facebook.com

♥ ♥ ♥ ♥ ♥ ♥ ♥ ♥ ♥ ♥ ♥ ♥ ♥ ♥

From the desk of Margaret Mallory

Dear Reader,

Ilysa is in love with her older brother's best friend. Sad to say, the lass doesn't have a chance with him.

As her clan chieftain, Connor MacDonald is the sixteenth-century Highland equivalent of a pro quarterback, movie star, Special Forces hero, and CEO all rolled into one. And the handsome, black-haired warrior never even noticed Ilysa *before* his unexpected rise to the chieftainship.

Other women, who are always attempting to lure Connor into bed—and failing, by the way—are drawn to him by his status, handsome face, and warrior's body. While no lass with a pulse could claim to be unaffected by Connor's devastating looks, Ilysa loves him for his noble heart. Connor MacDonald would give his life for the lowliest member of their clan, and Ilysa would give hers for him.

Connor MacDonald is the hope of his clan, a burden that weighs upon every decision he makes. Since becoming chieftain, he has devoted himself to raising his people from the ashes. With the help of his cousins (in *The Guardian* and *The Sinner*) and his best friend (in *The Warrior*), he has survived murder attempts by his own kin, threats from royals and rebels, and attacks by other clans. Now all that remains to secure his clan's future is to take back the lands that were stolen by the powerful MacLeods.

Through the first three books in The Return of the Highlander series, Ilysa has worked quietly and efficiently behind the scenes to support Connor and the clan. None of her efforts has made him look at her twice. Clearly, it's time for me to step in and give Connor a shake.

The poor lass does need help. Her mother thought she was protecting Ilysa in a violent world by covering her in severe kerchiefs and oversized gowns and admonishing her to never draw attention to herself. Ilysa's brief marriage left her feeling even less appealing.

But Ilysa underestimates her worth. After all, who helped our returning heroes in *The Guardian* sneak into the castle the night they took it from Connor's murderous uncle? And who healed Connor's wounds and brought him back from death's door? Even now, while Connor fights to protect the clan, Ilysa is willing to employ a bit of magic to protect him, whether from the threat of an assassin or a deceitful woman with silver-blue eyes.

Unfortunately, Ilysa's chances grow more dismal still when Connor decides he must marry to gain an ally for the clan's coming fight with the MacLeods. As I watched him consider one chieftain's daughter after another, I knew not one of them was the right wife for him or the clan. What our chieftain needs is a woman who can heal the wounds of his heart—and watch his back.

But Connor is no fool. With a little prodding, he finally opened his eyes and saw that Ilysa is the woman he wants. Passion burns! Yay! However, my relief is short lived because the stubborn man is determined to put the needs of the clan before his own desires. Admirable as that may be, I can't let him marry the wrong woman, can I?

Despite *all* my efforts, I fear Connor will lose everything before he realizes that love is the strongest ally.

With Ilysa's life and his clan's future hanging by a thread, will he be too late to save them?

I hope you enjoy the adventurous love story of Connor and Ilysa. I've found it hard to say goodbye to them and this series.

You can find me on Facebook, Twitter, and my website, www.MargaretMallory.com. I love to hear from readers!

Margaret Mallory

♥ ♥ ♥ ♥ ♥ ♥ ♥ ♥ ♥ ♥ ♥ ♥ ♥ ♥

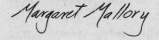

From the desk of Cynthia Garner

Dear Reader,

My latest novel, HEART OF THE DEMON, takes two of my favorite preternaturals—demon and fey—and puts them together. Tough guy Finn Evnissyen has met his match in Keira O'Brien!

I come by my fascination with the fey honestly. My family came to America from Donegal, Ireland, in 1795 and settled in the verdant hills of West Virginia. One item on my bucket list is to get to Donegal and see how many relatives still live there.

My fascination with demons, I guess, has its roots in my religious upbringing. Just as I have with vampires and werewolves, I've turned something considered wicked into

someone wickedly hawt! I hope after reading HEART OF
THE DEMON you'll agree.

To help me along, my Pandora account certainly
got its workout with this book. From my Filmscore station that played scores from *Iron Man*, *Sherlock Holmes*,
and *Halo 3*; to my metal station that rocked out with
Metallica, Ozzy Osbourne, and Rob Zombie; to my Celtic
punk station that rolled with the Dropkick Murphys,
Mumford & Sons, and Flatfoot 56, I had plenty of inspi-
ration to help me write.

I have a more complete playlist on my website extras
page, plus a detailed organizational chart of the Council
and their liaisons.

Happy Reading!

Cynthia Garner

cynthiagarnerbooks@gmail.com
http://cynthiagarnerbooks.com